D0098543

THE DEATH RELIC

THE
DEATH
RELIC

Chris Kuzneski

G.P. PUTNAM'S SONS
NEW YORK

PUTNAM

G. P. PUTNAM'S SONS
Publishers Since 1838
Published by the Penguin Group
Penguin Group (USA) Inc., 375 Hudson Street, New York, New York 10014,
USA • Penguin Group (Canada), 90 Eglinton Avenue East, Suite 700, Toronto,
Ontario M4P 2Y3, Canada (a division of Pearson Penguin Canada Inc.) •
Penguin Books Ltd, 80 Strand, London WC2R 0RL, England •
Penguin Ireland, 25 St Stephen's Green, Dublin 2, Ireland (a division of Penguin
Books Ltd) • Penguin Group (Australia), 707 Collins Street, Melbourne, Victoria
3008, Australia (a division of Pearson Australia Group Pty Ltd) •
Penguin Books India Pvt Ltd, 11 Community Centre, Panchsheel Park,
New Delhi–110 017, India • Penguin Group (NZ), 67 Apollo Drive, Rosedale,
Auckland 0632, New Zealand (a division of Pearson New Zealand Ltd) •
Penguin Books (South Africa), Rosebank Office Park, 181 Jan Smuts Avenue,
Parktown North 2193, South Africa • Penguin China, B7 Jiaming Center,
27 East Third Ring Road North, Chaoyang District, Beijing 100020, China

Penguin Books Ltd, Registered Offices:
80 Strand, London WC2R 0RL, England

Library of Congress Cataloging-in-Publication Data
Kuzneski, Chris.
The death relic/Chris Kuzneski.
p.   cm.
ISBN 978-0-399-15899-5
1. Archaeologists—Fiction.   2. Treasure troves—Fiction.
3. Missing persons—Fiction.   4. Yucatán Peninsula—Antiquities—Fiction.
5. Suspense fiction.   6. Mystery fiction.   I. Title.
PS3611.U98D43   2013   2012038476
813'.6—dc23

Printed in the United States of America
1   3   5   7   9   10   8   6   4   2

Book design by Lovedog Studio

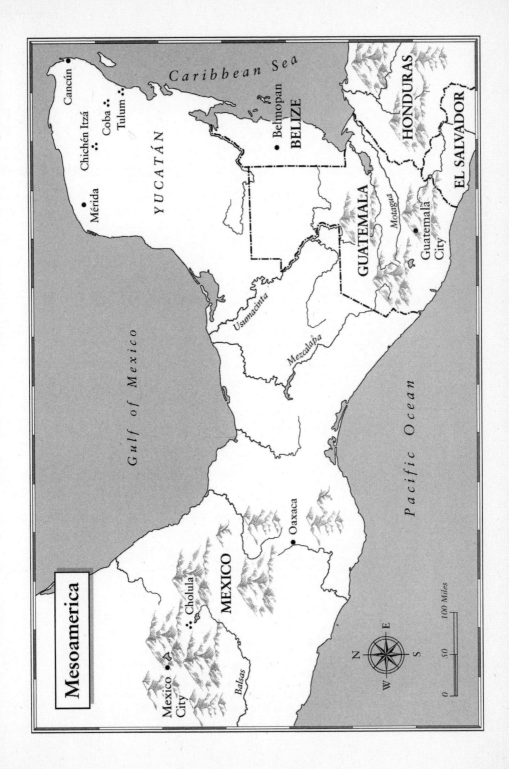

Mesoamerica

Caribbean Sea

Gulf of Mexico

Pacific Ocean

Cancún
Chichén Itzá
Coba
Tulum
Mérida
YUCATÁN
Belmopan
BELIZE
HONDURAS
EL SALVADOR
GUATEMALA
Guatemala City
Motagua
Usumacinta
Mezcalapa
Oaxaca
Cholula
MEXICO
Mexico City
Balsas

N E S W

100 Miles
0 50 100

THE PHONE RANG IN THE DEAD OF NIGHT. ONE RING, then a second. He sat up in bed and turned on the light. It rang a third time as he rubbed his eyes and focused on the clock.

It was 2:43 A.M.

Someone was going to pay.

No one was to bother him at this hour. Not his high-priced attorney, his top lieutenants, or anyone else in his organization. In his mind, they simply didn't deserve that kind of access. The only people he truly cared about slept under his roof. Everyone else could fend for themselves—especially after midnight.

He was the boss. Those were his rules. No one would dare to break them.

The last person who did was no longer alive.

On the fourth ring, he picked up his BlackBerry, only to discover that it wasn't ringing. He stared at the device, trying to make sense of things, wondering if it had been a dream. His question was answered when he heard the fifth ring. That's when he located the source of the sound. It was coming from his private cell phone on his dresser. *How could that be?* Only three people had the number: his wife, his daughter, and his son.

He glanced back at his wife, whose naked form was partially concealed in a tangle of sheets. God, she was beautiful. Dark hair, dark eyes, huge breasts. The perfect trophy wife. Three hours earlier, they had worn each other out. Now she was dead to the world. Except for the rise and fall of her chest, she hadn't moved in minutes. He knew she was capable of some amazing things in bed, but placing a call without a phone wasn't one of them.

That left two possibilities: his daughter or his son.

Suddenly anxious, he climbed out of bed and hustled to his phone. Thanks to technology, he knew it couldn't be a wrong number. He subscribed to a service that required callers to punch in an access code before the call was routed to his phone. The service cost a lot, but it was worth every peso. No solicitors. No crank calls. No one got through except the people he loved.

At least they hadn't until tonight.

It was now 2:44 A.M.

His nightmare was just starting.

He glanced at his phone. The screen said: DANIELA GARCIA. The call had been placed from his daughter's cell phone.

He answered. "Daniela?"

The caller replied in English. His voice, digitally altered to conceal his identity, sounded like something from a horror movie. "Is this Hector Garcia?"

"Yes. Who is this? Where is my daughter?"

The voice laughed. "I have the bitch. I have your son, too."

"No, you don't! You can't!" he said defiantly.

"Is that so? You want me to call you from your son's phone next?"

Hector nearly panicked. He ran his hand through his rumpled hair, imagining the worst. In his business, he had made a lot of enemies—the kind who would do *anything* to get even. Now someone had his children, the most important things in his life.

Or did they?

Hector hit the mute button on his phone and screamed at his wife. "Sofia!"

She rolled over and whined in Spanish, "I'm tired. What do you want?"

He snatched a book off his dresser and hurled it at her from across the room. It missed her face by a few inches. "Wake the fuck up!"

Used to his temper, she took the insult in stride. "What is it?"

"The kids! Check their rooms! Tell me if they're there."

"What?" she said, confused.

"Someone took my kids! Check their fucking rooms!"

She blinked a few times before it sank in, then she sprang into action. She snatched her bathrobe off the floor and sprinted toward the door while trying to get dressed. The entire time she was cursing the devil in rapid Spanish.

Hector waited for her to reach the hallway before he hit mute again. In situations like this, he couldn't show weakness. Not to one of his enemies. If he did, the problem would only get worse. "Do you know who I am? Do you know what I'm capable of?"

"Of course I do. That's why this is so much fun. After all these years, you're on the wrong end of a ransom call. I bet you're dying inside, not knowing if your children will make it through the night. Knowing you're *not* in control of who lives or dies."

Hector growled at him. "I swear to God, if you hurt my kids— if you so much as lay a finger on either of them—I will devote my life to finding you."

The voice laughed at his bravado. "*Your* life? Shouldn't you be more concerned about *their* lives? Or don't you care if they survive?"

He started to pace. "Of course I care! That's all I care about."

"Really? Then why haven't you asked the question?"

"What question?"

"Come on, Hector. You know the *question*. You hear it all the time."

"What are you talking about?" he demanded.

"Don't play dumb with me! I know all about your organization. I know how you make your money. Over the years, how many times have you placed this call? How many times have you heard the terror that you're feeling now? One hundred? Five hundred? A thousand? During those calls, I guarantee you've heard the same question over and over. Whether the families were rich or poor, I guarantee they asked you the same fucking question. And yet for some reason, you're refusing to ask it. Is it ego? Is it denial? Is it hubris?"

Hector burned with fury. He knew precisely what the caller was talking about, but the moment he asked the question, he knew he had lost control of the situation. With that in mind, he refused to ask it until he knew for sure that his children were missing.

A moment later, he heard his wife scream.

It was a sound that would haunt him for the rest of his life.

A sound that told him he had lost possession of his kids.

He took a deep breath to control his rage. "What do you want?"

"Finally, the magic question! I guess that means you believe me now?"

He repeated his words: "What do you want?"

"Does it matter? Whatever it is, you're going to give it to me. If not, my men are going to take turns on Daniela while your son watches. Then I'm going to upload the video to the Internet so the whole world can see it. Do I make myself clear?"

Hector said it louder: "What do you want?"

The caller laughed. "I want something *personal*. Something

that will hurt you to your very core. Something that *can't* be replaced."

Hector screamed into the phone. "*Personal?* You want something *personal*? You already have my fucking kids! What can be more personal than that?"

The caller grinned. "I want the medallion."

FRIDAY, FEBRUARY 10
CANCÚN, MEXICO

THE ARRANGEMENTS HAD BEEN MADE THE DAY BE-
fore by a man she had never met. A first-class ticket out of
Rome, a luxury suite in a five-star resort, and a stipend in the low
five figures. To earn the fee, all she had to do was fly to Mexico
and answer a few questions. The rest of the time, she could do
whatever she wanted—whether that was swimming, hiking, or
shopping.

Although the invitation was unexpected, she jumped at the
chance to escape the snow-covered streets of Italy for the tropical
beaches of Mexico, a country she had always wanted to visit. This
time of year, the average temperature was close to seventy degrees,
with daily lows near sixty. That was the only excuse she needed to
pack a bag and get away.

Located in the Mexican state of Quintana Roo, Cancún is a
coastal city on the northeast tip of the Yucatán Peninsula, just
north of a major corridor known as the Mayan Riviera. The popular tourist district stretches along the Caribbean coastline from

the seaport of Puerto Morelos to the ancient ruins of Tulum, nearly seventy miles to the south.

As her plane descended toward Cancún International Airport, she pressed her forehead against the glass and stared at the beach-front hotels that lined the light blue waters of the Yucatán Channel, a 135-mile strait that separates the Gulf of Mexico from the Caribbean Sea and Mexico from the island of Cuba. A self-proclaimed nerd, she was surprised to learn the channel marked the beginning of the Gulf Stream, the warm ocean current that follows the eastern coast of America before crossing the Atlantic Ocean toward Europe. From the air, the water looked calm and serene, but she knew the strong current influenced the climate on both sides of the Atlantic and was the source of many powerful storms.

Thankfully, hurricane season didn't start until June.

Minutes after landing, she strolled through the air-conditioned terminal, searching for a store where she could buy postcards and a local guidebook. She was a sucker for stuff like that, always wanting to know the best places to go and the best sites to see. When it came to travel, adventure was in her blood. Dressed in a cotton blouse and comfortable jeans, she blended in with most of the tourists she passed along the way. Unlike many of the major airports in Europe—which were often filled with businessmen in expensive suits and women in designer clothes—the vibe in Cancún was completely relaxed. Everything was laid-back and casual, like something out of a Jimmy Buffett song. People wore T-shirts, shorts, and sandals as they sipped on tropical drinks in the cantinas and restaurants that lined the long corridor.

Margaritas. Daiquiris. Coronas with lime.

She licked her lips at the possibilities.

Tempted to join the fun, she knew she'd better stay sober until she reached her hotel and met her employer. But, after that, all bets were off. This was a working vacation—with emphasis on the latter. She had been working nonstop since grad school and knew it was time for a break. Still in her twenties, she felt much older, thanks to a family tragedy that had made headline news in Italy. Hoping to avoid the spotlight, she poured herself into her work, refusing to take time off to grieve even though her friends and colleagues urged her to do so. In the short term, she powered through her sorrow and earned a doctorate in archaeology from a prestigious university in England, but eventually the emotions of the tragedy caught up with her. In many ways, she had been trying to regain her balance ever since.

"Excuse me," said a voice from behind. "Are you Dr. Pelati?"

Maria stopped in the hallway and turned around. Behind her was a squat, middle-aged man wearing an orange short-sleeved linen guayabera—a decorative shirt that was popular in Cuba and Latin America—and white slacks. In one hand, he held a white driver's cap; in the other, a small cardboard sign with the name DR. PELATI printed in neat black letters.

"Yes," she replied. "I'm Dr. Pelati."

He smiled warmly. "*Buenos días*, Dr. Pelati. *Bienvenida a México*. My name is Ernesto. I am your driver. I will be taking you to your hotel." He punctuated his statement with a slight bow of his head. "May I take your luggage?"

She glanced at her carry-on bag, then back at Ernesto. Standing five feet five in polished leather shoes, he was two inches shorter than Maria. Despite his height, he outweighed her by more than fifty pounds, a combination of his stocky build and protruding waistline.

"You're who?" she asked, confused.

He pointed to the name tag pinned to his breast pocket. It had one word on it: ERNESTO. "My name is Ernesto. I am your driver."

"My driver? I have a driver?"

He clicked his heels together and nodded. "*Sí!* And my name is Ernesto."

She smiled at the development. Over the years, she had heard dozens of stories about tourists being ripped off by unscrupulous cabdrivers in foreign countries. Now she wouldn't have to worry about it. "*Hola*, Ernesto. It's great to meet you. Please call me Maria."

He nodded again. "As you wish, Dr. Pelati. May I take your bag?"

Instead of waiting for her response, he politely grabbed the handle of her carry-on bag, pivoted it on its two wheels, and started pulling it toward the luggage carousel at the front of the terminal. "You have baggage, yes?"

Maria grimaced at his word choice. She had more "baggage" than he could possibly imagine—most of it family-related. Of course, that wasn't the type of baggage he was referring to. "I have two suitcases. One for my clothes, and one for all the souvenirs I'm going to buy."

Ernesto snorted with laughter. "You sound like my wife. Sometimes I wish she was addicted to drugs instead of shopping. It would be cheaper for me."

Maria smiled. "Have you been married long?"

"For thirty years," he said with pride. "Both of us grew up in villages near Playa del Carmen. I have loved her since childhood."

"How romantic."

"*Sí*, very romantic. *Y tú?*"

She shook her head. "Nope. Never married. Never been close."

Ernesto stopped suddenly—so suddenly that Maria nearly tripped over her carry-on bag. "How is that possible? A beautiful woman like you! Tell me, are you *looking* for boyfriend? If so, you would be perfect for Ernesto!"

The comment caught her completely off guard. She quickly flushed with embarrassment. She was used to being hit on by Italian men, who would whistle and occasionally grab her ass as she walked by, but she wasn't expecting it from her driver—someone who was married to his childhood sweetheart. "Ernesto, I'm flattered by your interest. I truly am. But somehow I don't think your wife would approve."

He dismissed her claim with a wave of his hand. "Of course she would approve! Who do you think told me to look?"

Maria's discomfort quickly turned to disgust. Because of her father, a lecherous man who couldn't be trusted, she had no patience when it came to deceitful men. "Your wife told you to find a girlfriend? Somehow I find that hard to believe."

Ernesto heard the tension in Maria's voice and saw the flaring of her nostrils. He instantly realized he had overstepped his bounds. "I have offended you, no? I swear to you, that was not my intent! I would never insult a guest. Please, do not tell my boss, or I will be fired!"

"Don't worry, I *won't* tell your boss. But I *should* tell your wife."

"My wife? Why would you tell my wife? I assure you, my wife would not be mad. She would be thrilled! She wants me to find someone for Ernesto. He needs all the help he can get."

Now it was Maria's turn to be confused. "Wait. Who is Ernesto?"

"Ernesto is my son." He reached into his shirt pocket and pulled out a photo. He showed it to her with pride. "He is very handsome, no? You would like him very much."

Maria laughed at the absurdity of the situation. All this time, she had thought Ernesto was hitting on her. Instead, he was simply playing matchmaker for Ernesto Jr. "You're right. Your son is very handsome. But I need more than good looks. Is he smart, too?"

Ernesto groaned. "Not really, but he is strong like bull. When he takes off shirt, all the girls swoon. He spends lots of time at the beach."

"As tempting as he sounds, I'm looking for someone with intelligence."

"Really?" He quickly pulled out a second photo, this one of a young woman with a flower in her hair. "My daughter is very pretty and very smart. Maybe you like her more?"

Maria laughed louder. This was getting more absurd by the minute. "Sorry, that won't work for me, either. Besides, I'm going back to Europe in a few days. No time for romance."

Ernesto shrugged and tucked the photos back into his pocket. "Oh well, a father must try."

A bittersweet smile crossed Maria's lips. "You're right. A father *should* try to help his kids. You're a good man, Ernesto. Your children are lucky to have someone like you."

He thanked her for the compliment, then grabbed the handle of her carry-on. "We better get moving. We still have to deal with your baggage."

She smiled at the irony of his statement. "Don't I know it."

3

T HE FIESTA AMERICANA GRAND CORAL BEACH IS A
luxury resort on the north end of Cancún's hotel district.
With sweeping views of Isla Mujeres and the Caribbean Sea, it
is annually recognized as one of the best hotels in all of Latin
America.

From the backseat of Ernesto's Town Car, Maria stared in awe
at the white beaches and the turquoise waters that lined Boulevard
Kukulcán, a causeway that juts away from the peninsula and into
the Caribbean. During her flight, she had assumed the color of the
water was an optical illusion because she had never seen that shade
of blue in a natural setting. But now that she was on the ground,
she knew that wasn't the case. The water *was* that color, and it
was calling to her. Suddenly, the thought of shopping had lost its
appeal. All she wanted to do was go to the beach and soak in the
surf while her troubles drifted away.

Ernesto studied her reaction in the rearview mirror. "I can tell
from your silence this is your first time in Cancún."

She nodded but refused to take her eyes off the beach. "How did you know?"

"You are—how you say?—hypnotized by beauty. I see it all the time when guests come from far away. They talk, talk, talk like parrots, until they see the water. Then they no speak until we get to hotel." He laughed at the behavior. "This color is new to you, no?"

She nodded. "I've never seen anything like it."

"This entire road was built atop the second-largest coral reef in the world. It stretches from Cancún all the way to Belize."

"How far is that?"

"Over two hundred and fifty miles. Up here in Cancún, the water is very shallow—no more than a few feet deep near shore. That is why the color is so blue. The sun shines on ocean floor."

"Whatever the reason, it's beautiful."

His chest puffed with pride. "Mexico is very different than most people think. Mexico is land of beauty, not violence. It is *not* like cowboy movie of Wild West." He paused, then corrected himself. "Actually, I take that back. Central Mexico is still like movie of Wild West. It is so bad even I, Ernesto Fernando Rodriguez, will not go there without a tank. But this part of Mexico—the Mayan Riviera—is very safe for tourists."

"That's good to know."

"You stay by hotel, you will be safe. I promise."

Palm trees and tropical flowers lined the stone driveway that led them to the front entrance of the Fiesta Americana, a massive resort that stretched for more than a city block and dwarfed every structure nearby. The hotel consisted of two twelve-story buildings connected by a central lobby and atrium; the outside had been painted sandy brown, an earthy color that fit perfectly with the blue sky above and the turquoise waters of the sea.

"Are you in a hurry?" Ernesto asked.

She glanced at her watch. "Not really. Why?"

"I would like to introduce you to the staff. They will make your stay very pleasant."

"Sounds good to me."

"Keep in mind, I don't do this for everyone, only special guests."

"I'm not sure if I qualify as special, but—"

"Of course you are special! You will marry my son."

Before she could argue, he stopped his Town Car underneath the covered entryway and honked his horn several times. Long, pronounced beeps that echoed throughout the resort. Within seconds, bellhops and valets arrived en masse, surrounding his car like a pack of wolves. But they weren't there for tips. They were there to watch the show.

Grinning like a child, Ernesto hopped out of the driver's seat and was greeted by a boisterous cheer. He milked the moment for as long as he could, blowing kisses to the crowd and speaking to everyone in rapid Spanish. Maria, who was fluent in the language, wasn't sure what he was waiting for, and then it happened. A mariachi band appeared out of nowhere. Five musicians, all dressed in silver-studded *charro* outfits with wide-brimmed hats, all of them ready to perform. The trumpet started first, followed by the guitar, two violins, and the Mexican *guitarrón*. As they played, Ernesto snapped his fingers to the beat and danced his way to Maria's side of the car while everyone clapped their hands and sang the song in unison.

It was like a scene from a movie.

Maria soaked it all in—the laughter, the teasing, the camaraderie—and tried to remember the last time she'd had this much fun with a group of her friends. Had it been months? Or years? She honestly couldn't remember. Then again, she didn't have many friends to begin with. A couple from school and a few from work, but none who lived in Italy. And when it came to dating, she put the "nun" in none, because she hadn't slept with a man in a very long time.

The thought was depressing, yet hardly surprising.

She knew her priorities were out of whack.

Over the past decade, the only thing she had cared about was work, and that single-mindedness had taken its toll on her personal life. So much so, she didn't have one. Ultimately, that was the main reason she had jumped at the chance to come to Cancún on a working vacation. She figured it might shake things up in her life. Might lead her into a new way of living, where having fun was just as important as having a career.

And if that didn't happen, at least she could work on her tan.

Grinning from ear to ear, Ernesto opened her door with a flourish. He extended his hand and helped her out of the car. "Welcome to the Fiesta Americana, your home away from home in beautiful Cancún, Mexico. As you know, I am Ernesto, and these are my friends!"

He turned and faced the crowd. "*Amigos*, this is Maria."

They shouted in unison: "*Hola*, Maria!"

"*Hola!*" she shouted back, energized by the scene.

"Maria will be staying here through the weekend," he explained in Spanish. "If you see her, I want you to give her extra-special treatment. She might marry my son!"

Maria gasped. "Wait! What?"

Over the next few minutes, she tried to set the record straight but to no avail. The staff was too festive and the music was too loud to dispute Ernesto's claim. After a while, she stopped arguing her case and started having fun instead. Before long, she was dancing with Ernesto and his friends in the middle of the driveway, her troubles a distant memory.

To her, this trip couldn't have come at a better time.

A week without stress was exactly what she needed.

✠   ✠   ✠

Sᴉᴛᴛɪɴɢ ɪɴ ᴀ ɴᴇᴀʀʙʏ ᴠᴀɴ, they watched the scene unfold in front of the hotel. They had been following Maria since the airport and would continue to watch her until she left Mexico.

That is, if they let her leave Mexico.

After all, she was the key to everything.

4

AMBRIDGE, PENNSYLVANIA
(16 MILES NORTHWEST OF PITTSBURGH)

DRESSED IN BLACK, THE MEN LOOKED LIKE SHAD-
ows as they crept through the forgotten tunnel system
underneath the city of Ambridge.

Built more than a century ago, the tunnels had been part of the
local sewer system until World War I, when the property was sold
to a wealthy industrialist who cleared the land and built a large
manufacturing complex on the north shore of the Ohio River.
According to the purchase agreement, the industrialist had vowed
to fill in the old tunnels at his expense and build new sewer lines
that would meet government standards. But when it came time to
do so, he decided it was a waste of money. Instead of filling in the
tunnels like he had promised, he sealed both ends and lied about it
to the city inspectors.

Decades later, when Payne Industries acquired the property,
the former owner failed to mention that the tunnels had never
been filled in. So they sat there, dormant, until they were recently
discovered by a demolition crew tasked with clearing the old steel
mill and blast furnace to make way for a new manufacturing

center that would house the Research and Development division of Payne Industries.

This type of demolition was fairly common in Pittsburgh. In recent years the city had undergone an amazing metamorphosis, one that had transformed it from an urban nightmare into one of the most scenic cities in America. First, the steel industry relocated, leaving plenty of land for new parks and businesses. Then Pittsburgh's three rivers—the Allegheny, the Monongahela, and the Ohio—were dredged, making them suitable for recreational use and riverfront entertainment. Buildings received face-lifts. Bridges received paint jobs. And the air was suddenly clean. Long gone were the days when the city had to turn on its streetlights in the middle of the afternoon so people could see through the smog. The city's transformation was so complete that Rand McNally, *Forbes*, and *The Economist* all recently named Pittsburgh as America's Most Livable City.

But below the surface, it was a different story.

More than twenty feet underground, the tunnels resembled *old* Pittsburgh—a dark, desolate place that smelled like a sewer, or something worse.

"This place is awesome," whispered David Jones, without a hint of sarcasm. Using next-generation night vision that resembled swimming goggles, he stared at the century-old architecture, marveling at the intricate pattern of the bricks. The diameter of the tunnel was nearly seven feet wide, and it seemed to go on forever. "Too bad you're tearing it down."

Annoyed by the comment, Jonathon Payne glanced over his shoulder. "I never said I was tearing it down. This is a piece of history. They don't make tunnels like this anymore. If it's structurally sound, I want to keep it."

Jones stared at the ankle-deep water on the tunnel floor. It was littered with bricks and mortar that had fallen from the roof, caused by leakage and decades of neglect. In his mind, there was no way in hell it was going to pass inspection. "Like I said, too bad you're tearing it down."

Payne ignored his best friend and continued forward.

To the outside world, the two of them didn't appear to have much in common, but that had more to do with their looks than anything else. Payne, the current CEO of Payne Industries, was a hulking six feet four. Muscles stacked upon muscles, his white skin littered with scars from bullets and blades. He had the look of an ex-athlete who had lived his life to the fullest but was forced to retire too soon. Raised by his paternal grandfather, a self-made millionaire who went from mill worker to mill owner in less than thirty years, Payne had shunned the family business for a career in the military. But when his grandfather passed away and left him controlling interest in Payne Industries, he felt obligated to return home and run the company.

Unfortunately, he'd been craving his old life ever since.

Jones, too, was an adrenaline junkie, but he looked more like an office clerk than an officer. Known for his brain rather than his brawn, he possessed the wiry build of a track star, someone who could run a marathon without breaking a sweat but wouldn't stand out in a crowd. Although his mocha skin and soft facial features made him look delicate, Jones was lethal on the battlefield, having completed the same military training as Payne.

The two of them used to lead the MANIACs, an elite Special Forces unit composed of the top soldiers from the Marines, Army, Navy, Intelligence, Air Force, and Coast Guard. They were specialists in every aspect of surveillance, reconnaissance, and combat. Classified above top secret, the MANIACs were essentially ghosts. And when it came to military operations that were strictly "off the book," the MANIACs were the best of the best.

Even though Payne and Jones had retired in their mid-thirties, they were still deadly. At the Pentagon's request, the duo was still actively involved with the Special Forces program. Officially, they were nothing more than *advisers*—trusted experts who gave their opinions on training, weapons, and tactics—but over the past few years, they had been placed in the field on more than one occasion. And they had loved every minute.

To stay sharp, the duo conducted field exercises on a regular basis. Sometimes to knock off their rust, other times to test young trainees in advanced warfare. On this particular night, they were trying out a new piece of technology that had been developed by Payne Industries. Known as the "puke light," the LED incapacitator is a nonlethal weapon that resembles a flashlight. The original device, which was designed by Intelligent Optical Systems (IOS), emits a bright, rapid, and well-focused series of "differently colored random pulses." Before the human eyes can focus on one frequency, another frequency comes on, causing intracranial pressure. This results in cluster headaches, nausea, vomiting, disorientation, and visual impairment of the target. At least, that was the intended effect. Unfortunately, some test subjects were completely unaffected by the light, which meant the design still needed to be tweaked before it could be trusted.

Based on years of combat experience, Payne and Jones recommended the addition of an auditory element to the device, something loud enough to disturb the fluid in the inner ear of their target without compromising their own equilibrium. They felt the combination of light and sound would produce the desired effect, leaving their opponent as defenseless as a victim of a stun grenade.

Of course, the only way to know for sure was to test it out.

To that end, Payne contacted the Army ROTC commander at the University of Pittsburgh, an old friend named Gregg Peterson, and requested the five best cadets from the Three Rivers Battalion. Young athletic men with lots of potential. Then he armed them with paintball guns and flashlights and dumped them at the other end of the tunnel system. Their lone goal was to shoot the unarmed

Payne and Jones before the duo could disarm them. If the cadets succeeded, Payne Industries would pay their tuition for the entire semester. If they failed, they would still be helping their country by testing a military prototype that would soon be used in close combat.

Not that they thought they'd fail.

The cadets were so confident they'd wipe out Payne and Jones that they were already planning a victory celebration back on campus. After all, how could two old guys take them out?

They would find out soon enough.

Thanks to his high-tech goggles, Payne saw the cadets long before he was in range of their flashlights or guns. Hustling to his left, he ducked behind a drainage pipe that smelled like old diapers. Meanwhile, Jones darted to his right, positioning himself next to a support beam that was ravaged with rust. In a narrow tunnel, both men knew they would be easy targets if the LED incapacitator didn't work, yet they weren't the least bit worried about failure. As Jones waited in the darkness, he had to stifle a yawn.

"So," he whispered to Payne, "where do you want to eat? How about that new place at Station Square?"

"Be quiet! They're coming."

"I know they're coming. That means this will be over soon, and we can get something to eat. Don't ask me why, but I'm craving Chinese."

"Don't mess with me, *Jonesy*. This is important."

Jones winced at the nickname. It was one he couldn't stand. "Why did you call me that?"

"You know how I feel about talking."

"You hate it during a mission."

"That's right, *Jonesy*."

Jones growled in the darkness. "Fine! I'll shut up. But once we're done here, we're getting Chinese—and you're paying for it!"

Payne grinned in victory. He had already promised to buy dinner in exchange for Jones's time and expertise, so the agreement didn't cost him anything extra. Furthermore, the deal assured his friend's full cooperation for the next few minutes. Not that he was actually concerned. Jones had a history of goofing around until the last possible second, but Payne knew when it was time for business, Jones would flip a mental switch and kick some serious ass.

And that time was now.

Shaped like a flashlight with an oversized head, the LED incapacitator had a maximum range of thirty feet. Positioned on both sides of the tunnel, Payne and Jones waited in the darkness until all of the cadets were within striking distance, then the duo turned on their devices. What happened next was like something out of a science-fiction movie. A rapid burst of bright, flashing lights blinded the cadets with a series of colored pulses, while a high-pitched squeal filled the tunnel with a torturous sound that didn't bother Payne or Jones because they were behind it. The five targets instantly dropped their rifles and fell to their knees as they tried to cover their eyes and ears at the exact same time. When that didn't work, things got progressively worse.

The second cadet was the first one to get sick. It started with nausea, then quickly turned to projectile vomiting that coated the back of the lead cadet. After that, it looked like a frat party gone wrong. One college student after another puking up whatever they had eaten in the past six hours: spaghetti, Doritos, and little bits of burger. Payne felt so bad for them that he turned off his device after only ten seconds of use and told Jones to do the same.

But Jones—who had heard some of the cadets' comments about his age—ignored the order until he had kicked away their weapons, which officially ended the drill. He punctuated his victory by blowing on the tip of the device like a gunslinger, then tucking it into an imaginary holster. "Call me crazy, but I think this sucker works."

Payne nodded. "I think you're right."

"Let's find out for sure." With his foot, Jones nudged one of the cadets, who was sprawled on the tunnel floor. "Hey, kid, what do you think? Does the device work?"

The cadet groaned, then vomited again.

Payne scrunched his face in disgust. "I think that's a yes."

"Definitely a yes," said Jones, who was already thinking about his next meal.

Blessed with an iron stomach, he studied the half-digested buffet that coated the tunnel walls, as if reading a menu. One entrée in particular caught his eye. "You know what? I think I changed my mind about dinner. Forget the beef and broccoli. Let's get pasta instead."

5

MARIA SHOWERED AND CHANGED INTO A SUNDRESS before heading downstairs to meet her new employer, an American scholar named Terrence Hamilton. Knowing little about him except his work in the field of anthropology, she was a bit nervous and more than a little curious. They were scheduled to meet for drinks at Isla Contoy, a casual poolside restaurant at the Fiesta Americana, where he had promised to explain why she had been summoned to Cancún on such short notice. Details over the phone had been vague at best, yet she had been willing to play along because of his sterling reputation and the first-class accommodations he had arranged.

Not to mention the tropical location of their meeting.

For Maria, that had been the clincher.

When she walked out of the rear entrance of the lobby and saw the view, she knew she had chosen wisely. Running parallel to the beach was a lagoon-style pool that stretched for as far as her eye could see. Bisected by an arched bridge that led toward the turquoise waters of the gulf, the pool was surrounded by swaying palms, white lounge chairs, and multiple tiki bars. Guests in various states of undress relaxed in the water and around the stone deck, soaking up the last rays of the day as the sun inched across the sky, casting a golden hue over the entire resort.

The temperature was in the low seventies but felt cooler, thanks to a gentle breeze that smelled like the sea. For Maria, the scent stirred up childhood memories of a family vacation to the Mediterranean. Though it had happened a lifetime ago, she could remember it clearly. She was playing with her brothers near the water's edge while her parents looked on from a picnic blanket, where they were eating cheese and drinking wine. There was no screaming. Or crying. Or drama of any kind. Nothing but fun, and love, and laughter. It was a stark contrast to the way things became in the years prior to her father's murder.

"Excuse me," said a voice from behind her.

Maria blinked a few times, then turned around, fully expecting to see her new boss. Instead, it was a member of the hotel staff, who was dressed in a tropical shirt and khaki pants. He had a broad, flat nose and hair the color of coal. A beach towel was draped over his left shoulder.

He smiled warmly. "You are Maria, no?"

She nodded. "Yes, I'm Maria."

"I thought that was you, but I wasn't sure. You were wearing different clothes earlier," he said with a thick accent. "My name is Carlos. I am a friend of Ernesto."

"Nice to meet you, Carlos."

"Nice to meet you, too. I like meeting pretty women, and you are *muy bonita*."

Suddenly uncomfortable, Maria thanked him for the compliment while brushing the hair out of her eyes. It was a nervous tic she had developed as a schoolgirl. "Did you need something, Carlos? Or did you just want to say hello?"

"Do you have a phone?" he asked.

She took a deep breath, worried that Carlos was about to ask for her number. How in the world was she supposed to relax if the staff kept asking her out? "Of course I do. Why?"

Carlos pointed at the scenery. "This is perfect time for photo. If you like, I can take picture with phone. Beautiful woman with beautiful view. Make all your friends jealous."

Maria flushed with guilt. She had been *this* close to brushing off Carlos, yet all he'd wanted to do was help. Obviously her people-reading skills had suffered from her recent lack of social interaction.

"Actually, that would be great. Thanks for offering."

"De nada."

Using her cell phone, Carlos took pictures of her from three different angles, making sure her smile was perfect before he snapped each one. When he was done, she thanked him with a quick hug, which he considered far more rewarding than a hand-ful of pesos. The love-struck grin on his face was proof of that. Afterward, she asked for directions to the restaurant. He pointed to the open-air structure between the beach and pool, and ex-plained how to get there.

Maria thanked him again, then hustled to her meeting.

Shaded by a massive thatched roof known as a *palapa*, Isla Contoy offered fabulous views of the ocean and the hotel's sandy beach. In the distance to the east, she could see the red-and-white-striped lighthouse at Punta Cancún, which is built on the tip of a rocky shoal that juts far into the channel. Waves crashed against the rocks, sending spray into the air like an angry whale. Yet some-how the water at the nearby beach was as calm and clear as a bath. Unsure how that was possible, she decided to spend the next few days doing research—while wearing a bikini and working on her tan.

Maria scanned the restaurant and spotted her employer at a small table near the back rail, as far from everyone else as possible.

Wearing a panama hat and an open-collared shirt, he could have passed for a tourist, if not for the briefcase sitting at his feet. In a restaurant filled with beachwear, it stood out like a surfboard on Wall Street.

"Dr. Hamilton," she said as she approached.

Deep in thought, the American took a few seconds to react to the sound of his name, but once he did, he hopped to his feet with so much energy he nearly knocked over the table. "I am indeed. Which means you must be Dr. Pelati."

She smiled and shook his hand. "Please, call me Maria."

"Only if you call me Terry. All my friends do."

"Okay, Terry."

A few inches taller than Maria, he was in good shape for someone twice her age, even though he hadn't been inside a gym in decades. Blessed with good genes and a high metabolism, his years in the field had kept him toned and tanned. A week's worth of whiskers covered his cheeks but couldn't hide the smile lines near the corners of his mouth. They peeked through the gray every time he grinned, which was quite often during their conversation.

Always the gentleman, he pulled out her chair and urged her to sit down. "So, what are you drinking? I'm halfway through a strawberry daiquiri, and let me tell you, it's heaven in a glass! They make it with fresh strawberries, Cuban rum, and clean ice—which is very important in Mexico. Coming from Italy, are you familiar with the term 'Montezuma's revenge'?"

She shook her head.

"Trust me, you *don't* want to become familiar with it. It's a miserable condition that affects nearly forty percent of all foreigners who visit this country. Down here, bottled water is a must. Never—and I mean *never*—drink from the tap, even if the locals say it's clean. And unless you're in a nice resort like this one, stay away from the ice. It will get you every time."

"Good to know."

"And fruit," he said as an afterthought. "Only eat fruit if you peel it yourself."

"Why's that?"

"Because fruit is washed with local water. Apples, pears, and the like are okay if you remove the skin, but I'd avoid grapes. Those rascals are tough to peel."

She laughed at the thought.

"So," he said as he called over the waiter, "what'll it be?"

"Tap water, extra ice. And a side of apple skins, please."

He burst out laughing, glad she had a sense of humor. "I can tell already we'll get along fine. For me, that's my biggest concern on any project. Not the academics or the science—those things tend to sort themselves out in the long run—but the personalities of my coworkers. I've been on digs where we've found *nothing*, yet I couldn't have been happier because I enjoyed my time in the field. On the other hand, I've made some major discoveries that were ruined by the miserable bastards I had to share my tent with."

Maria ordered a daiquiri as he continued to talk.

"When you reach a certain age—and mine shall remain a secret until it's chiseled on my tombstone—you learn there's more to life than your achievements. If at any point you find yourself not enjoying the journey, you need to find a different path."

She nodded in agreement. "It's funny you should mention that, because I've been struggling with that problem in recent months. Don't get me wrong: I love my work. But there has to be more to life than late nights in the library. There has to be something to balance it out."

He held up his drink. "You mean like daiquiris on a beach in the middle of winter?"

"That's a start. But I was thinking something bigger."

Hamilton smiled and leaned in closer. "In that case, this is your lucky day. Because I've stumbled across something that will blow your mind."

6

MARIA GLANCED ACROSS THE TABLE, TRYING TO decide if Hamilton was serious. One look at his cock-sure smile told her that he was.

"What did you find?" she demanded.

Hamilton laughed at her bluntness, enjoying the secret knowledge he possessed for as long as he could. To milk the moment a little while longer, he took a slow, pronounced sip of his daiquiri before wiping the corners of his mouth with his napkin. The whole time Maria stared at him with unblinking eyes.

"So," he asked, "how was your flight?"

"My *flight*?"

"I sprang for a first-class ticket. I hope you were comfortable."

"My flight was great."

"And your suite?"

"My *suite*?"

"Yes, your suite. Does it have a nice view?"

"My view is great. So are my bed, my bathroom, and the mini-bar. Now quit your stalling and tell me what you've found!"

"Boy," he teased, "you weren't kidding when you said you were all business. We'll have to work on that before you have a nervous breakdown."

Maria laughed, surprised the two of them were hitting it off so well after such a short amount of time. "Okay. Be that way. But keep something in mind: you invited me here for my expertise. Over the next few days, I'll have plenty of opportunities to get even."

"That, my dear, is a very good point! Perhaps you've waited long enough."

"Perhaps I have."

Hamilton glanced over her shoulder and frowned. "Unfortunately, it looks like you'll have to wait a few more seconds."

"Why's that?"

"We have company."

As if on cue, the waiter returned with Maria's daiquiri, plus a basket of tortilla chips and a dish of *pico de gallo*. Known locally as *salsa fresca*, the uncooked condiment was made from chopped tomatoes, onions, and serrano peppers. The aroma was so strong, Maria's nose started to run and her eyes started to water even though the dish had been placed in the middle of the table.

"*Santa Maria!*" she said, coughing. "I'm glad I'm sitting upwind from that concoction. The smell alone is giving me heartburn."

"I'll gladly eat your share," said Hamilton, who dipped one of the tortilla chips into the salsa before shoving it into his mouth. "I've been here so long I've fallen in love with spicy food. Now I put hot sauce on everything—from eggs in the morning to steaks at night. Believe it or not, I sometimes top off my dinner with jalapeño ice cream. It's a local favorite."

Maria scrunched her face at the thought. In her mind, a meal wasn't complete unless it ended with something sweet. Preferably something chocolate. "How long have you been here?"

"In Cancún? Less than an hour."

"Really? I thought your crew was based here."

"Heavens, no! Not a lot of research to do in these parts. This is a tourist city, not a historical one." Hamilton pointed at all the hotels that lined the beach. "Right now, there are approximately seven hundred thousand people living in Cancún, plus tens of thousands of tourists that visit on a daily basis. That being said, do you know what the local population was in 1970?"

She took a wild guess. "Fifty thousand."

He signaled lower. "Try again."

"Twenty thousand."

He shook his head. "Would you believe *three*?"

"Wow. Three thousand is pretty small."

"Not three thousand," he said, laughing. "I'm talking *three*—as in one, two, three."

The number shocked her. "You've got to be kidding."

"I assure you, my dear, I'm completely serious. I can't tell you how much money I've won over the years with that bit of trivia."

"Three people? How is that possible?"

He explained. "Back then, this entire stretch of land was part of a coconut plantation owned by Don José Gutiérrez. The only full-time residents of Cancún were the three caretakers of the plantation. I jokingly call them the Three Amigos."

Maria shook her head in disbelief. Based on everything she'd seen from the air, she had assumed Cancún had been around for centuries. "What happened in 1970?"

"Well," he said as he stuffed another tortilla chip into his mouth, "the Mexican government realized how important tourism could be for the local economy, so they financed the first nine hotels in the region and poured money into the infrastructure. Their goal was to build the best resort city in the Caribbean. Amazingly, they pulled it off in less than twenty years."

"That is amazing."

"Granted, there have been some bumps in the road over the

past four decades—most notably, Hurricane Gilbert and Hurricane Wilma—but that hasn't hurt the population growth in the city. It's practically doubled in size in the last ten years."

Maria sipped on her daiquiri, trying to remember how they had started on the topic to begin with. Mentally she traced the line of questioning back to when she had asked about Hamilton's time in the city. She had assumed he was based locally, since they were meeting at the Fiesta Americana, but he said he had been in Cancún for less than an hour.

"So," she asked, "where is your team stationed?"

"Wherever our research takes us. Right now, less than a hundred miles from here."

"Anywhere in particular?"

"Yes," he said cryptically as he dug through the wicker basket for the perfect-sized chip. "But if it's okay with you, I'd rather focus on your role in things, not mine. I'm sure you must be wondering why we brought you here on such short notice."

She nodded. "The question has crossed my mind."

"Any theories?"

"Plenty. Including some I'd rather not share."

He laughed at the insinuation. Somehow her statement had been playful and accusatory at the exact same time. "Well, now you've gone and done it. After a comment like that, I'm afraid you have to share."

"I'd rather not."

"I'm afraid you must. My reputation as a gentleman is at stake!"

She blushed, realizing she had little choice but to explain her remark. "Okay! But please keep something in mind: I had these thoughts before I knew anything about you, your research, or all the awards you've won in the field of anthropology."

He grinned. "If you're buttering me up, this has got to be good."

She nodded, then took a sip of her drink for some liquid courage. "What can I say? A man I've never met calls me out of the blue and offers to fly me halfway around the world and put me up at a five-star resort for the weekend. What do you think I thought?"

"That I was a dirty old man looking for action."

"Actually, I didn't know you were old during our initial phone call—but I did think you were *dirty*. I didn't find out about your age until I researched you on the Internet."

He gasped in mock horror. "Wait! Did you just call me *old*?"

She nodded. "However, I no longer think you're dirty."

"Well, then," he toasted, "here's to small victories."

She clinked his glass and smiled. "Trust me, it's a major victory in my eyes. Normally it takes a very long time to get on my good side. Yet you've managed to do it in two days."

"That's the daiquiri talking."

"Maybe a little. But I think it's more than that. I think it's your passion for history. That's what convinced me to accept your offer."

"My passion?"

She nodded. "Like I said, I looked you up on the Internet after you called. I wanted to get a better feel for your personality before I took a job so far from home, so I watched several of your lectures online. Let me tell you, I was impressed. Your passion for history oozed through the screen. No wonder you've won so many awards."

Now it was Hamilton's turn to blush. "Believe me, I don't do it for awards. I do it for myself. In my opinion, there's nothing better than making a discovery about the world we live in. It's the reason I live in a tent eleven months a year, the reason I never settled down or got married. History is my first and only love. It's the reason I breathe."

"Yep. That's the passion I was talking about."

He shrugged. "I can't help it. That's who I am."

She shook her head. "Never apologize for passion. Like I said, it's the main reason I'm here. I figured, if you've discovered something so secretive that you couldn't tell me about it over the phone, then it was bound to be important."

"Trust me, it is."

She studied his face. "How important are we talking?"

The cocksure grin returned to his lips. "Very."

7

IN THE LAST DECADE, MEXICO HAS PASSED COLOMBIA as the drug-trafficking center of the Americas, creating an atmosphere of crime and corruption. Border towns like Tijuana and Ciudad Juárez are particularly violent—the 2009 murder rate in Juárez was the highest in the world by more than 25 percent—but in terms of the sheer number of crimes, it is hard to beat Mexico City.

With a population of more than 21 million people and a police force that is undersized and underpaid, no one knows how many crimes actually occur in the capital city since most of them go unreported, a combination of distrust in the local police and a fear of retribution from criminals. The United Nations estimates that nearly 90 percent of all the cocaine sold in the United States is smuggled through Mexico, which is also the main foreign supplier of marijuana in America. With so much money at stake, it is cheaper for cartels to bribe the police in the federal district than to lose their products in raids.

Violent crimes are always a concern when drugs are involved, but most drug-related shootings take place in impoverished areas that are recognized as trouble zones. Unfortunately, the same cannot be said about kidnappings. In Mexico City, they can happen at any time and any place. And they happen with disturbing frequency. Last year, more than a thousand occurred in the metropolitan area, but experts believe that less than a quarter of all local kidnappings are reported. Assuming this is true, that's an average of *ten-plus kidnappings a day in a single city.*

Ten abductions a day. Every day. In one city.

Obviously, kidnappings are big business in this region. Tactics and techniques are practiced on the street. Vehicles are painted to resemble taxis or police cars. Foreign phrases are even learned, so criminals can make efficient demands from tourists. When the clock is ticking and weapons are involved, communication is vital—especially in the modern world of technology, where bank accounts are just sitting there, waiting to be exploited.

Kidnappings are so frequent in Mexico City that they are classified by type.

Locally, the most common form of abduction is known as a "flash kidnapping" or "express kidnapping." Most of these occur at night, and they usually last a few hours. Normally, the goal of a flash kidnapping is to make as much money as possible in the shortest amount of time, which is why most of these abductions happen between 11:00 P.M. and 12:00 A.M. Victims are taken to an ATM and forced to withdraw their maximum daily limit, whether that is a hundred, five hundred, or a thousand dollars. At midnight, bank computers reset their accounts for a new business day, which allows customers to make another maximum withdrawal at the same machine. If criminals time things right, they can double their take in less than five minutes.

Not surprisingly, banks in Mexico City are well aware of this problem. In order to fight back, many branches have imposed institutional limits on their ATMs, which prevent customers from withdrawing large amounts from their machines—even if customers haven't reached their cash limits for the day. Of course, all this usually does is prolong the terror of flash victims, who are then forced to spend more time with their kidnappers as they are driven from bank to bank to bank, slowly but surely accumulating their maximum amount before they are forced to repeat the process again after midnight. Afterward, victims are usually dropped off, penniless and scared, and far from help of any kind. This gives criminals plenty of time to escape.

In recent years, a new type of crime, known as "virtual kidnapping," has gained popularity in the region. Victims are called in the middle of the night and told a relative or close friend has been abducted. They are kept on the phone for several minutes, which prevents them from calling their loved one to check the veracity of the claim. They are warned that if they hang up or fail to meet their demands—which is usually a cash withdrawal or jewelry— the loved one will be harmed or killed. Of course, even if they tried to call the supposed victim for verification, the line would be busy because the kidnapper's partner would be running the same scam on the "kidnapped" party. For example, an elderly woman might think her daughter has been taken, while at the same time the daughter will think her mother has been abducted. These two are called at the exact same time, yet no one has actually been kidnapped.

This type of crime would be difficult to pull off in technologically advanced countries such as America or England. Too many people have cell phones, text messaging, and Internet connections, allowing them to make contact with their friends and family through alternative means. But in Mexico, home phones are still the primary method of communication. And since the police force isn't trusted, most victims would rather pay the ransom demand and guarantee the safety of their loved one than risk someone's life by calling the kidnapper's bluff—especially in a country where abductions are so common.

The final category is simply known as "traditional kidnapping." It is a long-term crime that has been around for centuries, one that targets people from wealthy families or organizations that have the means and motive to pay a substantial ransom demand. Though not as common as flash kidnappings, they can be far more lucrative because of the sums involved in a single abduction. One million. Five million. Ten million. It all depends on who was taken and how much they'll be missed. In Mexico City, most corporations hire bodyguards to accompany their executives around the clock, because it is far cheaper to pay for protection than to pay ransoms.

However, many foreign executives roll the dice when they come to Mexico. They figure they can slip in and out of the country without being noticed, especially if their business trips are planned at the last minute. They assume criminals won't have the time, the manpower, or the knowledge to stage a traditional kidnapping without plenty of advanced warning. And even if they did have the ability to pull off the crime, what are the odds that a criminal would target them? One in a hundred? One in a thousand? One in ten thousand?

Most executives are willing to take those chances.

Of course, some factors affect the odds. A person's size, age, and appearance can make all the difference in Mexico City. By considering risk versus reward, a young bodybuilder in a T-shirt is less likely to be abducted than an old man in a designer suit. Criminals are looking for the lowest amount of risk (someone who won't fight back) with the biggest potential for reward (the most money). And on those rare occasions when they spot someone who is low-risk and high-reward, they pounce as quickly as possible.

⊞ ⊞ ⊞

HECTOR GARCIA WAS WELL aware of the statistics. In fact, he knew them better than anyone, since he ran the kidnapping game in Mexico City. Although there were some independent crews floating around—mostly flash kidnappers who were desperate for quick scores—Hector's organization was so established that several multinational corporations paid him a "protection fee" to guarantee that their employees would not be kidnapped when they came to town for business.

With this type of reputation, Hector couldn't comprehend why he had been targeted, unless it was for revenge. He simply didn't fit the profile of low-risk, high-reward. Other than the President of Mexico, there was no one in the city who was a higher risk than Hector. He had thousands, literally thousands, of armed criminals working in his organization, yet someone had the cojones to abduct his children. Not only did they sneak into his mansion in the middle of the night—somehow getting past his world-class security system and a squad of military-trained guards—but the kidnappers had the audacity to taunt him during the initial call.

They had threatened to rape his daughter.

They had threatened to kill his son.

Now they were playing games with him.

The type of games that *he* was used to playing.

Every time the phone rang, his heart pounded so hard he could feel it in his feet. No longer the puppet master, he was forced to dance when *they* pulled his strings. Be here. Be there. Get this. Get that. Do whatever we say, or your kids will die. Despite their promises, it took him more than twenty-four hours to get a proof of life. And even then, they only let him talk to his daughter. The instant Hector asked about her brother's health—a question that he had been warned not to ask—they gagged the girl and hung up.

Several hours later, they still hadn't called back.

And all Hector could do was wait.

9

HAMILTON PUSHED THE CHIPS AND SALSA ASIDE. Now that he had established a rapport with Maria, he was ready to talk business. "Tell me, what do you know about the Maya?"

"The Maya?" she repeated, pausing for a moment to gather her thoughts. "Local civilization, very advanced for their time. They ruled this region for several hundred years until the Spanish conquistadores arrived in the sixteenth century. After that, they kind of faded away."

Hamilton considered her response for several seconds before shaking his head from side to side. He punctuated his thoughts by giving her a thumbs-down. "If you were my student, I'd give that answer a D-minus at best. About the only thing you got correct was their name."

Her face flushed with embarrassment. "Their name?"

He nodded. "Most people call them the Mayans, not the Maya. It's an error that drives me crazy. 'Maya' is the name of the people.

'Mayan' is an adjective that describes their things—Mayan art, Mayan language, and so on. At least you got their name right."

Sensing a shift in his tone, Maria lifted her glass and tried to ease the tension with a joke. "What did you say before? Here's to small victories!"

Hamilton forced a smile. "Sadly, I was hoping for more from you."

Her shoulders sagged, as if the wind had escaped her sails. "Listen, I think there's been some sort of misunderstanding. If you're looking for an expert in Mayan history, I'm definitely not your gal. In all my years, I think I took one course on Mesoamerica, and I only did that because it was a school requirement. My specialty is Christian history, not ancient civilizations."

A master of reading people, Hamilton studied her posture and realized he had been too tough on her. She had gone from eager to defensive in the blink of an eye. To ensure her involvement, he knew he had to walk a fine line between employer and friend. If he pushed her too hard, she was liable to walk away before she even got started.

With that in mind, he quickly apologized. "Please forgive my rudeness. For a brief second, I was back in the lecture hall, trying to motivate students at the beginning of a semester. Obviously I know what your specialty is. It's the reason I brought you here."

"Are you sure? Because—"

"Trust me, I'm positive. I could've called any scholar in the world, and yet I called you. I am fully confident that you are the right person for this project."

She breathed a sigh of relief. The last thing she wanted to do was disappoint him. "Just so you know, I'm a quick learner. It's one of my greatest strengths. Tell me what I need to know, and I'll remember it."

Hamilton nodded. "I'll keep that in mind."

Unsure where to begin, he removed his panama hat and ran his fingers through his stark white hair. Despite the mild temperature, it was plastered to his scalp with sweat. For the next few seconds he disappeared into his thoughts as he tried to decide what she needed to know about his project. No matter how bright she was, he couldn't afford to bog her down with too many details. All that would do was confuse her.

"Out of curiosity," she said, "what was wrong with it?"

He blinked a few times. "Excuse me?"

"My answer. What was wrong with it?"

"Just about everything."

She stared at him, defiant. Then she used the same words that he had used against her a moment earlier. "Sadly, I was hoping for more from you."

Slowly but surely, the corners of his lips curled upward. What had started as a grimace ended as a grin. Maybe hope wasn't lost after all. Maybe she was tougher than she looked.

Suddenly recharged, Hamilton placed his hat on his head. "All right, my dear, I'm willing to play this game if you're willing to listen. But don't expect me to pull any punches. You must under-stand, when it comes to facts, you *must* be precise. Otherwise, your answer is wrong."

"Sounds fair to me."

"Let's start with your initial statement about the Maya. They were *not* a local civilization, as you claimed. During the course of their history, their territory stretched from the Gulf of Mexico to the north to El Salvador in the south and as far west as central Mexico. And even though there were some minor sites found in Cancún, this area was never fully developed."

"Good to know."

He continued. "And your notion that they were advanced for their time? Talk about a general statement. What exactly does 'advanced' refer to?"

She shrugged. "Their culture?"

"Define 'culture.'"

"Everything that made them who they were—their beliefs, their customs, their technology. All of that encompasses their culture."

"In that case, the Maya weren't advanced at all—at least not according to Christian standards. As hard as this is to believe, the Maya never had the wheel. Or metal tools. Or draft animals, such as horses or donkeys. They did not have a monotheistic approach to religion, choosing instead to believe in many gods and supernatural beings. To appease these deities, humans were sacrificed in public ceremonies that make horror movies look humane."

Hamilton shook his head at the brutality. "Sorry, my dear, the Maya were not an advanced civilization, *unless* you broaden your definition to include other aspects of their life."

"Such as?"

"You tell me," he said, unwilling to do the work for her. "What are the Maya known for?"

She gave it some thought. "Their calendar."

"Now we're getting somewhere. Although they didn't create the Mesoamerican calendar that was used in this region, the Maya refined it in such a way that it was far more accurate than the original Gregorian calendar used in Europe. Do you know how?"

She nodded. "Astronomy."

"That's correct! The Maya were brilliant astronomers, able to calculate celestial events with amazing accuracy. Without the use of telescopes, they figured out the length of the solar year with a margin of error of only twenty-three seconds. The five-hundred-year cycle of Venus was only two hours off. Plus, they calculated the eclipses of the sun thirty-three years ahead of time. Most amazing of all, they accurately described the Orion Nebula more than a thousand years before it was officially discovered by a French astronomer in 1610."

"How'd they do that?"

Hamilton shrugged. "No one knows, but there's evidence to prove it."

"What about math?" she asked.

"What about it?"

"If the Maya could calculate solar cycles with that much accuracy, I'm guessing they had advanced knowledge of math."

His smile widened. "Now you're thinking! The Maya were very advanced in mathematics. In fact, they were one of the first civilizations to develop the concept of zero."

"Really? That seems pretty basic to me."

"To us, it is! But that wasn't the case in ancient times. Believe it or not, the greatest scholars in ancient Greece struggled with the status of zero as a number. To them, it wasn't about math. It was about philosophy. They constantly debated how *nothing* could actually be *something*."

She laughed at the thought. "Ancient Greeks loved their debates."

"But they weren't the only ones who struggled with zero. So did the Romans, Egyptians, and Babylonians—which is saying something, because the Babylonians were doing algebra two thousand years before Christ."

The mere mention of Christ grabbed Maria's attention. As an expert in Christian history, she prayed Hamilton would shift the conversation to her comfort zone because she was dying to know what her role would be in his project. But that didn't happen. Instead, he changed the topic to agriculture and the Maya's advanced methods of food production.

"As you probably know, the Maya relied on three main crops to survive: maize, squash, and beans. In this part of the world, those staples are referred to as the 'three sisters' because they complement each other in the ground and in one's diet. Unfortunately, growing those crops on a large-scale basis is more difficult than you'd think. To combat pH problems, the Maya introduced ash to the ground, which raised the level of phosphorous and other nutrients in the soil. They utilized crop rotation and raised field techniques that are still used to this day. They also built extensive canal systems that can still be seen in aerial pictures of the jungle."

Maria grimaced. "The jungle? What are they doing in the jungle?"

"Nothing. They're just sitting there."

"No, that's not what I meant. Why were they built in the jungle?"

"Aha! Now we're getting close."

"We are?"

He nodded. "We're finally going to discuss the most blatant error in your initial summation of the Maya."

"Which error was that?"

"The part where you claimed the Maya faded away *after* the conquistadores."

"That's not correct?"

He shook his head. "Believe it or not, the Maya started to disappear in the ninth century, nearly seven hundred years before the Spanish arrived."

"Wait," she said, confused. "What do you mean by 'disappear'?"

Hamilton smiled. "One day they were here, and the next they were gone."

10

DESPITE HER DOCTORATE IN HISTORY, MARIA WAS unfamiliar with the ninth-century disappearance of the Maya. As far as she knew, the Spanish had conquered them in the 1500s.

Hamilton noticed the confusion in her eyes. "Perhaps I was a bit melodramatic when I said the Maya disappeared. They didn't vanish into thin air. At least, I don't think they did."

"Then what happened?"

"The truth is no one knows. But sometime around A.D. 850, the Maya abandoned most of their major cities. No rhyme, no reason, no explanation of any kind. The Maya simply left and didn't come back. Within months, their cities were swallowed by vegetation. That's why so many canals and temples are still being found in the jungle. Sites from Mexico to Guatemala were deserted seven hundred years before the Spanish arrived, so explorers don't know where to look. Who knows what could still be out there hiding in the trees?"

"Where did the Maya go when they left the cities?"

Hamilton shrugged. "Somewhere. Nowhere. Everywhere in between. Our best guess is that they moved from place to place for a hundred years or so before they grew in numbers and reemerged as a force in the mid-tenth century."

"They abandoned their cities but reemerged as a force? How is that possible?"

"What do you know about Mayan politics?"

"Absolutely nothing."

He figured as much. "Unlike the Roman Empire, the Maya were never a unified nation. Instead, they were a series of tiny kingdoms that sometimes fought one another. A typical kingdom was usually nothing more than a city-state, headed by a hereditary ruler known as an *ajaw*. These kingdoms were generally small in size, consisting of a capital city and the nearby villages. Despite the geography involved, a kingdom was identified by the name of the ruling dynasty, not by its territory. Therefore, when the royal family was captured or killed, the kingdom ceased to exist."

"Did that happen often?"

He nodded. "Eventually, the kingdoms became bigger and bigger until they grew into powerful city-states that spread to all corners of Mesoamerica. This proved to be problematic for the Spanish. Without one true government to overthrow, they had to endure a brutal campaign against the Maya that lasted the better part of two centuries."

"Two centuries? I didn't know it lasted that long."

"One hundred and seventy years, to be precise."

Francisco de Montejo, a Spanish conquistador who had petitioned the King of Spain for the right to conquer the Yucatán, arrived on the east coast in 1527. Remarkably, the last Mayan stronghold—the Itzá capital of Tayasal in Guatemala—didn't fall until 1697. By comparison, Cortés and the Spanish conquered the Aztec Empire in a mere two years.

Hamilton continued. "During that time, the Spanish did everything they could to sever the Maya's connection with their past, including the burning of all Mayan texts. Not surprisingly, they did this in the name of God."

Maria shook her head in frustration. As a historian, one of the things that pissed her off more than anything else was the purposeful destruction of ancient documents. If not for the burning of the Library of Alexandria, the House of Wisdom in Baghdad, and countless other libraries around the world, she knew many of the mysteries of the past could be solved. She also realized most of the burnings had been done to promote a new ideology to a conquered civilization. In the case of the Maya, it was the introduction of Christianity.

"Are you familiar with Diego de Landa?" he asked.

She nodded. "He was a Franciscan monk who came here in the mid-1500s to teach the natives about Christ. At least, I think that's when he arrived. According to your timeline, the Spanish Conquest was just warming up, so I might be wrong."

"No," he assured her, "you are correct about the date. Landa arrived here in 1549 to encourage the Maya's conversion to Catholicism while the conquistadores continued their campaign in other parts of the Yucatán. By order of the Spanish Crown, the Franciscans were granted a spiritual monopoly over the entire region, and Landa was one of the leaders."

As a practicing Catholic, Maria frequently found herself embarrassed by the violent history of the Church, and this was one of those times. Although the term "spiritual monopoly" was new to her, she knew exactly what it meant. When it came to religion, the Maya had no choice in the matter. If they didn't convert to Catholicism, they were punished or killed.

Over the years, she had come across dozens of historical events when the Vatican or its representatives had encouraged similar acts of conversion. Some of the incidents were so abhorrent that they forced her to seriously question her devotion to the Church that had empowered the behavior. But in the end, she always came to the same conclusion.

The religion was pure, but humans were fallible.

Hamilton continued. "In the history of the Maya, there has never been a more controversial figure than Diego de Landa. To many, he is hated for his cruelty and his destruction of invaluable ancient documents. To others, he is praised for his personal preservation of the Mayan culture. In all of my years as a historian, he is the most complex man I have ever encountered."

Maria frowned. "How could he be known for such contradictory things? That doesn't seem possible."

"As I mentioned, Landa was complicated. When he first arrived in the Yucatán, he was stationed as a monk in the mission at Izamal, a small city to the west. While there, Landa noticed the Maya's use of glyphs and decided to translate them into Spanish. Working with Mayan royalty, he established a base for their glyphs—which were a mixture of syllables and words—that is still used by scholars today. Two decades later, on his return voyage to Spain, Landa started to write a book called *Relación de las cosas de Yucatán*, in which he chronicles the Mayan culture in remarkable depth. In it, he discusses their language, their religion, their writing, and their ethnology. Over the years, I have used it many times as a guide."

"I have to admit, none of that sounds bad to me. Why is he reviled?"

"Why?" Hamilton asked rhetorically. "The main reason that modern scholars like myself are reliant on Landa's book is because he personally burned the Mayan glyphs. If he hadn't done that, our knowledge of the Maya would be so much more advanced. We would be able to read Mayan history in the hand of the Maya, not his distilled version of ancient events."

"Landa translated the documents, then burned them?"

He nodded gravely. "Are you familiar with the term 'auto-da-fé'? It was a ritual used during the Spanish Inquisition."

She grimaced in disgust. The ceremony was one of the skeletons in the Church's closet that they would rather forget. "The term meant 'act of faith' in medieval Spanish. The ritual involved a Catholic Mass, followed by a public procession of the condemned, and a reading of their sentences. Torture was quite common. So was burning at the stake."

Hamilton lowered his voice to a whisper. "In July of 1562, Landa ordered an auto-da-fé in the city of Maní. At the end of the ceremony, he burned more than twenty thousand Mayan images and a reported five thousand Mayan idols, claiming they were the works of the devil. This marked the beginning of a new campaign where Mayan nobles were jailed, interrogated, and tortured to speed the mass adoption of Catholicism. Scared for their lives, thousands of Maya fled from the cities and into the jungles to avoid abuse."

"He burned twenty-five thousand items? The fire must have been huge."

"It could be seen for miles and signaled the start of Landa's brutal regime. Over the next several decades, the Spanish burned every Mayan document they could get their hands on—much to the dismay of the Maya, who were forced to watch their entire history go up in flames."

She took a deep breath. "The thought of it sickens me."

Hamilton nodded in agreement. "Do you know how many Maya are still living in Mesoamerica today?"

She shrugged. "I have no idea."

"Approximately ten million. That's a significant amount when you consider there are less than three million Native Americans still living in the United States."

"Ten million is way more than I figured."

"Amazingly, do you know how many Mayan codices managed to survive?"

She shook her head, unwilling to guess.

Hamilton held up his hand with his fingers spread. Then he tucked his little finger under his thumb. "Only three."

11

MARIA THOUGHT BACK TO HAMILTON'S EARLIER pronouncement—when he had claimed the Maya had vanished overnight during the ninth century—and figured he would amend his statement about the Mayan codices. But unlike before, no correction was forthcoming.

He wiggled his three extended fingers to illustrate his point. "I know it's tough to fathom, but only three codices survived the Spanish Conquest and the eventual spread of Christianity. Because of their near extinction, Mayan codices are considered priceless."

"Are they on display in Mexico? I'd love to see them."

He shook his head. "Like most items plundered from the New World, they are currently in Europe. As such, each of the codices is named for the city where it eventually settled. The Dresden Codex is being held in the Saxon State Library in Dresden. The Paris Codex is in the Bibliothèque Nationale in Paris. And the third one, the Madrid Codex, is in the Museo de América in Madrid."

"It's being guarded by Spain? That's disturbingly ironic."

"Trust me, that isn't lost upon Mayan scholars. If they had their way, all three of the codices would be returned to the Yucatán, where they rightfully belong."

In 1965, a fourth codex was supposedly discovered in a Mexican cave, but its authenticity has been questioned ever since. Named for the Grolier Club of New York City, an association of bibliophiles who first presented the document to the world, the Grolier Codex consists of eleven damaged pages from a presumed twenty-page book. Since its pages are far less detailed than the other codices and its information is very similar to the Dresden Codex, most experts believe it is a forgery. Therefore, it is usually ignored by academics.

"With your background, I assume you've worked with codices."

She nodded. "The Romans invented them as a replacement for scrolls in the first century A.D. Their widespread popularity is generally associated with the rise of Christianity, which used the format for the Bible from the very beginning. No pun intended."

The word *codex* derives from the Latin word *caudex*—which literally means "block of wood." In reality, a codex is a book with multiple sheets of paper (or papyrus, etc.) that have been folded, stitched, bound together, and given a cover. Developed by the Romans from wooden writing tablets, the codex has multiple advantages over the scroll, which had been the main form of book in the ancient world. In addition to its sturdiness, a codex provides random access to its information—meaning it could be opened to any page—as opposed to the scroll, which offers only sequential access. Furthermore, codices (the plural of *codex*) were much cheaper to make than scrolls because both sides of the page could be used, thus saving paper.

Hamilton took the napkin from his lap and placed it on the table. Then he began folding it lengthwise, as in the shape of a paper fan, one careful fold after another. "Mayan codices are different from Roman codices because they were painted on bark cloth, not paper, and screen-folded in this fashion. Made from the inner bark of fig trees, the cloth was far more durable than papyrus, and better for writing. Unfortunately, the three codices that survived are relatively new. They were written during the colonial period, an era that started with the arrival of the Spanish."

"That's less than five hundred years ago."

He nodded, all too familiar with the math. "Based on the carbon dating of a site in Belize, the Mayan civilization started as early as 2600 B.C. That means over four thousand years of history was destroyed by Landa and his men, information we may never recover."

As a historian, Maria knew the Maya had been around for a long time, but she had never grasped how long until that very moment. Growing up in Italy, she had heard many stories about Romulus and Remus, the mythical twin brothers who had founded the city of Rome on April 21, 753 B.C. Her father used to preach about the date's significance, saying it—and not the emergence of ancient Greece—was the "true" beginning of Western civilization. Despite her hatred of the man, his notion of history had wormed its way into her brain, somehow becoming the benchmark of comparison for anything she examined.

Constantinople? Founded a thousand years *after* Rome.

The Ottoman Empire? Two thousand years *after* Rome.

And so on.

In her field of study, she never had to go before that date. Her mental timeline started in 753 B.C. and marched toward the birth of Christianity and the present.

But the Maya? They were off the chart in the other direction.

Their civilization started 1,800 years *before* Rome.

Five hundred years *before* the first dynasty in China.

Even *before* the Great Pyramid of Giza.

Maria dwelled on the numbers as they danced through her

head. "Four thousand years of history is tough for me to comprehend. That's twice as long as the Catholic Church's."

Hamilton nodded. "Who knows what we might learn about the world if additional codices were found? They might change our view of everything."

When he said it, the cocksure grin returned to his face—the same grin that had been present when he had talked about blowing her mind. It had disappeared during their lengthy discussion of the Spanish Conquest, but it was now back in full force, tugging on the corners of his mouth like the strings of a marionette.

She lowered her voice to a whisper. "You found another codex?"

He refused to answer directly, but the twinkle in his eyes spoke volumes. "Let's just say the last few weeks have been interesting."

"That's great!" she said, trying hard to contain her enthusiasm. Although she barely knew Hamilton, she was thrilled he had found something to cap his illustrious career. For her, it was proof that good things happened to those who worked the hardest—a thought that had kept her going in the male-dominated world of archaeology. "What's the next step?"

"Funny you should ask."

"Why's that?"

"Because the next step . . . is *you*."

"Me?" she shrieked.

He laughed at her reaction. "Come now, Maria. Is it really that hard to believe? I mean, I flew you here for a reason—and it wasn't to drink daiquiris."

"I know, but . . ."

"But what?"

"I'm *not* a Maya expert."

"Thank goodness for that!" he said, laughing. "We already have one of those, and his name is Terrence Hamilton."

She cracked a smile, despite her continued confusion. As an

expert in the field of Christianity, she honestly didn't know how she could help his cause.

"Listen," he said in a soothing voice, "I know it doesn't make much sense right now, but trust me when I tell you I need your help more than you can possibly imagine."

"You do?"

"I certainly do."

"And it has something to do with my field?"

"Definitely. It's right up your alley."

She paused for a moment, thinking things through. "I have to admit I'm intrigued by your project. I can't imagine what it has to do with me. I really can't."

He smiled. "Just say the word and I'll fill you in on everything."

She took a deep breath, then nodded. "Okay. I'll do it."

"You'll do it?"

"Yes, I'll join your team. But only because I'm so intrigued."

Hamilton jumped from his seat with a burst of excitement. "Excellent! Truly excellent! You've made an old man very happy!"

"I can see that."

"Seriously, my dear, I am truly grateful."

Maria beamed with pride. It had been a long time since she had felt so appreciated. "Don't go thanking me yet. Let's hold off on the flattery until I've done something to merit it."

"Yes, of course," he said sheepishly. "It's just, I don't know. Now that you're in my corner, I feel like everything is going to be all right."

She laughed at him. "There you go again. More flattery."

He shook his head. "That wasn't flattery. Just confidence in our abilities. Nothing wrong with a little confidence, is there?"

"No. I guess not."

"What about gifts?"

"Gifts?" she said, confused.

"What's your stance on gifts?"

"Umm . . . I tend to like them."

"Wonderful!" he said, reaching into his pocket. "Because I have a gift for you."

She immediately tensed. "I hope it isn't jewelry. Otherwise, we might have to revisit the dirty-old-man conversation that we had earlier."

He brushed aside the remark. "Good heavens, Maria. It's nothing like that. In fact, it's the least romantic gift I can think of."

She relaxed slightly. "What is it?"

He extended his hand to reveal a metal cross. Approximately six inches in length, it appeared to be quite old. Accented by four red stones, which were mounted near the ends of the beams, the cross had a small hole in the middle. At first glance, she couldn't tell if a jewel had been pried from the center or something had fallen off over the years. Whatever the case, the cross was still beautiful despite the hole.

She took it in her hands. "Where did you get this?"

"On a recent dig," he explained. "Unlike you, I'm *not* a religious person—never have been, never will be—so I have no use for this trinket. I'm simply not the praying type. However, I thought someone in your field might appreciate it. If not, I'd be happy to return it to our box of goodies. You'd be surprised what you find when you search long enough."

12

AFTER DINNER, PAYNE AND JONES WENT TO A sports bar on East Carson Street, where they could shoot pool and watch the hockey game. Led by Sidney Crosby, one of the best players in the world, the Pittsburgh Penguins were playing a late-night game against the Vancouver Canucks. Despite the bad weather outside, the bar was packed with Penguins fans, many of whom wore the team's black and gold colors as they guzzled beer and shouted profanity at the dozens of TVs.

For Payne, a joint like this felt like home. Despite his military academy education and his title as CEO of Payne Industries, he was a blue-collar guy at heart. Raised by his grandfather, who had started out as a laborer at a local steel mill before starting his own company, Payne spent much of his childhood in a hard hat. During the school year, he was allowed to concentrate on academics and athletics, and he excelled at both, but during the summer months his grandfather put him to work on the floor alongside grizzled men who were more than twice his age and picked on him because of his surname. The experience did more than toughen Payne up.

It showed him how blessed he was to have opportunities outside the mill.

"Nice shot," Jones teased as he put down his beer and grabbed the cue stick from Payne. "Too bad you missed."

Payne shrugged. "The hockey game distracted me."

"Doesn't matter. It's still my turn. Let me show you how it's done." Jones eyed the table for a few seconds, then pointed to the far end. "Six ball, corner pocket."

He calmly lined up the shot, then buried the ball with one swift strike.

Payne grunted but said nothing, which was standard protocol for them. When they competed against each other, compliments were nonexistent unless someone did something miraculous—like a hole-in-one in golf or a 300 game in bowling—and even those comments came begrudgingly. Once their match was complete, their friendship returned to normal, but during the heat of battle, they were competitors who did just about anything to gain an advantage.

And that included mind games.

"So," Payne said, "I'm surprised you like eight ball as much as you do."

Jones moved around the table, looking for his next shot. "Why's that?"

"Because it's a blatantly racist game."

"You mean like hockey? I haven't seen a black player yet."

"No, I'm talking about the game's hidden meaning."

Jones shook his head, trying to ignore Payne. "You are so predictable. As soon as I start to win, you start your yapping. Yap, yap, yap. Like a little dog. It's pathetic."

Payne remained silent, patiently letting his remark fester. He knew the comment about race would eventually be addressed, and when it was, it would mess with his friend's mind.

Jones studied the table. "Four ball, side pocket . . . No, wait.

Scratch that. Two ball, far corner. I think I can squeeze it in past the twelve . . ."

"What's wrong?" Payne asked.

Jones repositioned himself for the shot. "Nothing's wrong."

"Are you sure? Because it *looks* like something's wrong."

He ignored the question and attempted the shot, which he missed by a few inches. Not because he was distracted but because it was a difficult shot. "Shit."

Payne fought the urge to smile as he snatched the cue back. "Wow. That was *really* close. You must be heartbroken. I'll tell you what: If you want, we can move the balls back and I'll let you try again. That's what my dad used to do . . . when I was three."

"Screw you."

"I can even pick you up so you can see over the edge of the table a little better. For a short guy like you, that's a pretty big disadvantage."

Jones sneered as he returned to their corner table. He took a long swig of beer before he spoke again. "What were you talking about before?"

"When?"

"Earlier."

"Yeah, that really narrows it down."

Jones growled softly. "That bullshit about eight ball."

"Oh, *that*. I was wondering when we'd get back to that. I heard some sociologist talking about it on TV. He claims eight ball is a racist game that should be boycotted by everyone."

"Really? Why's that?"

Payne explained the theory. "The cue ball—which is *white*—is used to knock around all the colored balls. The balls that are solid in color have the lowest numbers on them. In other words, they have the lowest value, according to society. Meanwhile, the striped balls—which are half white—have higher numbers, giving them more intrinsic value."

Jones grunted. "I never thought of it like that."

"But that's not the worst part."

"It's not?"

Payne shook his head. "The object of the game is to knock the eight ball—which is *black*—off the table. Nobody wins until the black ball gets eliminated. Once it does, we celebrate."

"Son of a bitch! We're playing a racist game."

"Just say the word and we can quit."

From his seat in the corner, Jones eyed the playing surface. He had a three-ball lead in their current game. "Not right now. I'm winning."

"Are you sure? Because I'm more than willing to quit—"

Jones interrupted him. "Not a chance in hell! It's funny how you didn't mention this racism when you were kicking my ass in the last game."

"I didn't think of it then."

"I wonder why."

"Wait! What are you suggesting? That I'd stoop so low as to use race issues to my personal advantage?"

Jones nodded. "Just like a whitey."

Payne faked indignation. More like brothers than friends, they constantly joked about race without offending each other. It had been that way for as long as they could remember. "How dare you call me whitey! I'm an honorary black guy. You said so yourself."

"You *were* until you made up that bullshit about a sociologist."

"Bullshit? What bullshit?"

Jones called his bluff. "Sociologist, my ass! That eight-ball-is-racist skit is one of the oldest jokes in the world. I've heard everyone from Martin Lawrence to Chris Rock talk about it. If you're gonna distract me, you need to come up with fresher material."

Before Payne could respond, he heard his phone ring above the din of the bar. It was sitting on their table, right next to Jones. "Can you grab that for me?"

"Not a chance. You'll use it as an excuse to quit."

"No, I won't."

"Yes, you will."

"At least tell me who's calling. I won't pick up unless it's important."

Jones sighed and grabbed the phone. He did a double take when he read the caller ID. The name on the screen was a blast from the past. Not Payne's past. His *own* past. For a moment, it took his breath away, like a sucker punch to the gut. Why in the hell was she calling Payne in the middle of the night? The two of them didn't talk—or did they? If so, his best friend had been keeping it from him.

Suddenly his world was filled with doubt.

Payne searched for his next shot. "Who is it?"

"Maria," he said softly.

"Who?"

Jones cleared his throat and spoke louder. "Maria."

"Maria who? I don't know any Marias."

He glared at his friend. "Maria Pelati."

Payne stopped what he was doing and focused on Jones. From the look in his eyes, it was obvious he wasn't happy about the call. "Really? Why's she calling me?"

He continued to glare. "I was about to ask you the same thing."

13

ANGEL RAMIREZ WAS THE SECOND IN COMMAND IN Hector's organization. He was phoned a few hours after Hector received the proof-of-life call from the kidnappers. Hector wouldn't tell him what was going on. He just told him to get his ass to the mansion as soon as possible. He would explain everything when Angel—the name is pronounced "AHN-hell" in Spanish—arrived.

Hector was waiting for him in his library. As he paced back and forth, the look on his face was one of rage. Not anger but all-out fury. Unaware of the crisis, Angel assumed that he had done something to upset his boss. He racked his brain and tried to remember any mistakes he had made in the last few days, but he came up empty. Still, Angel was so concerned about Hector's wrath that he glanced at the floor to make sure plastic hadn't been laid down to protect the wood. On more than one occasion, Hector had fired an employee by *literally* firing at him.

Angel breathed a sigh of relief when he saw the floor.

Still pacing, Hector blurted out, "They have my kids."

"What?" he said in Spanish.

"They have my fucking kids."

"Who does?"

"How should I fucking know? If I did, I would get them!"

Angel shook his head in confusion. His boss wasn't making sense. "Hector, what are you talking about? Someone stole your children?"

"Yes!" he screamed. "They got my kids!"

"When did this happen?"

Hector paused in thought. For him, the last thirty-six hours had been a long nightmare. At some point, one day had run into the next. "Yesterday. While we were sleeping."

"They took your kids from here?"

"Yes!"

"How did they get in?"

Hector glared at him. "I have no fucking idea! I'm not a detective!"

He picked up an antique globe and flung it across the room. Solidly constructed from a single piece of metal, the globe struck a series of Aztec masks that were displayed on the far wall. One of the masks was obliterated on impact, and another was damaged when it fell and bounced across the floor. Hector immediately regretted his outburst.

Other than his kids, artifacts were his pride and joy.

Growing up in Mexico City, Hector was fascinated by the history of the Aztecs, an indigenous group that had ruled the region through power and fear. Even as a small boy, when most of his friends were focused on baseball and soccer, he preferred the local museums to the neighborhood parks. He simply couldn't get enough of the Aztec culture. Eventually, once he reached a point in his life where he had more money than he could possibly spend, he returned to his childhood passion, buying artifacts through legal and illegal means. The shelves and walls in his library were lined with the relics he had collected in recent years.

Angel urged him to settle down. "Hector, listen to me. I know you're upset. You have every right to be. I can't even imagine the terror you're feeling. But I need you to tell me everything. Not a little. Not a lot. But *everything*. It's the only way I can help."

A few seconds passed before Hector nodded. Slightly at first, and then a full nod—as if it took that long to finally give in. For a man like Hector, it took a lot to admit that he needed help from anyone, even his best friend. Normally, he had the world by the balls, not the other way around. "Okay! I'll tell you. But it doesn't leave this room."

"Of course not. This is between us."

"I'm serious," he growled. "If this gets out, our enemies will pounce. I can't afford to show weakness."

Angel nodded in agreement. He knew what was at stake.

Over the next few minutes, Hector filled him in on everything. The phone calls. The threats. The initial request. And worst of all, the silence. Twelve hours had passed since Hector had received a proof of life. One from his daughter, but not from his son. Both men had been in the kidnapping game long enough to know that it was probably just a ploy. Nothing more than a scare tactic to speed up negotiations. On the other hand, they had also seen the alternative. Maybe something had happened and the boy was dead.

Hector tried not to think about it.

Angel asked, "What does your gut tell you?"

"About what?"

"The kidnappers. Why did they target you? For money? For power? For revenge?"

He shrugged. "Probably all three."

"Maybe. Or maybe not."

He wasn't in the mood for games. "Explain."

"If this was about power, why did they go after your kids? They were already in your house. They got past your guards and your security system without detection. If they cared about power, why didn't they just creep down the hall and shoot you in the head? That would have made a much bigger statement than a kidnapping."

Hector glared at him. "Are you trying to make me feel better?"

"As a matter of fact, I am. In our business, the only way to get power is to take it. They had their chance to steal your crown, but they passed on the opportunity. Why would they do that if they cared about power? The truth is they wouldn't."

Hector shrugged. He wasn't in the mood to think.

Angel continued: "I think revenge is the most likely reason. You make your living from kidnapping, and someone abducted your kids. I think that's too coincidental to ignore."

"You're probably right."

"I'm sure money will come into play at some point, but so far they haven't asked for cash. Or have they?"

"No money. Just the medallion."

Angel shook his head. It didn't make sense to him. Hector had millions upon millions of dollars, but so far the only thing the kidnappers had requested was a relic that Hector had bought at a private auction for less than twenty thousand dollars. Why would they do that?

"I don't get it. What's so special about this medallion?"

Hector sighed. "Everything."

14

PAYNE HAD NOTHING TO HIDE. HE TRULY DIDN'T
know why Maria was calling. The last he had heard, she had
earned her doctorate in archaeology and was living in Italy. Or
somewhere near there. He honestly didn't know because he wasn't
that close to her. Other than a work-related adventure a few years
back, the only connection they shared was his pissed-off best
friend, who had dated her briefly before things had fizzled out. To
this day, Payne still didn't know what had happened between the
two of them, because Jones refused to talk about it, but the glare
on his friend's face proved he wasn't over it. Or her.

With that in mind, Payne decided to tread cautiously.

He answered the phone in front of Jones. "Hello."

"Jon, is that you?"

"Yes. Who's this?"

"It's Maria Pelati. Do you remember me?"

"Of course I remember you." He pointed toward the exit and
urged Jones to follow. "Hang on just a minute. It's really loud in
here. Let me walk outside so I can hear you better."

"Please hurry. I think I'm in trouble."

Noticing the tension in her voice, Payne pushed his way through the crowd while Jones hustled to keep up. "Almost there. Give me two more seconds . . ."

Payne opened the door and stepped into the bitter cold. His clothes and hair were quickly coated with snow. Except for two smokers who huddled near the doorway for warmth, the sidewalk was completely deserted. On a night like this, even hookers stayed inside. Searching for privacy, Payne glanced in both directions and spotted an empty bus shelter about twenty feet to his left. Although it wasn't heated, it was better than nothing. Not only would it protect him from the gusting wind but it would save his lungs from the secondhand smoke.

Payne ignored the elements and headed that way.

Jones, who was slowed by the crowd and the bouncer, emerged a moment later without his coat or gloves. This time, he didn't shiver or complain about the weather. His emotions were keeping him warm. A little too warm.

"Where in the hell are you going?" he shouted.

"In here," Payne replied as he ducked into the shelter. Made of tempered safety glass, the walls were covered with ads for local businesses. A wooden bench was bolted to the ground. A fluorescent light glowed overhead.

"Jon, are you there?" she asked.

"I'm here," he assured her, as Jones joined him inside the shelter. "If it's okay with you, I'm going to put you on speakerphone, so DJ can listen in."

She took a deep breath. "David's there?"

"Yes. Is that a problem?"

She paused. "Maybe."

"Great," Payne said, completely ignoring her response. He didn't care how many problems it caused Maria. There was no way he was going to keep this conversation from Jones. Not with the anger in his best friend's eyes. Instead of condensation, Payne half expected to see flames coming out of Jones's nostrils. He was *that* pissed.

Payne turned on his speakerphone. "You're on with both of us."

She remained silent for the next few seconds, unsure of what to say.

The moment lingered a little too long for Jones.

"Are you there?" Jones blurted.

"Yes," she said meekly. "I'm here."

As soon as he heard her voice, the edge in his softened. He could tell something was wrong. "Are you all right?"

"I don't know. I honestly don't know."

His anger quickly turned to concern. "Where are you? At home?"

"No," she said. "I'm at a hotel."

"Where's the hotel?"

"Cancún."

"*Cancún?* What are you doing in Mexico?"

"I came here for a job, but . . ."

"But what?"

She swallowed hard. "Something happened."

Jones glanced at Payne, looking for an explanation, hoping he could fill in all the details that were currently missing. But Payne was at a loss for words. He was just as confused as Jones, maybe more so, since he had no idea why she would call him in the middle of the night. Then again, neither did Jones, which was why his temper had flared when he saw her name on Payne's caller ID. For a few terrible minutes, he had assumed his best friend had betrayed him.

Jones quickly regained his composure. "First things first. Are you hurt?"

"No."

"Are you safe?"

"Maybe."

"That's not good enough," Jones snapped.

Payne put his hand on his friend's shoulder and squeezed, urging him to calm down. Anxiety would only heighten the situation. "What do you mean by *maybe*?"

She tried to explain. "I'm locked in my bedroom inside my suite, but I don't know how safe it is. I think they grabbed him downstairs."

"Grabbed who?" Payne asked.

"My boss. His name is Terrence Hamilton."

Without delay, Jones punched the name into his smart phone and pulled up as much information as he could from the Internet. Within seconds, he knew Hamilton was an American anthropologist from a prestigious university, and he specialized in the Maya.

Payne continued the questioning. "Do you know who grabbed him?"

"I don't know. I didn't see it. But he left the restaurant and didn't come back. He said he would be gone for five minutes—he had to get something from his car—but he never returned. I waited there for an hour. I even ordered a second drink, but he never came back."

"Did you look for his car?"

She nodded. "It's still outside my hotel."

"What hotel?"

"The Fiesta Americana."

Payne whistled. "Nice place."

As a connoisseur of fine hotels, he was quite familiar with its extravagance. Although he had never stayed there, he knew it was the type of resort that had security guards and hundreds of cameras. That meant if Hamilton had been snatched from the property grounds, the odds were pretty good that someone knew something. With the right amount of persuasion, Payne was confident they could get to the bottom of things in less than an hour. Maybe two if they needed a translator who wouldn't faint at the sight of blood. Sometimes those were tough to find.

"Maria," Jones said as he reentered the conversation, "we can worry about your boss later. For now, I need to make sure you're not in danger. Are you safe in your room?"

"I don't know," she admitted.

"Why don't you know?"

She took a deep breath, trying to calm her nerves. "When I came back here, things had been moved around—like someone was looking for something."

"Could it have been a maid?" Jones asked.

"No," she snapped, "it wasn't a maid! My room was tossed. My clothes are everywhere. And my passport is missing. Someone took it from my nightstand."

"Your passport was stolen?"

"As far as I can tell—unless it's buried under this mess."

Payne tried to reassure her. "Don't worry about your passport. It happens all the time. We'll contact your embassy and get you a new one. No problem at all."

Maria shook her head. "I'm not worried about my passport. I'm worried about Hamilton. I think someone grabbed him when he went to his car."

"But you didn't see it?"

"No, I didn't see it."

"Then why would someone grab him? Is he rich? Does he have enemies? What can you tell us about him?"

"Not much," she admitted. "He called out of the blue and hired me for a job that he refused to discuss on the phone—but he hinted at a major discovery. We were in the middle of discussing the specifics when he disappeared."

"Hold up!" Payne demanded. "You met the guy today?"

"Yes."

"Are you sure he didn't ditch you?"

"Believe me, that's the first thing I thought when he didn't come back to the restaurant. But the more I thought about it, the less sense it made. He was in the middle of telling me about my role in things when he went to his car to get some documents. But his car is still here *and* he left his briefcase at the table. If he was ditching me, he would have taken both."

Payne agreed. "You're probably right."

"Couple that with my room being tossed, and . . ."

"You're right. It seems suspicious."

Jones interrupted them. "Speaking of your room, if someone searched it, there's always the chance they might come back. Did you barricade your door?"

She nodded. "With everything I could find."

"Good."

"Same with the glass door to my terrace. I rolled up newspapers and wedged them in the track so the door can't slide open."

"That's smart. How high is your room?"

"Top floor."

"Good. That'll be tough to access from outside."

She took a deep breath. "What else can I do?"

Jones shrugged. "Not much—unless you want to call the police. But I'll be honest: The police in Mexico are pretty damn corrupt. I know that from personal experience."

"No," she admitted, "I prefer this. I feel safer already."

Jones appreciated the sentiment but felt helpless being so far away. "You know, it's funny that you called when you did."

"Really? Why's that?"

Jones snatched the phone from Payne, then turned off the speakerphone so he could speak to her in private. "Because Jon and I were looking for somewhere to go this weekend. Somewhere warmer than Pittsburgh."

She smiled. "I forgot how much you hate the cold."

"I really do."

"Not to rub it in, but the weather is gorgeous here. I was going to try out my new bikini this weekend."

"Me, too!"

She laughed. "I'm serious. This was supposed to be a working vacation. Now I'm stuck in my room, worried for my safety. I feel like such an idiot."

"Listen," Jones said in a soothing voice, "I know you aren't the type of woman who needs to be rescued. Trust me, I know that better than anyone. But it sounds like your boss might be in serious trouble, the kind I can handle. If you'd like, I'd be more than happy—"

Payne cleared his throat loudly.

Jones smiled and corrected himself. "I mean, *we* would be more than happy to come to Cancún to look into things for you. That is, if you're interested."

She nodded. "Yes, I'm interested."

He grinned. "I was hoping you'd say that."

15

Because of the winter storm, the Payne Industries jet couldn't take off from the private airfield until early the next morning. Not only did the runway have to be cleared of snow, but their plane had to be deiced to prevent mechanical failure. Once they got off the ground and above the thick layer of gray clouds, their four-hour flight was smooth all the way to Cancún.

Having called ahead, a silver SUV was waiting for them at the hangar when they landed in Mexico. Payne handled the paperwork while Jones tossed their bags into the trunk and entered the hotel address into the vehicle's navigation system. Less than thirty minutes later, they were pulling up to the Fiesta Americana, where they were greeted by one valet and zero mariachi bands. To them, that was a good thing. No one should be forced to listen to trumpets before noon.

Not wanting to scare Maria, Jones called her from the lobby to let her know they were on their way up to her suite. By the time they got there, she had pulled the furniture away from the door and put down the steak knife she had clutched throughout the night. For her, sleep had been next to impossible. She had dozed off once or twice while reading a book on the Maya, but the smallest sound in the hall or outside her window had caused her to wake in a panic.

All in all, it had been a dreadful night.

Just before dawn, as the sun struggled to rise above the distant horizon, she tried to recall the last time she couldn't fall asleep because of fear. Was it during a thunderstorm when she was a child? Or the first time she went camping alone? Eventually, she reached an ironic conclusion, one that put a smile on her face and let her know that everything would be all right.

For as long as she could remember, she had always loved the saying "God works in mysterious ways." Her mother had taught it to her at an early age, and Maria believed it with all her heart—so much so that she had said it thousands of times over the years. Despite the constant repetition and her steadfast belief in its message, she was still amazed whenever the adage proved true. And in her mind, this was one of those times. Why? Because the last time fear had kept her awake was the night she had met Payne and Jones in Milan.

A night they had hunted her like prey.

A night they had threatened to kill her.

Now they were there to protect her.

✠　　✠　　✠

JONES KNOCKED SOFTLY ON the door. "Maria, it's us."

"Just a minute," she said as she glanced through the peephole.

Jones stood in front, a forced smile on his worried face, doing his best to put a positive spin on a bad situation. Behind him, Payne loomed in the background. A quiet pillar of strength, he stood there with his arms crossed, muscles bulging against his sleeves, his eyes looking for trouble. If possible, he looked even bigger than she remembered.

Years had passed since she had seen them last, and a lot of things had changed. But at that moment, as she stood there with her eye against the lens and the doorknob in her hand, she knew one thing had remained the same: her feelings for both of them.

After all this time, she still felt conflicted and confused.

Yet here they were, willing to help.

Maria took a deep breath and opened the door. "Thank you for coming."

"Thank you for calling." Jones gave her a friendly hug. "Pittsburgh's supposed to get six more inches of snow this weekend. That's six inches too many for me."

Payne hugged her next. As he did, he glanced over her shoulder and scanned the suite. "I'm not a wuss like DJ, but I have to admit, sunburn sounds better than frostbite."

She smiled at the notion. "Well, I brought a bottle of suntan lotion. You're welcome to it—if you can find it in here. It's kind of a mess."

Payne nodded as he stepped inside. Furniture was out of place. Paintings were off the walls. Clothes were scattered everywhere. Her suite looked like the movie set of *The Hangover*, minus Mike Tyson's tiger. "Man, I want to party with you. You live like a rock star."

She scoffed at the notion. "Hardly! I spent the whole night in bed, researching the Maya."

As he closed the door, Jones tried to lighten the mood. "Is that what the kids are calling it nowadays? 'Researching the Maya'?"

Payne smiled. "Hey, baby, want to come back to my place and research the Maya?"

Jones raised his voice an octave. "Only if you sacrifice a virgin."

She blushed as she laughed. "Trust me, I spent the night alone, trying to figure out why Hamilton brought me to Mexico. I even picked the lock on his briefcase to look for clues."

Payne stared at her. "You picked his lock? With what?"

"A paper clip—just like David taught me."

Jones gave her a high five. "That's my girl."

Payne glanced at him. "You taught her to pick a lock? When did you do that?"

He shrugged. "Second date."

"No, seriously."

"I *am* serious."

Maria laughed at the memory. "We had gone out for dinner in this trendy part of town. Afterward we went for a long walk and came across this old couple who had locked their keys in their car. They were trying to open their door with a rusty coat hanger. It looked like they had found it in a storm drain or something, because it had clearly seen better days. Anyway, David offered to help them, and—"

Payne interrupted her. "Let me guess: He beat them senseless and ended up stealing their car. Or is that more of a third-date kind of thing?"

Jones rolled his eyes, then ticked off an imaginary list. "Third date is firearms. Fourth date is self-defense. And the fifth date is . . . *researching the Maya*."

"Unfortunately," Payne teased, "I see a major flaw in your system. Once you teach them self-defense, you probably won't get to do any research."

Jones groaned. "Is that why I'm still single?"

Maria laughed at their antics and pointed toward the main bedroom. "Let me get the briefcase. I need to show you what I found."

Payne waved her off. "Take your time. I want to check out your place."

Known as a master suite, it looked more like a luxury condo-
minium than a hotel room. With 860 square feet of living space,
the corner suite was equipped with marble floors, a wet bar, a
sunken living room, two large bathrooms, an indoor Jacuzzi, and
a large TV. Outside, there was a private terrace with a teak patio
set from Spain. As far as Payne could tell, it was the only furniture
that hadn't been disturbed.

He stared out the window at the light blue sea. The water
reminded him of a diving trip he had taken near the Cayman
Islands. "Why toss the suite?"

Jones shrugged. "I was wondering the same thing."

"She flies into town. Comes here and unpacks. Then goes downstairs to meet Hamilton. That's what? Three hours at most?"

"Sounds about right."

"If that's the case, there are only three reasonable explanations
that I can think of—and one of them is pretty unlikely."

"Which one is that?"

"Random robbery."

"You're right. That seems doubtful. Nothing is missing except
her passport, and run-of-the-mill thieves wouldn't trash the place.
They'd want to make as little noise as possible."

"Agreed."

"Which leads us to number two."

Payne nodded. "Nonrandom robbery."

"They were looking for something specific. Maybe something
she brought from home, or something she was holding for Hamilton. They were confident she had it here, so they trashed the suite,
looking for it."

"If that's the case, they probably think she still has it—unless
they grabbed Hamilton to find out for sure."

"Any idea what it might be?"

Payne shook his head. "What about you?"

"Nope."

Maria cleared her throat from the back of the room. "Me, neither."

Jones turned and faced her. "Are you sure? Maybe a book, or a document of some kind?"

"Absolutely not."

"Were you supposed to bring anything at all?"

She placed the briefcase on the counter, then walked toward the window where they were standing. "A week's worth of clothes and toiletries. Other than that, I was on my own."

Payne grunted. "That's too bad."

"That's *bad*? Why is that bad?"

"Why? Because there's only one other scenario that I can think of."

"Which is?"

Payne looked at Jones. "You want to tell her?"

"No, you can tell her. It's your theory."

Maria stepped forward and poked Payne in his chest. She did it so hard she almost made a hole in his shirt. "I don't care who tells me, just tell me!"

Payne grimaced but admired her feistiness. That was more like the Maria that he remembered from Milan. She wasn't someone who cowered in her room, but someone who was willing to fight. "Fine! I'll tell you. But you aren't going to like it."

"Why not?"

"Because someone trashed your suite to scare you."

16

MARIA LOOKED TO JONES FOR CONFIRMATION. HE nodded and tried to assure her that everything would be all right, but she cut him off in the middle of his speech.

"Who would want to scare me?" she demanded.

Jones shrugged. "You would know better than us."

She glanced at Payne, looking for answers. "This is my first time here. Why would someone want to scare me?"

"I don't know, but I get the feeling it worked."

The comment pissed her off. "You're right! I got scared and locked myself in my room. Sorry for being human. Unlike you, most of us haven't been trained to kill."

Payne paused, unsure where her anger was coming from. He assumed it was a combination of fear, anxiety, and lack of sleep—as a former soldier, he knew how volatile that mix could be—yet he sensed something else was bubbling under the surface. Was it guilt over Hamilton's disappearance? Or embarrassment about calling them for help? Whatever the reason, he knew his comment had served as the catalyst to her outburst.

"Sorry, Maria. I didn't mean it as an insult. I honestly didn't. I simply meant if they were trying to scare you, they did a damn good job."

She took a deep breath and backed away. "I'm sorry, too."

"There's no need to apologize."

"Actually, there is. You came all this way to help, and I just yelled at you over nothing. I shouldn't have done that."

"Don't worry about it. I've been trained to ignore emotions."

She smiled but said nothing.

Jones cleared his throat to break the remaining tension. "Anyway, let's get back to the original topic. Who would want to scare you?"

She gave it some thought. "Someone who doesn't want me to work for Hamilton, I guess. But I don't know who that would be. Maybe a rival or something."

"Does he have one?" Payne wondered.

"Not that I know of, but I can make some calls and ask around."

Jones nodded. "That's a good place to start. We can also do some digging on our own. See if anything pops up. Who knows what we might find?"

Maria looked at him. "Do you still have connections with the government?"

"What kind are you referring to?"

"Police."

Jones nodded. As a licensed private detective, he had many friends in the law-enforcement community. "Why?"

"Can you run a criminal background check on Hamilton?"

"Of course I can. But why? What are you thinking?"

"I just want to make sure he isn't a bad guy."

"Why would you think that?" Payne asked.

"I don't. I mean, I didn't . . ."

"Until?"

"Until I opened his case. Now I'm not so sure."

Payne and Jones glanced at the briefcase. It was sitting on the counter on the other side of the suite. They had completely forgotten about it until that very moment. As Maria walked toward it, they followed closely behind, all the while wondering what she could have found that had put doubt in her mind. Payne thought it was pretty ironic that Maria didn't think Hamilton was a bad guy until *she* picked the lock on *his* briefcase, but he decided to hold his comment for another time—when she was in a better mood and his chest had fully healed from her claw marks.

Maria continued her explanation. "I was hoping there would be a map of the dig site or maybe some information about my role in things. Instead, I found this."

She opened the briefcase so they could see inside.

Tucked in a hand-stitched leather holster was a .38 Smith & Wesson single-action revolver. Made from bright nickel, it had a spur trigger, a flat-sided hammer, and an eight-inch barrel that would have looked at home in a cowboy movie. A gold eagle was engraved on both sides of the revolver between the cylinder and the top of the pearl grips. The engravings continued down the barrel, an intricate pattern of swirls and flourishes that was common on Mexican revolvers.

Jones started to salivate as soon as he saw it. He carefully removed it from its holster and held it up to the light to admire the craftsmanship. From the weight alone, he knew the revolver was fully loaded. With a practiced hand, he tilted out the cylinder, dumped the bullets into his opposite palm, then clicked the cylinder back in place. "If Hamilton is dead, I call dibs."

Maria smacked his arm. "I can't believe you just said that."

"Sorry. But it's a *really* nice revolver."

Payne admired it as well. "See the eagle on the side?"

She looked closer. "It's clutching something in its beak. . . . Is that a snake?"

Payne nodded. "That symbol is the Mexican coat of arms. Not the current version, but one from the forties. If I had to guess, I'd say the revolver is from that era."

"In other words, it's a collectible."

"A collectible that can kill."

Jones grunted his displeasure. "That being said, it's not the most efficient gun in the world. This is a single-action revolver, meaning you have to cock the hammer with your thumb after every shot. The movement of the hammer spins the cylinder, which moves the next round into place. Compared to a modern Glock or SIG Sauer, this is a relic from another time."

Payne argued his point. "But it's still a gun, right?"

"Yes."

"And it was loaded?"

"You know it was."

"Then Hamilton was prepared to use it."

"I completely agree. Now all we have to do is figure out when the next stagecoach is coming to town, and we can go down there and stop the robbery," cracked Jones.

"I'm serious."

"I'm serious, too. This *isn't* an offensive weapon."

She looked at him. "What do you mean by that?"

Jones paused in thought. "Are you familiar with the expression 'Don't bring a knife to a gunfight'? Well, I wouldn't bring this weapon, either. It's way too slow and inefficient. A gun like this was designed for appearance and little else. Do you know what they call a revolver like this in Texas?"

"I have no idea."

"A barbecue gun. Do you know why?"

She shook her head.

"Because it's the kind of gun you'd wear to a family barbecue. You'd strap it to your hip in a fancy holster like this one, and all your buddies would admire it."

She looked to Payne for clarification. "People wear guns to family barbecues in America?"

"Not in America, but they do in Texas."

"Really?"

Payne kept a straight face. "When kids play Cowboys and Indians in the great state of Texas, they use real guns. And *real* Indians."

She cracked a smile. "That's so wrong."

"Sorry. I meant Native Americans."

"Anyway," Jones concluded, "I don't think Hamilton had this revolver to rob a bank or do anything illegal. I think he had it with him for self-defense."

"Why do you say that?" she asked.

He aimed the revolver at the plasma TV and cocked the hammer. "This sucker might be slow, but people are going to think twice if you whip it out."

"Okay," she admitted, "that sounds plausible. He had it with him for self-defense. But why? Why did he think it was necessary?"

Jones pulled the trigger, and the hammer slammed shut. The metallic clack echoed in the trashed suite. "That's what we need to find out."

17

TIFFANY DUFFY DIDN'T KNOW WHAT TO EXPECT when she flew to Mexico City for a business trip, but she wasn't expecting this.

According to CIA estimates, Mexico City is the third most-populated metropolitan area in the world, behind only Tokyo, Japan, and Seoul, South Korea. With more than 21 million people, Mexico City accounts for nearly twenty percent of the population of Mexico and a significant portion of the nation's wealth. Because of its proximity to the United States, Mexico is often viewed as a secondary player on the global stage, but its population of 111 million people is the eleventh largest in the world. That is more than Canada, Ireland, and the United Kingdom combined.

The capital city is nestled in the Valley of Mexico in the high plateaus of the Trans-Mexican Volcanic Belt. Composed of more than twenty volcanoes, including some of Mexico's highest peaks, the belt stretches across southern Mexico from the Pacific coast to the Caribbean Sea. With a minimum altitude of 7,200 feet, Mexico City has a much different feel than tropical Cancún.

Instead of colorful resorts, there are drab apartment buildings. Instead of manicured streets, there is urban sprawl. And instead of white, sandy beaches, there are mountains topped with perpetual snow.

Sadly, many of those peaks are rarely seen by locals because of the thick layer of smog that hovers above the valley like a dirty blanket. Twenty times worse than any city in America, the smog reached such toxic levels in 1990 that a local newspaper estimated the life expectancy of its citizens was nearly ten years less than residents of other Mexican cities. To combat this problem, the local government instituted a program called "Hoy No Circula." In Spanish, it means "Today (your car) doesn't circulate," but it's more commonly known as "One Day Without a Car." Restrictions are based on the last digit of license plates and prohibit certain cars from being driven on certain days of the week.

Tiffany wasn't familiar with the program, but she would've had a hard time believing there were *any* traffic regulations on the city's busy streets. A constant stream of cars—more than she had ever seen in her native Ohio—whizzed past at an alarming speed. She tried to cross the road on multiple occasions, only to be greeted by a chorus of beeps and shouts of profanity. At least she *assumed* it was profanity. She didn't know for sure, since her street slang was rusty, but she had spent enough time in Cleveland to realize that motorists probably weren't welcoming her to their city while they were flipping her off.

With map in hand, Tiffany eventually made her way through the chaos and into the heart of the Centro Histórico, where the pace seemed to slow. She had seen several posters of Plaza de la Constitución at the airport and hoped to take a few pictures of her own.

Dressed in blue jeans and a beige sweater, Tiffany stood out in the crowd, thanks to her strawberry-blond hair and freckles. In Mexico City, redheads were almost as rare as clean air or good

French food, so she was noticed by Latino men and women alike. More cute than sexy, she was often classified as the girl next door—especially in the winter, when she packed on a few extra pounds. The truth was she wasn't obese or even overweight, but she was a little too thick to be mistaken for a fashion model. And she was fine with that. Unlike some of her friends, who starved themselves to fit into smaller dress sizes, she worked out just enough to keep the figure she had. In fact, when anyone questioned her weight, she always replied, *I would rather be happy and healthy than skinny and sad.*

Anxious to learn as much about the area as possible, she paid fifty pesos for a walking tour of the historic plaza. Led by an elderly guide named Paco, the group had thirteen people in total with a wide variety of ages and ethnicities.

"Good afternoon," he said in accented English. "Welcome to Constitution Square. Or, as most locals call it, Zócalo. Does anyone know what this word means?"

Someone shouted the answer: "The main square."

Paco pointed at him. "*Muy bien!* I see someone has taken my tour before! If I have questions, maybe I ask you? I am old and sometimes forget."

Tiffany smiled, glad he had a sense of humor.

"Okay," Paco said, "that was easy question. Let me see how you do with tricky one. Why do Mexicans call this place Zócalo instead of Plaza de la Constitución?"

This time nobody guessed.

Paco had anticipated the silence. "The answer is simple. The *Spanish* Constitution of 1812 was signed in the plaza, but the *Mexican* Constitution was not. My brothers *refuse* to call this Constitution Square until there is a Mexican Square in Madrid!" To drive home his point, he thrust his fist into the air, as if he had just delivered an impassioned speech to a group of armed rebels.

He held it there for a moment before he broke into a wide grin. "Who am I kidding? We call it Zócalo because it is easier to say."

Everybody laughed as he signaled for them to follow. Slowly but surely, he made his way across the gray plaza toward a gigantic Mexican flag that fluttered high above the center of the square. Not wanting to miss a word, Tiffany walked beside him.

"Long ago, *zócalo* did not mean 'main square.' The word comes from Italian word *zoccolo*, which means 'pedestal.' Back in 1800s, the government planned a monument to honor Mexican independence. They set up a giant pedestal but—oops!—never put up the statue. Locals, as a joke, referred to this place as *zócalo*, and the nickname became popular. Before long, it was a new word in our language. Now Zócalo is the name of many squares throughout Mexico."

"Why didn't they put up the statue?" someone asked.

Paco shrugged. "I do not know. That was before my time. But I can tell you that the Zócalo is one of the largest city squares in the world. I have heard Red Square in Moscow is the only one larger, but some visitors say that is wrong. I am too old to measure, so I do not know for sure." He glanced at Tiffany and winked. "But it is *much* bigger than any square in America."

She smiled at him. "How did you know I was American?"

"*Pelirroja.*"

"*Pelirroja*? What does that mean?"

He pointed at her hair. "It means 'redhead.' You are only second one this year. The other one look like hamburger girl from Wendy's. I called her Wendy, but she did not like."

Tiffany nodded. "I wouldn't like that, either."

He smiled. "That is why I no call you Wendy! Who said I am dumb?"

Everybody laughed, including Paco, who seemed to draw energy from the crowd. A stage actor in his younger years, he loved being the center of attention. For him, the size of his audience didn't matter. He wanted to put on the best show possible.

He turned his back to the north and pointed over his shoulders with both of his thumbs. "Okay, my friends. It is time to stop looking at me. There are better things to see. Behind me is Catedral Metropolitana de la Asunción de María. In English, that is Metropolitan Cathedral of the Assumption of Mary. It is the largest and oldest cathedral in the Americas. It is also the seat of the Roman Catholic Archdiocese of Mexico. The cathedral was built in sections from 1573 to 1813. Its design is a mixture of three different styles, but I do not remember what they are. If you want to find out, you can get a tour of the cathedral. But I warn you: the priests charge three times as much as me and are not nearly as funny."

He waited for the laughter to die down before he pointed to the east. A long building, half the height of the cathedral, stretched the entire length of the plaza. Its facade was decorated with *tezontle*, a porous red stone common in Mexican construction. "That is Palacio Nacional, or the National Palace. Once the presidential residence of Mexico, it is now a government building with offices for the treasury and collections from the National Archives. If you have the time, I recommend the giant mural painted by Diego Rivera. He is famous Mexican painter who was married to Frida Kahlo. She was even more famous than him. Do you know Frida?"

A few people nodded tentatively.

He smiled. "She had eyebrows like angry caterpillars."

The group laughed and nodded in understanding. Pictures and paintings of Frida—who grew up in Coyoacán, one of the sixteen boroughs of Mexico City—and her distinctive eyebrows were displayed throughout the city.

"Anyhow," he said, "the mural represents the entire history of Mexico. It is like the Sistine Chapel at the Vatican—except it is Mexican and on a wall, not Italian and on a ceiling. Actually, now that I think about it, it is nothing like the Sistine Chapel! Please forget I say anything."

Everyone laughed again.

Over the next ten minutes, he talked about the Old Portal de Mercaderes to the west and the Nacional Monte de Piedad building on the northwest corner of the plaza. He also mixed in facts and figures about the surrounding side streets and mentioned some of the festivals and religious events that were held annually in the Zócalo.

Tiffany, who knew very little about the region, thought the tour was coming to a close, but Paco was just getting to the good stuff. Until that point, everything he had mentioned was *modern* Mexican history. The true importance of the plaza had nothing to do with the Spanish and everything to do with the empire that had ruled the land prior to their arrival.

The Aztecs.

18

PAYNE AND JONES STRAIGHTENED UP HER SUITE FOR twenty minutes while they discussed their plan of attack. Meanwhile, Maria called the Italian embassy in Mexico City to find out what she had to do to get a new passport. Without one, she wouldn't be allowed to leave the country.

"Good news," she said as she emerged from her bedroom. "There's an Italian consulate in Cancún about five miles from the hotel. I can get new paperwork there."

Jones pushed the sofa into place. "Great. Do you need a lift?"

"Eventually. I'm not in a rush, though. I'm not leaving Mexico until I know why I was invited here, who trashed my suite, and what happened to Hamilton."

"Really? Because we're taking off today."

She glared at him. "You're leaving? Why?"

Jones sighed. "I miss the snow."

She laughed, glad he was only joking. "If you'd like, we can fill the Jacuzzi with ice and you can hop in for a while. It will remind you of home."

"Only if you join me, you kinky minx."

Payne grimaced. "No, thanks."

Jones pointed at Maria. "I was talking to *her*."

Payne scoffed at the notion. "I don't believe that for a second."

"Neither do I," Maria teased.

Jones was tempted to argue but realized it would get him nowhere. He opted to leave the suite instead. "I need to check something outside. When I return, I expect the two of you to be on your best behavior. That means no more childishness."

"What are you checking?" Payne wondered.

Jones opened the front door. "None of your damn business."

"Oh, I get it. *Don't ask, don't tell.*"

Jones stammered, trying to think of a witty response. When none came to mind, he stormed into the hallway and slammed the door shut.

Maria looked to Payne for an explanation. "I don't get it."

"Get what?"

"That expression. Why did he get so mad?"

Payne chuckled to himself. "I'd be happy to tell you, but it will be much funnier if you ask him about it—since the two of you dated for a while."

She shrugged and agreed to do it.

"Speaking of dating, do you mind if I ask you a personal question?"

She instantly tensed. "That depends on the question."

He sat on the arm of the couch. "Why did you two stop seeing each other? One minute it seemed like you were hot and heavy, and the next it was over."

In a flash, her face flushed with emotion. She didn't have to see her reflection in a mirror to know it. She could *feel* the burn in her cheeks. It was so intense it felt like an allergic reaction. She tried to hide her embarrassment from Payne by turning away and scooping up some magazines off the floor, but she didn't turn quickly enough.

"Why?" she asked over her shoulder. "What did David say?"

"Nothing. That's why I'm asking you."

She tried to play it cool. "Does it really matter?"

"I don't know. That's what I'm trying to figure out. Trust me, I'm doing it for his own good."

"How do you figure?"

"Just trying to see if there's a pattern. I figure, if his relationships keep ending in the same way, maybe I can do something to help. He's a great guy. He deserves to be happy."

She fiddled with the magazines. "He isn't happy?"

Payne laughed. "Not when it's cold outside."

"I meant in general."

"Happy, sad—it's tough to tell since he's always joking around."

"You're right about that—he *loves* to joke. But that's one of the things I miss the most about him. He kept me constantly laughing."

Payne leaned to his right and tried to see her face, but the angle of her body prevented it. "You miss him?"

She took a deep breath and let it out slowly. "Of course I miss him. I miss all of my friends when I'm out in the field. My job can be lonely at times."

"That's not what I meant."

"Trust me, I know what you meant. I'm not stupid."

"I didn't say that you were. In fact, I find the opposite to be true."

She turned and faced him from across the room. "Was that a *compliment*?"

He studied her face. "You sound surprised."

"I am," she admitted. "You're not exactly known for flattery."

"Hold up. Was that an *insult*?"

She shrugged off the claim. "Not necessarily. I've met many men who weren't known for their flattery. Some of them were wonderful. Others were idiots."

"Which am I?"

She smiled coyly. "I'd rather not say."

He laughed at the comment. "That doesn't surprise me. You're not exactly known for your openness."

"Well, I . . . Wait. What?"

"I asked you a question two minutes ago, and I'm still waiting for an answer. Why did you and DJ stop dating?"

She glanced away. "It's complicated."

"Isn't it always?"

"Not like this it isn't."

"Try me. I'm not as dumb as I look."

She shook her head. "I'd rather not."

"Come on. Give me a hint. Was it you?"

"Jon."

"Was it DJ?"

"Jon!"

"Was it mutual?"

"Enough! Can't you see I don't want to talk about it?"

Payne held up his hands in surrender. "Sorry. I didn't mean to freak you out. I'm just trying to protect my friend."

"Protect him from what?"

"Take a wild guess."

She pointed at herself. "*Me*? You're trying to protect him from *me*?"

"See! You are smart. I said you were, and you are."

"Trust me, Jon. You don't have to worry about me. I want the best for David. I really do. I'd never hurt him on purpose."

"Really? Then what's with the mind games?"

"*Mind games?* What are you talking about?"

"Give me a break. You know exactly what I'm talking about."

She shook her head violently. "I don't. I swear to God, I don't!"

He sensed she was telling the truth. "Last night's phone call. Why did you call me?"

"What?"

"You heard my question. Why in the world did you call me?"

She paused, searching for the words to explain her rationale. "I don't know. I was scared and needed advice from someone who had been in dangerous situations, and I thought you would be less emotional than David. I figured he might flip out if I told him my life was in danger, and I didn't want that to happen. I didn't want him to feel that pain. Besides, I didn't even know if he would answer my call. We haven't spoken in a very long time."

Payne rubbed his eyes in thought. After having doubts about her intentions, he realized maybe she wasn't playing games after all. Maybe she honestly didn't realize how much damage her phone call had caused. Although slightly naive, her explanation made a lot of sense. "Just so you know, calling the best friend of your ex is never the best thing to do—especially in the middle of the night."

She glared at him. "Sorry if I bothered you. I promise, it won't happen again."

He shook his head to let her know she had missed his point. "Maria, your call didn't bother me. It bothered *him*."

"It bothered David?"

"Of course it bothered him. You were in trouble, and you called me instead of him. How do you think that made him feel?"

She groaned in understanding. "Not very good."

Payne lowered his voice to a whisper. "Yet he was willing to swallow his pride and fly down here to make sure you were okay.

If you ask me, that says a hell of a lot about him and his feelings for you. Please keep that in mind over the next few days."

She nodded. "I promise I will."

"If not—if you start messing with his heart in any way—I swear to God we'll be on the next flight out of here, even if I have to kidnap him myself."

19

JONES RETURNED TO THE SUITE A FEW MINUTES LATER, completely unaware of the conversation that had taken place between Payne and Maria. Although he sensed some lingering tension in the room, he was too excited about his discovery to ask about it.

"I think we caught a major break," Jones proclaimed. "I figured a nice resort like this would have lots of surveillance, and I was right. They have cameras in the hallways, in the stairwells, and in the elevators. Unless the bastards jumped out of an airplane and landed on your terrace, the odds are pretty good we'll be able to see who trashed your suite."

"That's great," Maria said. "Do you think the hotel will show us the footage?"

Jones shrugged. "Only one way to find out."

Payne nodded. "Why don't you let me handle that? You two have better stuff to do."

Maria tensed, unsure what he was implying. "Such as?"

"Show DJ where Hamilton parked his car. Maybe you'll find something useful inside."

"Sure, no problem. But I don't have his keys."

Jones grinned. "We know. That's why we're going to the car while Jon is at the security office. He'll distract the guards while we break in."

She laughed. "Sounds like fun."

"It will be if we don't get caught. Mexican prisons are the worst."

"Are you speaking from experience, or . . . ?"

Jones glanced at Payne, then back at her. "Let's just say I'm glad you didn't call us from Tijuana, because we're no longer welcomed there."

"You're banned from Tijuana?"

"We were," Jones said as he opened the door for her. "But only for a decade."

"A decade?" she screeched. "What did you do?"

Jones temporarily ignored her. "You coming?"

Payne shook his head. "Not quite yet. I still have to call D.C. I'll text you when the coast is clear."

"Remember to grab the briefcase."

"Will do."

"Oh, and give my best to Randy."

Payne laughed. "I'm sure that will make his day."

✠   ✠   ✠

TECHNICALLY, RANDY RASKIN DIDN'T work in Washington, D.C. He actually worked across the Potomac River in Arlington, Virginia, inside a windowless office in the subbasement of the Pentagon, but due to his classified position as a computer researcher for the U.S. military, the data he compiled frequently found its way to the White House and Capitol Hill.

Amazingly, most of his friends thought he was nothing more than a low-level programmer, working a dead-end job in the world's largest office building—because that's what he was required to tell them. But in reality, he was a high-tech maestro, able to track down just about anything in cyberspace. Thanks to the next-generation technology and his high security clearance, Raskin was privy to many of the government's biggest secrets, a mountain of classified data that was there for the taking if someone knew how to access it. His job was to make sure the latest information got into the right hands at the best possible time.

Over the years, Payne and Jones had used his services on many occasions, which had eventually led to a friendship. Raskin often pretended he didn't have time for them, or their bimonthly favors, but the truth was he admired them greatly and would do just about anything to help. In fact, one of his biggest joys in life was living vicariously through them—whether that was during their stint with the MANIACs or their recent adventures around the globe. That included keeping tabs on them at all times.

Raskin answered his phone on the second ring. "Research."

Payne smiled. "Señor Raskin. How are you today?"

He leaned back in his chair. "I was doing great until I heard your voice. Now I'm worried about how many laws you're going to ask me to break during our conversation. I hope you know Big Brother is recording this."

"Wait a second. I thought *you* were Big Brother."

Raskin shook his head. "Sadly, I'm more like Big Brother's little brother. He accumulates all this cool information about the world, then I sneak into his room and play with his toys."

Payne laughed. "That describes you perfectly. You're such a little pest."

"I can't believe you just called me a pest. You're not even on active duty, yet you call me more often than Central Command."

"That's because CENTCOM is running a war, and I'm bored at the beach."

Raskin leaned forward and hit a few keys on his wireless keyboard. Instantly, a map of the world appeared on one of the screens in front of him. A moment later, the camera zoomed in on the east coast of Mexico, revealing a blinking dot in the city of Cancún. The camera kept zooming closer and closer until Raskin was able to see Payne's precise location on a digital map of the city.

"How's the Fiesta Americana? I hear it's lovely this time of year."

Payne grunted his displeasure at being tracked by satellite. To show his annoyance, he looked out the window and flipped off the sky. "I thought you were going to stop doing that."

"Doing what?"

"Tracking my cell signal for your personal pleasure."

"And I thought you were going to stop calling me at work."

"I would, but you never *leave* work."

"That's because I don't want you to call me."

Payne laughed at the comment. The truth was Raskin never left work because he was a raging workaholic who consumed more caffeine in a single day than Starbucks served in a week. "Fine! If you don't want to talk, I guess I won't tell you about Maria."

Raskin's ears perked up. "Maria? Who's Maria?"

"You mean you don't know? I figured with all of those fancy databases at your disposal, you'd already have her photo and dossier in front of you."

"Tell me her last name, and I will."

"Sorry, my friend, you have to earn your reward. Find out what I need to know, and I'll fill you in on everything else. And let me tell you, Maria is just your type."

"In other words, she's a woman."

"Exactly."

Raskin groaned. "Okay, okay, I'll help you out. But only because I crave estrogen. Do you know the last time I talked to a woman who wasn't my mother?"

"I have no idea."

"Well, I don't know, either. That's how long it's been."

Payne tried not to laugh. "Sorry."

"But it's not my fault. I swear it isn't. You've been to my office. You know what it's like down here. My coworkers are all *nerds*. If I was a woman, I'd stay away, too."

Payne remained silent for the next few seconds. "Are you done whining?"

Raskin nodded. "For now."

"Good. Because I need this information A-SAP."

Raskin cracked his knuckles. "Fire away."

"I need background information on a Dr. Terrence Hamilton. He's an American professor who specializes in anthropology."

"How deep?"

"Give me everything. Personal, criminal, financial, and social. He disappeared from this hotel sometime last night. If anything pops, and I mean *anything*—credit card, cell phone, ATM—I want to know immediately."

"Easy enough."

Payne walked across the room and grabbed Hamilton's gun. "I also need you to trace a weapon for me."

"What kind?"

"Smith and Wesson single-action revolver. It's a long-barreled thirty-eight. Probably fifty or sixty years old."

"Let me guess: a Mexican special."

"Well, we are in Mexico."

"Got a serial number?"

He carefully read it to Raskin. "Hamilton was carrying it in his briefcase. I don't know if he owns it, found it, stole it, or built it himself. Any info would be appreciated."

"I'll see what I can do. Might be tough, though. A gun like that will have a lot of history that isn't available online. Our amigos to the south are slightly behind in their data entry."

"Would a picture help?"

"Of Maria?" he asked excitedly.

"Of the revolver."

"Oh." Disappointment filled his voice. "Sure. Can't hurt."

Payne snapped one with his phone. "I'll send it as soon as I hang up."

"Anything else?"

"That's it for now. We just landed a few hours ago, so we're still playing catch-up. If we need something else, I'll let you know."

"Great," he said sarcastically. "Can't wait."

"By the way, DJ sends his love."

"I don't want his love. I *want* a photo of Maria."

"Sorry. Ain't gonna happen."

"In that case, I'll settle for a random chick in a bikini."

Payne smiled. "Fine. I'll see what I can do."

20

DRESSED IN KHAKI SHORTS, A COTTON BLOUSE, AND leather sandals, Maria Pelati looked like she was heading out for a day of shopping. Instead, she was on her way to the parking lot to break into Hamilton's car. The absurdity of the situation put a smile on her face.

"I have to admit," she said to Jones, who studied their surroundings with a suspicious eye, "things are never boring when we're together."

He grinned. "That's because you keep getting into trouble."

"You don't have to be so happy about it."

"As a matter of fact, I do. Without trouble, we never would have met."

A few years earlier, Maria was a graduate student on an archaeological dig in Umbria, a landlocked region in central Italy. Led by Dr. Charles Boyd, her longtime professor and mentor, they were searching for the catacombs of Orvieto, the legendary safe haven of the popes of the Middle Ages, when they stumbled across a discovery that threatened to destroy the foundation of the Catholic

Church. Fearing the damage it would cause, some high-ranking members of the Vatican tried to silence the problem by manufacturing false evidence against Boyd and leaking it to police agencies around the globe. In the blink of an eye, he went from a respected academic to one of the most sought-after fugitives in all of Europe.

And Maria was labeled as his accomplice.

Known for their ability to track and eliminate targets, Payne and Jones were coerced by the CIA to find Dr. Boyd and Maria before anyone else could grab them and capitalize on their discovery. Using their unique skill set and their vast network of connections, Payne and Jones found the fugitives in Milan and were threatening to turn them over to the authorities when they realized they had been set up by the men who had hired them. Over the next week, Payne and Jones protected the fugitives—and their shocking secret—like precious cargo, battling a private brigade of henchmen in Italy, Austria, and Switzerland, while staying one step ahead of the law.

Many had been killed to keep her alive, including Maria's brother.

During that period, Jones had saved her life on multiple occasions, and their romance had blossomed from there. It started with innocent flirtation, followed by dating, and eventually a long-distance relationship that had shown a lot of promise. The attraction was obvious, and so was the chemistry—the kind that was clear to everyone—yet the timing of things couldn't have been worse for the couple. Between Maria's graduate studies in England and the steady growth of Jones's detective agency in Pittsburgh, they didn't have enough time or energy to work through the main issue that eventually tore them apart.

Something that had been kept from Payne.

Out of respect for Maria, Jones had concealed the information from his best friend because he didn't think the three of them would ever be forced to interact again, but a late-night phone call had changed all of that. Suddenly, the three of them were working together in close proximity, which put Jones in a situation he had hoped to avoid. Although he was excited to see Maria, he knew her reemergence in their life would force him to have a difficult conversation with Payne, one that would test their friendship in a whole new way.

Jones had wanted to discuss it during their flight but had chickened out.

Some things scared even him.

✠　　　✠　　　✠

PAYNE TOOK THE ELEVATOR to the lobby, where he hoped to find a map of the resort. If none was available, he would have to get directions from the front desk attendant.

Guests of all ages scurried past him, the sound of flip-flops and bratty kids echoing in the atrium. Payne ignored the noise and admired the view. Green ferns dangled from the floors above, a splash of color clinging to the white walls that climbed all the way to the ceiling. Scattered throughout the lobby was artwork depicting native life in the region. Some statues, some paintings, and a few modern pieces that he didn't understand.

But that was common for Payne.

Art wasn't his thing.

"Excuse me," he said to a passing valet, who was pushing an empty luggage cart toward the front entrance. "Do you speak English?"

The valet nodded. *"Sí."*

"Where's the security office?"

Without saying a word, he pointed toward a side corridor that led to a private office. It was near the main lobby but just out of view of hotel guests.

Payne smiled. *"Gracias."*

The valet replied in perfect English. "You're welcome."

Payne laughed at the exchange because it reminded him of many conversations he'd had around the globe. Although language skills were never his strength, he had learned long ago that native speakers were much more likely to help a foreigner who *attempted* to use the native tongue during the conversation. It didn't matter if the language was completely butchered. All that mattered was the effort—because *effort* was viewed as a sign of respect.

A few seconds later, Payne knocked on the door of the security office, unsure how he would be received by the staff. Just to be safe, he had rehearsed the details of his cover story in his head, over and over again, until he was confident he wouldn't screw it up. Like most cover stories he had used over the years, this one contained a teaspoon of truth and a gallon of lies. The goal was to get the information he needed while covering his trail for would-be pursuers.

"Hola?" Payne said as he knocked again. "Anybody home?"

"Come in," someone shouted in English.

Payne opened the door slowly, then stuck his head through the crack. "Hello?"

"I'm in the back."

Payne closed the door behind him, walked past the unmanned desk on his left, and made his way to the back office, where more than twenty screens lined the far wall. Black-and-white video feeds, showing different areas of the resort, from the private beach to the guest parking lot, rotated through the monitors in regular intervals.

Watching them all was a single guard, who sat in front of a large panel that looked like the mixing board in a music studio. Without taking his eyes off the screens, he spoke over his shoulder. "How can I help you?"

"I'm here to report an incident."

The guard yawned. "What kind of incident?"

"A break-in."

The guard cocked his head to the side, as if he was trying to decide if the matter was worthy of his time. "This *isn't* a noise complaint?"

"No."

"Or a lost pet?"

"Nope."

"Or some kid shitting in the pool?"

"They do that?"

"Sometimes."

Payne winced. "No."

"You're sure?"

"I'm positive. No noise, no pets, no shit."

"In that case," said the guard as he whirled around, "you've come to the right place."

Until that moment, Payne hadn't realized that the guard was in a modified wheelchair, and the guard hadn't realized that Payne was nearly twice the size of an average man. The two of them stared at each other, reveling in their surprise but unwilling to comment on the other until the guard could hold it in no more.

"Wooeee! You sure are a big sucker. They don't grow 'em like you in this part of the world." He pointed to an office chair that had been pushed out of the way. "Would you mind sitting down for me? I already got a broken neck. I don't want to make it worse by staring up at you."

Payne grabbed the chair. "No problem at all."

"I'm sure glad you didn't lose your pet. I can't imagine how much damage Babe the Blue Ox could do in a place like this."

Payne laughed at the Paul Bunyan reference. A character from American folklore, Bunyan was a lumberjack of extraordinary size and skill whose lone companion was a massive blue ox named Babe. Working in unison, the two of them cleared tons of timber every day. "Unfortunately, I sold my ox when I lost my job. Damn tree huggers got me fired."

The guard, whose name was Jody DeJute, shook Payne's hand. "Nice to meet another unemployed American. I came south when I lost my gig at a high-tech firm in Houston. Corporate downsizing or some bullshit like that. But I landed on my feet—so to speak."

"How long have you been here?"

"A year or so. I helped put in this system. Did such a good job they kept me on to run it. About the only running I get to do."

Payne forced a smile. One of his best friends from the military had lost both of his legs when an IED—an improvised explosive device—blew up under his Humvee while he was doing advanced surveillance in Iraq. For the first several months, his buddy was so ashamed of his condition and so afraid that everyone was going to tease him about it that he tried to beat everyone to the punch by making wheelchair jokes every chance that he got. "What can the system do?"

"What *can't* it do!" DeJute proclaimed as he whirled back toward the control panel. "With the touch of a button, I can access any camera I want. I can pan, or zoom, or both. For insurance purposes, we store videos on-site for a month. After that, we delete the local files, but we keep backup copies on some server in the middle of nowhere. I still have access, but it takes a while."

Payne shook his head. "Don't worry. The break-in occurred yesterday afternoon."

"*Yesterday?* Shit, I worked yesterday. Did you report this to anyone else?"

"Nope. You're the first."

"And hopefully the last. I can't afford to lose another job."

21

Paco was proud of his Aztec ancestry. He stood in the middle of the plaza and urged everyone to gather around. He didn't care if they were part of his tour group or not. His goal was to educate as many people as possible about the city that his ancestors had built, a city so spectacular that conquistadores wept when they saw it because they thought they had found heaven.

"Imagine a lake," he said as he spread his arms out wide, "one that stretches farther than your eyes can see. No cathedrals, no palaces, no buildings. Just a lake, hidden from the world by volcanoes and snow-covered mountains. Can you picture such a place?"

Tiffany closed her eyes and nodded. She could see it in her mind.

"Now imagine an island, no more than a hundred yards wide, in the middle of the vast water. The land is flat and unremarkable. It is surrounded by marshes, thick with vegetation. And yet, as you stare at it from the distant shore, you see potential. For the past hundred years, your people, known as the Mexica, have been wandering through the wasteland, searching for somewhere to live. You are used to deserts, not lakes. Cactuses, not trees. Everything about this island is foreign to you, but you are guided here by a vision: an eagle with a serpent in its beak, sent as a sign from your main god, Huitzilopochtli. Despite cries of protest from your tribe, you choose this island—this tiny island—as the place to build a city."

Paco paused briefly, just long enough for the crowd to open their eyes and focus on his weathered face. With his words, he was about to create a kingdom.

"Amazingly, the gods reward your courage with a miracle. As the northern wind howls, the summer rain fades away. Over the course of a week, the waters of the lake slowly recede and your island starts to grow. What was once a pebble becomes a rock. What was once a rock becomes a boulder. And what was once a boulder becomes your home."

Tiffany shivered as he said it. Goose bumps covered her arms.

"The city's name is Tenochtitlan, and it is founded in the shallows of Lake Texcoco. In less than six months, the rains will return and your home will be underwater unless you can defeat nature. Channels are dug to great depths. Levees are built to soaring heights. Fires burn throughout the night to light your workers' way. If you fail, you will be killed—whether by flood or revolt—but in your heart, you know you will succeed. You have seen the city in your dreams, one of astonishing size and beauty."

Paco lifted his arms above his head, then wiggled his fingers to indicate rain. The crowd was so transfixed that they half expected the skies to open at that moment.

"*Whooooosh* goes the wind! *Crash* goes the thunder! And the dark waters start to rise. Standing in the middle of a growing lake, you do not know if you will survive. You pray to Huitzilopochtli with all your might, unsure if he will reward your bravery.

Eventually, he gives you his response. Whether by fate or fortune, he answers your prayer and the water is held at bay. The year is A.D. 1325. The island is underneath our feet. It is time to build an empire."

Paco pointed toward the northeast, somewhere between the Metropolitan Cathedral and the National Palace. "To honor Huitzilopochtli, construction begins on a temple made of earth and wood. To protect it, you build canals to funnel the lake and rainwater away. Before long, your island is interlaced with bridges and canals that allow you to visit every section of the city on foot or canoe. But there is a problem. The water that flows through your city is brown, muddied by runoff from the mountains. To fix the issue, your engineers build a dike that is ten miles long. It separates the spring-fed waters to the west from the dirty waters of the east. Next comes a pair of aqueducts—three miles each and made of terra-cotta—that pumps fresh water into the city from the springs at Chapultepec. But this water is not for drinking. It is for bathing and toilets. Unlike the *savages* who came from Europe, our ancestors bathed twice a day and went to the bathroom indoors instead of in the woods."

Tiffany laughed at the description, as did most of the group. She had never heard Europeans described as "savages" before. Normally, the natives were the "savages," and the conquerors were the "enlightened"—not the other way around. But from Paco's perspective, the roles were reversed. Until that moment, she had never thought of things in a *foreign* way. Whether right or wrong, she had always viewed things from an American standpoint.

It was probably why so many people hated her countrymen.

Paco was ready to explain a crucial part of Mexico's history. He waited for the laughter to stop before he continued. "In 1428, barely a century after the birth of your kingdom, a pact is made with two neighboring city-states. Suddenly, three different groups—the Mexica of Tenochtitlan, the Acolhua of Texcoco, and the Tepanec of Tlacopan—are fighting under one name. This Triple Alliance of Nahua tribes is known as the Aztec Empire."

He spread his arms out wide. "For the next hundred years, the Aztecs dominate this valley and beyond. Led by rulers such as Montezuma, Tlacaelel, and Ahuitzotl, the empire stretches from the Pacific Ocean to the Gulf of Mexico. And our city—our tiny little island in the middle of the lake—becomes a capital unlike any the world has ever seen."

Once again, he pointed to the northeast. "Remember our temple? The one made of earth and wood? It is no longer suitable for our city. It is rebuilt over and over, seven times in all, until it is an enormous pyramid of stucco and stone. Unlike Egyptian pyramids, the Templo Mayor has no apex. Instead, there is a great platform on top that is over three hundred feet wide. The platform is divided into two shrines—one for Huitzilopochtli, and one for Tlaloc, the god of rain. The shrines are over a hundred feet in height. They house sacred fires that always burn."

Paco raised his arms while wiggling his fingers to indicate smoke.

"Surrounding the Templo Mayor is a walled square. It is known as the temple precinct. It is home to more than forty buildings. This includes a temple honoring Quetzalcoatl, the feathered serpent, and several smaller shrines honoring minor gods. We do this to keep the gods happy. We expand our city even further by building miles of roads upon the water. They stretch west to the mainland and connect us to smaller islands that we have raised in the lake. But these are not normal causeways. They have special bridges that allow boats and people to pass freely. Amazingly, if we are ever attacked, the bridges can be pulled away instantly to protect our city from invading forces."

Tenochtitlan was divided into four zones called *campan* that surrounded the temple precinct in the middle. Each *campan* had twenty districts, and each district was crisscrossed by perpendicular streets that were half land, half water. This allowed boat and foot traffic throughout the city. Each district, or *calpulli*, had its own marketplace where the Aztecs went to buy products, but they paled in comparison to the main market to the north.

"By 1492, the year Columbus *discovered* the Americas, the population of Tenochtitlan is more than three hundred thousand people. That is bigger than London, Madrid, or Rome. On a normal day, more than fifty thousand people work and shop at our marketplace in Tlatelolco. Money is not used there. Goods and services are bartered for. Small trades are made. Differences in price are settled with cacao beans. They are small, brown, and practically worthless—just like an American penny."

He winked at Tiffany, who responded with a smile.

"There are restaurants and hairdressers. Pharmacies and butchers. Art shops and fruit stands. Everything you can imagine in one immense plaza. Best of all, the marketplace is clean and orderly. No chaos, little crime, no garbage in the streets. More than a thousand men work as cleaners. This includes men in small boats who collect the trash and haul it away."

Paco lowered his voice to a whisper. "Do not get me wrong. Our city is not perfect. At night, half-naked women with heavy makeup and painted teeth—yes, painted teeth—roam the alleys, looking for men. To attract attention, they chew Aztec gum called *tzictli* as loud as they can. The clicking noise echoes throughout the streets. When the noise finally stops, you know their mouths are doing something else, like . . . *talking*."

Everybody laughed at the misdirection. They thought for sure that he was going to say something much dirtier than "talking."

Paco gasped in mock disgust. "What you think I going to say? I am a classy tour guide!"

22

DEJUTE FIDDLED WITH HIS WHEELCHAIR UNTIL HE was perfectly positioned in front of the control panel. "Much better. Now, let's get down to business. What's your room number?"

Payne gave him the number of Maria's suite.

DeJute punched the information into his computer and pulled up her registration. He studied it intently. "Hmmm. Must be some kind of mistake. You don't look like a Maria."

"I'm not. I'm Miss Pelati's bodyguard."

"Her bodyguard?" He glanced over his shoulder and stared at Payne's biceps. His muscular arms were almost as thick as DeJute's withered legs. "Now, *that* I believe. What, is she an Italian princess or something?"

Payne scoffed at the notion. "Sometimes she acts that way, but she's just a regular person. No better than you or I."

"I hear ya, chief. Rich people piss me off."

"Me, too," he joked.

"Is she gonna fire you?"

"If this goes public, she probably will. You know how rich people hate bad publicity. That's why I didn't go to the police with any of this. If they get involved, my ass is grass."

DeJute reached behind him and tapped Payne's arm. "Don't worry, chief. You came to the right place. We only call the cops if it's absolutely necessary. They're bad for business."

"Tell me about it."

"So, when did this break-in occur?"

"Late afternoon, early evening. She was having drinks at that bistro by the beach. When she returned to her suite, the place was trashed."

"Someone trashed it?"

"Like a rock star," Payne replied. "Don't worry, we straightened things up. Looks almost as good as new."

"What did they steal?"

"Not much. Maybe a few trinkets. The main thing was her passport. Someone swiped it from her nightstand. We're still trying to figure out if they got anything else."

"Jewelry? Laptops? Anything like that?"

"Nope. Nothing big. Just her passport."

"Hmmm." DeJute stroked his chin in thought. "Something smells fishy."

"Fishy? What do you mean?"

He turned back and stared at Payne. "I mean, I'm not buying it for a second."

✠   ✠   ✠

JONES LINGERED AT THE edge of the parking lot, waiting for the all-clear signal from Payne. Just to be safe, he checked the reception on his cell phone. Several bars were visible.

"What's taking so long?" Maria wondered.

"Could be anything. Won't know for sure until he calls."

"You're sure he'll remember?"

"Of course he'll remember. He's the most dependable person I've ever met."

"Ever?"

"Ever," he proclaimed.

Maria struggled with his statement, since she'd never had anyone like that in her life. Not a family member, or a classmate, or a long-term boyfriend. No one that she truly felt she could count on if times got rough. But it wasn't through lack of trying. Over the years, she had made a number of friends, but it seemed like something bad happened whenever she got close to any of them—whether it was a death, a fight, or a personal betrayal. After a while, she became so sick of the heartbreak that she decided to put up walls to keep everyone out.

She glanced at Jones. "I know this is going to sound like a funny question, but I've always wondered something about you and Jon—"

He cut her off. "We've never kissed, and we never will."

She laughed. "Good to know, but that wasn't the direction I was heading."

"In that case, fire away."

She gathered her thoughts. "When the two of you first met, did you click right away? Or did it take a while to build your friendship?"

Jones grinned. "I never told you about this?"

"You said you met in the military but never gave me the specifics. I think I would have remembered because I've always wondered."

"Trust me, you *definitely* would have remembered. Because the first time I met Jon, I thought he was the biggest asshole in the world."

"Really?"

"Really."

The comment surprised her. "What didn't you like about him?"

"Just about everything. He was Navy; I was Air Force. He was white; I was black. He was rich; I was broke. He was tall; I was not. Not much common ground to work with."

"I guess not."

"The worst part? We were up for the same command, and he got the post instead of me. Pissed me off something fierce. I figured he got the unit because of his connections, or his skin color, or something that shouldn't have made a damn bit of difference, and I held it against him for the longest time. I'm sure this will come as a huge shock to you, since you hold me in such high esteem, but I can be a royal pain in the ass when I want to be."

"Noooooo!" she said sarcastically.

"Hard to believe, huh?" He laughed at himself. "Anyway, the military—in their infinite wisdom—made things worse by making me his second in command. New unit, new rules, and the two officers in charge couldn't stand each other. I'm telling you, for the first month or so, I was a prickly SOB. I was never technically insubordinate because I didn't want to get thrown in the stockade, but every chance I got I made his life a living hell."

"For a month?"

"Or three."

"How'd he handle it?"

"Much better than I would have," Jones assured her. He paused for a moment as he thought back to his younger days. "That's when I realized he was *special*, not some pampered rich kid who had been given a job for the wrong reason, but someone who deserved the command. As hard as this is to admit—and you'll *never* get me to do it in front of Jon—the Pentagon made the right choice. Not only was he the better soldier, he's also the better man."

Maria shook her head. "I find that hard to believe."

He shrugged. "Believe what you want to believe, but I'm telling you the truth. That's how I honestly feel. If I didn't, do you really think I would've stayed by his side for so long?"

✠   ✠   ✠

YEARS IN THE TRENCHES had taught Payne to remain calm in the worst of circumstances, so he barely blinked an eye when DeJute challenged his story. "What aren't you buying?"

"The entire thing about the break-in. Something else is going on. Something bigger."

"Such as?"

DeJute looked at him. "Identity theft."

"Identity theft? Why do you think that?"

"We see it all the time in Mexico. A wealthy gringo comes to town, and the locals take advantage. I mean, why else would they steal her passport? They got her name, her photo, and her country of origin. I wouldn't be surprised if they were applying for credit cards as we speak."

Payne doubted the possibility but didn't want to hurt the feelings of the one guy who could help. "You might be on to something."

"I know I'm on to something."

"In that case, we need to see who broke into her room immediately. Maybe we can stop the bastards before they bleed her dry. Maybe even save my job."

"You got it, chief. We'll nail their Mexican asses to the wall."

Payne ignored the racism and pointed at the control panel. "While you're pulling up the video feed, mind if I call my assistant? I want to see if they grabbed anything else, like her driver's license or a credit card."

"Good idea. The more they know about her, the more damage they can do."

Payne hit the speed dial as he walked toward the outer office.

Jones answered on the second ring. "How's it look?"

"Great. We're pulling up the feed now. The head honcho is an American who really knows his shit. He wants to nail their Mexican asses to the wall."

DeJute heard the comment from across the room and gave him a thumbs-up. "We'll get the spics and beat them like piñatas."

Jones grunted. "Sounds like a real winner."

Payne smiled at the sarcasm. "He thinks it might be identity theft because of the stolen passport. Says it happens a lot down here."

"Maybe so, but I highly doubt it in this case. Identity thieves wouldn't trash her room. They'd try to slip away unnoticed because it would give them more time to operate."

"I couldn't agree more."

Jones glanced across the parking lot. The only person in sight was Maria, who was quickly running out of patience. "How much time do I have?"

"More than you possibly need. There are cameras all over the place, which means tons of footage to examine. Odds are pretty good I'll get eyes on the incident."

"You talking about the break-in or Hamilton's disappearance?"

"Both. If something happened here, I'll definitely get to see it."

23

DeJute PUNCHED A FEW BUTTONS AND PULLED UP the data from the camera near Maria's suite. He tapped another key and moved the live feed—a feed that they could rewind like a TV show stored on a DVR—to the center monitor. The screen was four times as large as the others and would give them a better view of the break-in. "Not much going on right now. Just an empty hallway."

Payne glanced over DeJute's shoulder and got a feel for the control panel, just in case he needed to pull up some footage on his own. "Empty is good."

"Unless you're talking about my glass at happy hour. Then empty is *bad*."

"You got me there."

"Of course, I have to be careful when I drink. Don't want to get a DUI in my wheelchair. No telling who I might run over in this thing."

Payne pushed his personal feeling aside—he had lost his parents to a drunk driver—and ignored the comment. "The incident took place some time between four and seven P.M."

DeJute entered the data with his keyboard, and the video skipped back to 4:00 P.M. the previous afternoon. From there, he grabbed the joystick on the control panel and tilted it to the right. This sped the video forward. "Pretty cool, huh? I control every-thing with this little lever. I can go forward or backward, up or down, in or out. Whatever I want to do."

"Let's go forward until we see someone in the hallway."

"You got it, chief."

Nothing appeared on the monitor until Maria departed the suite. Wearing a sundress and sandals, she opened the door, closed it behind her, then made sure it was locked. After that, she strolled down the corridor toward the elevator.

DeJute pointed at the screen. "Is that your boss?"

"Yep. That's her."

"I'll be damned. I know who that is!"

Payne tensed. "You do?"

"I sure as shit do. That's Mariachi Maria!"

"Excuse me?"

DeJute laughed to himself. "Your boss is Mariachi Maria. How funny is that?"

Payne stared at him. "I think you better explain."

He leaned forward and tapped a few buttons. "I can do better than that. I'll let you see the video for yourself."

"The video? Of what?"

"Sometimes when we get a really important client, the hotel mariachi band is summoned to greet them by the front door. Well, your boss lady was selected for the royal treatment."

"She was?"

DeJute nodded. "I've been playing this video all day long. It's actually kind of sexy. After a while, she gets into the music and starts to shake her chi-chis."

Payne watched the video of Maria's arrival and couldn't help but smile. In a span of five minutes, she went from confused to embarrassed to downright festive. For him, it was a pleasant surprise because it revealed a side of her personality that he wasn't familiar with. Jones had always claimed that she was fun—that she liked to dance and goof around—but Payne had never seen it for himself because of the imminent threat of danger during their only encounters.

"If you can, please burn me a copy. I'd love to have it in case she fires my ass. You know, as blackmail material."

"Dude, I like the way you think." DeJute reached to his right and opened a small filing cabinet under his desk. Inside, there were hundreds of DVDs. He grabbed the first disc in the stack and handed it to Payne. It was labeled MARIACHI MARIA. "You can have my copy. I'll burn another one later for my personal collection."

"Thanks. I appreciate it."

"No problem at all."

"If it's okay with you, can we go back to the other feed now? Maybe I can save my job before I have to play this card."

"You got it, chief."

DeJute hit a few keys, and the hallway video returned to the point where they had left off: Maria had just departed her suite and was headed for the elevator. DeJute grabbed the joystick and tilted it to the right. The video sped forward at ten times the normal speed. He stared at the screen intently, patiently waiting for someone to make an appearance in the corridor.

Several seconds passed before someone finally did.

✠　　✠　　✠

JONES AND MARIA WALKED across the parking lot at a leisurely pace. Not from overconfidence, but to draw as little attention as possible.

"Hamilton's car is just ahead. It's the maroon Hummer H2."

"How do you know?" Jones asked.

"Because he told me he was driving a maroon Hummer H2. And when I checked the parking lot last night, it was the only one here."

"In that case, I'm going to go out on a limb and say it's probably his vehicle."

She gave him a friendly punch. "Thank goodness you're here. I never would have figured that out on my own."

Jones smiled. "Well, I am a trained professional."

"I know you are. That's why I gave you a call."

A few seconds passed before he spoke again. When he did, his voice was a little less jovial. "Actually, you didn't give me a call. You called Jon, not me."

The comment stung her so much she stopped walking. She paused for a moment, took a deep breath, then hustled to catch up to Jones, who never broke stride until he reached the H2.

"About that," she said as she grabbed his arm.

He shook his head. "Not now. We got a job to do. Can't lose focus."

"Right. Sorry. You're right. We can talk about it later."

"Or not."

"No," she said firmly, "we *will* talk about it later."

"Fine! We'll talk about it later. But if it's okay with you, I'd prefer if our conversation didn't take place inside a Mexican prison."

"Right. Of course. Sorry."

"Don't be sorry. Do your job. Stand over there and let me know if anyone's coming."

✠   ✠   ✠

DEJUTE STOPPED THE VIDEO and zoomed in on the elevator, a few seconds after the doors had opened. Standing in the hallway were two Latin men with short black hair and stocky builds.

Dressed in casual clothes and designer sunglasses that obscured their faces, they took a moment to get their bearings before they walked down the corridor toward Maria's suite.

"Look familiar?" Payne asked.

"Not at all."

"Can you print that image for me? I'd like to have it."

"No problem."

The men stopped in front of her door and glanced in both directions. With no one in sight, one of them pulled out a keycard and inserted it into the slot. A moment later, the light turned green, and the men entered the suite.

Payne pointed at the screen. "Did you see that? They had a key."

He nodded. "I can't walk, but I *can* see."

"Where did they get a key?"

"Honestly, any number of places. The front desk, a maid's cart, even your boss's pocket. That's the problem with keycards. They can be duplicated with ease."

"Then why do you use them?"

"Two reasons," he explained. "First of all, they're inexpensive. If someone loses a card, it costs us less than a nickel to replace it, which is a lot cheaper than calling a locksmith."

Payne grunted in disgust. "In other words, hotels care more about saving money than protecting their guests."

"And that surprises you?"

"No, I guess not."

DeJute glanced back at him. "Don't worry, chief. In cases like this, the hotel's cheapness actually works to your advantage."

"How do you figure?"

"Anytime a keycard is used, my computer keeps track. If you give me a minute, I can tell you when their keycard was made, who it was given to, and where it's been used before."

Payne smiled. "In that case, all is forgiven."

24

J ONES SPOTTED TWO CAMERAS IN THE PARKING LOT during his advance surveillance. One was on the far side of the complex; the other was facing the driver's side of the H2 from roughly twenty feet away. Fearing detection, he purposely kept his back to the camera by working on the driver's-side door. Not only would it keep his face off the surveillance footage, but it would also block the camera's view of his lock-picking expertise.

"Am I clear?" Jones whispered into his headset, which was synched to his cell phone via a Bluetooth connection.

Maria answered from the edge of the parking lot. "Looks clear to me."

Using the homemade lock picks that he carried in his wallet, Jones went to work on the door. Fifteen seconds later, it popped open with a click. "I'm in."

"Already?"

"Actually, that was slow. With a bump key, I can beat ten seconds."

"Really?"

"Yes, really."

"Wow. That's awesome . . . Wait. What's a bump key?"

He sighed. "Can we talk about it later?"

"Sorry."

Jones climbed into the Hummer and quietly closed the door. Once inside, he felt a lot less vulnerable. The heavily tinted windows and the reflective sunshade—which protected the H2's interior from the heat of the Mexican sun—concealed his actions and identity from the outside world. As long as no one had spotted him breaking in, he knew he was reasonably safe.

"Still clear?"

"Yes," she assured him.

Jones leaned across the center armrest and opened the glove compartment. Inside there was a pair of sunglasses, a spare set of keys, and a rental agreement for the Hummer. He grabbed the paperwork and tucked it into his cargo pants, hoping it would give them a better understanding of Hamilton's movements before his trip to Cancún. If they figured out where he had come from, perhaps they could locate the other members of Hamilton's research team and get to the bottom of his disappearance. Or, at the very least, find out why Maria had been invited to Mexico.

For Jones, that was the most important thing of all.

✠   ✠   ✠

WHILE DEJUTE PULLED UP the keycard data on his computer, Payne kept his eyes on the monitors. He tried not to fixate on the action in the parking lot, but his gaze naturally drifted toward his best friend as he approached the H2 on one of the smaller screens.

"So," Payne said, trying to keep DeJute distracted from the video feed, "do you always work alone, or did I catch you at the worst possible moment?"

"Normally, there's someone working in the outer office, but he went to take a piss or something. Unfortunately, I can't use that excuse, since I piss in a bag."

Payne grunted, unsure how to respond.

DeJute sensed his discomfort. "It's got some advantages, though. I never miss any action when I go to a ballgame. Same thing at the movies. For all you know, I'm pissing right now."

"Now you're just showing off."

"Maybe a little."

Payne laughed and glanced back at the monitor. Jones was no longer visible. He was safely inside the H2. "How's that data coming?"

A printer chattered on the desk behind him.

DeJute pointed over his shoulder. "It's printing right now."

"Can you make me a copy?"

"That is your copy. I'll just use my computer."

Payne grabbed the two pages from the printer, then sat next to DeJute, who was studying the numbers on his screen. "Okay, what am I looking at?"

DeJute explained. "The data's divided into three columns. First column lists a portal. Second lists a card number. Third lists a time stamp."

"What's a portal?"

"That's my nickname for the individual card readers. Not only is 'portal' easier to say than 'individual card readers,' but it sounds a hell of a lot cooler."

"You're right. It does."

He pointed at the first column on his screen. "Most portals are simply room numbers, but some are coded for common areas— like the spa or the workout center. Anything that requires a card for entry has a unique portal number. Swipe your card, and we get a record."

Following along on his printout, Payne shifted his focus to the second column. "How are the card numbers assigned?"

"We erase the cards as soon as they're turned in at checkout. After that, we recode the blank cards with new information, using a digital encoder at the front desk. Each card is given a new list of permissions, which grants access to different portals on the property. Not only individual rooms, but things like elevator access, and so on."

"What about employees?"

"Different employees have different permission codes installed on their cards. Managers can go anywhere they want. Same with certain members of the security staff. Maids have unlimited access in some parts of the hotel, but they can't use their cards outside their assigned areas. If they try, we'll know about it." DeJute smiled to himself. "Actually, if *anyone* tries, we know about it. Our system records all card swipes, whether successful or not."

Payne took a moment to study the report. DeJute had filtered the data by portal number on the first sheet, listing every card that had accessed Maria's suite (Room 1257) in the last twenty-four hours. According to the data, three cards had opened her room a total of four times.

Portal	Card #	Time
1257-1	19420114	13:27:34
1257-1	19771004	15:47:45
1257-1	19690902	17:32:11
1257-1	19771004	19:03:21

As a former soldier, Payne was quite familiar with military time. He quickly recognized the significance of 17:32:11, because it corresponded with the time stamp on the video feed of the break-in, which had occurred at 5:32 P.M. (plus eleven seconds) on the twelve-hour clock. The image of Maria's door was still paused on the center monitor, allowing him to double-check the time.

Payne pointed at the video feed. "They opened her door at five thirty-two P.M."

DeJute nodded. "Yep."

"That means their card number is one-niner-six-niner-zero-niner-zero-two."

"You got it, chief."

Payne glanced up the column and studied the numbers. Two other cards had been granted access to her suite earlier in the day. One of them, 19771004, also accessed the suite *after* the break-in. By process of elimination, Payne knew it probably belonged to Maria. "The card ending in one-zero-zero-four must be my boss's. She used her suite when she checked in, then used it again after her meeting at the bistro."

Using his computer mouse, DeJute clicked on the card number and was whisked to a separate window that displayed registration information. The keycard was assigned to Maria Pelati. As proof, her signature appeared at the bottom of the page. "You nailed it, chief."

"Can you go back to the other screen?"

"Of course." DeJute clicked a button and returned to the master list. "Before you even ask, I can tell you the first keycard belongs to a maid. One-nine-four-two is a staff prefix, and one twenty-seven P.M. is in the gap between checkout and check-in. She was probably preparing the suite."

Payne nodded. "I kind of figured as much. I was actually more concerned with the Hispanic gentlemen we saw on the screen. I want to know who their card belongs to."

DeJute moved his cursor over 19690902 and clicked once. A new window appeared on the screen. Strangely, it listed the same registration information as a moment before—with one major exception. Instead of Maria Pelati's signature, a different name was scrawled across the bottom of the page. Payne leaned closer and tried to decipher the handwriting. A few seconds passed before he figured it out, and when he did, he grunted with surprise.

The name was Terrence Hamilton.

25

P ACO'S HUMOR FADED AS HE APPROACHED THE END of his speech. The final part of his tour always made him gloomy. After building a kingdom with his words, he was forced to tear it down.

"Sadly," he explained, "our city did not survive the treachery of Spain. Less than thirty years after Columbus arrived in the Americas, a conquistador named Hernán Cortés saw Tenochtitlan from a distance. He marveled at its wealth and size while his men wept at its beauty. They cried out to Cortés: *Are we dead? Are we dreaming? How can this vision be real?* But he could not answer them. How can you explain what you do not understand?"

He paused for a moment to let that sink in. "The date was November 8, 1519. Our city had reached its glorious peak. Within two years, it was all but destroyed."

A murmur went through the crowd. Even though the conquest of Tenochtitlan had happened nearly five hundred years ago, they could hear the pain in Paco's voice.

"Our ruler at the time was Montezuma the Second. Under his

leadership, the Aztec Empire reached its largest size. According to diplomatic custom, Montezuma allowed Cortés and some of his men to march into our city. He greeted them with gold and silver. They gave us smallpox in return. Still, he invited them to stay at the royal palace, where they remained for months. During this time, Aztec nobles slowly began to doubt the motives of Cortés. They voiced their concerns to Montezuma, who eventually asked Cortés and his men to leave. But the Spaniards refused. Instead, they captured our ruler and used him as a hostage to guarantee their safety."

Paco took a deep breath. "What happened next is still unknown to my people. Some claim Cortés killed Montezuma as a sign of his power. Others claim Montezuma was stoned to death by the Aztecs as punishment for being captured. In many ways, the truth does not matter. All that matters is what happened to our beautiful city."

He pointed to the south. "In May of 1521, the Iztapalapa Causeway was blocked by the Spanish. Then the Tlacopan Causeway to the west and the Tepeyácac Causeway to the north. Next they ruptured our aqueducts, which cut off freshwater to our city. For the next three months, the Aztec people suffered. Without food and water, they became weak and the smallpox started to spread. Before long, they were no match for Spain. Cortés landed his troops on the south end of our island and went from house to house, slaughtering everyone. Finally, in August of 1521, our new ruler, Cuauhtémoc, was forced to surrender to Cortés."

"Did Cortés kill him?" someone asked from the crowd.

"Not at first," Paco said while shaking his head. "The Spanish believed the Aztecs were hiding a great treasure—one of gold and jewels—so Cuauhtémoc was tortured to reveal its location. The barbaric Spaniards placed his feet in a raging fire, trying to burn the information from him, but he refused to tell them anything. For his bravery, he is still honored to this day. There is a giant statue of Cuauhtémoc on Avenida Reforma. Plus, there is a bust over there."

He pointed to the far side of the plaza.

Everyone turned except Tiffany, who remained focused on Paco.

"What happened to the treasure?" she wondered.

He looked at her and smiled. There was one in every group.

"Ahhhh," he said, "the Aztec treasure. More extravagant than you can possibly imagine. Thanks to Cuauhtémoc, the Spanish never found it. Or maybe they did. The truth is I do not know. According to some, the treasure never existed—nothing but a myth to entertain children. According to others, it is still waiting to be found. Over the centuries, many explorers have crossed the sea to discover it. Most of them never returned home."

"What about you? Do you think there was a treasure?" she asked.

"In my dreams, I picture a cave filled with gold. It is buried deep underneath Mexican soil. Who knows?" He stomped his foot three times. "Maybe it is underneath this plaza."

The group laughed at his comment because they assumed it was a joke. But Paco shook his head. He had one more story to tell them before he finished the tour.

"I know what you are thinking: How could this be? How could something so big be sleeping underneath the Zócalo? Well, I am about to tell you—and you will be impressed. Once Cortés took control of Tenochtitlan, he ordered its destruction. He kept the four districts and the basic layout of our city, but the buildings didn't survive. He had the main temple completely razed. Then he took the stones and used them to pave this plaza."

He turned north and pointed at the cathedral. "Next, Cortés built a church where the four districts merged. He built it there so everyone in the city would learn about Jesus. To make sure we got his message, he built a church or shrine on top of every Aztec temple in Tenochtitlan. From that point on, if we worshipped our gods, we were sentenced to death."

He took a deep breath. The thought of it made him angry. "By 1573, the year the Spanish started the cathedral, most natives had converted. Not by blood, but in their minds. They no longer thought like Aztecs. Now they thought like Spaniards. This was not their fault, for this was all they knew. Tales of our city had been passed from father to son, but that was not the same as being there. How can one learn if one cannot see for oneself? Before long, Tenochtitlan was gone from memory. Forgotten by history until 1978."

"What happened then?" someone shouted.

Paco grinned at the group. "Another miracle."

He explained that a worker for the electric company was digging a block away from the plaza. Known as the "island of the dogs," the area was slightly elevated from the rest of the neighborhood. Any time there was flooding, which happened every rainy season, street dogs would gather there to avoid the rising water. Approximately six feet underground, the worker's shovel hit something solid. He summoned other workers to the "island," who helped him uncover a pink andesite monolith. Weighing 8.5 tons and measuring nearly eleven feet in diameter, the stone disk depicted the Aztec moon goddess Coyolxauhqui, and dated back to the fifteenth century. Upon closer inspection, historians realized it had been placed at the foot of the Huitzilopochtli temple during Axayacatl's reign, sometime between 1469 and 1481.

Following its discovery, the Mexican government gave permission to tear down an entire city block to excavate the Templo Mayor site. Over the next four years, they uncovered the construction history of the central temple and numerous artifacts that overturned our basic understanding of Aztec religion, culture, and ideology. The project, led by Mexican archaeologist Eduardo Matos Moctezuma, culminated with the creation of the Templo

Mayor Museum, where the monolith and other relics are displayed a block from the plaza.

Paco pointed out the location of the museum before he concluded his tour. "Like I say earlier, who knows what is underneath our feet? Maybe it is dirt, maybe it is lake, or maybe it is gold. In a country like Mexico, you never know what you might find until you dig."

26

JONES GLANCED IN THE HUMMER'S REARVIEW MIRROR and noticed the backseat had been folded down to accommodate a large object of some kind. He didn't know what the item was, since a black tarp had been strapped over the top of it with multiple bungee cords, but he figured it had to be important if Hamilton had dragged it all the way to Cancún.

He spoke into his headset. "Refresh my memory. What was Hamilton getting from the car when he disappeared?"

Maria answered from across the parking lot. "Some documents that he wanted me to translate. He wouldn't tell me what they were, though. I think he wanted to test my knowledge."

"Documents, huh?"

"That's what he said. Why?"

"I think he brought more than documents."

"Like what?"

Jones reached out and pushed the tarp. The object underneath didn't budge. It just sat there, veiled, like a forgotten treasure waiting to be found. "Well, I don't think it's a corpse."

"What?" she shrieked.

He flinched from the shrill in his ear. "Calm down, Maria. I said I *don't* think it's a corpse. Can't be sure, though. It's covered with a big-ass tarp."

"Is it Hamilton?"

"Wow. You get something in your head, and you won't let go. I said I *don't* think it's a corpse. How many times do I have to say that?"

"But how do you know? If you can't see it, how do you know?"

"Because it's a hundred degrees in here, and nothing stinks. If Hamilton had been stashed in here overnight, you could smell him from where you're standing."

She took a deep breath—partly to calm down, partly to smell the air. As far as she could tell, nothing reeked in the vicinity. "Then why would you say that?"

"Say what?"

"*I don't think it's a corpse.* The only reason I thought it *might* be a corpse was because you brought it up."

"Really? That expression is a figure of speech."

"Bullshit! That is *not* a figure of speech."

"Maybe not in Europe, but it is in America," he fibbed.

"You're so full of shit."

Jones cracked a smile. "Honestly. Ask any American."

"Trust me, I will."

"I know you will. In the meantime, can we focus on the corpse?"

Maria seethed. "Not funny at all."

☒   ☒   ☒

PAYNE STARED AT THE NAME on the computer and tried to make sense of it. The keycard used for the break-in belonged to Terrence Hamilton.

DeJute glanced at Payne, then the screen, then back at Payne. He sensed something was wrong. "From the expression on your face, I get the feeling you know the dude."

Payne shook his head. "Never met him, but I know his name. He was meeting with my boss at the time of the break-in."

DeJute laughed to himself. "Man, oh, man. That takes some balls!"

"What does?"

"The V.A. scam. You can't pull that off without some serious cojones."

Payne looked at him. "I'm not familiar with that term."

"Sorry. It means 'balls' in Spanish."

"Not cojones. I know what that means. I meant the V.A. scam."

"Oops, my bad. The V stands for victim. The A stands for alibi. It's when the victim of a crime is actually the alibi for the person who set it up. We don't see it a lot at the high-end resorts. It's much more common at the cheaper hotels down the beach. Normally it involves a pretty girl in a bathing suit. She distracts a guy at the bar while her partner goes through his room. If security gets involved, the victim actually provides the alibi for the babe."

"That's devious."

"And fairly common. Happens all the time in resort towns."

Payne shook his head. "Not like this it doesn't."

"Meaning?"

"Hamilton's name is on the registration. The keycard belonged to him. Technically speaking, I don't think you can break into a room that you're entitled to enter."

"Good point, chief."

"And if he wanted to rob her, why in the hell did he give those guys his personal keycard? That kind of defeats the purpose of the V.A. scam. His signature is on the registration."

DeJute paused in thought. "So, Hamilton *isn't* involved in the robbery?"

"I don't think so, but I'd love to find out how they got his keycard."

"Me, too. But how do we do that?"

Payne pointed at the monitor. "We go to the tape."

DeJute knocked twice on his own head. As he did, he made a hollow sound with his mouth. "Duh! I should have thought of that. I mean, I *am* the video supervisor."

"Despite your impressive title, can I make a suggestion on where to begin?"

"No problem, chief."

"Hamilton had a meeting with my boss, sometime around five P.M. She said he left their table at the bistro and never returned. I figure, if we track him from there, we can see if he does anything suspicious."

DeJute grabbed a clipboard from his desk and flipped through the pages until he figured out which camera covered the Isla Contoy bistro. He punched the camera number into his computer and waited for the live feed of the restaurant to appear on the center screen. The image flickered briefly before the interior of the thatched hut came into view. Unfortunately, it wasn't as clear as the other video feeds. Dark splotches obscured half of the scene.

Payne grimaced. "What's wrong with the feed?"

"Nothing," he assured him. "The camera's mounted near the top of the thatched roof, so it has to battle the sun reflecting off the water and the shadows from the hut. What can I say? Sometimes the picture is a little shitty. I'd climb up there myself and tweak the settings, but in case you didn't notice, I'm in a wheelchair."

"Nope. Didn't notice."

DeJute entered the time of the meeting into his computer and waited for the footage to appear on the screen. "Fortunately for you, the sun shouldn't be a problem at dinnertime."

He was right. Yesterday's scene was much clearer than the live feed from the bistro because of the position of the sun. Using his joystick, DeJute zoomed in on the restaurant's clientele until he spotted Maria and Hamilton sitting at a small table near the back rail. The two of them appeared to be friends. They casually sipped on daiquiris while engaged in a lively conversation. The two smiled, and laughed, and enjoyed their drinks.

Payne continued to watch closely as DeJute fast-forwarded the scene. At no point did anyone approach their table except for the waiter. And as far as he could tell, Hamilton didn't slip the waiter a keycard, or anything else, for that matter. In fact, Hamilton barely looked at the waiter at all. His eyes were glued on Maria the entire time, as if he were a poker player looking for tells. To Payne, it was a little bit creepy. But he quickly blamed Hamilton's conduct on the combination of three things that had caused millions of men to act like idiots over the years: alcohol, a romantic setting, and the beauty of an exotic woman.

Even Payne had fallen victim to that potent mix on a few occasions.

Eventually, they reached the part of the footage where Hamilton excused himself from the table. DeJute moved his joystick to the center position, which slowed the feed to normal time.

"Okay," Payne said. "Let's see where he goes."

Using one camera feed after another, DeJute traced Hamilton's path from the bistro, to the pool deck, and into a corridor that led to the atrium. During his journey, there were occasional gaps in the camera coverage, but they were usually able to spot him quickly on the next video feed, thanks to his distinctive panama hat. It stood out in a crowd, even from across the lobby.

Slowly but surely, they tracked him to a side door that led to the parking lot where he had parked his H2. He pushed it open and stepped outside, the door closing gently behind him.

Fighting a yawn, DeJute glanced at his clipboard and punched in the number of the next camera, the one on the other side of the door. The live feed popped on the screen, revealing the exterior of the hotel from the edge of the parking lot. DeJute typed in the time period he wanted to view, and the footage from the previous evening appeared.

Payne glanced at the time. "You're two minutes early."

DeJute nodded and tilted his joystick to the right. The video sped forward at an accelerated rate. As it approached the span they wanted to view, he slowed it to its normal pace.

The two of them stared at the screen, waiting for Hamilton to open the door.

According to the time stamp, he would do it in five seconds.

Then four. Then three. Then two. Then one.

Then nothing.

Nothing at all.

Because the monitor turned black.

27

PAYNE GLARED AT DeJUTE. "WHAT THE HELL HAP-
pened?"

DeJute frantically hit buttons on his keyboard while staring at
the black screen. "I have no idea! I've never seen this before!"

Boiling with frustration, Payne glanced back at the monitor.
Despite the absence of a picture, the time counter continued to
tick forward at the bottom of the screen. One second after another,
ticking away in darkness. "I'll be damned. They erased the tape."

"What? Not a chance. I bet the monitor went bad. I'll just move
the feed to—"

Payne cut him off. "It's not the screen. Take a look at the counter. It's still working fine. I'm telling you, someone erased this portion of the tape—or somehow blocked the camera."

"No way," he argued, sounding less confident than he had a
moment before. "I bet if I move the feed to another screen—"

Payne shook his head. "Don't waste your time. It won't make
any difference."

"But—"

"Listen," he said in a calming voice, "if you need proof, just fast-forward the video for a few minutes. I bet the picture returns pretty quickly."

DeJute grabbed the joystick and cranked it to the right. Instantly, the counter whizzed forward at twenty times its normal speed. The picture remained solid black for several seconds, temporarily stoking DeJute's doubt, but before he had a chance to voice it, the video returned to the center monitor—just as Payne had promised.

DeJute released the joystick. "Son of a bitch. Someone erased the tape."

"I know."

"But why? Why would someone do that?"

Payne shrugged, offering nothing.

Still trying to process things in his own head, DeJute rewound the video to the point where it went black. He watched the feed again, this time at a slower speed, hoping he would notice something useful on the screen. Payne watched, too, as the feed went from an exterior shot of the hotel to solid black. Then they watched it again. And again. The same thing, over and over, looking for a scrap of evidence to help them piece together what had happened.

Payne cleared his throat. "Nothing's there."

"But—"

"Trust me, if they took the time to erase the feed, they took the time to get it all."

"All of what?"

"Whatever happened outside."

DeJute looked over his shoulder. "Which was what?"

Payne shook his head, unwilling to voice an opinion. "Let me ask you a better question. How did they erase the tape?"

He groaned. "Beats the hell out of me. I don't even know how to do that."

"You don't?"

"Not like that, I don't." He glanced back at the screen. "Then again, I'm not a high-tech surgeon. I'm more of a sledgehammer kind of guy."

"Meaning?"

"Why erase five minutes when you could delete the entire file? Because that's what I would have done. I would have found the file on the server and trashed the bitch."

"Good point."

DeJute stared at his keyboard, unsure what to do next. "So . . ."

"I'm thinking," Payne said.

"If you want, I can switch to the parking lot feed. Maybe we can see something from there."

Although it was a good suggestion—one that might provide important clues about Hamilton's disappearance—Payne knew he couldn't risk it, not with Jones rummaging through the Hummer in the parking lot. Even if they rewound the video to the previous night, the live feed would appear on the main screen for a few seconds while DeJute entered the data, and the last thing Payne needed was for Jones, or Maria, to be spotted outside.

Payne spoke decisively. "Actually, let's go back to the lobby camera for a while. I want to see if Hamilton heads back into the hotel through that same door. Maybe we can pick up his scent from there."

✠　　✠　　✠

THE BUNGEE CORDS WERE attached to tiny hooks in the side panels of the Hummer's trunk. Jones reached between the front seats and unclipped the closest cord, making sure it didn't snap back and take out his eye like the Red Ryder BB Gun from *A Christmas Story*.

For some reason, that movie always cracked him up.

He carefully moved the first cord out of the way and went to work on the second. Using extra caution, he unclipped the hook and tossed the cord on the passenger side's floor.

"What's happening?" Maria asked.

"Hold your horses. I'm almost done."

"Easy for you to say. I'm the one exposed out here."

Jones leaned forward and grabbed the third cord. "You're exposed? You're sitting on a bench outside a five-star resort. Meanwhile, I'm rifling through someone's car. Are you sure you want to make that argument?"

She conceded his point. "Sorry. I'm not used to this."

"And I am? Just because I'm black doesn't mean I do this all the time."

Despite his claim of racism, she knew he was joking. "Are you sure? Because you're pretty darn good at it."

"True, but that has *nothing* to do with my skin color. I break into cars because I'm nosy, not because I'm black."

"That's good to know. I'll be sure to explain that to the *policía* when they arrive."

Jones smiled as he unclipped the cord and loosened the tarp in the back of the H2. He hadn't talked to Maria in months, yet their repartee had picked up right where it had left off. For Jones, it was the rarest of things. Over the years, he had met very few women who got his sense of humor. Most were offended by his comments, or didn't understand his obscure references, but Maria was different. Not only did she find him funny, but she had enough feistiness to keep him in line when he strayed a little bit too far.

In that regard, she was like Payne—with breasts.

"Still clear?" he asked as he pulled up the corner of the tarp.

"Yes."

"Are you sure? Because I might need to turn on a light."

"Why?"

"Because it's dark under the tarp."

She scanned the parking lot. "Yes, I'm sure."

Jones knew the dome light wouldn't be bright enough to let him see clearly, so he opted to pull back the reflective sunshade that covered the windshield. Starting on the passenger side, he folded it twice on its creases until a third of the glass was exposed. Sunlight streamed through the gap, filling the cargo space with more than enough light to suit his needs.

"That's more like it," he mumbled to himself.

Wasting no time, Jones turned in his seat and reached into the trunk. But instead of loosening additional cords, he grabbed the edge of the tarp and peered underneath.

Directly in front of him was a narrow wooden crate that ran parallel to the dashboard. Made of thick plywood, it had three latches that held its lid in place. It reminded him of his old foot-locker from the military. Durable but light, it was the type of crate that could hold just about anything: books, digging equipment, personal effects, even rations.

Farther back was a second crate, which was much different from the first. More of a display case than a footlocker, it stretched across the remainder of the trunk and was filled with dozens of objects that had been sealed in plastic. Some were big, and some were small. But he couldn't really tell what they were from where he was sitting.

"What did you find?" Maria asked.

"Two boxes filled with stuff. Not sure what it is, though, because I haven't had time to look."

"Sorry. I'll shut up now."

Jones laughed as he shifted his attention to the footlocker. He flicked open the two side latches before he focused on the center lock. Although it required a key, this type of lock was one of the simplest to pick. Jones could have done it with a paper clip or ballpoint pen. With his tools, he could've done it blindfolded. Less than five seconds later, it clicked open.

Grinning cockily, Jones put his tools away, then opened the lid. His eyes quickly doubled in size.

"Holy shit," he blurted into the headset.

"What's wrong?"

"Nothing's wrong. Nothing at all."

"Don't lie to me, David."

"I'm not lying," he assured her as he closed the lid and pulled up the tarp. One glance was all it took. He knew what he needed to do next. "But we have to move the Hummer."

"Why? Is there a bomb?" she demanded.

"A *bomb*? Why in the hell would there be a bomb?"

"Because you want to move the Hummer."

He scoffed at the notion. "No corpse. No bomb. No threat to mankind. I promise you that, but we still have to move the Hummer."

"But—"

"Maria!" he growled into his headset. "Read between the lines. I don't want to talk about this over the phone. Do you understand me?"

"Yes," she whispered.

"Good." He reached into the glove compartment and grabbed the spare set of keys. They would make stealing the H2 that much easier. "Then this is what I need you to do. I'm going to toss the keys for the SUV on the ground. Once I pull out of this space, I want you to pick up my keys and walk into the hotel lobby, where I want you to wait for Jon. Do not leave the lobby for any reason unless Jon is by your side. Do you understand?"

"Yes," she repeated.

"I'll keep an eye on you until you're inside the hotel. I'll text Jon and let him know what is going on. After that, he is in charge of you. Do whatever he says, whenever he says it. No arguments. No backtalk. No bullshit. Okay?"

She took a deep breath. "Okay."

He sensed her tension. "Maria, don't worry about this. Everything is going to be all right."

"Do you promise?"

"Yes," he lied. "I promise everything will be fine."

28

Because of their training, Payne and Jones understood the importance of advance planning, especially on foreign terrain. While most tourists focused on the basics—like hotel reservations and plane tickets—Payne and Jones always planned for the worst. They didn't care about fun-filled excursions for the entire family; they worried about the procurement of weapons and the feasibility of secondary transportation. Some viewed it as overkill, but their precaution had saved their lives on many occasions, so they weren't about to change their ways.

Not even on a trip to Cancún.

Before their jet had reached Mexican airspace, they had an exit plan in place. It included the establishment of multiple rendezvous points across the Yucatán Peninsula, just in case they were separated in the field and couldn't risk cellular communication. In addition, they chose two meeting spots across the nearest borders—one in Guatemala, and one in Belize. Thankfully, their current predicament didn't warrant a jungle-crossing trek to a neighboring country. They simply needed to meet somewhere secluded, away from security cameras and prying eyes, where they could discuss the best way to handle the latest development.

Less than ten miles from the Fiesta Americana, Jones parked the H2 near Punta Nizac, a rocky shoal that jutted into the Caribbean Sea on the southern end of Boulevard Kukulcán. The surrounding water offered some of the best snorkeling in the world—where stingrays and schools of brightly colored fish fed on the coral reefs—but a strong undertow and jagged rocks kept swimmers away from the point, which was one of the reasons that Jones had selected it.

He knew they would be alone out there.

Having spent a lot of time at MacDill Air Force Base in Tampa, Jones was used to the cawing of seagulls that flocked to the Gulf Coast of Florida. But for some reason, they were nowhere to be seen (or heard) in Cancún. Instead, the air was filled with frigate birds, massive creatures with black iridescent feathers that have wingspans of nearly eight feet. With the largest wings-to-body-weight ratio of any bird, they are essentially aerial, able to stay aloft for more than a week at a time. They cannot swim or walk very well, nor take off from flat surfaces, so the only time they land is to roost or breed on trees or cliffs. They even feed in the air, swooping down across the water to scoop up fish or to rob other seabirds of their catch, which is known as kleptoparasitic feeding. Strangely, they will also chase smaller birds that have recently fed, using their speed and endurance to outrun and harass their victims until they regurgitate their meals. At which point the frigate birds enjoy some in-flight dining.

While watching this odd behavior from afar, Jones's mind drifted back to the previous night, and he realized very little had changed, despite the radical shift in scenery. Less than twenty-four hours earlier, he was trudging through the sewers of Ambridge, Pennsylvania, while testing out the LED incapacitator, which resulted in a bunch of college boys throwing up on his boots. Now he was standing on one of the most scenic spots on earth, surrounded by the opulent waters of the Caribbean, and he was watching birds puke in the sky.

Jones shook his head in frustration.

Although he appreciated the symmetry, he had been hoping for something slightly more romantic than puking birds when he had left for Mexico. Maybe not a full reconciliation with Maria—he knew that would take a lot longer than a weekend to navigate—but he had wanted to test the waters for the future, whether it was a casual relationship or something more serious. Now that conversation would have to wait until they dealt with Hamilton's discovery and all the problems that were sure to follow.

Jones turned from the sea when he heard the sound of tires on gravel behind him. As expected, it was Payne and Maria. The silver SUV crawled down the unpaved road, easily navigating the sand and stone that led to the point. Payne eyed the terrain as he approached the H2. Although the location was secluded, it was less than ideal in many ways. Excluding the water, the only way off the rocky shoal was down the path he was currently on. With that in mind, he made a narrow three-point turn and backed the SUV into position. Now, if they needed to make a quick getaway, at least they were facing in the right direction.

Payne glanced at Maria. "Stay in here. I want to make sure everything's okay."

Maria was about to object when she remembered her promise to Jones. No back talk or bullshit of any kind. "Okay. I'll stay in the car."

"Don't worry. I'll leave the AC on. Feel free to change the radio station if you want."

She glared at him. "I wish you two would stop telling me not to worry. The more you do it, the more I worry."

Payne smiled as he opened the door. "Don't worry. We'll stop doing that soon."

Before she could respond, Payne closed the door in her face and shifted his focus to Jones. He was leaning against the side of the Hummer, his arms crossed in front of him and his face angled toward the sky. He had a distant look in his eyes, as if he were trying to grasp what they had stumbled into and didn't quite know how they were going to get out of it.

It was a look that Payne had seen hundreds of times.

A look that meant Jones was thinking.

Not wanting to disturb him, Payne walked down the path and sidled up to the Hummer. The wind was blowing in from the sea, and the sun was shining bright. All in all, it wasn't a bad place to be in the middle of February.

"So," he eventually said, "I got your text."

"I see that," Jones replied.

"Is everything all right?"

He shrugged. "I checked the Hummer for tracking devices and disabled the GPS before I arrived. As long as you weren't followed, we should be clear."

"Nope, we weren't followed. I made sure of that."

"In that case, we should be fine."

"Good. Then I'm going to close my eyes and work on my tan."

"That's what I've been doing."

Payne looked at him. "I can tell. You're much darker than I am."

Jones smiled. "That's what I was going for."

"Well, mission accomplished."

"Jon?"

"Yeah?"

"Please shut up now."

After that, Payne waited patiently, not wanting to push the conversation until Jones was ready to talk. Everybody had his own way of processing information, and this was Jones's method to work through complex problems. When it came to missions, he was a brilliant strategist. He had received the highest score in the history of the Air Force Academy's MSAE (Military Strategy Acumen Examination) and had organized hundreds of operations with the MANIACs. He had a way of seeing things several steps ahead, like a chess master. And sometimes high-level thinking took a little extra time.

A few minutes passed before Jones spoke again. When he finally did, there was a confidence in his voice that had been missing earlier. Plus, his sense of humor had returned.

Jones cleared his throat and pointed toward the sky. "Did you see the pterodactyls? They're particularly lovely this time of year."

Payne nodded. "One just swooped down and snatched a baby off the beach. I was going to save it, but I didn't want to disturb you."

"Thanks, Jon. I appreciate it."

"So," he said as he pointed toward the back of the Hummer, "are you ready to show me what you found? Maria said something about a bomb."

"Did she really?"

Payne shrugged. "I think she did, but I wasn't really listening. I was too preoccupied with evasive driving techniques and the threat of aerial pursuit."

"You say that like it's a bad thing."

"Actually, you're right. It was kind of fun."

"Glad to hear it."

Payne looked at him and waited for an explanation. "So?"

Jones stared back. "What?"

"Don't play dumb with me! I was in the middle of a productive meeting with Deputy Dawg when I got your text. I think something bad happened to Hamilton, and I was *this* close to figuring it out. I hope to hell you can shed some light on it."

"I think I can."

"Well?"

"Give me a hand with the trunk, and I'll show you."

A spare tire was mounted to the back gate of the H2. It swung left to right and had to be pushed out of the way before the back window could be lifted open. Payne handled both while Jones removed the last few bungee cords from the rear of the tarp. He would have done it earlier, but he didn't want to subject his cargo to the elements until it was completely necessary.

Jones spoke as he worked. "This is one of those good news/bad news situations. Don't be blinded by the good until I tell you about the bad."

"How bad?"

"Pretty bad."

"Okay, I'll keep that in mind."

Staring out the rear of the SUV, Maria saw them removing the final cord from the tarp and decided to take a closer look. After all, this was supposed to be her job, not theirs. She quietly opened her door and slipped out of the vehicle without making a sound. One step after another, she crept across the rocky shoal until she was close enough to gaze into the back of the H2. When she did, her eyes widened in surprise and a single phrase slipped from her mouth.

Two foreign words that summed up Payne's feelings as well.

Santa Maria!

29

TIFFANY WAITED FOR THE CROWD TO DISPERSE BE-
fore she approached Paco. She had thoroughly enjoyed
the walking tour and wanted to ask him a few more questions
about the area. She thanked him for his time and tipped him
twenty pesos. "I thought you did a wonderful job. You were very
informative."

He graciously took the money. "And entertaining."

"Yes," she said, laughing. "Informative *and* entertaining."

He grinned. *"Muchas gracias."*

"If you have a moment, may I ask you another question?"

"For you, *pelirroja*, anything."

She blushed slightly. She wasn't used to this kind of attention.
On most trips, she was rarely noticed. "I was wondering about the
lake."

"Which lake?"

"Lake, um, Texaco? You know, the one around the city?"

He smiled at her attempt. "It's Texcoco."

"Texcoco," she echoed.

He nodded. "*Texcoco* is a lake. *Texaco* is a gas station."

"Sorry about that. I knew it sounded wrong when I said it."

"That is okay. Americans say it like that all the time."

"You must get sick of us."

He shook his head. "Not at all. Without dumb Americans, I do not make money!"

She laughed at the comment. She sensed he was only teasing. "After that remark, I'm afraid to ask you my question. You're going to think I'm *really* stupid."

"Not stupid. Just unaware. Most people who live here are unaware, too. Tell me, what brings you to Mexico City?"

"A business trip."

"What kind of business?"

"International banking. I have a big meeting with a key contributor."

Paco grinned. "See! You are not stupid. You have important job with important company. You are much more important than me. I am just a tour guide. Your question could never be stupid. Tell me, what is question?"

"You said the Aztecs built their city in the middle of the lake. And the Spanish built this city on top of the Aztec city, right?"

"That is correct."

"That's what I thought. In that case, what happened to the lake? I don't remember seeing it when I flew into the airport."

"Sadly, the lake is no more. The Spanish killed it."

"They killed it? How do you kill a lake?"

"By building a giant drain to let the water out."

She stared at him, unsure if he was joking. "Are you serious?"

He nodded. "Flooding was a problem for the Spanish. They expanded our city without strengthening the levees, and that was a big mistake. The flood in 1629 was so bad that parts of the city remained underwater for five years. Eventually, the Spanish Crown did something desperate. They built a drain to save the city. First they took our island, then they took our lake."

"That's horrible. I bet the Aztec city looked gorgeous in the middle of the water."

He shrugged. He had never seen Tenochtitlan. He had been born five hundred years too late. "I must admit, there is one thing that gives me comfort about the fate of the Aztecs."

"What's that?" she asked.

He pointed at the Metropolitan Cathedral. It loomed high above the plaza, its bell towers stretching toward the sky. It truly was an impressive church.

She nodded solemnly. "Your faith in God."

He laughed at the suggestion. "No! I am not a religious man. I am talking about the building. The *building* brings me comfort."

"You mean its beauty?"

"I mean its *condition*. The stupid thing is falling down."

"Really?"

He laughed louder. "The Spanish thought they were so smart when they drained the lake. But guess what? The water had to go somewhere. In this case, it went under our island. For centuries, it has been eating away at the rock. The lake bed is dry, but our city is sinking—several inches every year. Look at the towers. They are all crooked. I call them the Leaning Towers of Zócalo. I am an old man, but my spine is straighter than them. Someday they will fall over. And when they do, I will laugh and thank Cuauhtémoc. I will tell tourists that his ghost knocked them over as revenge for losing his city."

Until that moment, she hadn't really noticed the towers. But after his comments, she couldn't help but notice how crooked they were. "I'll be damned. I totally missed that."

"Have you been inside the cathedral?" he asked.

"Not yet."

"Do not waste your time—unless you like scaffolding. Everywhere you look, there is scaffolding. It is holding up the arches. It is holding up the ceiling. It is even holding up Jesús. He should be on a cross, *not* on scaffolding. I am not Catholic, and even I know that."

She fought the urge to smile.

"Tell me," he said, "have you heard of 'the watch list'?"

"You mean the criminal watch list?"

He shook his head. "I mean, the *monument* watch list."

"Nope. Never heard of it."

"Historians studied famous monuments all around the world, and they picked the ones that you should visit before it is too late. Catedral Metropolitana is high on that list."

She considered his statement. "In that case, would you mind taking my picture in front of it? I want to get a photo before it falls down."

✠   ✠   ✠

OVER THE NEXT FIFTEEN MINUTES, Tiffany took several photographs of the plaza. She walked to one end of the square and snapped some pictures. Then she walked to the other end and did the same. But instead of focusing her lens on the buildings and monuments—like every other tourist in the Zócalo—she was more concerned with traffic patterns and escape routes.

As families strolled past and young kids played, she tried to imagine what they would do if they heard a gunshot. Would they freeze? Would they scatter? Or would they put their faith in God and run toward the cathedral? And what about the guards at the National Palace? It was no longer the official residence of the Mexican president, but it was still a government building. Would they come running, or would they lock their doors to protect their own?

Tiffany continued to ponder such things as she walked toward the northeast corner of the plaza. She noticed a steady stream of people coming and going from that direction, but she couldn't understand why. As far as she could tell, there was nothing over there except an intersection. And then she saw it. A set of stairs leading *under* the plaza.

She hustled closer and peered into the stairwell, unsure what she would find in the shadows. Several feet underground, there was a blue-and-white sign that read ZÓCALO. Next to it was the symbol for the Mexico City metro system. For some reason, this major station on Line 2 was practically hidden from the plaza. No signs or symbols on the street above. Just two iron railings and a long set of stone stairs that led into the depths of Paco's island.

Just to be safe, she made sure there were no surprises in the station before she called in her field assessment. Using a burner phone, she dialed the number from memory and waited for the team leader to answer. She knew what was at stake. The next phase of their mission would be based on her evaluation. If the plaza wouldn't work for a ransom drop, she had the authority to move it to a secondary location—even if that meant waiting for another day.

"So," he asked her, "what do you think?"

"I think it's perfect."

"Are you sure?"

"I'm positive. There's no way they'll catch me."

"If they do, they'll kill you."

She smiled. "Not if I kill them first."

30

PAYNE DIDN'T BOTHER TO CRITICIZE MARIA FOR leaving the SUV. He was too focused on Hamilton's cargo to worry about her disobedience.

The back of the Hummer was filled with artifacts, each divided by category and stored in a handmade display case with removable wooden slats. The case stretched almost the whole length and width of the trunk, as if it were custom-fitted to the vehicle. Large objects—such as painted ceramic vases, clay statues, and intricate jade masks—were packed in Bubble Wrap and given their own individual compartments. Meanwhile, smaller items—such as jewelry, stone figurines, and pottery shards—were relegated to plastic bags and crammed in the remaining spaces. With a depth of twenty-four inches, the case held more than a hundred items.

As the lone archaeologist in the group, Maria stepped forward and examined the relics. Despite having very little experience with Mesoamerican art, she had spent enough time in museums around the world to know an important find when she saw one. And this qualified.

Maria held up a plastic bag. Inside was a carved stone figure depicting a Mayan god with an elaborate headdress. "Do you know what a collector would pay for this?"

Payne shrugged. "No idea."

"Depending on its age, probably tens of thousands of dollars."

"For an action figure? It's not even in its original box."

She ignored his wisecrack. "The Mayan civilization is more than four thousand years old. If this object came from the Pre-classic Era, it might even predate Christ." She handed it to Jones, who gazed at its features. "I'll be the first to admit that this isn't my area of specialty, but at first glance, I'd say that Hamilton made a substantial discovery. On the open market, the contents of this trunk are worth . . . well . . . I honestly don't know. But I *guarantee* it's a lot."

Jones grimaced at her assessment but said nothing. In his mind, it still wasn't the right time to ruin their moods. He would wait until they had a little more time to examine the bounty before he revealed the bad news about Hamilton.

Payne glanced at Maria. "What did you mean by that?"

"Which part?" she asked.

"The part where you said this wasn't your area of expertise."

"Well, it *isn't* my area of expertise. Furthermore, you know that it isn't."

Payne didn't like her tone, and he didn't like her use of the word "furthermore." The word was dripping with condescension. "Excuse me?"

She glared at him. "You know damn well what my specialty is. Or don't you remember roughing me up while I was searching for Christian artifacts in Italy?"

"Roughing you up? What in the hell are you talking about?"

Her voice was filled with venom. "Oh, I see how it is. You've beaten up so many women that you can't possibly remember them all. Well, let me refresh your memory. When you tracked me down in Milan, you grabbed me by my hair, threw me on the hood of a car, then shoved a gun under my chin while threatening to blow my head off. Or was that someone else?"

"Hold up," he said, confused. "Is that how you remember it?"

"Yes! That's how I remember it!"

He shook his head. "Funny, because I remember it different than you. I remember you and your mentor being international fugitives at the time, accused of mass murder and twenty other charges that would've gotten you fried. That forced me to take extra precaution during our first encounter. *Furthermore*—to use your word—I recall saving your ass on multiple occasions, clearing both of your names, and helping you with the biggest discovery of your career."

"Yeah, but—"

"*Furthermore,*" he said angrily, "I also remember a phone call from you less than twenty-four hours ago where you were crying like a schoolgirl and begging for my help. So it might be nice if you dropped the arrogance for a little while and showed me some goddamned respect."

Furious, she cursed at him in Italian.

Payne turned toward Jones. "I don't deserve this shit! I really don't! You need to talk to your wife right now and get her ass in line, or you can handle this mess on your own. As far as I'm concerned, there are more than enough ungrateful people in the world. If they happen to lose their queen, it isn't going to bother me in the least."

"Jon—"

"DJ, I'm serious! She's been giving me attitude since our arrival. First at the hotel, then in the car. Now she's accusing me of beating women? What the hell is that about? I asked her a legitimate question about her area of expertise, and she hits me with a 'furthermore.' Really? After all I've done for her? I ought to take that 'furthermore' and shove it up her ass."

Payne turned his head and glared at Maria. "But I would never do that, because *I don't hurt women.*"

Cursing under his breath, he stormed away from the Hummer and headed to the far end of the rocky shoal. Not only to calm down but to give the unhappy couple a chance to talk in private. Payne knew his verbal confrontation with Maria would put Jones in an awkward position—forcing him to get between his best friend and his ex-girlfriend—but Payne didn't regret anything he had said. He truly meant it when he claimed he would walk away from the situation. Although it was against his nature to turn his back on someone in trouble, the only person who appeared to be in peril was Terrence Hamilton, a total stranger to them. With Payne's military connections, he knew he could place a single call to the U.S. embassy in Mexico and convince them to assemble a team to investigate Hamilton's disappearance. In fact, the more he thought about it, the more he regretted not doing that from the very beginning.

Heck, the only reason he hadn't was because of Jones.

Or, more specifically, Jones's feelings for Maria.

Payne knew Jones cared about her—more than Jones was willing to admit—and wanted to prove his worth by rescuing her from danger. As someone who had been through a similar situation with his ex-girlfriend, Ariane, he understood Jones's desire to be a protector and wanted to help him in any way possible. But at the same time, he knew he had to step in at some point and speak up for Hamilton. It was one thing to be a good wingman and help his buddy work things out with an ex-flame. It was another thing completely if Hamilton died or got hurt while Jones and Maria struggled through their issues.

Payne thought Hamilton deserved better than that.

He deserved their full attention.

If Jones and Maria didn't get their act together soon, he would be forced to step aside and call in reinforcements from the U.S. embassy. His conscience wouldn't give him a choice.

Trying to calm down, Payne picked up a flat rock and tried to skip it across the undulating surface of the Caribbean. The rock skipped four times before it was swallowed by a turquoise wave. A split second later, the wave crashed into a nearby reef, sending spray high into the air. Other than the surf and the wind, the only other sound was the rumble of a distant motor. Shielding his eyes from the sun, he gazed to the northwest and spotted two Jet Skis running parallel to the crowded beach, both riders zipping along at a high rate of speed.

Payne smiled as he thought back to a recent trip to Clearwater, Florida. He and Jones had rented WaveRunners near Pier 60 and taken them into the Gulf of Mexico, where they had lucked upon a school of dolphins. For more than ten minutes, the dolphins followed them wherever they went. Not in a predatory way. More like a game of follow-the-leader. Back and forth, side by side, as fast as they could go. It was, without a doubt, one of the coolest things he had ever experienced. Two species, each intrigued by the other, sharing the open sea.

Unfortunately, his smile quickly faded when he refocused on his current situation. For whatever reason, Maria was harboring some serious anger toward him, and it had reared its ugly head on two occasions in the past few hours. Thankfully, neither instance had put them at risk, but he realized it was only a matter of time before it did. If the two of them were going to work together, Payne knew they had to come to some sort of understanding. Otherwise, his involvement would cause more damage than good.

For the sake of Jones, he was willing to try.

He hoped Maria would, too.

31

PAYNE KEPT HIS DISTANCE FOR A FEW MORE MINUTES before he headed back to the Hummer. Jones spotted his approach and intercepted him about twenty feet from the vehicle.

"How ya doin'?" Jones asked in a playful voice.

"Not great, but better than before."

"Are you sure? Because I'd be happy to drive into the city to buy you some Prozac. Down here, they make it themselves and sell it *behind* the pharmacy."

Payne smiled. "As tempting as that sounds, I think I'll pass."

"What about a beer? Maybe a Dos Equis or a Tecate. Oh, I know! What about a hooker? I bet they're in the same alley as the Prozac."

Payne declined again. "No, thanks."

Jones took a step closer and lowered his voice. "Listen, I know you're tempted to bail on this, and if you did, I wouldn't blame you at all. Maria's behavior was way out of line. That being said, I'm asking as your best friend, please hang in there a little while longer. I really need your help on this one."

"I know you do, but—"

"But what?"

Payne leaned away from him. "First of all, you're a little too close to me right now. Please back up before I'm forced to give you a mint."

He smiled and took a giant step back. "Sorry."

"Second, you know how I feel about begging."

Jones rolled his eyes. "It should only be done by children in Third World countries, or in movies for comic effect."

"Exactly."

"In my defense, I act like a child quite frequently, and Mexico isn't exactly a superpower."

"Those are very good points."

"I thought so."

Payne continued. "Third, despite my recent outburst and my obvious frustration, I am not the main problem here. I think both of us know that Maria has a bigger issue with me than I do with her. As long as she harbors that animosity, there is very little I can do besides staying out of her way—and that will be tough to do if I'm trying to protect her."

"Trust me, we're in complete agreement on this one. As soon as she calmed down, I let her know that she was at fault and her childish behavior would not be tolerated."

Payne smirked. "Yeah, I'm sure you said it just like that."

"Or words to that effect."

"That means you begged her to give me one more chance."

Jones laughed. "I will not confirm or deny the allegation."

"Personally, I don't care what you said or how you said it, as long as her behavior improves. If she pulls that argumentative shit when we're in a dangerous situation, there's a very good chance that someone ends up dead."

"I agree."

"Does she know that?"

"I'll make sure she does."

Payne pointed at the Hummer. "Speaking of danger, I think it's time you told me what you found with the artifacts. I need to know what we're facing here."

Jones stared at him. "How do you know I found something?"

"How? Because I'm fucking psychic."

"If that's the case, then you already know what I found."

"Shit, I walked right into that one."

"Which proves you *aren't* a psychic."

Payne conceded the point. "Actually, when I pulled up, you said this was a good news/bad news thing. I'm guessing the artifacts are the good news. I'm still waiting for the bad."

Jones turned and faced the Hummer. "Then follow me. There's something that you and Maria need to see before we leave Cancún."

"We're leaving Cancún?"

He nodded. "The sooner, the better."

As they walked, Payne briefed Jones on the surveillance video and everything else he had learned at the security office. He also showed him a photo of the two Latin men who had broken into the suite. Maria heard the tail end of the conversation but was reluctant to ask any questions before she had a chance to clear the air with Payne. Then again, even if she had questioned him, it wouldn't have bothered him in the least. During his military career, he had crossed paths with many people he didn't get along with, but it had never prevented him from doing his job. That was a skill he had learned at the Academy and had mastered during Special Forces training. Instructors had taught him how to compartmentalize his feelings, which allowed him to focus on the task at hand while blocking out everything else. Compared to the horrors he had suppressed on the battlefield, his issues with Maria would be easy to ignore.

Jones opened the driver's-side door and reached between the seats. "As soon as I saw this in the trunk, I knew something bad was going on. I don't know what, but *something*."

Maria stared through the open hatch. "Saw what?"

The tarp, which had been rolled up from the rear of the vehicle to uncover the box of artifacts, had been stored behind the front seat. Payne and Maria had assumed that it had been wedged in an empty space, but it had actually been draped over a second box that was smaller than the first. Jones grabbed the middle of the tarp and yanked it into the front seat.

Payne, who was standing nearby, opened the rear driver's-side door for a better view of the hidden crate. Painted Army green and made out of thick plywood, it looked like a thousand other crates that he had seen in his former profession. Most of them filled with danger. As soon as he saw it, a surge of adrenaline coursed through his veins. "What's inside?"

Jones answered. "A little bit of everything."

Payne leaned forward and opened the three front clasps. Then he tilted the lid back to see what they were dealing with. "Holy shit."

Jones nodded. "My sentiments exactly."

Known in Russia as an Avtomat Kalashnikova, or Kalash for short, the weapon was commonly called an AK-47 in other parts of the world. First developed in the Soviet Union during the 1940s, it is a selective-fire, gas-operated 7.62x39-millimeter assault rifle that had a killing range of more than a thousand feet. Unlike the Mexican handgun stashed in Hamilton's briefcase, the AK-47 was an offensive weapon, capable of doing serious damage.

Payne grabbed the top rifle and showed it to Maria.

She gasped at the sight. "What's that for?"

Jones answered, "It's not for a Texas barbecue."

"I know that," she stammered. "I mean, why does he have it?"

Payne gazed into the crate. "You mean *them*."

"Them?" she asked.

He nodded. "Two AKs, plenty of ammo, some plastic explosives, a few detonators, and a set of binoculars."

Jones corrected him. "Actually, they're field glasses."

"Oh, in that case I feel *much* better about his box of weapons."

"Well, you should. They're much more durable than binoculars. Believe it or not, field glasses have no internal prisms."

Payne rolled his eyes. "Thank God for that! I'm sure all of us will sleep a little more soundly with that nugget tucked under our pillows. Hamilton was armed for war, but at least we know his field glasses will survive if we knock them off a nightstand."

Maria ignored the sarcasm and focused on Jones. "But why does he have that stuff? He's a scholar, not a soldier."

"I honestly don't know. But it's pretty obvious that he was keeping some secrets from you."

"I guess he was."

Payne returned the weapon to the crate, then walked toward them. "Now comes the hard part. You have to decide what you want to do about it."

"What do you mean?"

"Do you want to wash your hands of the situation, or do you want to press forward?"

She answered without hesitation. "I want to press forward."

"Are you sure?" Jones asked.

"I'm absolutely positive. I need to know why I'm here. I need to know why someone trashed my suite and stole my passport. I need to know what happened to Hamilton. How can I ever feel safe without those answers?"

She took a deep breath, then flashed a weary smile. "Besides, I can't go home even if I wanted to. I'm stuck in Mexico until I get a new passport."

"True," Jones said, "but that doesn't mean you have to stay involved. We can call the authorities and let them handle things."

She scoffed at the notion. "And what are they going to do? Impound the weapons, take the artifacts, maybe fill out some paperwork. Hamilton's been gone less than a day, and there's no hard evidence that he's been abducted. The local cops won't do a thing except get in our way."

Payne stared at her. "You're assuming that I want to stay involved."

"Why wouldn't you?"

"Why? Because I never met the guy, and he had a box of weapons. Where's my incentive? I felt bad for Hamilton when I thought he was an innocent victim. But now it's pretty obvious that he was into something shady. For all I know, he might've had it coming."

"And what about me? Do I have it coming?"

"How should I know? I haven't talked to you in years."

Sensing an argument, Jones quickly intervened. "Of course you don't have it coming. You came here for a job, and things went sour. It's not your fault."

"Listen," she said, her voice much softer than it had been a moment before, "I know I screwed up. I know I shouldn't have come here without knowing all the details about the job before I left Italy. What can I say? I tried to be spontaneous for once in my life, and it kind of blew up in my face. Unfortunately, there's no turning back now. I'm caught up in this mess—whatever it is—and I'm looking for a way out. Obviously, you guys know a lot more about these situations than I do, but I don't think the police are the best way to go. I think we need to press forward. I think we need to find Hamilton so I can ask him about my involvement. I need to know who trashed my suite and stole my passport. That's the only way I'll feel safe."

Jones put his arm around her shoulder and squeezed. "Don't worry, Maria. Nothing is going to happen to you. We won't let it. Isn't that right, Jon?"

Payne sighed and nodded slightly. He wasn't thrilled with the idea, not with so many unknowns, but at least her rationale made sense.

Hamilton was the key to everything.

He possessed all the answers.

32

WHILE PAYNE AND JONES TALKED STRATEGY, MARIA glanced through the artifacts, hoping to find the document that Hamilton had gone to retrieve at the time of his disappearance. Before he had left the bistro, he had claimed that her role in the project would be "right up her alley," but so far everything in the back of the Hummer was foreign to her. Although she could appreciate the intrinsic beauty of the statues and vases, she simply didn't know enough about the Mayan culture to assess their value. Were they first century? Ninth century? Twelfth century?

Were they from the Yucatán, or were they from Belize?

Did the colors and patterns have any significance?

She honestly didn't know.

To her, it was like trying to learn an ancient language without a primer of any kind. If she was given several months and the proper tools, she could probably grasp the basics and reach some general conclusions about the artifacts. But considering the time constraints and her current location, she knew it was an impossible task. So much so, she didn't take any of the items out of the plastic bags or the Bubble Wrap to examine them. Why risk potential damage if there was nothing to gain?

About the only thing that made sense to her was a map of the region. She found it folded up and stuffed next to the center console. Three places had been circled, all of them known for their Mayan ruins: Tulum, Cobá, and Chichén Itzá. She didn't know if Hamilton had been to the sites or had hoped to visit them, but at least it was *something*.

Frustrated by her lack of success, she sat on the back bumper of the Hummer and tried to recall her conversation with Hamilton. She figured if she thought about it long enough, she might remember an important fact that had slipped her mind. Maybe a hint about his predicament, or a subtle clue about her role in things. Ultimately, that's what bothered her the most—not knowing why she was there. Why, after being in the field for several weeks, had Hamilton picked up the phone and reached out to her? Why was he willing to fly her halfway around the world and put her up in a five-star hotel? What did she bring to the table that no one else could?

Maria rubbed her eyes in thought.

Despite her youth and inexperience, she had an impressive résumé, one that put most others to shame. While working with her professor, Dr. Charles Boyd, they had discovered the catacombs of Orvieto and had revealed evidence that gave the academic world new insights into the life of Tiberius, the second emperor of ancient Rome. When these discoveries were brought to light, she had been labeled a rising star in the academic community, someone who had done so much at such a young age. Couple that with her famous surname—her father had been Italy's Minister of Antiquities at the time of his death—and she had her choice of jobs around the globe.

Instead of cashing in on her sudden fame, she did the unexpected and returned to England, where she worked on her thesis and earned her doctorate, all the while trying to avoid the guilt caused by losing her brother and father in the same adventure that had made her a celebrity. Between the remorse and the sorrow and all the other emotions that kept her up at night, she found herself running away from society and all the amazing opportunities that had surfaced. Subconsciously, she did this to punish herself for their deaths. It simply felt wrong to capitalize on a situation that had caused her family irreparable harm—even though she wasn't to blame for their downfall. Unfortunately, the mind is a tricky thing, and somewhere deep inside her conscience she was still struggling with the events that led to their demise.

Ironically, some of the same emotions that she had felt in Orvieto had resurfaced with Hamilton's disappearance. After years of avoiding team projects, she had finally decided to get back in the game with a working vacation, but less than an hour after meeting and bonding with her new boss, her world was turned upside down once again.

He was missing.

She was in danger.

Yet somehow *she* felt responsible.

It didn't matter that he had kept secrets from her about the project, his team, and all the weapons that he had in his Hummer. All she could focus on was the reason for his disappearance. In her mind, it all boiled down to one thing. If he hadn't driven to Cancún to meet her, none of this would have happened. Hamilton would still be a free, and . . .

Wait a minute! That was it!

Hamilton had driven there to meet her.

She hopped off the back bumper of the H2 and rushed to the front passenger door. A few seconds later, she was digging through the glove compartment, looking for Hamilton's rental agreement.

Payne and Jones noticed her excitement and came over to investigate.

"What are you looking for?" Jones asked.

"Hamilton's paperwork."

He reached into his cargo pocket. "I have it right here."

"May I see it?" she asked.

"Of course."

She glanced at the paperwork. It was divided into two columns. Spanish on the left; English on the right. She was fluent in both but felt far more comfortable with English, so she concentrated on the right-hand side. When she didn't see what she was looking for, she flipped to page two, then to page three. Finally, toward the bottom of page four, she spotted the elusive piece of information. "No! That can't be right."

Payne stared at her. "What can't be right?"

"Cancún! How can it be Cancún?"

"I have no idea. Then again, I have no idea what you're talking about."

She looked at him. "During my conversation with Hamilton, he said he had driven to Cancún for our meeting. I asked him where he had come from, and he was somewhat vague on the topic. He told me his team was less than a hundred miles from here."

"Good to know."

"I was hoping this agreement would list the town where he rented the vehicle, and that would narrow our search even further. But he rented the vehicle *here*."

"In Cancún?" Payne asked.

"Yes! He rented it *here*."

Jones nodded. "I know."

"You know? How do you know?" she demanded.

"Because I looked at the agreement about an hour ago. I would have been happy to tell you if you had been a little bit nicer to me, but you were too busy being Nancy Drew to let me get a word in."

Payne glanced at him. "Was Nancy Drew *mean*? I don't remember her being mean. Sexually frustrated, yes. Maybe even a lesbian. But definitely not mean."

Jones shook his head. "She *wasn't* a lesbian. I can tell you that. I'm pretty sure she banged the Hardy Boys."

"Wait! The Hardy Boys *weren't* gay? I thought they were married."

"No, they were brothers. Not husbands."

"I'll be damned. All this time I thought they were gay."

Jones stroked his chin in thought. "Unless . . ."

"Unless, what?"

"Maybe *they* were lesbians."

She slammed the glove compartment shut. "Okay! I get it. I was mean to both of you, and I should have told you what I was thinking instead of bossing you around. I promise I won't let it happen again."

Jones ignored her tone and opted to move on. "Somehow I doubt that, but I'll let it slide for now—if only to get back on task."

"Thank you."

He continued. "So, while you were playing detective, did you happen to notice the date of the rental agreement?"

She glanced at the paperwork. "No, why?"

"He rented the vehicle a few weeks ago, which leads me to believe that he wasn't lying to you. He probably did drive to Cancún for your meeting."

She spotted the date on the contract and nodded in relief. It was one thing to keep secrets from her. It was quite another if he had been lying. "Good."

"Now all we have to do is figure out where his team is."

Payne spoke up. "A hundred miles is a reasonable distance to search—especially since we're against the coast. That eliminates half of our search grid right away. No need to go east."

Jones nodded. "That's true."

"Plus, I have Randy running down his financials. If he stopped to buy gas or supplies with a credit card, we'll be able to narrow our focus even more."

"When will he call?"

Payne shrugged. "Depends on the world. As long as nothing major happens in the next few hours, I'm sure we'll hear from him today. If something comes up, who knows?"

"Fuckin' world. Always screwing things up!"

"Don't I know it."

She looked at them, concerned. "We aren't going to wait, are we? I mean, can't we start the search without Randy's information?"

Jones nodded. "We could, but we don't know which direction to go. And even if we did, we wouldn't know what to look for, since we don't know anything about Hamilton's team. Are they men, women, old, young, white, Hispanic? Heck, we don't even have a head count."

"That's true," she said, "but we do have his Hummer. He's been driving around in this thing for a few weeks now. Maybe someone will recognize it."

Payne glanced at the vehicle. The H2 had a distinctive look. Much larger than most vehicles he had seen in Mexico, it also had extra-long running boards and a roof rack that was large enough to accommodate a steamer trunk. To handle the rugged terrain, the H2 was equipped with oversized tires and a snorkel that allowed it to ford streams without drowning out the engine. Throw in the maroon color, and it probably would stand out to the locals—especially in the poor villages that dotted the region. From his duties at Payne Industries, he knew the average income in Mexico was roughly a third of the average income in America, which was why so many companies were looking for workers south of the border. Less money meant fewer luxury purchases, so the odds were pretty good that there weren't many new Hummers being driven around the Yucatán.

He nodded. "She does have a point. This vehicle certainly stands out."

Jones considered their logic. Although he viewed it as a long shot, he liked the fact that Payne and Maria had actually agreed on something. In his mind, that was almost as important as finding a clue. "That's fine with me. If you want to take a road trip, I'm willing to go. Of course, we still need to pick a direction."

She held up the map of the region. "I found this wedged next to the driver's seat. Three Mayan sites are circled on it. If we're lucky, maybe Hamilton visited them. If we're *really* lucky, maybe he talked to some of the experts at the sites."

Payne shrugged. "Couldn't hurt to look—unless we're talking about a ten-hour drive. My ass can't handle that."

"No," she assured them, "all of them are close. Less than a hundred miles away."

"Works for me. Where are we headed first?"

She tapped on the circle to the south. "We're going to Tulum."

33

Initially, Tiffany had some doubts about her assignment. She thought too much blood would have to be spilled to achieve their objective. Not that she minded violence. She actually enjoyed it in a way that few women did. It was one of the traits that made her special. Her girl-next-door looks and her taste for blood made her perfect for undercover work. She could get to places that most men couldn't. And once she got there, she could finish the job on her own.

Still, she was smart enough to realize that targeting Hector Garcia, one of the most powerful criminals in Mexico, was a dangerous game. The only way to survive was to make sure that nothing, absolutely nothing, could be traced back to her. She certainly couldn't be caught, but she also needed to make sure that she wasn't seen by anyone in his organization. To pull that off, she brought in a crew of her own. Handpicked from previous missions, each of them had a specialty. If they did their jobs and did them well, there was no doubt in her mind that they could accomplish the impossible: they could make her disappear in the middle of an open plaza.

Her crew had been in town for nearly a week. They had scouted the city, handled the kidnapping, and guarded the children in a local safe house, while she took care of Hamilton in Cancún. She wasn't used to dealing with so many issues at once, but she viewed this as a once-in-a-lifetime opportunity that she couldn't pass up. If everything went according to plan, she would make more money in one job than she could ever make in a lifetime of regular jobs.

It was why she was taking so many risks.

To prepare the plaza for the ransom drop, members of her crew walked the periphery of the Zócalo. Every time they came across a garbage can—more than thirty were distributed throughout the square—they tossed in a plastic bottle filled with a special concoction. Controlled by a remote detonator and designed for maximum coverage in an urban environment, the bottles would ignite on cue. One of her men, an ex-soldier in the U.S. military who specialized in explosives, had suggested the devices based on the flatness of the terrain and the atmospheric conditions in the city. Due to its location in a highland valley, cold air sinks down from the mountains, trapping smoke and pollution near the surface. As long as the wind didn't pick up in the next hour or so, the entire plaza would be overwhelmed by the blasts.

Obviously, this would be a huge advantage for Tiffany's crew. With the push of a single button, they would be able to neutralize Hector's entire army. It didn't matter if he brought in snipers, or mercenaries, or hired the entire police force to lock down the area during the ransom drop. If they were in the plaza when the devices went off, they would be rendered useless.

✠   ✠   ✠

IN THE PAST SIXTY HOURS, Hector had fallen apart. He couldn't eat. He couldn't sleep. He couldn't focus on anything except his children. Overwhelmed by guilt and rage, he went through stretches of depression followed by bursts of anger. If he wasn't brooding or cursing, he was breaking mirrors and lamps while threatening to kill anyone who tried to stop him.

It got so bad that Angel, his second in command, ordered everyone from the house. That included Hector's wife, Sofia. Fearing for her safety, she gladly left the scene for a few days of pampering at a local resort. Married for two years, she wanted to be there for Hector in his time of crisis but not if it meant putting herself at risk. There was only so much she was willing to do for a life of luxury. As it was, she didn't have a biological connection with the kids, so Angel thought it would be best if she disappeared for a while.

Neither Hector nor Sofia argued with the decision.

The kidnappers had been playing games with Hector for two and a half days. They had changed their demands more than once. At first, they had requested the medallion. Then it was the medallion *plus* a million dollars. Then it was the medallion and *five* million dollars. He figured that number would continue to climb higher and higher. After all, his organization raked in several million dollars every month. Anyone with the courage to abduct his children would have the guts to ask for more than five million dollars. Taking no chances, Hector and Angel pulled twenty million dollars in U.S. currency from their vaults and had it waiting at the mansion.

To some, this would be a staggering amount.

To them, it was a few months of revenue.

In the kidnapping and drug game, large pallets of cash were exchanged so often that the latest generation of criminal had started to refer to money by total weight instead of total value. In the United States and Mexico, American one-hundred-dollar bills were the denomination of choice. Hector knew that ten thousand hundred-dollar bills equaled a million dollars. He also knew that a million dollars weighed nearly twenty-two pounds. Five million dollars weighed nearly 110 pounds. With that much money, it was far easier to weigh it than to count it, so modern-day criminals might request 110 pounds of cash to complete a deal. Just to be safe, Hector had nearly 440 pounds of cash on hand.

All of it in hundred-dollar bills.

One hundred bills per stack, wrapped in paper bands.

One hundred stacks per million, sealed in clear plastic.

Twenty sealed million-dollar blocks, ready to be delivered.

All he needed was a time, a place, and an amount.

☧   ☧   ☧

HECTOR'S PRIVATE LINE RANG shortly after his wife had left the mansion. Thinking it was Sofia, he was ready to curse her out for tying up his phone when he noticed the caller ID. The screen said: DANIELA GARCIA (MOBILE). The call had been placed from his daughter's cell phone. He used the speakerphone to answer so Angel could listen in.

"Hello?" Hector said.

"*Papá!*" Daniela cried.

"Baby, is that you? Are you all right?"

"*Papá!* Please get me!"

"I'm trying, baby. I'm trying."

Her cell phone quickly changed hands. Suddenly, her brother, Antonio, was on the line. It was the first time he had been allowed to speak to Hector since the abduction.

"Father!" he wailed in Spanish. "Please pay them. *Please!*"

"Antonio! My son! You're alive!"

"Yes, Father. But please—"

Hector heard a slight struggle on the other end of the line. Then silence.

The next voice he heard was the kidnapper's. It was digitally altered, as it had been in all the previous calls. Only this time, he was straight to the point.

"Both kids are alive. *That's* your proof of life. There won't be another until we make the exchange. I want the medallion and ten million dollars in cash. Do you have the money?"

"Yes."

"You have thirty minutes to get to the site. For every minute you're late, I cut off an appendage. Might be a finger, might be an ear. If you love your kids, you won't be late."

"Where?"

He ignored the question. "Each kid will be wired with explosives. If I see anything that looks suspicious—and I mean *anything*—I'll blow the little fuckers to smithereens."

"I swear to God, if you—"

"*What?* You'll do *what*? Now isn't the time for threats. Now is the time to listen. I'm in charge, and I'll stay in charge until we make the exchange. Once I have the ransom and you have your kids, you can threaten me all you want. Until that moment, you need to do exactly what I say, or I'll start cutting off limbs. Do you understand?"

Hector clenched his jaw. "Yes."

"Excuse me?"

"Yes! I understand."

The caller laughed. "Is Angel there?"

Hector glanced at Angel, confused. "What?"

"Is Angel Ramirez, your lieutenant, there with you?"

Angel answered. "Yes. I am here."

"I figured as much. Hector had to trust someone; I figured it would be you. After all, I know how damaging it would be to your organization if word got out that Hector's children had been kidnapped. He wouldn't seem so powerful after something like that. Am I correct?"

Angel reluctantly nodded. "Yes."

"I also assume that a man in his position will want revenge."

"Yes."

"And because of his distress, he'll probably assign you with that task."

"Perhaps."

"Do me a favor. Look at your phone. I sent you a gift."

As if by magic, Angel's cell phone vibrated in his pocket. He quickly pulled it out and stared at the screen. A picture file had been attached to a text message. To view the photo, he pushed a button on his phone. Suddenly, he was staring at a woman pushing a baby stroller through a local park. He gasped when he saw it. He quickly showed it to Hector, who started to curse.

The caller laughed. "From your reaction, I'll assume that we found the correct Ramirez woman. That is your wife, is it not?"

Angel cursed loudly. "Yes."

"And your baby boy?"

"Yes."

"Right now, they're safe. Well, maybe not *safe*—but they are currently free. They'll stay that way as long as this exchange goes smoothly. If not, we'll scoop them up quicker than you can kill me. Am I clear?"

"Yes."

"Good!" the caller said. "Now be a good amigo and start loading the money into the back of Hector's SUV. Oh, in case you were wondering, I know all about its custom features: the armor plating, the bulletproof glass, and the fuel-tank safety system. I mention that in case you think it gives you some kind of tactical advantage. Trust me, it doesn't."

Angel stared at Hector, and Hector stared back.

Neither man could understand how the caller knew so much.

The caller laughed at their silence. He knew he had them on

their heels. "Come on, Angel! Time to get moving! The money won't load itself."

Hector nodded his approval, and Angel ran off.

The caller waited a few seconds. "Is he gone?"

Hector answered. "Yes."

"Despite my deterrents, I know you'll be tempted to put up a fight at the exchange. You're tired, and stressed, and thirsty for revenge. If I were you, I'd be tempted, too. But keep something in mind: the guilt you feel now will be *nothing* compared to the guilt you'll feel if you force me to incinerate your kids. Do you understand?"

"Yes. I understand."

"Are you sure?"

"Yes," he said definitively. "I understand."

"You have thirty minutes, and the clock is ticking. I'll meet you near the Mexican flag in the center of the Zócalo. Do you know where that is?"

"Yes."

"Don't be late."

34

TULUM, MEXICO
(81 MILES SOUTH OF CANCÚN)

THE DRIVE TO TULUM WAS A SIMPLE ONE. THE DECIsion on what to drive was not.

Neither vehicle was large enough to accommodate the artifacts, the weapons, and three people, and everyone had a different opinion on the best solution. Payne wanted to cover the items with the tarp and leave the H2 in an all-day parking lot in Cancún, but Jones and Maria thought that was too risky. As to be expected, she was most concerned about the artifacts, which she felt might provide valuable clues about Hamilton's research. Meanwhile, Jones was focused on the weapons. He figured if Hamilton was lugging them around for his team's safety, maybe they should, too. Eventually, Payne got sick of arguing and made a decision for the group. They would take *both* vehicles to Tulum—if only to give himself some time alone.

Relishing the peace and quiet, Payne led the way in the Hummer. He made a single turn in Cancún onto Federal Highway 307, then headed southwest along the coast. Jones and Maria followed a quarter mile back in the SUV, each of them looking for potential trouble. The journey took them through a number of tourist towns, including Puerto Morelos, Playa del Carmen, Paamul, Xel-Há, and Akumal. They stopped briefly at a beachside restaurant, where they ordered grilled fish tacos, Mexican rice, and Pepsi, which was served in old-fashioned glass bottles. For Payne, they brought back so many memories of his childhood—listening to baseball games with his grandfather while drinking soda from glass bottles—that he ended up buying an entire case for nostalgia. He also loaded up on water, snacks, sunscreen, and bug spray, just in case they had to trek through the jungle to see the ruins at Tulum.

Conversation was limited during lunch, but not because of lingering tension. All three of them were so mesmerized by the tropical scenery that words weren't needed for entertainment. The turquoise water, the white powdery sand, and the warm winter sun relaxed their bodies and calmed their minds. Suddenly, the anger that had been pushing them apart had temporarily drifted away. It had been replaced by a solitary goal: finding information about Hamilton.

First discovered by the Spanish in 1518, Tulum was a walled city built atop a thirty-nine-foot bluff that overlooked the Caribbean Sea. One of the last cities occupied by the Maya, it flourished between the thirteenth and fifteenth centuries and served as a port for Cobá, a major city to the northwest. Because of its positioning along the shore and the strength of its fortified walls, Tulum managed to survive seventy years after the Spanish occupation of Mexico. Ironically, its downfall was not attributed to war but rather the Old World diseases brought by the settlers.

Once the Maya got sick, they were no match for the Spanish.

Payne and Jones parked their vehicles on opposite sides of the parking lot and met outside the visitor center, which sat near the western wall of the city. Maria bought a map of the site and a guidebook of the region, hoping to increase her knowledge of the

Mayan civilization. She figured the more she knew about the Maya, the better. Before she left the center, she asked the clerk if he was familiar with Dr. Hamilton. She even pulled out her phone and showed him a photo that she had downloaded from the Internet, but the clerk didn't recognize him.

Maria thanked him, then headed outside.

"Any luck?" Jones asked her.

"No—not that I was expecting any. I know this is a long shot at best."

"Better than sitting around the hotel, waiting for a call from Randy. Besides, I've always wanted to see this place."

She studied his face, trying to gauge his sincerity. "You're familiar with Tulum?"

He nodded. "Of course I'm familiar with Tulum. Isn't everybody?"

Payne grimaced. "I'm not."

"Actually, you are," Jones assured him. "They filmed that movie here. You know, the one with Jeff Bridges and James Woods. Both of them fall in love with the same brunette."

"Sorry. Not ringing any bells."

"We watched the movie on cable last month."

"We did?"

"Bridges is a football player who gets hurt and comes down here to find her. Alex Karras is a bad guy. Phil Collins sang the title song. . . . Crap, what was it called?"

Maria supplied the answer: *"Against All Odds."*

"Yes!" Jones blurted. *"Against All Odds.* Thank you for remembering. That would have driven me crazy."

"Actually, I've never seen it," she said.

"Then how did you know the name?"

She held up a brochure. It featured a screen shot of the movie— a shirtless Jeff Bridges and a scantily clad Rachel Ward were making out in the Caribbean surf—along with a proclamation in

Spanish and English that *Against All Odds* was filmed here in the early 1980s.

Payne pointed at the photo. "Now I remember it. Those two did it in the ruins."

She glanced at the image. "Really?"

Jones nodded. "Oh, yeah. They were *researching the Maya.*"

Maria laughed at the term that he had coined earlier that morning. "Apparently, I chose the wrong field of study. Researching the Vatican is not nearly as sexy."

Jones scrunched his face. "It *really* isn't."

The roar of an engine and the squealing of heavy brakes caught their attention. They turned and spotted two large tour buses pulling into the parking lot. A tour guide hopped out first, followed by dozens of people from all parts of the globe. Wanting to beat the crowd, Payne, Jones, and Maria hustled through the main gate and entered the pre-Columbian city before they got caught up in the stampede of tourists.

Named after the Mayan word for "wall," Tulum is one of the most scenic sites in the Caribbean and the third most visited archaeological site in Mexico. Protected by steep cliffs to the east, the city was guarded by massive walls to the north, south, and west. They were made from large stones excavated from a nearby quarry. During the city's heyday, its walls averaged 13 feet in height and over 20 feet in width. The largest of these was the western wall. Nearly 1300 feet in length, it took years to build and ran parallel to the coastline. For additional safety, guard towers were installed in the northwest and southwest corners of the city, high above the walls that protected the northern and southern flanks. These two walls, approximately 560 feet in length, had narrow gates that allowed people to enter and exit the city.

At least that used to be the case.

Now the walls were barely there.

Centuries of erosion and neglect had reduced the mighty

barricades to rubble. Though a few sections were still standing, the once impenetrable fortress was a shell of its former self. And yet there was an unmistakable magic about the place. Payne felt it as he walked along the dirt path, snaking his way past the crumbling palaces and temples. He sensed it when the wind whipped through the palm trees that dotted the terrain and ruffled his hair. And he saw it when he stared at El Castillo, the main building on the site. Rising high above the other structures, the "castle" was situated against the cliffs to the east. Outlined by the blue sky and the turquoise sea, the gray stones seemed to glow in the afternoon sun.

Payne stopped and stared in amazement. Having circled the globe on several occasions, he tried to remember the last time he had seen something as breathtaking as Tulum, but he struggled with the task. The ruins and the sea were a startling combination.

Maria noticed the look on his face and sidled up next to him. "Pretty impressive."

He nodded. "It sure is."

"Amazingly, the Maya built this place more than a century before Columbus. Imagine how startling it must have been for the Spanish when they spotted Tulum from the sea. They were expecting a land full of savages. They found this instead."

Payne smiled at the notion. "They probably shit their pants. Trust me, there's nothing worse than bad reconnaissance—especially that far from home. Without the proper supplies, they had no choice but to go forward. Maybe make some allies and hope for the best."

Maria pointed at El Castillo. "Notice the rounded columns and the clean line of the stairs. They did all of that without metal tools."

"Really? How'd they cut the stone?"

"According to this guidebook, they used obsidian."

"Obsidian? Isn't that glass?"

She nodded. "Volcanic glass. They also used it for weapons. Their swords were made of wood, but the blades were made from obsidian."

He glanced at the book in her hand. "Is there a picture in there? I'd love to see what they looked like."

"Sorry, no picture. But Hamilton might have one."

"A sword?"

"Maybe. But I was talking about a picture."

Payne grunted and returned his gaze to the architecture. Without the precision of metal tools, the Maya had accomplished some amazing things. "For the record, I'd love to get my hands on a Mayan sword. I have a collection of ancient weapons, but nothing from this region."

"Really? I didn't know that," she fibbed. In truth, Jones had told her all about the collection during their drive to Tulum and had encouraged her to bring it up. It was his attempt to give Payne and Maria something to talk about other than their mutual frustration. "I'll tell you what I'm willing to do. If you help me find Hamilton, I'll try to make that happen."

Payne smiled, even though he sensed that Jones had put her up to it. But in his mind, that didn't matter. At least she was trying.

35

TIFFANY HAD HEARD HORROR STORIES ABOUT THE way women were treated in Mexico City. She knew females were groped so often on the metro trains that a third of the cars were deemed "women only" during rush hour—a rule that was enforced by armed guards. She also knew women were abducted so frequently in the Federal District that the government approved the use of "pink taxis," a fleet of pink cars driven by women, for women, that were equipped with safety locks and alarm buttons. And yet here she was—a "lowly" woman—ready to rip off the most powerful criminal in the region.

The irony of the situation made her smile.

Wearing oversized sunglasses and a white floppy hat that kept her red hair hidden, Tiffany was confident that no one would suspect her of anything as she strolled through the busy plaza. Here, among the tourists, she was just another face in the crowd. The rest of her crew blended in as well. Her point man was sitting on a bench in front of the Metropolitan Cathedral, where he was able to keep his eyes on traffic from the east. They had mapped out the most direct route from Hector's house, so they knew this was the road he would likely take to the Zócalo.

Meanwhile, the explosives expert was positioned high above the plaza to the west. He monitored action from the rooftop restaurant on the Portal de Mercaderes building. From his elevated vantage point, he had a bird's-eye view of the square, which would allow him to call out possible threats via their radio earpieces. In addition, he would be able to judge the best moment to ignite his devices, using a laptop computer that sat next to his lunch. The program on his screen was designed to look like a Sudoku puzzle. In actuality, the numbers corresponded to garbage cans in the plaza. He could ignite them together, in rows, or individually.

It all depended on the events below.

To keep their names off the airwaves, every member of the team was given a code name that corresponded to the role they would play. The man by the cathedral was called Church. The explosives expert was called Boom. And Tiffany was called Red. In a life-or-death mission, names didn't have to be creative; they needed to be memorable.

⌖   ⌖   ⌖

ON THE DRIVE TO the plaza, Angel tried to call his wife to warn her about the threat, but his call didn't go through. He hung up and frantically tried to call her sister instead. Unfortunately, that call died as well. In fact, every call that Angel and Hector tried to make from the SUV died as soon as they hit SEND. Why? Because Tiffany's crew had installed a cell phone jammer in Hector's vehicle on the night they had abducted his children.

Tiffany didn't activate the device until the final ransom call had been made, but now that it was turned on, any cell phone inside the SUV would not be able to get a signal because of radio spectrum interference. Not only would it prevent Angel from warning his wife, but it would also prevent them from calling in reinforcements to meet them at the Zócalo. Of course, the downside was their inability to contact her if something went horribly wrong—they were involved in an accident, or blew a tire, et cetera—which is why she had a car following Hector's SUV just in case.

The driver went by the name of Chase.

✠   ✠   ✠

INSTEAD OF A PLAIN SEDAN, Chase was driving a bright green Volkswagen Beetle. It had a white roof, an illuminated TAXI sign, and the word TAXI painted on its two doors. With its rounded frame and neon paint job, it would stand out in most places like a lightning bug on a dark night, but not in Mexico City, where the bright green cars swarmed the streets by the thousand. Chase didn't voice it, but he assumed some Mexican official had received a huge kickback when he had agreed to buy that many Beetles. They were fun little cars, but they weren't practical as taxis.

Unbeknownst to him, the Mexico City government agreed with the sentiment, which is why they had recently outlawed the use of VW Beetles as licensed taxis in the city. The vehicles were still popular as "street" or "gypsy" cabs—independent taxis that picked up fares—but licensed companies had to remove them from their fleets, since they were unsafe for passengers. With two doors instead of four, they realized it was too easy to abduct people in the cars, since it was nearly impossible to escape from the backseat.

Fittingly, Hector and Angel were quite familiar with the Beetle.

Their flash kidnapping business thrived because of that car.

Now one was tracking them to the ransom drop.

Two others were bringing Hector's kids to the site.

✠   ✠   ✠

THE DRIVER IN CHARGE of Daniela was code-named Cash. At first he had been dubbed Girl—since he was delivering the girl to the plaza—but he objected so vehemently to the feminine code name that they changed it. He claimed that his duty of picking up the ransom money was just as important as dropping off the girl, so he fought for Cash and won.

Of course, Tiffany failed to tell him that his code name of Girl had nothing to do with Daniela, and everything to do with his whining during the trip. The truth was the other guys had wanted to call him Bitch because he had been acting like one since their arrival in Mexico City. She had softened it to Girl because she didn't want the crew swearing in Daniela's presence, but the more Cash complained, the more tempted Tiffany was to change his name again.

Somehow Bitch seemed more appropriate.

The third driver, who was in charge of Antonio, was nick-named Bro. Not only because he was in charge of the brother but because he had the annoying habit of calling everyone "bro." She figured if his own name were Bro, it would force him to stop using that term on the radio. Plus, she hoped he would hear how stupid it sounded when everyone called him Bro.

Unfortunately, it had the opposite effect.

It made him use the term even more.

✠   ✠   ✠

TIFFANY—WHOSE NOSE, EARS, and cheeks were slathered in a thick layer of zinc oxide ointment to conceal her face—strolled around the plaza. As luck should have it, several dozen protesters were holding a small rally on the southeast corner of the Zócalo. Some people held sheets that were painted with slogans. Others were chanting while passing out literature. She didn't know what they were protesting and honestly didn't care, as long as they kept it peaceful. The last thing she wanted was an increased police presence in the plaza—not with Hector set to arrive.

She glanced at her watch. He had less than five minutes to meet his deadline. After that, things would get tricky. She had done everything in her power to make the children as comfortable as possible during the last sixty hours. They were fed their favorite meals. They watched their favorite movies. They were treated like guests, not hostages. In her mind, the children were nothing more than bargaining chips. They had done nothing wrong, so they were treated with kindness and respect. She knew they couldn't control who their father was. In fact, they were so young that they probably didn't even know what he did for a living. To them, he was simply their father—not a violent criminal who made his living off other people's pain.

Unfortunately, if their father didn't hurry up, she was supposed to penalize the kids for his tardiness. To encourage Hector's promptness, her boss had told him that one appendage would be cut off for every minute that he was late. She understood her boss's rationale. The threat of physical violence against a loved one was a common ploy in the abduction game. Hector's men used it constantly during virtual and traditional kidnappings. But it was something she didn't want to do. Blowing a bad guy's head off was one thing, but chopping off a child's finger was quite another. There were some things that even she wasn't willing to do.

"Chase," she said into her earpiece, "what's your ETA?"

He answered. "About two minutes out."

She glanced at her watch. They would barely make the deadline. "Keep me posted."

"Will do, Red."

"How's it looking, Boom?"

He scanned the plaza from his bird's-eye view. "Looks clear, but not for very long."

She froze, concerned. "Why?"

Boom laughed. "Because I'm about to blow this fucker up."

She cracked a smile. "Church, what about you?"

"I was fine until I heard some tourist say the cathedral is falling down."

She nodded. "I heard that, too."

Church glanced up at the cathedral, paranoid. "You what?"

"Don't worry! I promise you'll die fast," Boom assured him.

"Not funny. Not funny at all."

Chase spoke again. "One minute out."

Boom continued to tease Church. "Jesus Christ, will you look at all that scaffolding? And that isn't *American* scaffolding. That's *Mexican* scaffolding. No way that stuff holds. That shit's gonna look like a game of pickup sticks when I'm done with it."

Church leapt off his bench. "That does it. I'm out of here."

She turned toward the cathedral. "Stay put, and that's an order."

"But—"

She cut him off. "If you leave your post, you lose your share."

He growled at her but said nothing.

She continued her rundown. "Cash, where are you?"

"Circling the fucking block. Like I have been. For an hour."

She rolled her eyes. "Bro, what about you?"

"I'm in position, bro. Just say the word, and I'll be there."

She nodded, confident, as she glanced toward the road from the east.

The fun was about to begin.

36

WITH WEAPONS ON HIS MIND AND TWO BUSLOADS of tourists pouring through the gates of Tulum, Payne excused himself from the site and headed back to the H2, where he could call the Pentagon. Payne knew he walked a fine line with Raskin, who wasn't obligated to help but did so out of a sense of loyalty and friendship, and was reluctant to phone him again. But the more he pondered the cache of weapons in the Hummer, the more apprehensive he became.

Something about them felt *off*.

Like they didn't belong to Hamilton.

Known for his gut instincts, Payne decided to follow his hunch and pursue the gun angle—even if it meant pissing off his friend.

Raskin answered on the first ring. "Research."

"Randy, it's Jon."

He immediately tensed. "Are you all right?"

"Yeah, I'm fine."

"What about DJ?"

"He's fine, too."

Raskin breathed a sigh of relief. "Then why are you calling me?"

"I need your help."

"No shit! The only time you call is when you need my help. I'm pretty sure we established that in our earlier conversation."

"I know we did, but—"

"Listen," Raskin said, "things are a little bit hectic for me at the moment. I haven't had a chance to run down your information yet."

"Good."

"*Good?* Did you say 'good'? I have to admit, I wasn't expecting that. Why is it good?"

"Because I have something else to add to my list."

"Okay! *That's* more like it. *That's* the Jon I know. You're not pulling back. You're merely piling on. Just once I'd like you to call me and say, 'Thanks, anyway, but I figured it out on my own.' That would truly make my day."

Payne smiled at the sarcasm. "I wouldn't hold my breath."

"Don't worry, I won't."

"If it makes you feel any better, I'm merely tweaking your original search. I'm not adding a brand-new category. In my opinion, *that* would be rude."

"Fine. Which part are you tweaking?"

"We found more weapons."

Raskin opened a digital notepad on his screen. It contained information about Hamilton's single-action revolver from their earlier conversation. "Another Mexican special?"

"Nope. Two AKs and some C-four."

"Where?"

"In Hamilton's vehicle."

Raskin grunted. "Is he an anthropologist or a mercenary?"

Payne smiled. "That's what I'm trying to find out."

"Well, I'll see what I can do. The AKs might be easier to trace than the revolver. Big guns tend to get more attention in Mexico."

"That's what I figured. That's why I called you back."

"Fine. Give me their serial numbers."

"Hold on. Give me a second. I gotta open the Hummer."

Raskin grumbled. "Come on, man. I'm in a hurry."

"Sorry about that, but I'm in a public setting. I have to do this discreetly."

"In that case, just text me the numbers."

Payne nodded. He didn't want to press his luck with Raskin. "Good idea. I'll send you a text as soon as I can."

"Great. Can't wait."

"And as a token of thanks, I'll send you that bikini photo you asked for. I snapped a picture during lunch that I'm sure you'll enjoy."

"Awesome. I'm looking forward to it."

Payne was about to hang up when he remembered one last thing. "Wait!"

Raskin sighed. "What is it now?"

"Quick computer question."

"Holy fuck! Can't you tell that I'm busy?"

"Yes, I can, but this is important. I actually talked to another computer guy about this because I didn't want to disturb you, but—"

Raskin cut him off. "Hold up! You did *what*?"

"I said I talked to anoth—"

"Oh, no! I heard you the first time," Raskin snapped. "You talked to *another* computer guy behind my back. Why would you do that?"

"I didn't want to bother you."

"You didn't want to *bother* me?" he mocked. "Do I know this nerd?"

Payne shook his head. "I don't think so. He lives in Mexico."

"He lives in *Mexico*? Oh, I see how you are. You leave the country for a little R and R, and you immediately forget about your man in D.C. Well, Captain Payne, the only R and R you should be worried about is Randy Raskin."

Payne laughed at the jealous rant. He knew Raskin was only kidding. At least he *hoped* he was kidding. If not, they needed to have a serious conversation. "Just a minute. I thought you said you were busy?"

"I am, but I couldn't resist. I needed to blow off some steam."

"No apologies necessary. Glad I could help."

"So, what's your computer question?"

"I tracked down some security footage from the hotel. A second before Hamilton disappears, the screen goes black. No static. No disruption of power. The image simply goes black."

"For how long?"

"Precisely five minutes."

"Precisely? What, did you time it?"

"Didn't have to. The video counter kept rolling during the blackout."

Raskin leaned back in his chair. "Is that so?"

"I checked the camera before I left the hotel. No way to access it without a ladder. It's mounted high on a wall in the front driveway."

"Did your boyfriend do a system check?"

"You mean DJ?"

Raskin laughed. "Not your girlfriend. I meant the *other* computer guy."

Payne smiled. He was used to Raskin busting his balls about Jones, not about other people. "He did, and he claims everything is running fine. The thing that confused him the most is the file itself. He said the simplest solution would have been to delete the whole video. Just wipe it out completely. But that isn't what happened here. Someone took the time to conceal one tiny sliver. He can't figure out how it was done, and I can't figure out why."

Intrigued by the problem, Raskin leaned back even farther. His chair groaned in protest as he considered the pieces of the puzzle. "Your boyfriend's right. The simplest solution would have been to wipe out the entire file. Of course, that might have been noticed."

"Why's that?"

"Most security systems have a series of checks and balances to guarantee a clean operation. Scans are scheduled throughout the day to monitor the health of the most important files. If a file is missing or a hobbit is detected, the operator is notified."

"Did you say 'hobbit'?"

"Yes, I did."

"Like the character from *The Lord of the Rings*?"

Raskin corrected him. "Hobbits are a race of diminutive beings that occupy Middle-earth, not a single character."

"Good Lord! You are a nerd."

"I never said I wasn't."

"Well, I'm not, so I need you to explain what a computer hobbit is."

"It used to be the name of an eight-bit Soviet computer system, but those suckers are obsolete. And by 'suckers,' I mean the computer systems and the Soviets themselves. We sure kicked their asses in the Cold War, didn't we?"

Payne ignored the taunt. "And what does it mean now?"

"It's a file that comes up short. You know, like a hobbit."

"Define short."

Raskin put his feet up on the desk. "Most security systems are set up in loops. Five hours, ten hours, twelve hours, whatever. At the end of that period, the old file is saved and a new file is hatched. Because of these time limits, every file should have the same amount of information. The images will be different, but the size of the files is identical."

"I'm with you so far."

"Now, if something happens to one of these files—the camera goes down, the software malfunctions, or someone deletes a section—the size of the file is going to be shortened."

"Making it a hobbit."

"Exactly. But that's not what happened in Mexico. Someone actually took the time to black out a section of the video. That means its size will be the same as the other files."

"Meaning the operator *wouldn't* be notified of a system error."

Raskin nodded. "If you didn't spot the gap with your own eyes, the odds are pretty damn good that no one would have noticed it."

Payne stroked his chin in thought. "To black out a video like that, how good would a hacker have to be?"

Raskin whistled. "Pretty damn good."

"Too skilled for you to catch?"

"That depends. How hot is the bikini photo that you're going to send?"

"Pretty damn hot."

Raskin grinned. "In that case, I can catch him."

37

ANGEL WEAVED HIS WAY ACROSS SEVERAL LANES OF traffic until the SUV was in the innermost lane. The road encircled the Zócalo like a racetrack around a stone infield. Sitting in the passenger seat, Hector stared at the giant Mexican flag in the center of the historic plaza. In all his years, he couldn't remember it being so still. Normally, it flapped and fluttered in the violent breeze. Today, it looked like a hanged man, dangling lifeless above the square.

Fraught with guilt, Hector viewed it as a sign.

This was where he would be punished for his sins.

Angel eased the wheels of the SUV over the curb, then drove toward the center of the plaza. Despite the confused looks from the locals, who weren't used to seeing vehicles in the square, he parked fifteen feet north of the flagpole. Three tourists were standing in front of them. Two were posing for a picture; the third was the photographer. Other than that, the area around the flag was completely clear.

No cars. No gunmen. No drama.

Just another day at the Zócalo.

Hector glanced at his watch and noted the time. They were one minute early for the meeting. If the caller kept his promise, Hector's kids wouldn't be injured. For that, he breathed a sigh of relief. If anything happened to them, he wouldn't be able to forgive himself. He truly wouldn't. Despite his history of violence, he was still a father, one who cared deeply about the welfare of his kids. Otherwise, he wouldn't be willing to give up so much to get them back.

Angel glanced at him. "Now what?"

Hector shrugged. "I have no idea."

Unsure what to do, they just sat there. Helpless.

They had the medallion. They had the money. They were on time.

They had no choice but to wait.

✠   ✠   ✠

WITH HER SUNGLASSES AND floppy hat, Tiffany blended in with the curious crowd. But unlike them, she was ready to launch an attack.

"Light the east," she ordered.

From his perch at the restaurant, Boom pushed a few keys on his computer. A split second later, a series of devices were ignited on the far side of the plaza.

Whoosh! Whoosh! Whoosh!

One after another, garbage cans erupted in thick plumes of white smoke. The explosions were virtually harmless but terrifying nonetheless—especially for the people near the cans. One person screamed, then a dozen more followed. Before long, screaming and crying could be heard around the plaza as the chaos spread like an invisible plague. Then people started to run.

"Where are they going?" she demanded.

Boom studied the commotion in the plaza below and noted their movement. As expected, most of them were running toward him, trying to get as far from the smoke as possible. With very little wind to contend with, he could turn them any way he wanted. "They're going west."

She figured as much. "Light the north."

Boom grinned and pushed another key.

Whoosh! Whoosh! Whoosh!

This time all the garbage cans on the cathedral's side of the plaza erupted like volcanoes, spewing smoke and an occasional piece of trash. Church stood from the bench, calmly slipped on his gas mask, then strolled through the smoke toward the square. As he did, he fired a few shots into the air, trying to drive everyone to the southwest. The reason for this was simple: Tiffany's preferred escape route was to the north. The last thing they wanted was a bunch of people blocking traffic in that direction, so they tried to steer the crowd to the south.

"How's it looking?" she asked.

Boom laughed. "They're stampeding like a herd of cattle."

"What about Hector?"

"Still there."

"Good," she said as she slipped on her gas mask. "Light him up."

✠ ✠ ✠

DESPITE THE SMOKE IN the plaza and the gunshots behind them, Hector and Angel felt reasonably safe inside their SUV. With its armor plating and bulletproof windows, they knew it would take a serious weapon—like a rocket launcher—to threaten them.

Tiffany knew that, too, which is why her goal was to force them out of the vehicle as soon as possible. With that in mind, her crew had placed a small incendiary device under the driver's seat on the night they had installed the cell phone jammer. Known as a smoke canister, it was designed by the military to cover troop movement in the field. Once ignited, it produced an intense chemical reaction that released a stream of smoke for a short period of time.

From his perch above the plaza, Boom activated the device with the touch of a button. A few seconds later, Hector and Angel stumbled out of the SUV and fell to the ground. Both men were gasping and coughing, desperately fighting for breath. More concerned with air than bullets, they paid little attention to their surroundings until their eyes and lungs had started to clear. Only then did they notice the two people standing in front of them.

Both were wearing gas masks. Both were holding guns.

Hector and Angel were at their mercy.

Sensing that his life was about to end, Angel decided to go out in a blaze of glory. From his knees, he reached behind his back and grabbed the handle of his Glock. He had it halfway out of his belt when Church fired a bullet into his shoulder. Angel crumpled to the ground in agony as blood oozed from the wound. Before long, his entire sleeve was bright red. Church rushed forward and kicked the Glock out of his hand, then checked him for additional weapons. Other than a small flask, he found nothing noteworthy in Angel's pockets.

Meanwhile, Tiffany kept her eyes on Hector. He was on all fours, still trying to catch his breath. Three days earlier, he had been considered an untouchable criminal. Now he was a broken man. His eyes still watering from the smoke, he glared at her through tears.

"Chase," she announced, "the bank is open."

✠   ✠   ✠

POSITIONED NEAR THE NORTHEAST corner of the plaza, Chase drove his bright green cab toward the giant flag, which was one of the few things still visible in the square. By now, a light breeze had started blowing in from the east. It pushed the smoke toward the middle of the Zócalo like a fog bank drifting toward shore. Chase turned on his headlights to help guide his way.

Ten seconds later, he pulled directly behind the SUV.

Thanks to the placement of his trunk—it was located in the front of older Beetles—Chase was able to load the money with relative ease. He took three sealed bricks, each containing a million dollars, and placed them inside a large duffel bag. Although there was room for a few more bricks, they had agreed to split the money among three cars. No sense giving the entire score to one driver. This way, if someone got killed or captured, it wouldn't be a total loss.

Chase closed his trunk as Cash pulled in next to him.

They nodded at each other but didn't say a word.

There was still work to be done.

By this time, the canister inside the SUV had run out of smoke. As the final fumes escaped through the open hatch, Chase peered into the vehicle. Sitting in the backseat was a small wooden cube. It was nondescript in every way. No carvings. No keyhole. No markings of any kind. Less than two feet in height, it had been strapped down like a baby seat. Chase opened the back door and undid the seat belt, careful not to scratch the wood. Then, without opening the lid, he carried the box toward Tiffany, who was the only one who knew what was supposed to be inside. Though he was tempted to peek, he was being paid a million dollars to fight the urge. That was part of the deal from the very beginning. Acquire the object, but don't look at it.

He knew it was probably for the best.

Most secrets weren't worth dying for.

✠   ✠   ✠

TIFFANY WASN'T AN ARCHAEOLOGIST. She was a field operative who specialized in acquisitions. Before this mission, she didn't
know the first thing about ancient artifacts.

Aztec. Mayan. Spanish. *Whatever.*

She honestly couldn't care less.

In this business, all she wanted to know was enough to complete the job. Get in, get out, and move on to the next operation.
Anything more would just slow her down.

At least that's how she used to think.

But something had changed during her tour of the plaza. Suddenly, she was interested in knowing more than just the basics.
Not because of a sudden passion for history, but because Paco had
mentioned something that had piqued her interest. According to
legend, there was an extravagant treasure buried deep underneath
Mexican soil—one that had never been found by explorers.
Whether it existed or not, the mere possibility made her think.

Is that what this mission was all about?

A cave filled with gold?

In many ways, it made perfect sense. It would explain why they
had risked so much to get something so little. What good was an
artifact unless it led to something more?

She would try to figure that out in the days ahead.

38

PAYNE REALIZED HIS MISTAKE AS SOON AS HE OPENED the door. He had forgotten to put the sunshade in the windshield when he had parked the Hummer, and now he would be forced to suffer. A wall of heat greeted him like a dragon's sneeze. In many ways, it reminded him of his days at the mill. Working near the blast furnaces in the dead of summer. Sweating so much that he had a permanent thirst. It was so bad at times that he actually looked forward to the rigors of two-a-day football practices, because they would be a vacation by comparison.

Years later, when he was stationed in the Middle East, everyone bitched and moaned about the desert heat. The air was dry. The sun was brutal. Lips cracked and skin chafed. To combat the conditions, American soldiers were *forced* to hydrate on a regular basis. Commanding officers were *required* to stand there and watch their soldiers drink their daily dose of fluids, whether they were thirsty or not. During this ritual, Payne did his best to lift their spirits by downplaying the heat. He assured his squad that it had been much hotter in Pittsburgh when he was a teenager. Everyone assumed he was kidding. But he was quite serious.

Nothing was hotter than the mill.

Payne reached inside the Hummer and started the ignition. Then he turned the AC on full blast. He wasn't as worried about the weapons as he was the artifacts. He didn't know if the heat would damage ancient relics. He assumed it wouldn't be a problem—otherwise Hamilton wouldn't have stored them in the H2—but he didn't want to take any chances. As long as he was in charge of the items, he would do his best to keep them safe.

A few minutes passed before he climbed into the Hummer. The engine was purring, and the vents were spitting out cool air. It was still uncomfortable but not nearly as bad as it had been a moment before. More concerned about his cargo than himself, he angled the vents toward the crates, then closed the door with a thud. He casually glanced in the side and rearview mirrors, looking for witnesses of any kind, then turned in his seat and opened the footlocker.

He needed to get some serial numbers.

He grabbed the first AK-47 and inspected its receiver, the main body of the weapon. The number was stamped into the metal, right where it was supposed to be. That meant there was a decent chance that it was manufactured in a proper facility, not a second-rate sweatshop in Africa. According to World Bank estimates, there are more than 75 million AK-47s in existence, which account for 15 percent of all firearms in the world. Many of which are counterfeit.

He quickly entered the alphanumeric code into a text message, double-checked it for accuracy, then returned the rifle to the crate. He repeated the process with the second rifle. The serial number was almost identical to the first, meaning it was probably part of the same shipment. With any luck, Raskin would be able to track both weapons rather easily.

Before sending the text, Payne used the encryption feature on his phone. It was a handy little tool that he was forced to use anytime he sent messages to Raskin—even for the bikini photo. Not because the Pentagon required it, but because Raskin wanted to train Payne and Jones in the latest technology. That way, if they ever needed to send a classified document to his office, they would be comfortable with the protocol.

Once the message was encrypted, Payne hit SEND.

Then he stared at his screen until it went through.

From the harried tone of Raskin's voice, Payne knew there was a good chance that he wouldn't get his information today. But that was okay with him. He felt privileged to have someone like Raskin in his corner. He was one of the top researchers in the world, someone who was so good at what he did that the Pentagon overlooked his quirks because they didn't have anybody who could replace him. Where most military personnel went to work in business uniforms or dress clothes, Raskin usually wore T-shirts, gym shorts, and canvas tennis shoes. According to Raskin, that was the price of genius. He also claimed that he went through a two-week stretch wearing nothing but a bathrobe and boxer shorts to work, but since very few people have access to his subbasement office, no one was willing or able to confirm it.

Payne laughed at the image in his head as he tried to close the lid on the footlocker. His first attempt was unsuccessful, so he shifted the rifles and ammunition around until there was plenty of clearance space. Unfortunately, that didn't make a difference when he tried again. Getting annoyed, Payne was about to slam the crate shut when a horrible thought entered his mind. What if the lid weren't closing because he had accidentally snagged one of the relics in the back of the crate? For all he knew, something might have shifted during his drive to Tulum, and he could be in the middle of smashing a priceless artifact without even knowing it.

The thought was not a pleasant one.

It was even worse than the image of Raskin in a bathrobe.

Cursing to himself, he climbed out of the H2 and opened the back door for a better view. He breathed a sigh of relief when he saw a small gap between the two crates and realized nothing from the display case was interfering with the lid. At least, he didn't think so. Just to be sure, he shoved the footlocker against the back of the front seats, widening the gap by a few inches.

With the back door open, sunlight streamed over his shoulder, illuminating the trunk and a whole lot more. For the first time, Payne noticed something between the crates. The manila envelope had been sitting on top of the footlocker when Jones had unfastened the bungee cords in the hotel parking lot, but it had slipped between the crates when Jones had pushed back the tarp. Now, through a combination of bad luck and good fortune, the corner of the envelope was caught in the back seam of the crate, preventing its closure.

Payne wedged his hand between the boxes and removed the envelope by wiggling it back and forth. It was larger than letter-size—made for legal documents and small catalogs—and was stuffed with several sheets of paper. Sealed with a brass clasp, it had no address or stamps or writing of any kind. It was merely a vessel for the document within.

Payne opened the clasp and peered inside.

Several pages were stapled together, hastily assembled by Hamilton a few hours before his disappearance. Payne removed the packet and stared at the title page.

A single name had been typed on the front.

It was a name he didn't know.

Payne flipped through the document and cursed at what he saw. Everything was handwritten in Spanish. One photocopied page after another, filled with elaborate prose that he was unable to read. Every once in a while, he spotted a word or two that he recognized from high school Spanish but not nearly enough to make sense of things. He would need Maria for that.

Not ready to call in reinforcements, Payne decided to run a search of his own. He typed the name into his phone's search engine and waited for the results, but a poor connection slowed his effort. His phone chugged through the data, giving him plenty of time to speculate.

He assumed the man would be local. Maybe a member of Hamilton's team. Or his supplier of weapons. Whoever it was, Payne hoped they could track him down for a long conversation, because at this stage of the game, they needed all the help they could get.

Unfortunately, a chat with this guy wasn't going to happen.

Not without a psychic.

Because the man was already dead.

39

RICARDO CÓRDOVA WAS A MIDLEVEL EMPLOYEE IN Hector's organization. He had started out as muscle for one of the local crews, but he had recently been promoted to talent scout because of his great eye for details. In his new role, he was expected to spot the best candidates for flash kidnappings and point them out to his associates. Whether they were wealthy locals or foreign businessmen, it didn't matter, as long as they had money. On weekends, his favorite place to work was the Zócalo, since it was always packed with clueless tourists.

His afternoon had started like any other. He strolled through the plaza while scanning the crowd for signs of wealth. Expensive shoes. Designer clothes. Fancy jewelry. The type of items that only the rich could afford. He had just spotted an elderly couple with high-priced watches when he was distracted by a black SUV. He turned and stared as it climbed over the curb on the edge of the plaza, then headed directly for the flagpole. Although it was uncommon for cars to be driven into the square, the intrusion didn't catch his attention. But the vehicle did.

He had seen it many times before.

It belonged to his boss, Hector Garcia.

Like most employees, Ricardo knew how important it was to impress his boss. Careers were often made or broken based on personal connections, especially in an organization where trust and loyalty were so important. At first, he was tempted to go over and introduce himself—just so Hector could put a face to his name—but then he realized it was the wrong play in this situation. Obviously, *something* was about to go down; otherwise, Hector wouldn't be drawing so much attention to himself in the middle of a public plaza.

So Ricardo decided to sit back and wait.

He figured he would keep an eye on things for the next few minutes and hope for the best. If an opening surfaced, he would hustle over and introduce himself. If not, he would go back to work like every other Saturday. After all, there was money to be made.

Then it happened.

Among the smoke and gunshots, he spotted the opportunity of a lifetime.

Not only did he have a chance to meet Hector.

He had a chance to save him.

FROM TIFFANY'S PERSPECTIVE, everything was going smoothly until that moment. The money was being loaded. The medallion was in their hands. And the police were slow to arrive. Thirty more seconds, and her crew would have left the plaza as they had planned.

But one bullet changed everything.

Because of the smoke, no one saw Ricardo until it was too late. He emerged from the haze like a thief in the night. One moment he wasn't there, the next he was. Severely outnumbered, he knew his only chance at success was a surprise attack. No hostages. No threats. No questions of any kind. His gun would do all the talking.

Church was feeling good about the mission until he felt the barrel of the gun against the base of his skull. A moment later, he couldn't feel anything at all. Ricardo squeezed his trigger and the bullet did the rest, tearing through Church's brain like a drill through wet clay. Blood splattered as Church fell, collapsing ten feet in front of Angel, who was kneeling on the ground in agony. Still bleeding from his shoulder wound, Angel ignored the pain and rolled underneath the SUV for cover. Much to his surprise, the gun that had been kicked out of his hand earlier was now within his reach. He grabbed it and looked for targets.

Tiffany, who was guarding Hector, spun toward Ricardo and fired two shots, both of which narrowly missed. Ricardo returned the favor, firing two shots of his own. The first whizzed past her face while the second missed high, partially because she had dropped to a knee. In close combat, she knew the smaller she was, the harder she would be to hit.

✠　　✠　　✠

HECTOR DIDN'T KNOW WHO the gunman was, and the truth was he didn't care. All that mattered was the chance to get away. Temporarily forgetting about his kids, he scrambled from the ground and sprinted into the smoke. By then, his lone goal was to survive. Within seconds, he had lost all sense of direction because of the haze that surrounded him.

North became south. East became west.

Everything looked the same.

From the flagpole in the center, the plaza extended for several hundred feet in every direction. No cross streets. No landmarks.

No signs. Just thousands of stone tiles, laid in straight rows, for as far as his eye could see. If Hector had taken a moment to collect his thoughts, he would have made it through the smoke in a hurry. Since the rows were straight, he could have followed any of them to the edge of the square. There was no mystery. No code to decipher. Every row led to freedom. All he had to do was pick one, and he would have survived.

Unfortunately for him, he didn't think of that.

He simply started to run.

WHILE CROUCHING ON ONE KNEE, Tiffany fired a third shot at Ricardo. It caught him flush in his stomach, three inches above his right hip. He screamed out in pain and fired wildly. The bullet struck the left side of the SUV as he stumbled forward, nearly falling to the ground before he caught his balance with his free hand. By this time, Chase had entered the fray. Known more for his driving than his marksmanship, he fired several shots at Ricardo, hoping to avenge the death of his fallen comrade. One of the shots came *close*—missing by less than a foot—but the others were way off the mark. Somewhere in the distance, a car window shattered.

"Shit!" he screamed in frustration.

Tiffany glanced to her left, expecting to see Hector on his hands and knees, but the bastard was no longer there. At that point, she had a decision to make. Either risk their freedom and try to find him, or hit the road before the police appeared. For her, it was an easy choice.

They had the medallion *and* the money.

It was time for them to leave.

"Clear out," she said into her earpiece.

✠   ✠   ✠

DESPITE THE SHOOTOUT THAT raged nearby, Cash remained near his car. His job had been to deliver the girl to the plaza and to pick up the money. Nothing more, nothing less. Now he wasn't sure what to do. His share of the ransom was in his vehicle, but so was the kid.

He spoke up. "What about the girl?"

Tiffany fired, trying to keep Ricardo pinned down. "Cut her loose."

He struggled to hear. "Say again?"

"Cut her loose!"

Cash rolled his eyes. He hated working for a woman. "You don't have to scream."

She fired again. "Fuck you, Cash! Cut her loose."

Daniela had been stashed in the backseat of the Beetle, where she had been freaking out for the last several minutes. Blindfolded and gagged, she could barely make a sound—at least none that could be heard over gunfire. Angered by Tiffany's comment, Cash reached into the car and yanked Daniela through the narrow gap between the folded seat and the door. He banged her shoulder and her arm on the door frame while he pulled her out. With her hands and her feet duct-taped together, she flopped like a rag doll when he threw her to the ground.

Cash stood over her. "The bitch is free."

✠   ✠   ✠

FROM HIS HIDING SPOT underneath the SUV, Angel heard something fall a few feet behind him. Using his good arm, he struggled to turn himself around, only to find himself staring at Hector's daughter. As far as he could tell, she was still in one piece—although maybe not for long. One of the kidnappers was hovering over her in a threatening manner.

Until that moment, Angel had planned on staying hidden, doing nothing to give his position away until the kidnappers had left the scene. But all that changed when he saw Daniela. Thoughts of his wife and baby boy danced through his head. If the situation had been reversed, he would fully expect Hector to try to save them, so he decided to do the same.

He inched forward on his stomach, using his elbows and feet. One inch after another, moving as silently as possible. Blood oozing as he crawled. The pain in his shoulder was excruciating, but he did his best to ignore it. He had to protect Daniela. He had to save the girl.

Unwilling to expose his torso, Angel did the next best thing.

He brought the battle to his level.

He aimed his gun at the kidnapper's knee and fired a single shot.

One moment Cash was upright; the next he was on the ground—so was much of his knee, which had been blown into tiny pieces. Writhing in agony, Cash paid no attention to the man lying in front of him until he saw the gun. It was pointed directly at his face.

The last thing that Cash saw was the smile on Angel's lips.

✠　　✠　　✠

HECTOR HEARD THE GUNSHOT and slowed to a halt. Somehow, some way, the shot had come from directly in front of him. Although he had been running nonstop since he had left the scene, he was back where he had first started—like an athlete on an oval track.

In his state of delirium, he interpreted this as a sign. It was

God's way of giving him a second chance. Instead of running like a coward, he should have charged forward and rescued his kids from danger. They were somewhere in the smoke. All he had to do was find them.

Struggling to catch his breath, he spotted Church's body on the ground. It was just lying there, missing a chunk of its head. Hector crouched and pried the gun from the dead man's grasp. It would come in handy for the fight ahead.

✠   ✠   ✠

By THIS TIME, Ricardo had lost a lot of blood. Sitting on the ground, he leaned against the front tire of the SUV. He tried to keep pressure on his stomach with his free hand, but the damn wound kept leaking. Blood oozed between his fingers. It felt warm and sticky.

He closed his eyes and prayed for help.

It wouldn't be coming from Tiffany.

She saw him helpless and went in for the kill.

Using the smoke for cover, she crept around the front bumper of the SUV and raised her weapon. Then, in a fitting tribute to Church—who had died in a similar fashion—she put the gun against Ricardo's head and calmly pulled the trigger.

Blood sprayed as he slumped over, dead.

His dreams of meeting Hector died with him.

✠   ✠   ✠

OVER THE YEARS, Hector had killed a lot of women. Most of them for business, but a few out of passion. In all that time, he had never wanted to kill one as badly as he did the bitch in front of him.

Hector didn't know her name, but he knew she was one of *them*—one of the assholes who had stolen his kids. To him, that was all that mattered. He would make her pay for their sins.

She was twelve feet ahead and didn't know he was coming.

He would enjoy this immensely.

✝ ✝ ✝

TIFFANY TURNED WHEN SHE heard the sound. To her surprise, Hector was standing behind her with his gun raised. Another moment and she would have been dead for sure.

Thankfully, he never had a chance to pull the trigger.

✝ ✝ ✝

HECTOR HEARD THE ROAR of the engine and whirled to see what it was. In his confusion, he swore a monster was lurking behind him. It was actually something worse.

A split second before impact, he saw the headlights of the Volkswagen Beetle shining through the smoke and a smiling face behind the wheel. Bro sadistically stomped on the gas and plowed into Hector at a high rate of speed. The curvature of the car's frame swept his legs out from under him, which was unfortunate for Hector, because it meant his face struck the front windshield like a bug on the highway. The glass cracked, and so did his head, which sent a spray of red across the white roof of the car.

The force was so great, Hector died instantly.

But there wasn't time to rejoice.

With the vehicle headed straight for her, Tiffany jumped onto the hood of the SUV, hoping to avoid the same bloody fate. Except her leap wasn't necessary. Bro slammed on the brakes and expertly spun the wheel, skidding to a stop a few feet from the SUV.

Laughing to himself, Bro rolled down his window. "Now, *that's* how you catch a cab!"

✠   ✠   ✠

ANGEL PULLED DANIELA UNDERNEATH the SUV and urged her to stay quiet. For the first time in his life, he looked forward to police interference.

The wail of approaching sirens was music to his ears.

Tiffany heard the sirens, too, and urged her crew to hurry. Bro's car was no longer viable, so they split the remaining money between the other two taxis. Chase would drive Tiffany. Bro would pick up Boom. They would meet later that day to discuss what went right and what went wrong. Until then, their main goal was to evade capture.

Tiffany pulled off her gas mask and tossed it into the back of the SUV. Chase and Bro followed her lead. To get away clean, they needed to destroy as much evidence as possible. That included the bodies of their fallen friends, which they lifted into the SUV.

"Hold up," she blurted. "Where are the kids?"

Chase shrugged. "Cash cut the girl loose. I don't know where she ran to."

"And the boy?"

Bro answered. "I dumped him near the street *before* I killed his father. What can I say? I'm a softy when it comes to kids."

Chase nodded his approval. "Good thinking, Bro."

"Thanks, bro."

She spoke into her earpiece. "Boom, you still there?"

"Sure am," he said from the balcony.

"Give us thirty seconds, then light the firecracker."

Boom smiled. "With pleasure."

She surveyed the scene one last time before she hopped into the bright green Beetle. Chase floored it in reverse, yanked the steering wheel hard, then shifted into drive. Tires smoked as he peeled out of the plaza.

☩　　☩　　☩

ANGEL SAW TIFFANY'S FACE and her red hair. He also heard her side of the conversation. He wasn't sure what "firecracker" referred to, but he knew it probably wasn't good.

His theory was confirmed when he saw the yellow light. It started blinking two feet in front of his face. Until that moment, he hadn't noticed the tiny detonator that had been mounted to the bottom of the SUV. Now it was the only thing he could see. Somewhere inside the vehicle there were enough explosives to kill a small army, and he was hiding directly underneath.

He cursed in Spanish as he crawled to the side of the SUV. Then he reached back and grabbed Daniela's arm. He yanked her out, heaved her over his good shoulder, then sprinted as fast as he could toward the south side of the Zócalo.

Boom stared at the plaza below. Despite the lingering cloud of smoke, he had used only half of his homemade arsenal. More than a dozen devices remained in the garbage cans to the west and south—devices that could possibly be traced back to him. Just to be safe, he decided to ignite them, too. From his perch, he pushed a few keys on his computer.

Whoosh! Whoosh! Whoosh!

One after another, garbage cans to the south erupted in smoke.

Whoosh! Whoosh! Whoosh!

So did all the cans to the west.

Angel heard the explosions and quickly veered to the east. Daniela bounced on his good shoulder as he continued to run. He had no idea where he was going, but he wouldn't stop running until he saw the street. And he wouldn't stop searching until he got revenge.

✠   ✠   ✠

BOOM GLANCED AT HIS watch and smiled. He lived for moments like this.

Four seconds until the firecracker.

The thunder. The fire. The destruction.

Then three seconds.

The plaza would never be the same.

And two seconds.

His grin widened.

Then one.

He whispered a single word: "Boom."

40

PAYNE HAD MANY TALENTS, BUT GETTING SECRETS from the dead wasn't one of them. He figured that was more Maria's field than his own. In fact, their two specialties couldn't be more different. He was great at finding live people and making them dead. She was great at finding dead people and making their pasts come alive. No wonder they kept arguing about everything.

Putting their differences aside, Payne called Maria and told her that he had found something in the Hummer that she needed to see. She wanted to know what it was, but he refused to tell her over the phone. He simply said it was significant and she needed to trust him. She sighed in protest but said she would be there shortly.

Five minutes later, she arrived with Jones.

"I hope this is important," she said. "We were making progress in there. We were talking to a tour guide who vaguely remembers Hamilton."

Payne was hoping for more. "And?"

Jones shook his head. "That's pretty much it."

"Wow," he said sarcastically. "Sorry I pulled you away from that. It sounds like you cracked this case wide open. Maybe we can get a sketch artist to do a drawing. Oh, wait! We already know what Hamilton looks like."

She smiled, knowing she couldn't argue that point. "Which means you found something better?"

He held up the manila envelope. "It's the document that Hamilton went to retrieve when he disappeared. At least I think it is. It was in the Hummer."

"Where?" Jones asked.

"Between the two crates. It was wedged in there pretty good."

She pointed at it. "What does it say?"

"I don't know. It's written in Spanish. But I think I know who wrote it."

"Who?" she demanded.

"A Franciscan named Diego de Landa."

Her mouth fell open. "Are you serious?"

"Of course I'm serious. I wouldn't have called you as a joke." He handed her the envelope. As he did, he shook his head. "You gotta start trusting me more."

She pulled out the packet and stared at the name on the title page: DIEGO DE LANDA. The possibilities gave her chills. "You're right, I do. I need to start trusting you more. And you're right about this, too. This is much more important than what we were doing."

"I know. That's why I called."

She pointed at the Hummer. "May I read this inside? I'd like to take some notes as I translate."

"The engine's running, and the AC's on. Be my guest."

She hustled around the front end and climbed into the passenger seat. Jones waited until she had closed the door before he turned his attention to Payne.

"Thanks for that. She's pretty excited."

"No problem. I'm trying to play nice."

"I know, and I appreciate it."

Payne nodded but said nothing.

"So," Jones said as he lowered his voice to a whisper, "can I ask you a personal question? You know, *confidential*. Just between us."

"Of course you can. What's up?"

Jones made sure Maria wasn't listening before he spoke again. "Who in the hell is Diego de Landa?"

Payne grinned. "You mean you don't know?"

"Well," he stammered, "the name is *vaguely* familiar, but I can't really spout a bunch of facts off the top of my head."

"In other words, you have no idea."

"Absolutely none."

"Don't worry. I had to run a search myself. I thought he might be a local gunrunner. Turns out he's a dead bishop from Spain."

"Wow. Your hunch was way off."

"I know. Thank God for Google."

Jones laughed. "So, what does a dead bishop have to do with Hamilton? Did they know each other?"

"If they did, we've stumbled into something significant. Landa died in the 1500s."

"In that case, I'll go out on a limb. I doubt they ever met."

"Probably not."

"Then what's the connection?"

Payne summarized what he had read online. "Landa came to Mexico as a Franciscan monk in 1549. His job was to teach the natives about the Church and to convert them to Christianity. While he was here, he studied the Mayan language and wrote a detailed account of their culture. To this day, it is still considered the most important book ever written about the Maya."

"Landa was a scholar?"

Payne shook his head. "He was a Nazi."

"A Nazi? In what way?"

"He organized the largest book-burning ceremony in the history of Mexico. If an object had anything to do with the Maya—images, idols, codices, whatever—he tossed it into the flames."

Jones grimaced. "Was it an auto-da-fé?"

He nodded. "You've heard of it?"

"Not the one you're referring to, but I'm familiar with the ritual. It was popular during the Spanish Inquisition. They did it all the time. It means 'act of faith.'"

"Maybe so, but I guess Landa's ceremony was particularly vicious. When word got back to the King of Spain, Landa was ordered to return home to defend himself."

According to historical records, Landa was accused of extreme cruelty and mistreatment of the Maya, including the torture of men, women, and children. Worst of all, he claimed he did it in the name of God. The Council of the Indies condemned Landa for his behavior. As a result, a committee of doctors was appointed to investigate Landa's alleged crimes.

Despite firsthand testimony from Francisco de Toral, the first Bishop of the Yucatán, who had filed the original complaint with the King, Landa was absolved of the charges. Then, in an unexpected move, Landa was named as the Bishop's replacement when Toral died in 1571. Somehow, in a span of less than ten years, Landa had gone from a prisoner who had been banished from the New World to the most powerful man in the Yucatán. Upon his return, Landa continued his brutal campaign against the Maya, drawing the ire of natives, monks, and Spanish soldiers because of his excessive cruelty.

This continued until his death in 1579.

Jones shook his head in disgust. "Landa was allowed to return?"

Payne nodded. "But no one knows why. According to the article that I read, records of that particular decision are missing from the archives."

"Imagine that. A government conspiracy. Some things never change."

"Actually, they've changed quite a bit. Back then, church and state had virtually no separation. There's no way of knowing who was responsible for Landa's freedom or promotion. Was it the King of Spain, the Pope, or some random cardinal? Then again, what do I know? Maybe Landa was totally innocent of all charges."

Jones scoffed at the notion. "Jon, I'm an angry black man. We think *everybody* is innocent. But I'm not buying it. The guy burned half the books in Mexico. He was guilty of something."

Payne laughed at the comment. "And as an honorary black man, I tend to agree with you. The guy sounds like scum to me. That being said, Landa's crimes happened over four hundred years ago. The only thing I care about is his connection to Hamilton."

"Which is?"

He shrugged. "I have no idea. The document was handwritten in Spanish—with lots of little symbols."

"What kind of symbols?"

"The Maya equivalent of hieroglyphics, whatever they're called."

"I think they're called glyphs. Mayan glyphs."

Payne shrugged. "If you say so. That isn't my specialty."

Jones glanced inside the Hummer. Maria was hard at work on the document and well out of earshot. "Unfortunately, it's not Maria's specialty, either. I was talking to her on the drive down here, and she's really confused about her role in this. I mean *really* confused. I think that's why she's been so short-tempered with us. That, and a few other things."

"What other things?"

Jones peeked again to make sure she wasn't listening. "Well, to be perfectly blunt, she's got some major father issues."

"I know. Otherwise, she wouldn't have dated an old fart like you."

"Jon, I'm being serious."

"Sorry. Couldn't resist. I'll be good from now on."

Jones took a deep breath. "Anyway, you know all about her father, Benito. We dealt with him in Orvieto. That man was old-school crazy. He pampered his sons like princes and treated his wife and daughter like servants. As soon as she showed some backbone, he sent her away to a boarding school so he wouldn't have to deal with her anymore."

"England, right?"

"That's right. A boarding school in England."

Payne nodded. He hadn't thought about these things in years, not since Jones had broken up with her. He knew bits and pieces of Maria's history, but not enough to understand her psyche. Not enough to know what made her tick. It took much longer than a week to learn those types of things, but that was all the time he had spent with her. Granted, it was a particularly brutal week, during which half the police in Europe were looking for them, but a week nonetheless.

Jones continued: "After her mother died, her family cut her off. They didn't talk to her, or write to her, or invite her home for the holidays. They ignored her, and she ignored them. At least she tried to. But the fact is her hatred toward her father actually made her stronger. Everything she did was fueled by her desire to rub it in his face. Her grades, her accolades, even her decision to become an archaeologist were because of him. He had assured her that women weren't cut out for that type of work, so she did everything to prove him wrong."

Payne raised an eyebrow. "Where are you going with this?"

"Relax. I'm almost there."

He sighed. "Good. Go on."

"Ever since then, she's been looking for a father figure. Someone who would take her under his wing and mentor her. She temporarily had that with her college professor, but he ended up using her for her connections to Benito."

Payne nodded. "Dr. Boyd. I remember."

Jones glanced into the Hummer again. "I'm not positive about this, but I think she was hoping that Hamilton would fill that role, at least temporarily. She kept going on and on about his passion for history, and how much of a connection they made during their brief conversation. I know it's kind of crazy—I mean, she barely knows the guy—but I think that's messing with her mind. Every time she lets someone into her life, something bad happens."

"Did you ask her about it?"

He winced. "Are you nuts? She would kick my ass if I suggested it. Heck, she'd kick my ass twice if she knew I told you about any of this, so please keep it to yourself."

Payne smiled. "Don't worry. I have no intention of making her mad. The last thing I want to worry about is friendly fire."

41

SEVERAL MINUTES PASSED BEFORE MARIA EMERGED from the Hummer. When she finally did, she had a strange look on her face, one that was impossible to read because of the wide range of emotions that she was experiencing. There were hints of excitement, confusion, determination, and anger—as if whatever she'd read had only complicated her outlook on things.

"What's wrong?" Jones asked.

"Nothing's wrong," she assured them, despite the turmoil that danced in her eyes. "It's just . . . if this document is correct, then I'm in over my head. *Way* over my head. I mean, I know some of the basics about Landa, but not nearly enough to confirm these claims."

"What claims?" Payne wondered.

She glanced at him, then lowered her eyes in shame. "Claims against the Church."

Jones, who knew she was a practicing Catholic and had been for her entire life, realized this would be a sensitive topic—especially since her father had been embroiled in a scandal at the

Vatican at the time of his death. With that in mind, he shook his head to warn Payne. It let him know that he needed to tread cautiously or risk her wrath. Payne nodded in understanding.

"What type of claims?" Jones asked softly.

She took a deep breath, then tried to brush it off. "Nothing I haven't seen before. Corruption, greed, hypocrisy. You know, the big three."

"Sorry to hear that."

She shrugged. "It's okay. I mean, it's *not* okay, but I've seen this crap so many times that it barely registers anymore. During the Middle Ages and the Renaissance, the Catholic Church was run by immoral men who used their positions to acquire power, wealth, and sex. Not everyone was like that—some priests and bishops were *actual* saints—but misbehavior was more common than you'd think. If I had a thousand dollars for every time the Pope got somebody pregnant, I could buy a very nice condo in Rome."

Payne was tempted to say that a condo in Rome is probably *where* the popes got most of the women pregnant, but he decided to heed Jones's warning and hold his tongue.

Jones pointed at the packet in her grasp. She was holding it so tightly that her fingertips were turning white. "You might want to ease up. A tree died for that document."

She glanced at her hands and nodded. "Sorry. I'm just a little rattled."

"Why? What does it say?"

She took another deep breath, trying to calm down. "Before I try to explain, what do you know about Landa?"

"Quite a bit, actually. I was filling Jon in while you worked on the translation."

Payne rolled his eyes but didn't contradict the claim. He knew Jones was trying to impress her. "That's right. He told me all about the book burnings, and the cruelty, and the charges of persecution. It was like having a conversation with an encyclopedia."

"Really?" she said, surprised. "That's great to hear, because I need all the help I can get. Maybe you can fill me in on some things. I'm somewhat hazy on his later years."

Payne couldn't help but smile. "Yes, David, please enlighten us."

Jones played it off perfectly. "Actually, I doubt I'll be much help to a historian like you. My knowledge of Landa is pretty superficial—you know, the type of stuff you could find on the Internet. I doubt I'll be able to tell you anything that you don't already know."

She smiled. "That's okay. Most guys wouldn't know Landa from a hole in the ground. I'm impressed that you know him at all."

Jones nodded smugly. "That's the beauty of an Air Force Academy education."

"What is?" demanded Payne, who had attended the rival Naval Academy. "Your superficial understanding of things, or the fact that you can get the same education on the Internet?"

Maria tried not to laugh, but she couldn't help herself. It was a funny line that helped to take the edge off the situation. Jones quickly insulted him back, and before long the three of them were engaged in some good-natured teasing. Payne hated to see the laughter end—it was the first time during the trip that he had felt comfortable with Maria, like she was a friend instead of a client—but he realized they were wasting precious time.

"So," Payne said, "I hate to be the bad guy, but I'm really curious about the document. What can you tell us?"

She nodded in understanding. It was time to get back to work. "What do you know about Landa's appointment as Bishop of Yucatán?"

"Not much, other than it was controversial."

"Controversial is an understatement. Not only did the committee find him innocent of his crimes, but he was eventually selected to replace the man who had brought the charges against him.

Needless to say, the governors of Yucatán were outraged by this decision. Everyone—and I mean *everyone*—in Mexico was familiar with Diego de Landa and his abusive ways, yet somehow he managed to convince the Church to send him back."

"Jon and I were just talking about that. We couldn't figure out how Landa pulled that off, unless there was some kind of conspiracy."

She held up the document. "According to this, Landa bought his freedom with the promise of a vast treasure. He convinced the Church that he had assembled a massive stockpile of Mayan artifacts—items that he had deemed too valuable to burn. In exchange for his release, he was willing to hide these items from the King and smuggle them to the Church instead."

"Landa admitted to this?" Payne asked.

She shook her head. "This journal wasn't written by Landa. It was written by a young priest named Marcos de Mercado. He was assigned by the Church to chronicle Landa's movement upon his return to the Yucatán. Prior to the priesthood, Mercado had trained as a soldier, so they felt he was the perfect choice to spy on Landa in hostile terrain. Not only did he know religion, but he knew the ways of the blade."

Jones grimaced. "Sounds like a bad movie. *Marcos de Mercado: Warrior Priest.*"

"Actually," she said, "I think you would have liked the guy. He had a quiet, intellectual side that came across in his writing. Underneath, he had the heart of a fighter."

"Tell me more about the document," Payne said to Maria. "Now that you've read it, do you have a better understanding of your role in things?"

"Not at all," she admitted. "If anything, I'm even more confused about my invitation. Obviously, Landa was involved with the Church in some type of scheme, but you don't have to be an expert in Christian history to know that. All I needed was the ability to read Spanish, which is a skill that Hamilton possesses."

"What about Landa's treasure? Are you familiar with that?"

She shook her head. "It's news to me. But . . ."

"But what?" Jones asked.

"If there was a treasure—and that's still a big *if* in my mind—it would certainly explain some of Hamilton's comments during our meeting. He kept bragging about something they had found. He hinted at its historical ramifications and said it would blow my mind. There was something about his tone that led me to believe that they were close to a major discovery. Real close."

Payne considered her words. "Hamilton was bragging?"

She nodded. "He could barely keep a grin off his face."

"Crap. That's not good. I didn't know he was a braggart."

"Not to everyone. Just to me. I think he was trying to impress me so I would take the job."

"Still," Payne said, "you'd be surprised how many plans fall apart because of bragging. What if someone at the hotel overheard his boasts? They might have grabbed him in the parking lot to get a big payday."

She dismissed his claim. "No way. He was careful. We sat far away from everyone else. There's no way anyone overheard us."

"Which way was the wind blowing?" Payne wondered.

"Excuse me?"

"Was it blowing toward the bar or toward the beach? You'd be surprised how far sound can travel. Believe it or not, sound is louder and more intense downwind."

Jones nodded. "He's right."

"I'm telling you, no one overheard us."

Payne let it slide. "Fine. Maybe you're right. But that's just a single conversation. What if you weren't the first person contacted by Hamilton? Maybe he bragged to someone else and they decided to make a play for the treasure. You said this guy was a drinker, right? What if he threw back too many tequilas one night and ended up spilling the news? There's no telling who knows about the treasure, or what they would do to find it."

Maria nodded and brushed the hair from her eyes. Until that moment, she had been shouldering a lot of guilt about Hamilton's disappearance, figuring if he hadn't driven to Cancún to meet with her, then he wouldn't have been abducted. But now, thanks to Payne's comment, she realized that Hamilton might have screwed up on his own. Somehow that made her feel slightly better about the situation. "If that's the case, what should we do now? Do we try to figure out who he talked to? Or is there some other angle to pursue?"

Payne looked at Jones. "What do you think?"

"Personally, I don't think there's any way we can figure out who Hamilton talked to or if anyone overheard his conversation, not without a lot of legwork. For the time being, I think the best thing to do is concentrate on what we know—and what we *don't* know."

"Meaning?"

"We need to talk to our expert about Landa's treasure. If it possibly exists, then there's a damn good chance it's connected to Hamilton's disappearance. If not, then we need to focus our attention on other motives."

Maria held up the document. "That sounds great and all, but I told you this isn't my area of expertise. This is the first time I've read anything about a treasure."

Jones smiled and patted her on the shoulder. "Don't worry. I wasn't talking about you. I was talking about our *other* expert."

42

PETR ULSTER, A ROUND MAN WITH A THICK BROWN beard, soaked in a marble tub filled with warm water and scented oils from Singapore. With bubbles up to his chin, he hummed softly to one of his favorite symphonies as he conducted an imaginary orchestra, flailing his arms to the rhythmic beat of the strings. Water sloshed back and forth with such ferocity that it exceeded the constraints of the tub and spilled onto the floor of his private bathroom. Not that he really cared. He was a man who lived for the moment, someone who relished the simple things in life—like a gourmet meal, a vintage bottle of wine, and the company of friends. Besides, he had a staff of servants who would clean up his mess when he was done with his performance.

The ringing of his telephone brought it to an early end.

Known for his brilliant mind and boyish enthusiasm, he groused about the interruption while reaching for the phone that was just beyond his grasp. While stretching for it, he pushed so much water onto the floor that it looked like a tropical storm had hit his bathroom. Thankfully, the only victim was a novelty toy that had been given to him as a joke by David Jones. Instead of a rubber ducky, it was a swan named Ludwig with a gold crown on its head. It had been knocked off the edge of the tub by a tidal wave. Only then did he realize how much of a mess he had made.

"Oh, dear," he mumbled to himself. "Winston will be peeved."

Worried about his butler's reaction, he leapt from the tub with reckless abandon, grabbed the lone towel from the heated rack, and threw it onto the flood to stop the spread of water before it reached the carpeted floor of his dressing room. This, of course, left him soaking wet, shivering, flustered, and bare ass naked when he answered the phone.

"Hello," he said, out of breath. "This is Petr."

"Petr? It's Jonathon Payne. Are you all right?"

A smile burst across his face. "I am now, my boy!"

"Are you sure? Because you sound, um, disheveled."

Ulster laughed as he turned down the music on the overhead speakers. "Though English is my fourth language, I'm not quite sure one can *sound* disheveled. I believe that is more of a visual condition than an auditory one."

"And yet you sound disheveled. Leave it to you to break new ground."

"If you say so! Who am I to argue with the great Jonathon Payne?"

Payne grinned. "Actually, I can think of quite a few times when we've argued, but I'm glad you have selective memory. It'll be easier to stay on your good side."

"No worries there, my friend, and you know it!"

Built in the mid-1960s by Austrian philanthropist Conrad Ulster, the Ulster Archives was the most extensive private collection of documents and antiquities in the world. Unlike most private collections, the main goal of the Archives wasn't to hoard artifacts. Instead, it attempted to bridge the ever-growing gap that existed between scholars and connoisseurs.

Ever since the Archives had opened, it had promoted the radical concept of sharing. In order to gain admittance, a visitor had to bring something of value—such as an ancient object or unpublished research—or be willing to donate his time and expertise to the facility. Whatever it was, it had to be approved in advance by the Archives staff. If for some reason they deemed it unworthy, then admission to the facility was denied until a suitable arrangement could be made.

It was their way to encourage sharing.

For more than a decade, the Archives have been run by Petr Ulster, Conrad's grandson. He had befriended Payne and Jones a few years ago when they had escorted two frightened academics, Dr. Charles Boyd and Maria Pelati, to the facility to conduct research on Tiberius. While they were there, a group of religious zealots had tried to burn the Archives to the ground. Their goal had been to kill Boyd and Pelati, and to destroy a collection of ancient documents that threatened the foundation of the Catholic Church. Fortunately, Payne and Jones had managed to intervene, thwarting the attack and saving the facility from irreparable damage.

Ever since that day, Ulster had considered them family.

Payne, who was aware of the time difference, felt the need to apologize despite their closeness. "Sorry to bother you on a Saturday night. I hope I didn't interrupt your dinner plans. I know how you like to entertain on the weekend."

Ulster stared at his naked form in the bathroom mirror. His round belly made him look like the Buddha. He patted it a few times before answering. "Actually, I'm trying to curtail my gluttonous ways. I tend to pack on the pounds during the winter months."

"Petr, you live on top of the Alps. They're all winter months."

Ulster laughed. "I think that's part of the problem!"

Payne knew if he wasn't careful, Ulster would talk his ear off about his diet, the snowfall in Küsendorf, or whatever else was on his mind. He had the ability to turn a two-second response into a ten-minute lecture. With that in mind, Payne decided to get aggressive. He knew if he didn't define the terms of the conversation, he was asking for trouble.

"If you have a moment," Payne said, "I was hoping to ask you a question or two about the Maya. I'm currently in Mexico, and—"

"Did you say the Maya? I love the Maya. They're one of my ten favorite civilizations of all time. Obviously, you'd have the Greeks and the Romans. I think most people would have them on their lists. Then there are the Egyptians and the Mongols—"

"Petr!" he shouted, to cut him off. "Did you hear what I said? I'm actually *in* Mexico right now, and I need some information about the Maya. Time is not my friend."

Ulster, who was familiar with Payne's military background, lowered his voice to a conspiratorial whisper. "Are you on a mission?"

"Something like that."

Ulster stomped his foot and whooped with glee. Regrettably, it wasn't the smartest thing to do while standing in a puddle. The force of his stomp shot water in every direction like a cannonball in a community pool. "Oh, goodness. I shouldn't have done that."

"Done what? Petr, are you all right?"

"One moment, my boy. I need to fetch a towel. I'm feeling a tad moist."

"Hold up! Were you exercising?"

Ulster grinned as he grabbed his bathrobe from the back of the door. He was far too embarrassed to tell him what he had actually been doing. "Yes. Something like that."

Payne covered the phone and whispered to Jones. "You're not going to believe this, but Petr was exercising."

Jones winced. "Are you sure you called the right Petr?"

"I'm positive. He just tried to tell me his top ten civilizations of all time."

Jones laughed. "Yep. That's the right Petr."

Freshly wrapped in a designer robe, Ulster grabbed the phone and collapsed into his favorite chair. It was tucked into the corner of his master bedroom. "There we go. Much better. Sorry for the delay. The walls and floors are literally dripping because of me."

"Don't overdo it, Petr. You need to ease into your workouts."

Feeling guilty about his deception, Ulster changed the topic. "Enough about that. Let's focus on you. What are you doing in Mexico?"

"DJ and I are helping a friend. Do you remember Maria Pelati?"

"Of course I remember Maria. She spent several weeks here after the fire, doing research and pitching in. What a lovely girl." Ulster paused in thought. "Wait a moment! Are David and Maria together again? They were *such* a cute couple. Their babies would be adorable!"

Payne nearly gagged. "Petr, how about we make a deal? I'll stop asking you questions about your workouts, and you stop mentioning things like that."

Ulster laughed. "That sounds fair to me."

"Anyway, as I was saying, we're here to help Maria. She was hired by a team of historians that are looking for a Mayan treasure, and most of the information is over her head."

"I bet it is. Not to be rude, but why would they hire Maria? That doesn't make any sense. Her specialty is Christianity, not Mesoamerican cultures."

Jesus, Payne thought, *am I the only one who didn't know that?*

"Apparently, this has something to do with a bishop named Diego de Landa. I guess they thought her background would be useful with him."

"Diego de Landa," he repeated with venom. "You know how I

feel about violence, but that's a man I wish you'd had a crack at. Actually, calling him a *man* is an insult to men everywhere. That, um, *bishop* was the devil incarnate."

Payne smiled. In all their time together, he had never heard Ulster curse. "For a moment there, I thought you were going to say 'bastard.'"

"For a moment there, I was tempted. But in the end, decorum won out."

"Anyway, the team leader gave Maria a document to translate. It describes a treasure and several other things that she isn't familiar with. We were hoping you could fill us in."

"I'd be happy to. That is, if you have permission from the team leader. I would hate to step on any toes."

Payne scratched his chin. "Actually, that might be a little bit difficult. One of the reasons that we're helping Maria is because the team leader has disappeared."

"Disappeared? As in lost in the jungle?"

He shook his head. "As in abducted from a hotel. At least that's what we think happened. We're still sorting through some of the facts."

"Good heavens! Is there anything I can do to help?"

"Yeah. You can answer some questions about the Maya."

"No, my boy, I meant in regards to the abduction. I know quite a few people in the academic community. Perhaps I can put you in touch with some of his colleagues."

Payne smiled at the suggestion. It was an angle he hadn't considered. "Actually, now that you mention it, that's a wonderful idea. Maria never had a chance to meet the rest of her team. If we can figure out who's involved with this, perhaps they can help us find Hamilton."

"Did you say 'Hamilton'? As in *Terrence* Hamilton?"

"Yep, that's the guy. Why? Have you heard of him?"

Ulster swallowed hard. "Indeed I have. He's a friend of mine."

43

Payne cursed his own stupidity. Until that moment, he hadn't even considered the possibility that Ulster and Hamilton might know each other, even though the connection should have been obvious. Because of the size and scope of the Archives, Ulster was considered royalty in the academic community, a man who could launch a career with a phone call or a letter of recommendation. And since Hamilton was considered one of the preeminent Mayan scholars in the world, it made sense that their two paths would have crossed at some point.

Payne quickly apologized. "Petr, I am so sorry. It never dawned on me that you might be friends. Are you two close?"

Ulster shook his head. "Not socially, but we chatted from time to time about his research. He had some fascinating theories about Mesoamerican cultures, particularly the shared terminology of the Maya and the Aztecs. Truly groundbreaking concepts."

"Is that so?" Payne asked as he considered the information. "How groundbreaking are we talking about?"

"I'm not sure I follow."

"I mean, would this be the kind of research that certain groups would want to stop?"

"Stop? Why would someone want to stop his research?"

Payne shrugged. "I don't know. Maybe political reasons."

"Political? Good heavens, no! The Maya and the Aztecs were once warring nations, but their descendants have long since assimilated into the Mexican culture. Now they stand in unison under the flag of Mexico. His research would not be controversial. Not at all!"

"Sorry, I'm just brainstorming here. Trying to figure out why someone would abduct Hamilton. As you know, I'm slightly out of my element when it comes to history."

Ulster took a deep breath. "Yes, of course, how silly of me. I didn't mean to snap at you. I guess I'm a tad unnerved by your news. Was there any sign of violence?"

"No, nothing like that."

Payne took a few minutes to fill Ulster in on the basics, everything from Maria's initial invitation to the translation of the Mercado document. Out of everything discussed, the thing that bothered Ulster the most was the cargo in the Hummer. He simply couldn't understand why Hamilton would have a crate filled with weapons and a trunk full of relics.

Ulster said, "That's not the Terrence that I know. He was always the cautious sort when it came to protecting his discoveries. He definitely wasn't the type to put explosives and artifacts in the same space. That's just asking for trouble."

"Unless, of course, he'd already found trouble and had no other choice but to protect himself. I mean, his captors must have been desperate. They grabbed him at a luxury hotel during daylight hours."

Ulster grimaced. "That doesn't sound like Terrence, either."

"What doesn't?"

"A luxury hotel. He was more of a tent kind of fellow."

"Hamilton wasn't staying there. Maria was. He got her a nice suite for the weekend. I think he used it to entice her to make the trip. That and a healthy stipend."

Ulster leaned forward in his chair. "Now, that *definitely* doesn't sound like Terrence. I wonder what he got himself involved in?"

"What are you talking about?"

"I don't want to speak ill of the dead—um, I mean *missing*—but when I said he was 'a tent kind of fellow,' that was a polite way of saying that he was thrifty. No, not thrifty. That would imply that he had wealth and chose not to spend it. Hmmm, how should I put this?"

"Bluntly."

"Yes, of course. No sense in holding back now. I think the most accurate term to describe Terrence would be *destitute*."

"Broke? He was broke? Why do you think that?"

"Why? Because it's common knowledge in the academic community. Terrence was something of a control freak when it came to his research. He hated external input—especially the kind that came from big-money donors who knew nothing about his field—so he tended to fund his expeditions out of his own pocket. That meant sleeping in a tent instead of an air-conditioned camper, using unpaid interns instead of a highly trained staff, and eating beans by the campfire instead of a feast prepared by a personal chef."

"In other words, he was the opposite of you."

Ulster laughed. "Exactly!"

Payne paused in thought. "But still respected?"

"Definitely! In fact, some scholars respected him even more because of his suffering. It takes a certain type of courage to turn down corporate money and academic funding to work for oneself. In many ways, I bet it was liberating. To make your own choices, to control your own destiny. Most people can't do that because of familial responsibilities. Between children and spouses, food and rent, there's no money left over for research. In today's economy, most tenured professors have to forgo sabbaticals because they don't have the funds to follow through with their research. What used to be a full year at half pay is now a half year at even less. It's sad, really. The best academic minds in the world are languishing on campuses because they can't afford to explore the world. How do we expect to learn new things about the past if our greatest scholars are tethered to their classrooms?"

Payne answered. "By breaking the rules."

"Actually, my boy, that was a rhetorical question."

"Maybe so, but I stand by my response. When people get desperate, they tend to do things that are out of character—whether it's stealing food when they're hungry or buying guns when they're scared. I might not know much about history, but I know a lot about people. And since our arrival in Mexico, everything that I've learned about this case—Maria's last-minute invitation, the break-in at her suite, even the crate of weapons—reeks of desperation."

"And how does that apply to Terrence?"

Payne shrugged. "I don't know. Maybe he got desperate and borrowed money from the wrong people to finance his dig? And when he didn't pay them back, maybe they came looking for him."

"Good heavens! That doesn't sound promising at all."

"Relax, it's just a theory. Then again, it would explain just about everything—including the Hail Mary to Maria."

"Hail Mary to Maria? I'm afraid you just lost me."

Payne smiled. It was rare to find a topic that confused Ulster. "That's an American football term. A losing team calls that play in the last seconds of a game. The quarterback throws the ball as far as he can and hopes that one of his teammates catches it. It's called a Hail Mary because it's nothing more than a prayer."

Ulster laughed. "A Hail Mary! Such an ironic term for a barbarous game. I'll have to remember that." He paused for a moment. "Now, how does that apply to Maria?"

Payne sensed that Ulster didn't quite understand the term, so he decided to spell it out for him. "For the sake of discussion, let's say that Hamilton borrowed fifty thousand dollars to finance his dig, and repayment was due this weekend. Let's also pretend that he borrowed this money from the wrong type of person: a loan shark or a criminal of some kind."

"Okay, I'm with you so far."

"According to Hamilton, he was really close to a major discovery, but he realized time was running out, and his investor wasn't the type of person that he could disappoint."

"Terrence was scared for his life."

Payne nodded. "So what does he do? He calls a Hail Mary—or in this case, a Hail Maria—a last-ditch attempt to make his discovery before time runs out."

Ulster sighed. "I'm afraid you lost me again on the last part."

"Which part of the last part?"

"Don't get me wrong: I understand your analogy. It's clever and apropos. Hamilton is desperate, so he makes a desperate call before time runs out. The part that confuses me is Maria. Of all the historians in the world, why would he call her? And that's not a knock on her. She's a talented researcher in her particular field, but I don't understand how she fits. If this was about Christ, Maria makes sense. But if this is about the Maya, he could have done a lot better."

Payne lowered his voice. "Just so you know, Maria is in total agreement. She can't figure out why she was chosen for this job. According to her, Hamilton assured her that the project was right up her alley, but she's in over her head and she knows it."

Ulster groaned. "She must feel horrible."

"She does. And she's taking it out on me."

"A big, tough guy like you—I think you can handle it."

"I could, but DJ won't let me shoot her."

Ulster smiled. "A hundred years ago, that would have been perfectly legal in Mexico. Nowadays, I'm fairly certain it's frowned upon."

"Yeah. That's what DJ said, too."

Ulster laughed loudly. Even though he loved his work at the Archives, he missed spending time in the field. Over the past few years, the most thrilling moments in his life had occurred with Payne and Jones by his side. Or, more accurately, with him at their side. Actually, that wasn't correct, either. Most of the time, he was cowering behind a tree or running in the opposite direction while they fought their way to safety. The truth was, when the three of them got together, Payne and Jones called the shots—and fired them, too.

Ulster cleared his throat. "I know you haven't asked—so if I'm overstepping my bounds, please let me know—but I'm more than willing to fly to Mexico to assist your efforts."

"Jeez, I don't know," teased Payne, who had been hoping for the offer all along.

Unaware of this, Ulster pleaded his case. "Between the Maya and Maria, it sounds like you have your hands full. Not to mention my dear friend Terrence. I would like to be there for him. You know, as a friendly face in a trying time."

Payne sighed for effect. "Fine! I'll let you come—on one condition."

"Anything. Just name it!"

"If I happen to shoot Maria, you have to help me bury the body."

Ulster laughed at the joke. "No worries, my boy. I've done a lot of digging over the years. I have the perfect shovel."

44

A S LONG AS THE WEATHER IN SWITZERLAND COOP-
erated, Ulster's private jet would arrive in Cancún in less
than twenty-four hours. In the meantime, Payne had a few ideas
about what they should do. That is, if he could convince Jones and
Maria to go along with his plan.

Payne spotted them near the main entrance to Tulum. They
had wandered off during the phone call and were now sitting on a
massive slab of gray stone that had once been a part of the western
wall. From their vantage point, they could see most of the site and
the turquoise waters of the Caribbean. It was truly a beautiful
spot.

Jones sensed Payne's approach from behind. "How'd it go?"

"Just as I expected," Payne said.

"In other words, Petr's packing for the airport—with an erec-
tion."

Maria smacked his arm. "David!"

"What? It's just a figure of speech. I simply meant he's excited
about the trip."

"Then you should have said *that*. Why be so crass?"

Payne sensed a lecture coming, so he saved his buddy by changing the topic. "Maria, I've got some good news for you. Petr is friends with the Italian ambassador to Switzerland. He felt very confident that we could get you a new passport by Monday."

"Really? That's wonderful."

"Unfortunately, it means we have to drive back to Cancún today."

"Why today? The Italian consulate is closed on weekends."

Payne smiled. "Not for Petr it isn't. He said he'll call us with a name and a time. All you have to do is show up and fill out some paperwork."

"That's great, I guess. But I feel kind of guilty about heading back to Cancún. Didn't we leave there to get away from danger?"

"I'm glad you brought that up. I've been giving it a lot of thought, and I think danger might be a good thing."

Maria stared at him. "Excuse me?"

"Yeah," Jones said, "you might need to explain that one."

Payne obliged. "After talking to Petr, I strongly believe we're dealing with some desperate people. Unfortunately, we don't know who they are or what they want. In my opinion, the worst way to handle a faceless enemy is to run away from them. On the road, everyone is a potential threat, and every place is a potential trap. It would be different if we were chasing a solid lead or trying to get across the border, but what we're doing is foolish. I'd rather hunker down and take a stand than stumble around Mexico."

Jones nodded in agreement. "Actually, that makes a lot of sense. Worst-case scenario, they make a move and we get to see who we're dealing with. That sounds good to me."

"Really?" she argued. "Isn't the worst-case scenario actually death?"

Payne grimaced. "Death? Who said anything about death?"

"I'm just making an argument."

"No, you're making this difficult. I thought you said you were going to start trusting me? Hell, it's not even about me. It's about *us*. When are you going to start trusting *us*? DJ's in full agreement on this one, yet you're arguing with him, too."

She glared at Payne. "What? I can't have an opinion?"

"Of course you can have an opinion. Have as many goddamned opinions as you want. But things would go a lot smoother if you kept some of them to yourself—especially when they're outside your area of expertise. Seriously! Did I challenge a single thing about your Spanish translation? No, I didn't. And do you know why? Because I can't *sprechen de Spanish*."

"That's completely different, and you know it."

"No, it's not. It's the same damn thing," he argued. "Do you know anything about defending a perimeter? Or choke points? Or kill zones? What about surveillance techniques? Well, DJ and I could teach a class on that shit because we've lived it and breathed it for two decades. That's our foreign language. We speak it better than anyone else in the world, yet you constantly challenge our conclusions. That has got to stop now."

She turned toward Jones for support. "David?"

He shrugged. "Sorry, Maria. I'm with Jon on this one. You called us to help you out, and you're making it awfully tough. How can we protect you if you fight us on everything?"

Maria seethed but realized she wasn't going to win the argument. "Fine. We'll do it your way. Whatever you guys say, I'll just keep my mouth shut!"

Without saying another word, she hopped off her perch and stormed toward the SUV. The entire time, she was kicking rocks and cursing them out in Italian.

Jones watched this unfold without saying a word. Eventually, he took a deep breath and let it out slowly. He knew he was in for a grueling trip back to Cancún. "There's no way she'll keep quiet for the whole trip. I'll give you a thousand dollars if you drive her to the consulate."

"Not a chance in hell."

"Come on, man. Be a friend. How about five thousand?"

"Only if I can use a gag."

Jones glanced at him. "Wait. We have a gag?"

Payne laughed at the sheer desperation in his buddy's eyes. He almost felt bad for him. "Hang on just a minute. I thought you liked her feistiness."

"Feisty is one thing. Crazy is another. I'm beginning to wonder which one she is."

Payne pointed at the SUV. "Only one way to find out."

Jones sighed. "Would it be rude to frisk her before I unlocked the door?"

"Probably."

He reluctantly nodded. "Can I borrow a rifle?"

"Sorry, soldier. Can't let you do that."

"Then how am I supposed to defend myself?"

Payne studied her from afar and shivered. "I honestly have no idea. We weren't trained for someone like her."

45

CONVERSATION WAS NONEXISTENT FOR THE FIRST seventeen minutes of the trip, which shocked and pleased Jones. He had expected a one-sided verbal barrage that would leave him hard of hearing in his right ear. Instead, he got the silent treatment. No words. No profanity. Not even a growl to express her anger.

In Jones's mind, it couldn't have gone better.

Unfortunately, he made a rookie mistake while weaving through traffic on Federal Highway 307. He leaned forward to check the side mirror and accidentally made eye contact with Maria. It lasted less than a second—nothing more than a fleeting glance in which no words were spoken—but somehow it opened the floodgates. Before he knew it, emotions were pouring out like water through a broken dam.

She said, "I'm sorry about my behavior back there. I didn't mean to yell at you guys over something so stupid. But sometimes, I don't know, sometimes I feel so unappreciated, like my opinions don't make a damn bit of difference." Tears formed in the corners of her eyes. She wiped them away with the back of her hand. "Do you ever feel like that?"

Jones, who rarely shared his feelings with anyone, squirmed in his seat. Normally, he would crack a joke to avoid a serious conversation, but he sensed that simply wouldn't cut it. He knew he was dealing with someone in a fragile state, and the wrong response would make things worse. So he opted to talk about his past. "Not anymore. But I used to feel that way all the time."

"Really? What changed?"

"Just about everything."

She looked at him, waiting for details. "Like what?"

He took a deep breath. This was going to get messy. "You and me, we come from completely different backgrounds—different countries, different families, different lifestyles—but we ended up in the same place because we let something beat us down. Unlike you, I had all the love and support I could get at home. My parents were great. They worked hard to make sure I had everything I needed, but they always had time for me, whether it was to help me with my homework or to smack my ass with a wooden spoon when I was bad. And let me tell you, I was a handful at times. Even worse than I am now."

She smiled when she pictured him as a child.

"For me, problems were nonexistent at home. They started the moment I walked out the door and tried to fit in with my classmates. In my hometown, white faces were the norm. In a town of three thousand people, there were less than fifty minorities. Not black people, mind you, *minorities*. It was so bad that I used to keep track of them in a notebook." He laughed at the memory. "I've always been a numbers guy, so I used to find solace in charts and graphs. At any one time, I could tell you exactly how many blacks, or Asians, or Hispanics there were in my town and where they lived. I actually learned about Venn diagrams when the

Chang family moved down the street. They were Chinese Jews, which forced me to change my entire system."

She laughed despite her confusion. "Why did you track minorities?"

"Why? Because I was looking for allies. If the shit ever hit the fan, I wanted to know where I should run to first. I figured the Jacksons were more likely to help me than Billy Bob's parents. By the way, that's the name of a real kid. The bastard kicked my ass. Twice."

"Did that happen a lot?"

"What?"

"Fights."

He shrugged. "I was smart, skinny, and black. I was a walking kick-me sign."

"I didn't know that," she said sympathetically.

"Really? I thought I told you I was black."

She smiled. "Nope. Never came up."

"Well," he said, "it came up quite a bit for me. Believe it or not, the physical beatings were easier to handle than the mental ones. Most of the times it wasn't blatant. I didn't grow up in the Deep South or the 1800s. It's not like people called me nigger to my face—at least not very often. I'm talking about small things, the things that make a person feel bad about themselves. Snide remarks, backhanded compliments, jokes that went a little too far. My teenage years were pretty rough. I felt like I was alone in the world, and, no matter what I did or how hard I tried, I would always be looked down upon by society. I was a person without self-esteem."

She nodded in understanding. She felt the same way after years of abuse from her father. Not physical abuse, but mental. Whether it was his comments about her intelligence, his insults about her looks or weight, or his general disregard for women, she learned to hate herself at a very early age. Her mother tried to comfort her and tell her everything would be all right, but when she died, there was no one left to protect Maria. By then, she had already been shipped off to a boarding school, where she fought long and hard to turn her life around.

Eventually, she learned to use the hatred that she had felt for her father as fuel for her revenge. She scratched and clawed and beat all the odds to become a rising star in the field of archaeology. Unfortunately, what should have been her crowning achievement—the discovery of the catacombs of Orvieto and all of the secrets that were hidden within—was marred by the death of her father. Instead of having the chance to rub it in his face, she found herself linked to the crimes he had committed before his murder. Crimes against the Vatican itself.

Even in death, her father made her suffer.

"What did you do to change?" she asked.

He glanced at her. "Well, I was tired of being an outcast in my hometown, so I joined the one team in the world where they treat everybody the same."

"Which team is that?"

"The military," he said with a smile. "Of course, *everybody* is treated like shit in the military, but that was a lot better than being the only one treated like shit."

"Misery loves company."

He nodded. "Before long, I was getting more respect at the Academy than I had in high school—probably because I had been toughened up over the years. Other cadets in my class struggled with the abuse. They weren't used to the insults or the cruelty. For me, it felt like home. I figured, there was only so much they could do to me. They could scream, and rant, and get in my face, but they weren't allowed to kick my ass like Billy Bob. If they did, their ass was grass, not mine. That fact alone gave me inner peace. So did my performance at SERE. That's when I knew I had found my calling."

"What's SERE?" she asked.

"It used to be a training program at the Academy. It stands for Survival, Evasion, Resistance, and Escape. I'm not allowed to talk about the specifics, but let's just say it was so difficult that the Academy was forced to shut it down because it was too damn hard. During my first year, I had heard all kinds of horror stories about it from the upperclassmen. They made it sound like a concentration camp, as if only the lucky ones survived. I figured a skinny sucker like myself would be broken within hours, but somehow I thrived. By the end of the program, I was so damn confident I felt like I could take on the world. Ironically, the thing that was supposed to break me actually made me stronger. Ever since then, I haven't looked back."

She took a deep breath. "I'm having trouble with that."

"With what?"

"The past," she said quietly. "I don't know how to let go of it. That's something I never learned how to do. Sometimes I let it consume me."

He nodded. "I know."

"You know?"

"Of course I know. I've known since I met you in Milan. But guess what? That's not necessarily a bad thing for an archaeologist. You *should* be worried about the past."

She smiled. "That's a very good point."

"Besides, the past made you into the person that you are today, so it can't be all bad. Now all you have to do is figure out how to use it to your advantage. You need to find a new direction to channel your passion. If you'd like, I'd be happy to make a suggestion."

"Is that so?" she said, laughing. "What did you have in mind?"

He grinned. "Let's go back to the hotel and *research the Maya.*"

46

THE ITALIAN CONSULATE WAS LESS THAN FIVE MILES from the Fiesta Americana hotel. Payne, who had driven the lead vehicle on their journey back to Cancún, circled the block twice before he gave Jones permission to pull down the street behind him. Unlike the Italian embassy in Mexico City, which was housed in a stone building that resembled a fortress, the local consulate was contained in a small suite that looked like a condo.

No sentries. Or guard dogs. Or snipers on the roof.

Just a plaque by the door and a flag inside.

In a past life, it could have been a dentist's office.

A small man, wearing a sport coat and dress pants, sat on the front stoop. His hair was gray, and his smile was wide. Designer sunglasses covered his eyes. He had been on his way to a cocktail party at a local hotel when he had received an urgent call from his boss. An Italian VIP had lost her passport and needed a replacement. He was ordered to report to the consulate at once. Normally, he would have argued with his boss. He would have said that he was too busy and had other plans. But all of that changed when the boss mentioned the VIP's name.

It was Maria Pelati.

Daughter of *Benito* Pelati.

Suddenly, he was more than happy to help.

Giuseppe leapt to his feet when the two vehicles stopped in front of the consulate. He spotted Maria in the passenger seat of the SUV and rushed to open her door. But Payne was a little too fast. He hustled from the H2 and intercepted Giuseppe before he reached the sidewalk.

Payne ordered him to stop. "Whoa! Slow down! What's the hurry?"

Giuseppe took off his sunglasses and stared at the mountain of a man. "I am sorry. My name is Giuseppe Amato. I am here to assist Miss Pelati."

Payne corrected him. "Actually, *I'm* here to assist her."

"Yes, of course. My apologies."

Payne tried not to smile. He could tell the guy wasn't a threat. He simply wanted to make a point. "Let me see your identification."

Giuseppe slowly reached into his jacket pocket and pulled out his ID. It identified him as an employee of the consulate. "I was phoned by my boss, who was phoned by his boss, who was phoned by Petr Ulster. I am to help her with her passport."

Payne stared at him. "I think you're missing one or two bosses in there."

Giuseppe shrugged. "That is entirely possible."

"And why were you waiting outside?"

"I am anxious to meet Miss Pelati. There is so much I would like to ask her."

"Really? About what?"

"Her father!" Giuseppe exclaimed. "Where I come from, Benito

Pelati is considered a hero. He did so much to preserve the history of my homeland, so much to preserve our culture. I remember hearing him speak at a function in Venice. He had such passion, such fire. It was like watching an emperor at the Colosseum. We gave him a standing ovation!"

Payne was quite familiar with Benito Pelati and his stellar reputation. As Italy's Minister of Antiquities, Benito had accomplished many wonderful feats during his decades of service. He had spent years preaching to the masses about the importance of history, fighting to protect the treasures of ancient Rome. After a while, his name became synonymous with the effort, known by young and old alike. To many, he was viewed as a savior. But like many politicians, the real man was quite different from his public persona. Having dealt with him firsthand, Payne knew Benito had been a cruel, power-hungry bastard. Nearly everything he had done had been for his own personal gain rather than the welfare of his church or country.

Naturally, none of this came out at the time of his death. The Vatican, quite familiar with the effects of a scandal, felt some things were best kept secret. The Parliament quickly agreed and sealed his records. This made for an interesting dichotomy. While the media praised Benito's achievements, cardinals and senators secretly celebrated his demise. Millions held vigils and wept in the streets while his peers rejoiced in private. Meanwhile, Maria did everything she possibly could to avoid the spotlight. Her surviving brother, Dante, handled the press while she slipped out of the country unnoticed. She spent the next several days in seclusion at the Ulster Archives before heading back to England to finish her education.

In many ways, she had been running ever since.

"Listen," Payne said to Giuseppe in a decisive tone, "I can understand your curiosity. I really can. I know how much Benito meant to Italy, and I can tell that you're genuinely excited to talk about his exploits. Unfortunately, I'm going to have to insist that you don't mention his name. The topic is far too painful for her to discuss."

Giuseppe lowered his head in shame. "Yes, of course, how selfish of me. I mourned the loss of a patriot. She mourned the loss of her father. Her grief must be unbearable."

Payne nodded but said nothing.

"Tell me," Giuseppe whispered, "what can I talk about?"

Payne wanted to say, *It beats the hell out of me,* but he caught himself before it slipped out. Instead, he decided to focus on something positive. Something that might help them in the long run. "How long have you lived here?"

"Almost four years."

"And you're a fan of history?"

"Yes, very much so. Benito taught—" He quickly covered his mouth, as if he had just cursed in front of a nun. "I mean, I learned to appreciate history back in Italy. I have been to all of the local sites and museums."

"Then talk about that. She loves local history."

Giuseppe nodded. "Then that's what I will do. Thank you very much."

By this time, Jones was standing next to Maria's door, waiting for the all-clear signal. He sensed that the man posed no threat but was being put through his paces for Maria's benefit. Not to impress her but to make her feel threatened. Sometimes fear was needed to gain control. The sooner she started to view herself as a potential target, the sooner she would start following orders. At least that was the goal. In the long run, her compliance would benefit everyone.

Payne signaled to Jones, who helped her out of the SUV. After a brief introduction, the four of them headed inside the consulate, where Maria and Giuseppe started her paperwork. Meanwhile, Payne asked if he could use the fax machine to send the Mercado document to Petr Ulster, who wanted a chance to read it on his flight to Mexico. Giuseppe showed him where it was and how to use it—the buttons were labeled in Italian—then hustled back to Maria.

Jones watched with amusement. "I've never seen you do this before. Normally you make your secretary do everything."

Payne scoffed at the notion. "My secretary doesn't do office work, and you know it. I hired her for her tits."

Most people would have viewed his comment as sexist, but Jones knew the truth about his secretary. She was an eighty-two-year-old firecracker, who had started working for Payne Industries long before Payne was even born. That included thirty years as his grandfather's secretary. Not as his assistant but as his *secretary*. Even though she knew more about the company than Payne did, she still insisted on being called a secretary because that was her job title when she was originally hired and she didn't think there was anything wrong with it. Known for her foul mouth and quick wit, she had a saltier sense of humor than most comedians.

Jones laughed loudly. "I'm going to tell her you said that."

Payne smiled. "I hope you do. I like keeping her sharp."

Jones watched intently as Payne fed the document through the machine. Several seconds passed before a confirmation notice appeared on the screen. As soon as it did, Payne deleted the document from the system's memory and erased the number he had sent it to. No sense in taking any chances.

"So," Payne said, "did you need something? You're kind of creeping me out."

"Actually, I wanted to thank you."

"For what?"

"For what you said to Giuseppe. I had a long talk with Maria about her issues on the way here. The last thing she needed was to answer a bunch of questions about Benito."

"I didn't do it for her. I did it for me. I'm sick of her yapping."

He shook his head. "No, you didn't. You did it for her. And I appreciate it."

Payne stared at him. "You've been thanking me a lot on this trip. I didn't think we did that. You know, the whole thank-you thing. Are you dying or something?"

"Nope, not dying. Just trying to keep the peace."

"No, you're trying to *get a piece*. Big difference."

Jones laughed. "Either way, I appreciate it."

Payne smiled and pointed at Jones's crotch. "Both of you are welcome."

47

MARIA FINISHED THE PAPERWORK FOR HER NEW passport in less than twenty minutes. She thanked Giuseppe for his time before Payne and Jones asked him for a huge favor. They were looking for a place to store Hamilton's Hummer—and its delicate cargo—and asked if the consulate had a warehouse they could use. As luck would have it, the consulate included a private garage attached to the back of the building. Not only would it keep the vehicle off the street but the garage was technically Italian soil, which meant they didn't have to worry about Mexican authorities catching them with Mayan artifacts or a crate full of rifles and explosives.

Payne pulled the vehicle around back, parked it in Giuseppe's personal spot, and then grabbed everything they needed for their night at the Fiesta Americana. Maria still wasn't thrilled about putting herself in danger to flush out the men who had trashed her room, but Payne and Jones were so confident in their decision that she decided to go along without complaint.

Jones, who had started his day in Pittsburgh, showered as soon as they reached the suite. When he emerged, he felt like a brand-new person. Dressed in shorts and a T-shirt, he raided the minibar for caffeine and candy even though they still had plenty of snacks left over from lunch. He had spent the whole day looking for Terrence Hamilton. He figured the least Hamilton could do was buy him a Coke and some Reese's Peanut Butter Cups.

That is, if the guy was still alive.

Meanwhile, Payne took his turn in the guest bathroom. As a hotel aficionado, he paid close attention to the small details in the suite: the marble floor, the jetted tubs, the Italian towels and bathrobes. All the little things that made a guest feel like royalty. Some people were surprised that he cared about such comforts, especially those who knew about his military career. But he told them it was *because* of his military career that he cared about such things. After years of sleeping in the desert and the jungle, he vowed to see the world from a different perspective on his next go-around. It was one of the few guilty pleasures that he had.

Like many people, Payne did some of his best thinking in the shower. Time when he could block out the world. Time he could spend alone with his thoughts. He ran through the last twenty-four hours in his mind, searching for irregularities. Years of experience had taught him the value of this. Little was gained by focusing on the norm. It was the anomalies—the things that went against the grain—that tended to define a situation.

Unfortunately, there were so many irregularities with Hamilton's disappearance that Payne didn't know where to begin. According to Petr Ulster, Hamilton was a thrifty academic who didn't have enough money to pay for research assistants, let alone a corner suite at a five-star resort. Yet he paid for Maria's first-class airfare from Rome and rented her a suite for the entire weekend. Why would he do that? Was it, as Maria speculated, an enticement for her to make the journey? And even if it was, why in the world did he choose her for the job? Not even Maria could explain that.

But the oddities didn't end there. Hamilton had a trunk full of artifacts and a crate filled with weapons, even though both were out of character for him. These things reeked of desperation, but desperation related to what? Did he borrow money from the wrong people? Or was this merely a precaution because of his expected windfall? He had told Maria that they were close to finding something that would blow her mind. Maybe the weapons were nothing more than insurance.

For Payne, it was tough to get a read on things because he had never met the man. He had never looked him in the eye or had a conversation with him. Other than a few photos from the Internet, his only experience with Hamilton was the hotel's security feed—a feed that had been partially erased by a top-notch hacker. That was another thing that didn't make much sense. Why take the time to do that? Payne was quite familiar with the abduction racket in Latin America. Several of his military buddies had left the service to work as independent contractors in the kidnap-and-ransom (K&R) industry, including a few who worked in Mexico. He knew kidnappings were so common in certain parts of the world that corporations paid big bucks for K&R insurance (policies that would reimburse them for money lost on ransom payments). Yet in all the articles he had read, he couldn't recall anything about a high-end hacker covering up an abduction. Then again, maybe that was because hackers covered up the cover-up.

Payne put on a golf shirt and shorts, and then headed into the living room, where he fully expected to find Jones and Maria flirting, or fighting, or both. But neither of them was there. Instead, Maria was taking a much-needed nap in the bedroom, and Jones was admiring the ocean view from their private terrace. Payne grabbed a bottle of water, then joined him outside.

"Nice view," he said as he pushed a teak chair against the patio wall. From there, he could see the Caribbean and the interior of the suite. "But not as nice as Pittsburgh."

Jones laughed. "Apples and oranges."

Payne nodded in agreement. Both views were spectacular, but in completely different ways. "Speaking of fruit, I'm *starving*. We might need to get room service."

"When aren't you starving?"

"Good point." Blessed with a freakishly high metabolism, Payne had to consume more than eight thousand calories a day or else he lost weight. "How long has she been sleeping?"

"Four hours or so. Pretty much the entire time you were in the bathroom. I swear, you are such a princess when it comes to hotels. Did you enjoy the guava shampoo and the papaya soap? What about the towels? Did they meet your impeccably high standards?"

"First off, I was in there for ten minutes, not four hours."

"Bullshit."

"Second, I thoroughly enjoyed the bathroom accoutrements. Thank you for asking."

Jones stared at him. "God as my witness, if you ever say 'accoutrements' again, I'm going to punch you in the face. That word is way too fancy for an American."

Payne laughed. "You're probably right."

"I know I'm right."

Payne cracked open the bottle and took a long swig. "Anyway, while I was in the bathroom, I was pondering the circumstances of Hamilton's disappearance, and I realized something important."

"That water is a valuable resource and shouldn't be wasted in a four-hour shower?"

"No, I thought of someone we should call."

"The African village that won't have anything to drink because of you?"

Payne ignored him. "Don Stillwagon."

Jones paused in thought. It was a name he hadn't heard in a very long time. "Stillwagon? Why should we call Stillwagon? Isn't he in Eastern Europe?"

Payne shook his head. "Stillwagon's in Mexico."

"Really? Doing what?"

"K-and-R."

"No shit. I haven't talked to him in years."

"Me, neither. That's why I didn't think of him at first. The last I heard, he was working for an insurance company in Mexico City."

"That's a thousand miles away."

"True, but it's still Mexico. He has to know some of the players who work around here. And even if he doesn't, he'll know a lot more about K-and-R than us."

Jones nodded in agreement. "Do you have his number?"

"Probably. If not, I'm sure I can get it. That is, if you think it's worth my time. Remember, you're running the show down here, not me. I don't want to step on any toes."

"Hell, yeah, it's worth your time. What else are you going to do tonight? I mean, besides ordering room service ten times and watching pay-per-view."

Payne laughed. "Actually, I'm glad you just said that. I've been meaning to tell you something all day. The head of security gave me a movie that you have to see. Go get your computer. It's one you should watch without Maria. I don't think she would approve."

Jones glanced inside the suite. Thankfully, she was still sleeping in the other room. "Why? How perverted is it?"

"Just get your laptop. I don't want to ruin the surprise."

48

JONES SET UP HIS COMPUTER ON THE PRIVATE TERRACE.
He angled the screen away from the sliding glass door—just in case *she* woke up in the middle of the viewing—then grabbed the DVD from Payne. The label read MARIACHI MARIA. From the title alone, he would have assumed it was a Mexican adult film, but the grin on Payne's face suggested otherwise. So did Payne's presence. In all their years of friendship, they had never hung out and watched porn together.

Not knowing what to expect, Jones was temporarily confused when the video opened in the driveway in front of the Fiesta Americana. A Town Car pulled under the covered entryway and was quickly surrounded by bellboys and valets. The driver hopped out of the car and started blowing kisses to everyone, as if he were a bullfighter who had just entered the ring. A few seconds later, a mariachi band appeared out of nowhere. Five musicians in all, dressed in silver-studded *charro* outfits with wide-brimmed hats. The movie had no sound, but it was obvious that the band had started to play because everyone was clapping in unison.

Jones glanced at Payne. "Worst. Porn. Ever. Why am I watching this?"

Payne laughed. "Just keep watching."

"If the band gets naked, you owe me a new computer, because I'm going to throw this one over the railing. I'm pretty sure I can reach the ocean from here."

"Trust me, it gets better."

"It would have to get better. It can't get worse."

Suddenly, the driver started snapping his fingers and dancing in the middle of the driveway. He didn't care who was watching. This was his moment to shine, and he performed without shame. He just danced, danced, danced around the front of the car. Then he danced, danced, danced toward the passenger-side door. The driver was so theatrical, so over-the-top, that Jones couldn't help smiling. The whole scene was just too funny.

And then it happened.

The moment Payne had been waiting for.

Mariachi Maria stepped out of the car.

The instant Jones saw her, his eyes doubled in size—and so did his smile. He quickly covered his mouth with both of his hands, trying to hold in the laughter for as long as possible, because he knew when he let it out he would wake her in the other room. Not that he really cared. The truth was there was no way in hell that he would be able to keep this from Maria for very long. His desire to share it with her was far too great. And not in a negative way. He didn't want to tease her about her dancing. At least not much. Instead, he wanted to point at the screen and say, *That's the Maria I remember.* The fun-loving girl who smiled, and laughed, and loved life. Not the grumpy one who had been picking fights with everyone in sight.

That was the Maria he had fallen for.

The one he missed.

"Holy crap!" Payne blurted as he pointed at the screen.

Jones laughed. "I know! Isn't this great? I want five copies—"

"No! Go back!" He started hitting keys on the laptop, trying to figure out its controls in the darkness of the patio. "How do you stop this thing?"

Jones stared at him. "Why? What's wrong?"

"Stop the damn movie and go back."

"Back? To where?"

"Twenty seconds or so. I think I saw something."

Jones clicked PAUSE. Then REWIND. The footage inched back in time, slowly crawling toward the segment that Payne wanted to see. "Want to tell me what I'm looking for?"

Payne ignored him and focused on the screen. "Okay . . . stop!"

Jones paused the film. "Now what?"

"I'll be damned. Will you look at that?"

"What?"

"That!"

Jones crouched next to the screen and studied the image. He searched the crowd of bellboys and valets for faces that didn't belong. He looked for guns. He looked for nudity. He looked for anything that might have piqued his best friend's interest, but he came up empty. "Come on! You know I hate when you do this."

"I know. *That's* why I do it."

Jones glanced back at the screen. "Aha! I see it. Right there!"

Payne smiled. "You're lying."

"No, I'm not."

"Yes, you are."

Jones growled at him. "You're right. I'm lying. I have no idea what you're talking about. Now, stop being a dick and tell m—"

"Look at the van."

"What van?"

Payne pointed in the background of the video. A van was parked twenty feet behind the Town Car. Two men were sitting in the front seat of the van, surveying the scene in front of them. They were Latin men with short black hair and stocky builds. They were dressed in casual clothes and designer sunglasses—the same outfits they had been wearing when they broke into Maria's suite. "Recognize them?"

"Not really."

"Those are the bastards that trashed this place. I showed you their picture."

Jones squinted. "Are you sure? All Mexicans look alike to me."

Payne winced. "I can't believe you just said that."

"Why? I'm black. I'm allowed to be racist."

"Toward other blacks, *maybe*. But not toward other races."

Jones grimaced. "Really?"

"Yes, really."

"No wonder I have no ethnic friends. I mean, other than *you*. Of course, you're a Polack, so you don't know any better."

Payne glared at him. "Are you done?"

"I don't know. All that sugar and caffeine is kicking in."

"Well, try to focus. We're talking about Maria's safety."

"How do you figure?"

He pointed at the screen. "Those guys pulled in *after* the Town Car. That means there's a damn good chance they followed her from the airport. All this time, we thought this was about Hamilton. Maybe this is actually about Maria."

Jones considered the possibility. "I doubt it. If they wanted Maria, why didn't they just grab her? They had plenty of chances before we showed up. They could have nabbed her at the airport. They could have nabbed her at the bistro. Hell, they could have run the Town Car off the road on its way to the hotel. What would the driver have done to protect her? The tango?"

Payne nodded. "Yeah, I guess you're right. They had plenty of chances. In that case, why follow her from the airport? What were they hoping to achieve?"

"Maybe they lost track of Hamilton and followed her to find him."

"How did they know about her to begin with?"

"Beats the hell out of me."

"And why trash her room?"

Jones shrugged. "I thought we decided it was to scare her."

"But scare her from what?"

"I don't know. Maybe to scare her from Hamilton. Maybe it was their way to say their problem was with him, not with her. Maybe it was their way to tell her to back off."

"If that's the case, she *really* misread the sign."

Jones leaned back in his chair and smiled. "It wouldn't be the first time she had misread a sign."

"What does that mean?"

"Whatever you do, do *not* get in a car if she's driving. I made that mistake once, and I'll never do it again. Seriously, I'd rather play Russian roulette."

"She's that bad?"

He cringed at the memory. "You and me, we've been through some serious shit in our lifetimes. Iraq. Afghanistan. That weekend in Bangkok. But nothing—and I mean *nothing*—was as frightening as that car ride in Switzerland. In a span of thirty minutes, I thought I was going to die fifty times. No exaggeration. Fifty times. That's almost two per minute."

Payne waved off the claim. "Come on! She can't be *that* bad."

"Here's the thing: She *isn't* that bad of a driver. In fact, she's pretty good. She knows how to steer, and brake, and parallel park. She even uses her turn signal, unlike most people in the world. If we put her on a racetrack, I'm sure she would do pretty well."

"Then what's her problem?"

Jones glanced inside the suite to make sure she was still sleeping. "She tends to forget what country she's in."

"What does that mean?"

"I mean, she grew up in Italy, where they drive on the right, but she learned how to drive in England, where they drive on the left. For some reason, she has a mental block when she's behind the wheel. She simply can't remember which side to drive on."

"You're shitting me."

"I wish I was, but I swear I'm not."

"I can't believe you never told me this. Give me details."

Jones leaned forward to explain. "This happened right after the incident at the Archives. She was there doing research with Petr, and I was there helping with security after the fire."

"Where was I?"

"You were with Nick Dial at Interpol, cleaning up our mess."

Payne nodded. "That's right. I forgot about the bodies."

"Anyway, I asked Maria out to dinner, and she said, *Hell, yes*— because I'm attractive, and funny, and hung like a donkey. I borrowed one of Petr's cars, a tiny convertible, and we drove halfway down the mountain to this restaurant with a spectacular view. I ended up having a few drinks at dinner, so I gladly surrendered the keys to Maria. At the time, I thought it was the smart thing to do. Now I realize a Klan meeting would have been safer."

Payne laughed. "Go on."

"She started off perfectly fine because all she had to do was follow the flow of cars in front of her as we left town. It wasn't until we hit the rural road—the one that weaved up the mountain to Küsendorf—that I detected a problem. I knew we were in deep shit when she pointed at a road sign and said, 'Look, the sign is backward.'"

"Wait! You mean she was looking on the wrong side of the road?"

Jones nodded. "I thought she was joking until she took the next blind curve on the left side. A truck was headed directly toward us, and she was beeping at him like it was *his* fault. At the last minute, she must have realized her mistake because she swerved into the right lane—and by 'right,' I mean the right lane *and* I mean the correct lane. Same lane, in this case."

"What did you do?"

"You mean *after* I shit myself? I asked her if she was okay. She assured me that she was fine—she had a single glass of wine at dinner—so I figured it was just some bad steering on her part. Could've happened to anyone. You know those Alpine roads. They're death traps. No cops. No guardrails. No yellow lines. I assumed it was a onetime thing that wouldn't happen again. Boy, was I wrong. Every time we went through a tight curve, she ended up on the wrong side of the road. Not once. Not twice. Fifty fucking times. My adrenaline was pumping so hard, I was probably sober by turn six. By turn fifteen, my blood-alcohol level was a negative number. And yes, I know that isn't possible, but I'm telling you I was fine—except for my face. My face was so white that I looked like you."

"In other words, you got better-looking during the trip."

"No, but I aged fifty years. That's probably why we looked alike."

Payne rolled his eyes. His friend always had to get in the last word. "Did you say anything when you got back to the Archives?"

"Of course I did. I said, 'Thank you.'"

"You thanked her?"

"Hell, no! I thanked *God*. I got on my knees and thanked Him for saving me."

"You prayed to God?"

"Don't be silly. I wasn't on my knees to pray. I was on my knees to puke. But since I was down there, I figured it couldn't hurt."

"But you're not religious."

"I know I'm not, but Maria is. I figured God saved her ass—I mean, she prays all the time—so I decided to thank Him for saving me, too."

Payne stared at him. "Is that why you two broke up?"

"Because of her driving?"

"No. Because of her religion."

Jones shook his head. "Not at all. I mean, we didn't see eye to eye on certain things, but she respected my beliefs and I respected hers. Both of us were cool with that."

"Then why?"

"Why what?"

"Why did she break up with you?"

Jones took a deep breath, then he hit the power button on his computer. The image of Maria, dancing and smiling, disappeared from the screen. "Who said she did?"

49

SUNDAY, FEBRUARY 12

PETR ULSTER ARRIVED IN CANCÚN EARLY ON SUNDAY morning—so early that he took a taxi from the private airfield to the hotel because he didn't think his friends would be awake to pick him up. He waited in the lobby until 8:00 A.M., when his patience finally ran out. Bubbling with enthusiasm, he simply had to get the adventure started, or he was going to burst.

Payne, who had spent a restless night on the couch, heard the knock on the door at 8:04 A.M. He was less than amused by the disturbance. He grabbed his gun and hustled to the entryway while Jones covered his position from behind. Even in retirement, they could put their game faces on in the blink of an eye—even if their eyes were bloodshot. "Who is it?"

"It's Petr . . . Petr Ulster."

Payne groaned. It was too early for this. "What's the password?"

"Password? You didn't tell me a password."

"Sorry. You need the password." Payne turned and shouted over his shoulder. "Come back when you have the password."

Jones laughed at the scene. He was quite familiar with Payne's early-morning grumpiness. It hadn't been an issue in the military—they woke up when they were told to wake up—but in recent years, it had become more and more prevalent. "You're not going to let him in?"

Payne shook his head. "Not until noon."

Jones squeezed past him in the hallway and looked through the peephole, just to make sure Ulster was alone. He was standing in the corridor, bags near his feet and confusion on his face. For a moment, it looked like he was going to pick up his luggage and walk away, but at the last second, he paused and scratched his brown beard in thought. One of the best academic minds in the world was standing outside the door, trying to figure out a password that didn't exist. Jones was so amused by the possibilities that he decided to egg him on.

Jones said, "The clock is ticking. What's the password?"

Ulster, still clueless, took a wild guess. "Shovel."

"Shovel?" It was such a random word that Jones opened the door to find out why he had guessed it. "Did you say 'shovel'?"

"Was that correct?" he asked, hopeful.

"No, it wasn't correct. Jon was just messing with you. There is no password."

"Oh."

Jones greeted him with a hug. They briefly exchanged pleasantries before Jones refocused the conversation on the password. "Out of curiosity, why did you guess 'shovel'?"

"Because I told Jonathon I would bring one in case . . . um . . . never mind."

"In case, what?"

Ulster blushed. "I would rather not say. You might think less of me."

Jones stared at him. "Come on, Petr. There are no secrets here."

Ulster nodded and lowered his voice to a whisper. "I said I would bring a shovel in case Jonathon shot Maria. You know, to stop her yapping." His face flushed from embarrassment. His cheeks were so red that his beard appeared to change colors. "Oh my goodness, I can't believe I just said that. I swear, we were just joking on the phone. I would never condone violence against Maria. I think the world of her."

Jones laughed. "Don't worry. I believe you."

"Please," he begged, "feel free to check my bags. I am shovel-free."

"Petr, relax! I know you were just kidding." He threw his arm around Ulster's shoulder and squeezed. "Remember, I'm the guy who bought you a rubber duck shaped like the Swan King. We tend to joke around here. That's why you like hanging with us."

Ulster smiled at the thought of the bathtub toy. "Is that why?"

"That's one of the reasons. You also like it when we shoot bad guys."

"I know it sounds barbaric, but I do enjoy a good bloodletting every now and again—especially when I feel imperiled. It happens so infrequently at the Archives."

"And the one time it did, we were there to save the day."

Ulster nodded. "That, of course, is why I am so eager to return the favor."

"Maybe *too* eager. We're still waking up."

"Yes, I figured as much. Shall I leave and come back?"

Jones grabbed a suitcase. "Of course not. Come in and make yourself at home."

"Are you sure? Because—"

"Of course I'm sure. But just to be safe, why don't you wait on the deck? The sun is shining, the birds are singing, and you'll be out of the path of Hurricane Payne."

⊞   ⊞   ⊞

An hour later, the four of them were eating breakfast on the terrace. Ulster, who'd had nothing better to do while everyone else got ready, ordered them a Mexican feast from room service: breakfast burritos, scrambled eggs with chorizo, chiles rellenos, jalapeño corn cakes, plus an assortment of fruits, breads, and juices. With every bite of food, Payne became less and less irritable. Some people needed coffee in the morning to start their day, but he needed food. Because of his high metabolism, he woke up every day, running on fumes.

"So," Payne said after a few minutes of small talk, "did you get a chance to read the document that I faxed from the consulate?"

Ulster nodded. "I did indeed. It was a *fascinating* read, one filled with secrets and subtext. As I mentioned on the phone, I was familiar with Marcos de Mercado, the young priest assigned to Diego de Landa upon his return to the New World, but this document was a revelation. In fact, I'm fairly confident that its discovery was recent."

"Why do you say that?" Maria asked.

"I have this wonderful piece of software at the Archives that searches through every scholastic database in the world. I scan my text into the system, then it searches for common words and phrases in every document that has ever been mentioned in the digital world—whether that's a foreign translation, a short passage, or a quote in a doctoral thesis. In a matter of seconds, I find out if my document has ever been examined. It really is quite remarkable."

"Thanks," Payne said, "I'm glad you like it."

Maria glanced at him, confused. "What does that mean?"

"It means I'm glad he liked my software."

"Yours?" she asked.

"Well, not *mine*. But my company's. Petr told me about a problem he was having—"

"—accessing academic databases in multiple languages," Ulster explained.

Payne nodded. "And my Research and Development division tried to find a solution. It took a while to work out the kinks, but after some helpful advice from a friend of ours—"

"To Randy!" Jones blurted as he raised his glass of juice.

"—we developed a working prototype for the Archives. It's still in the beta phase, but someday we hope to release it as open-source software. Then everyone can use it for free."

"Why would you do that? Your company could lose millions," she said.

"It's not about money. It's about the freedom of historical information. You know, the concept that Petr encourages at the Archives."

She nodded, impressed. "Don't get me wrong: I think that's wonderful. I just . . ."

Payne smiled. "Didn't expect it from me?"

"Something like that," she admitted.

"Well, maybe one of these days, you'll realize I'm not such a bad guy after all."

"I never said that you were."

Worried about the direction of the conversation, Jones intervened. "Speaking of bad guys, what did you find out about Landa in the document?"

Ulster answered excitedly. "Quite a bit! For centuries, scholars have debated why the Spanish Crown would appoint him as the Bishop of Yucatán. After all, he was hated by just about everyone in the New World—the Maya, the soldiers, and the clergy—because of his sadistic behavior. Furthermore, he had embarrassed several key political figures in Spain with the auto-da-fé of Maní in 1562. No one could understand why he was rewarded with such a plum role in the colonization of the Americas less than ten years later, but now we know. He bribed his way back to the New World with the promise of treasure."

"You think the document is real?" she asked.

Ulster nodded. "Considering the source, I think that's a logical assumption. Terrence Hamilton is a leading expert in his field. If he had the document in his possession, I'm willing to give him the benefit of the doubt—at least for the time being. We'll know for sure once we get to see the original. *If* we get to see the original."

Payne grimaced. "Right now, that's a pretty big *if*."

"Why do you say that?" she demanded.

"Last night I tracked down a friend of mine who works K-and-R in Mexi—"

She cut him off. "What's K-and-R?"

"Sorry. That means kidnap and ransom. It's a booming industry in Latin America, and my friend works as a retrieval specialist in Mexico City."

Jones tried to reassure her. "His name is Don Stillwagon. We've known him for years. He's very good at what he does. He knows what he's talking about."

She nodded in acceptance.

"Anyway," Payne continued, "he's very familiar with the gangs that run eastern Mexico. He said in ninety-five percent of all cases, a ransom demand will be issued within forty-eight hours. After that, the odds of recovery go down significantly."

Ulster gulped. "You mean they'll kill him?"

"No, I mean the odds are pretty good he's *already* dead."

"What?" she blurted.

Payne shook his head. "Don't misunderstand me: I didn't say Hamilton is dead. I said if a demand hasn't been issued in forty-eight hours, there's probably a pretty good reason. Most of the time, it means something happened to the target. Maybe he fought back. Maybe he saw their faces. Or maybe he was killed during the abduction. Whatever the reason, the gang chalks it up as a loss and moves on to its next victim. Down here, time is money."

"Just like that?" she asked.

Payne nodded. "Just like that."

Ulster glanced at his watch. It was nearly 9:30 A.M. "When was Terrence grabbed?"

"Roughly five P.M. on Friday. That means seven and a half hours to go."

"That isn't a lot of time," Ulster said.

"True, but keep something in mind: The odds are pretty damn good they're not going to call *us*. They'll call Hamilton's family, or his university, or whoever would be willing to pay for his release. For all we know, that call was made yesterday."

"Then what should we do?" she asked.

"We're already doing it. We're following the clues that were left behind. With any luck, we'll stumble across something significant. And if we do, we'll be ready to help."

50

B Y THE END OF BREAKFAST, ULSTER WAS BOUNCING with anticipation. Ever since the phone call from Payne, he had been eager to examine the Mayan artifacts that Hamilton had discovered. Based on their colors, materials, and designs, Ulster felt he could take an educated guess about their city of origin. By doing so, he hoped to figure out where Hamilton and his team had been working in the weeks prior to his disappearance.

"Where shall we have the unveiling?" Ulster asked.

"That depends," Payne said. "What do you need to examine them?"

"Not a lot. I brought everything I need, with one tiny exception."

"What's that?"

"Maria."

She flinched at the mention of her name. "Me?"

Ulster laughed. "Of course *you*. The last time I checked, you were a world-class historian. That hasn't changed, has it?"

"No."

"Then your expertise will be invaluable. I certainly can't count on these brutes to handle delicate artifacts. I've seen them play catch with a priceless vase."

Jones laughed. "In my defense, I thought 'priceless' meant it was free."

Payne nodded. "And in my defense, he threw it at me. All I did was catch it. Technically, I saved the damn thing."

"Regardless of the circumstances," Ulster said, grinning, "I would prefer to work with an expert in the field—someone like Maria."

"No problem. I'd be happy to help." She leaned toward Ulster, who was sitting on her right, and whispered, "Just so you know, I'm far from an expert when it comes to the Maya."

He whispered back, "That makes two of us. Perhaps we can put our heads together and fake it. These guys won't know any better."

She giggled and put her hand on his shoulder. "I'm so glad you're here. I really am."

He smiled at her. "I'm so glad I was invited. It's been far too long, my dear. How come you haven't visited me in Küsendorf? You know you're always welcome."

"I am?" she said, surprised.

"Of course! In fact, after the time we spent together at the Archives, I was secretly hoping that you would view me as a mentor. Not that you need one. I mean, you have achieved so much at such a tender age, more than I had in my twenties. Nevertheless, sometimes it might be comforting to have someone in your corner, someone who has faced the same battles as you, someone with a similar background. Keep in mind, my father and grandfather were both revered for the work they did in the preservation of artifacts, so I know how difficult it is to live up to a family reputation. In many ways, my name is a blessing. In other ways, it is a curse."

She nodded. "Trust me, I'm quite familiar with the curse part."

"Yes," he said knowingly, "I guess you've beaten me in *that* category. Still, consider this an open invitation. If you ever want to talk, I'd love to hear from you, day or night."

"Thanks. That means the world to me."

Payne cleared his throat from across the table. "Sorry to interrupt your whispering—I know how you ladies love to gossip—but shouldn't we get the show on the road?"

Ulster nodded. "I've been ready since sunrise. Just lead the way, and I shall follow."

⛨   ⛨   ⛨

THE FOURSOME RODE TOGETHER to the Italian consulate, where Hamilton's H2 had been stashed overnight. Jones parked the SUV in the alley, not far from the private garage, and kept watch while Payne opened the door. He punched in the access code, given to them by Giuseppe, and waited for the light to turn green. As soon as it did, he signaled for the others to join him.

Ulster took charge once they got inside. Although he wasn't an expert in any particular field, he had a working knowledge of every historical topic imaginable. In a recent interview, he had compared himself to a family physician. He didn't have a concentrated specialty, like a cardiovascular surgeon, who knew the inner workings of the heart better than anyone. Instead, he was more like a general practitioner, someone who knew a lot about a lot, which enabled him to jump comfortably from one field to another. Compared to Maria, who'd had limited exposure to the Maya, Ulster was an authority on Mesoamerica. He had downplayed his knowledge at breakfast to boost her confidence, but it was obvious to everyone that he was running the show.

While studying the contents of the crate in the H2, he tried to make sense of Hamilton's ordering system. The artifacts were divided by size and stored in a display case with removable wooden slats. Large objects were packed in Bubble Wrap and given their own individual compartments. But smaller items, such as stone figurines and pottery shards, were relegated to plastic bags and crammed into the remaining spaces. "Did any of you move *any-thing*?"

Maria shook her head. "I examined a couple of bags to see what we were dealing with, but I put them back exactly where I found them."

"Did you open them?"

"Definitely not. I didn't think it was worth the risk."

"Then this is how they were arranged?"

"Yes," she assured him. "Why?"

"Because none of this makes sense."

Ulster picked up a plastic bag to illustrate his point. Inside were two stone figurines that looked nothing alike. One was quite vibrant. It depicted a half-naked warrior with an elaborate head-dress that had been painted in a rainbow of colors. Everything about it was loud and flashy, like a child's toy from an ancient era. The other was a simple carved head. It was solid and subtle. No wild colors or funky designs. It had a quiet dignity that the other one lacked.

Wearing a pair of cotton archival gloves, Ulster reached into the bag and pulled out the carved head. He held it up for everyone to see. "This figurine is Mayan. It has a distinctive face, particularly the curvature of its nose. The carvings along the base are fairly typical of this region during the Postclassic period. That's the era right before the arrival of the Spanish. If I had to guess, I would say this is from the fourteenth or fifteenth century."

He handed it to Maria, who was also wearing gloves, so she could show it to Payne and Jones. They stared at it intently while Ulster removed the second figurine from the bag.

"Now, this one," he proclaimed, "is remarkably different. Everything about it—its color, its shape, its place of origin—is dissimilar to the first. Of course, there's a very good reason for their differences. This one *isn't* Mayan. This one is *Aztec*."

"Aztec?" she blurted. "Are you sure?"

He nodded. "I am absolutely certain. Over the years, I have worked with artwork from both civilizations, and there are some basic differences between the two. In this case, it's pretty straightforward. These figurines are prototypical of their individual cultures."

"And that's bad?" Jones wondered.

Ulster shook his head. "Not bad, just confusing. For the life of me, I can't figure out why he would have placed these items together. It makes no sense."

Payne knew very little about the Maya, other than what he had heard or read in the past two days, and his knowledge of the Aztec was virtually nonexistent. So he needed further clarification to make sense of the problem. "Both groups are from Mexico, right? But you're saying you *wouldn't* find these pieces in the same place?"

Ulster nodded. "Even though the Maya and the Aztecs shared the land that is now known as Mexico, the two civilizations were bitter enemies. The only time they came together was on the battlefield. Thankfully, the two groups were separated by hundreds of miles of desert, or else they would have fought more frequently."

"But I thought you said . . . ah, never mind. You'd know better than I."

Ulster encouraged him to continue. "Go on. Speak your mind."

He shrugged reluctantly. "Yesterday on the phone, didn't you say Hamilton had a theory about the Maya and the Aztecs? Something about a shared language."

"Not a language, my boy, but you are correct: I did mention a theory during our conversation. I have to admit I'm surprised that you remembered. You normally tune me out."

"It was a quick chat. I didn't have time to tune you out."

Ulster laughed. "Unfortunately, the theory Terrence mentioned was quite speculative. As far as I know, he never had definitive proof. He based his entire hypothesis on some shared terminology that he had discovered in the histories of both civilizations."

Maria furrowed her brow. "What kind of terminology?"

Ulster explained. "As you probably know, the written languages of the Maya and the Aztec were radically different. The Mayan language was a mixture of phonetic symbols and logograms, which are visual characters that represent words. In later years, it evolved into a highly complex language that was used to describe their way of life in great detail. Instead of a pure alphabet, glyphs were used to correspond to nouns, verbs, adjectives, and so forth. In many ways, the structure is similar to the modern languages of the Americas."

"What about the Aztecs?" she asked.

"By comparison, the Aztec language was rudimentary. It was nothing more than a series of mnemonics and logograms that weren't meant to be read. It was a language that was meant to be *told*. Their codices were essentially pictographic aids for recalling events. The details and the flourishes of the story came from the orator, not from the written word itself."

Jones frowned. "If that's the case, how could they have shared terminology?"

"The same way that a word in English can have the same meaning as a character in Mandarin Chinese. They may look nothing alike, yet the translation is similar."

Jones scratched his head. "Then what's the big deal? If two languages from halfway around the world have similarities, what's so remarkable about shared terminology between the Aztec and the Maya? I would think it would be a bigger deal if they *didn't* share similarities."

"You are correct. Two languages from the same region should have occasional traits in common, and the Aztec and Maya languages certainly did. But what Hamilton was suggesting went beyond terminology. During the course of his research, he came across what he called 'a shared perspective' in the two languages—and that is something entirely different."

"'A shared perspective'? What does that mean?" Maria asked.

Hundreds of examples from ancient history rushed through his head, but he knew most of them would be far too advanced for Payne and Jones. With that in mind, he chose something from modern history to illustrate his point. "For as long as I can remember, there has been conflict in the Middle East. Egypt, Iraq, Israel, Jordan, Lebanon, Saudi Arabia, Syria, and so on—they are constantly arguing about every topic under the sun. Correct?"

Payne, Jones, and Maria nodded in agreement.

"Jonathon," Ulster said, "you have spent a lot of time in that region. If you had to wager, do you think you'll see peace in the Middle East in your lifetime?"

"Not a chance."

"Why not?"

"There's no middle ground for a settlement. Each country has its own set of beliefs, which prevents them from giving in."

"In other words, they have different ideologies."

"For the most part, yes."

Ulster nodded. "As hard as this is to believe, those countries are less than three hundred miles apart. That's much closer than the major cities of the Aztec and the Maya ever were. And yet the basic ideologies of those countries are so drastically different they can't agree on anything."

"I think all of them would agree with that," Jones said, smiling.

Ulster missed the joke. "Now, let's shine the spotlight on one place in particular: the city of Jerusalem. It is considered a holy city by three major religions: Judaism, Christianity, and Islam. In less than one square mile, the Old City contains key sites from all three religions, including the Western Wall, the Temple Mount, the Church of the Holy Sepulchre, the Dome of the Rock, and al-Aqsa Mosque. Needless to say, this proximity breeds conflict. During its long history, Jerusalem has been captured and recaptured a remarkable forty-four times."

Familiar with Ulster's methods, Payne knew how important it was to keep him on task. Otherwise, he would ramble all day. "What's your point?"

"My point? Ah, yes, my point! Let me ask you a simple question, one with a complex answer. If a terrorist blew up the city of Jerusalem, who would get blamed?"

"A black guy," Jones cracked.

Payne couldn't help but laugh.

Maria, who was still trying to understand the concept of a shared perspective, managed to stay focused. "Everyone would get blamed. The Jews would blame the Christians. The Christians would blame the Muslims. The Muslims would blame the Jews, and so on."

Ulster nodded. "One catastrophic event in a single city, yet multiple perspectives. Why? Because all of these groups have different ideologies. And different ideologies lead to different points of view. And different points of view lead to different interpretations. And different interpretations lead to different historical records. As a historian, that leads to an interesting dilemma: How do you determine what really happened? If you're truly neutral, the odds are pretty good that it will be a combination of all of these accounts rolled into one. Right?"

"Right," she said. "You look for the common ground."

"But what do you do if there's only one perspective? Do you trust it?"

"I guess that depends."

"Of course it does. It depends on a lot of things, most of which are so transparent I won't even bother discussing them. What about two perspectives?"

"The same thing. It depends."

"On what?"

"Whether or not the perspectives are too similar to be distinct. For instance, if I interviewed two Christians about the bombing of Jerusalem, there's a good chance they would agree on certain things that were influenced by their beliefs. The odds are pretty good they wouldn't blame a fellow Christian for the violence. They would blame a Muslim or a Jew."

Ulster nodded in agreement. "Let's go one step further. What if you were given two accounts of the bombing, one from a Christian and one from a Muslim, and both of them said the exact same thing? Would that make a difference?"

"Definitely."

"Why?"

"Because they never agree on anything, yet they agreed on this."

Ulster smiled. "That, my dear, is a *shared perspective*. As a historian, you live for that moment when all of your sources—even countries at war—are saying the exact same thing. That is when you know you have probably found the truth."

Maria paused in thought, trying to remember how they had started down this path. "And Hamilton found something with the Aztec and the Maya? A shared perspective?"

Ulster nodded. "Or so he claimed."

"On what topic?"

"On what *really* happened when the Spanish arrived in the Americas."

51

MARIA STARED AT ULSTER, WAITING FOR AN EX-
planation. "What does *that* mean?"

Ulster grinned with delight. He loved when people were passionate about history. "In the grand scheme of things, what do we
really know about the Spanish colonization of the Americas? After
all, it happened five hundred years ago, long before any of us were
born. And unlike the Jerusalem scenario, we don't have multiple
accounts to sort through, because the Spanish burned every native
codex that they could get their hands on. That means everything
in our modern history books was written from one perspective:
the perspective of Spain."

"What are you saying? Hamilton found something contradictory?"

"Not only contradictory, but *shared*. The last time we spoke,
which was a few weeks ago, he hinted that he had found a shared
perspective between the Aztec and the Maya that would cast doubt
on what really happened in the 1500s. He didn't talk specifics—so

I don't know what aspect of the colonization he was referring to—but he was genuinely excited about it."

"He was excited when I talked to him, too. But he was reluctant to tell me the specifics. He was getting ready to, but he disappeared before he had a chance."

"Sorry to interrupt," Payne said, "but let's get back to the artifacts. Could they possibly relate to any of this? I certainly hope so. Otherwise, we just wasted an hour of daylight on a history lesson that could have waited."

Having worked with Payne before, Ulster wasn't the least bit offended by his bluntness. He knew the clock was ticking, and Hamilton's life was possibly at stake. "Yes, of course, let's talk about the artifacts. Obviously, I haven't examined them in depth, but based on first impressions, I would say the only possible connection between the Aztec and the Mayan relics is one I'm not familiar with. In other words, we'll need Hamilton or a member of his team to tell us how they are related."

"Speaking of his team, did you have any luck running down their names?"

Ulster shook his head. "I made a number of calls last evening to colleagues who know Hamilton a lot better than I, and all of them said the same thing. He was working on a passion project that he refused to talk about. As for possible names, no one was forthcoming. Either they didn't know, or they weren't willing to tell me."

"If you had to guess, which one was it?"

Ulster puffed out his chest. "I'd say they didn't know whom he was working with. As you know, I am pretty good at sniffing out the truth."

"Really?" Jones said. "Because we lie to you *all* the time."

"You do?"

"No," he said, laughing, "but I think I just proved a point."

Payne rolled his eyes. It wasn't the time for jokes. "Petr, do me a favor. Keep looking through the artifacts. The more we know about Hamilton's project, the better."

"No problem."

"And, Maria, if it's okay with you, please give him a hand."

"Of course," she said.

"What about me?" Jones asked.

"Inspect Hamilton's weapons and make sure they're in working order. If push comes to shove, I want to know what we can count on."

He smiled at the possibilities. "Gladly."

✠   ✠   ✠

NEARLY TWENTY HOURS HAD passed since he had spoken to Randy Raskin. In the real world, that wasn't a lot of time. During a mission, that was an eternity. Although he knew his friend was constantly busy, it was unlike Raskin to take so long on such a simple request. Payne decided to call him at the Pentagon to find out why.

Raskin answered his office line. "Research."

"Hey, Randy, it's Jon. Do you have a minute?"

Raskin paused momentarily. Then he cleared his throat as if making a point. "I'm sorry, Mr. Payne, I can't assist you today. Perhaps I can transfer your call to another extension."

Payne froze. Something was wrong. In all their time working together, Raskin had never referred to him as Mr. Payne or acted in such a professional manner. Normally, Raskin greeted him with an insult or threatened to hang up on him. He certainly never asked to transfer his call. To Payne, it meant one of two things: Either a superior was standing in Raskin's office, or Payne's request had infringed upon an active mission of the U.S. government—in which case, a superior was monitoring Raskin's calls. Either way, Big Brother was definitely listening in. With that in mind, Payne decided to fish for information without getting Raskin in any additional trouble.

"No problem, Randy. Unfortunately, I'm on the road right now, so I don't have a list of extensions in front of me. Do me a favor and transfer me to the correct department."

"Sure thing, Mr. Payne."

Raskin punched a few keys on his computer, and the call was rerouted to a female operator at the George Bush Center for Intelligence in Fairfax County, Virginia. It was only a few miles from Arlington, but a completely different world. One filled with spooks and deceit.

She answered in a monotone. "ID number, please."

"ID?" he said, confused. "Who am I speaking to?"

"ID number, please."

"Sorry, ma'am, I'm kind of at a loss right now. I was transferred from a research analyst at the Pentagon to this extension. What department is this?"

She paused a few seconds before answering. "Langley."

"Langley?" he said, surprised. He had been in Langley, Virginia, twice in the past ten years, and on both occasions it was to visit the headquarters of the Central Intelligence Agency. The thought of those trips made him squirm. Although he had worked with a number of operatives over the years—the I in MANIACs stood for Intelligence—he found the Executive Office to be way too political for his taste. Based on his experience, they cared more about covering their asses in the media than covering their assets in the field. "Is this the CIA?"

"ID number, please."

"Ma'am, I just told you, I was transferred to this extension by the Pentagon. How do I know what number to give you if I don't know what department this is?"

Click. She hung up.

"Thanks, sweetie. You've been a big help."

Afterward, he stared at his phone for several seconds. He hoped Raskin would send him a text message to apologize for his professionalism or, better yet, to explain the situation they had stumbled into. But after a minute of nothing, he gave up hope and went to discuss things with Jones. He ducked his head into the garage and said, "Hey, DJ, do you have a second?"

"Sure," said Jones, who had just started to inspect Hamilton's weapons. He wiped his hands on a rag as he walked past Maria and Ulster. "We'll be outside. Scream if you need us."

Lost in a world of artifacts, they barely noticed his departure.

Payne waited for him in the driveway. He tried to play it cool by leaning against a stone wall that defined the rear of the property, but his stress level was obvious. Jones could see it on his face and in his posture. Something had happened.

"What's wrong?" Jones demanded.

"What do you mean?"

"You came out here to talk to Randy. Five minutes later, you're talking to me. Obviously, something's wrong."

"You're right. Something *is* wrong, but I don't know what it is."

"Meaning?"

"Randy wouldn't talk to me."

"What's he pouting about now?"

"He wasn't pouting. He wasn't *allowed* to talk to me."

"Why not?" Jones asked.

"I don't know. But he called me *Mr. Payne*—"

"He did *what*?"

"Then he transferred my call to Langley."

"Langley?"

"Yes, Langley."

"Shit."

Payne nodded. "Yeah. That pretty much sums it up."

Jones paused in thought. It took a moment for everything to

sink in. Even then, the picture in his head was still fuzzy. "What triggered their interest?"

"Could've been anything: Hamilton's financials, the serial numbers on the rifles, his disappearance. For all we know, the Agency grabbed Hamilton."

"Not a chance in hell. The CIA would *never* abduct an American on foreign soil." Jones kept a straight face for less than three seconds before he cracked up. "Damn! I thought I could say that without laughing."

"Come on, DJ, *focus*. We need to figure out our next step."

Jones shook his head. "No, we need to figure out his *last* step."

"Whose last step? Hamilton's?"

"No. Randy's."

52

PAYNE WAS CONFUSED BY JONES'S COMMENT ABOUT Raskin. "What good will that do?"

"You know how the Agency works. They have ten thousand analysts whose sole job is to search data streams for red flags. As soon as one of those pops up, they make a call and their supervisors intervene. Obviously Randy did *something* to get noticed. If we can figure out what he did, maybe we can figure out why the CIA is interested in this mess."

"Why don't we just call one of our contacts at Langley?"

Jones shook his head. "Randy has a higher security clearance than anyone we know at the Agency. Hell, *we* have a higher security clearance than anyone we know at the Agency. If he wasn't allowed to tell us, then we're on our own when it comes to Hamilton."

"Wait. Should we stop looking for him?"

"That depends. Did Randy tell you to stop?"

"No."

"Did anyone at the CIA?"

"Not really. They hung up on me."

Jones laughed. "In that case, fuck 'em! No one told us to stand down, so we have every right to look for Hamilton."

"Yeah, you're probably right. But . . ."

"But, what?"

Payne pointed at the garage. "I don't think we should tell Petr and Maria."

"Why not?"

"Technically speaking, we wouldn't be violating any laws by mentioning the Agency's interest—especially since we don't know what their interest is—but I doubt they would want two foreign nationals to know anything about their involvement."

"That's too bad."

"Why's that?"

"Petr would get a boner if he knew the CIA was involved."

Payne grimaced. "Why are you obsessed with that?"

"With what?"

"Petr's groin. That's the second time you've used that joke in the last twenty-four hours."

"Really?"

"Yeah, really. Maria yelled at you the last time. She called you 'crass.'"

"Oh," he said, "that explains it. I tend to block out things when she starts yelling."

Payne smiled. "I guess that means you have no idea why we're in Mexico, because she's been yelling since we got here."

Jones stared at him. "We're in *Mexico*?"

Payne laughed. "Anyway, let's get back to Randy. How do we figure out what got him noticed?"

Jones scratched his head in thought. "I wasn't privy to any of your calls, so I don't know what was said. How many were there?"

"Three, counting today."

"Forget about today. Whatever got him flagged happened before today. What did you ask him to do first?"

Payne tried to remember the details of their first conversation. "I asked him to run a background search on Hamilton. Personal, criminal, financial, the works."

"Anything else?"

"Not in the first call, but . . ." Payne paused for a moment. "Actually, I take that back. I also asked him to run the serial number on Hamilton's gun. You know, the Mexican Special from his briefcase. Because of its age, he told me not to get my hopes up."

"What about the second call?"

Payne closed his eyes in thought. "I asked him to run the serial numbers on the AKs. After that, we discussed the blacked-out security feed from the hotel. He wasn't sure how it was done, but he promised to look into it."

"Randy didn't know how it was done?"

"No, but he was fairly confident he could catch the hacker."

"Just a second. What if it was also the other way around?"

"I don't follow."

"What if Randy *tried* to trace the hack—and traced it right back to the CIA? I'm sure that would have set off all kinds of bells and whistles at the Agency."

Payne considered the theory. "I don't know. Randy's a sneaky son of a bitch. Do you really think they would have caught him?"

"Good point. Then how about this? Randy traced it back to the CIA and was legally obligated to get clearance before he could tell us anything. They told him to fuck off, and he had no choice but to deny our request for assistance."

Payne nodded. "Now, *that* sounds more realistic."

"Okay, then let's assume that's what happened. If so, there's a very good chance that he ran background on Hamilton before he was cock-blocked by the CIA. Same thing with his weapons search. He would have done those first because they aren't labor-intensive. Punch in some names and numbers, and his computer would have done the rest."

"So, what are you saying?"

"I'm saying there's a damn good chance he compiled our data before the CIA got involved. If so, that's very good news."

"Good? How can that be good? If he can't send it, we can't use it."

Jones smiled. "Who said he didn't send it?"

In recent years, Payne's knowledge of computers and gadgets had increased exponentially, mostly because Jones had given him so much crap about being the CEO and majority owner of a technology-based company and having less computer ability than the average third grader. With a lot of hard work, Payne's expertise would now rival most college students', which was an amazing leap in such a short amount of time. Unfortunately, that meant his comprehension was still *way* behind Jones's, who actually built computers in his workshop for fun. Jones wasn't as skilled as Raskin—then again, who was?—but he had enough know-how to develop a backdoor file-sharing system that allowed him to access encrypted documents from anywhere in the world.

Payne said, "I checked my in-box. Nothing from Randy."

"Does that surprise you? He was probably afraid you were going to accidentally forward it to everyone on your contact list. Again."

"That happened *once*. Can you please let it die?"

"Not while I'm alive."

"*That* can be arranged."

Jones dismissed the threat as he pulled out his phone. He punched in his password, then opened the program that allowed him to view all the files that had been transferred to his computer system in Pittsburgh. "I got something."

"From Randy?"

He nodded. "Came in late last night. I'm downloading it now."

"What is it?"

He glanced at Payne. "I don't know. I'm downloading it now."

"Sorry. I'm anxious."

Jones laughed as he waited. "Okay, I got it. Let's take a look."

He hit a few keys and opened the file on his phone. As suspected, it was a comprehensive background report on Hamilton. It included personal data (addresses, phone numbers, et cetera), criminal records (nothing but a few traffic citations), and a financial profile (he was practically broke). For the most part, nothing helped Payne and Jones with their search until they came across a credit card that Raskin had highlighted. It showed several minor purchases in recent weeks, including one at a gas station in Piste, Mexico.

Jones pointed at the screen. "Will you look at that?"

Payne nodded, intrigued. "Piste? What's near Piste?"

"I don't know. Let's go ask."

The two of them ducked inside the garage, where Maria and Ulster were still hard at work on the artifacts. She glanced back when they heard the door open.

"Where have you two been?" she asked.

"Outside," Jones said. "Are either of you familiar with Piste, Mexico?"

Ulster turned and nodded. "It's a dusty little town, a few hours west of here. Nothing more than a speck on the map. Why do you ask?"

"If it's just a speck, why do you know it?"

"Why? Because it's the closest town to a famous Mayan site called Chichén Itzá. It's less than a mile away."

Maria stared at Jones. "Why? What's going on?"

"We just got a financial report on Hamilton. One of the items was a credit card statement, which lists a recent purchase at a gas station in Piste."

"That's great! He probably filled up there before he drove to Cancún."

Payne shook his head. "Somehow I doubt it."

"You doubt it? Why do you say that?"

He stared at her. "The purchase happened last night."

53

C H I C H É N   I T Z Á ,   M E X I C O
(1 1 1   M I L E S   S O U T H W E S T   O F   C A N C Ú N)

THICK VEGETATION LINED BOTH SIDES OF THE ROAD. It blocked their view of the countryside as they drove toward Chichén Itzá. Nearly three hours in length, the trip was uneventful. Except for an occasional tour bus, the only other sign of civilization was a constant stream of tollbooths that seemed to pop up every other mile. By the time they reached Piste, a rural town by the famous archaeological site, Jones had counted more tollbooths than exits.

During their journey, the four of them discussed the significance of Hamilton's credit card activity. Ulster assured the group that his personal credit card purchases were commonly off by a few days when he traveled abroad. This was particularly common in developing countries like Mexico, where technology lagged behind. Eventually, his bank in Switzerland would straighten out the transaction dates, but sometimes that wouldn't occur for a week or two after he had received his statement.

Payne and Jones were familiar with the lag time, but they still thought it was worth the drive. With little else to go on, they wanted to investigate the possibility that the purchase had been made by a member of Hamilton's team. According to Ulster, Hamilton often worked with unpaid interns on his research trips, so it stood to reason that he might have given them access to his credit card in order to buy supplies for their campsite. If so, they hoped to track down his research team somewhere near the Mayan site and get information about Hamilton.

To do so, they had to start at the beginning.

The place where the purchase had been made the night before.

Much to their surprise, the gas station was fairly modern—at least compared to the rest of the area, which seemed to be a few decades behind the times. There was a hospital, a fruit market, and a few restaurants near the main road, but there were also packs of feral dogs that roamed the dusty alleyways. Houses, for the most part, were hidden from view, tucked behind a thick wall of vegetation that looked remarkably similar to the jungle they had been staring at for miles. It was the main reason that so many Mayan sites were still being discovered today.

They were hidden in the jungle.

Jones pulled the SUV next to the pump and took a few minutes to top off the SUV's tank. Out here, in the middle of nowhere, gas stations were few and far between. No sense taking any chances. Meanwhile, Payne headed into the station with Maria, who would serve as his interpreter in case the clerk couldn't speak English. A bell mounted above the door announced their arrival with a loud jingle. Payne walked to the front counter and waited for the owner, who had been stocking shelves in the back of the store.

Wearing a white apron with green trim, the gray-haired man shuffled forward. He had a name tag that read EDUARDO. He greeted them with a friendly wave. *"Hola."*

"Hola," Maria said. *"Hablas inglés?"*

Eduardo nodded and smiled. "Yes."

Maria glanced at Payne. "He said yes."

"Thanks, honey. I figured that one out. Now go wait in the car."

She wandered off. "No, thanks. I think I'll shop instead."

"Great. Go do that."

Eduardo said nothing. He just kept smiling.

Payne focused on him. "Sir, I was hoping you could help us out."

"Do you need directions? I am bad with directions. All the signs are written in Spanish."

Payne laughed. "That's pretty funny. How many times have you used that line?"

Eduardo frowned. "Funny? What is funny about my problem? I cannot read Spanish. I can only read Mayan. And you make jokes?"

"Oh, man, I am *so* sorry. I didn't mean to offend you. I thought . . ."

Eduardo kept a straight face for a few seconds. Then he burst out laughing. "Now, that is funny! You should see your face. It is red like tomato. You thought I only read Mayan."

Payne stammered. "Well, how should I know?"

"How? Look around the store! Everything is written in Spanish."

Payne groaned. "Okay, I guess you're right. Now I feel like an idiot."

Eduardo kept laughing. "Do not feel dumb. I trick people all the time. This job is boring without jokes. I hope you are not mad."

"Mad? Not at all. In fact, I'm glad you tricked me."

"Really? Why is that?"

"Now you owe me."

Eduardo shrugged. "Maybe. What you need?"

"Were you working last night?"

"*Sí*. That means 'yes.'"

"Yeah, I know."

"If you knew I was working, why did you ask?"

Payne rolled his eyes. This guy joked more than Jones. He needed to put a stop to the levity, or this would take all day. "On Friday night, a friend of ours was kidnapped in Cancún. We've been waiting for a ransom call ever since."

Eduardo blushed. Now he was the one who felt like an idiot. "I am sorry for your loss. Mexico is dangerous place."

"Last night, someone used his credit card at your store. We were hoping you could remember what the person looked like. It might give us our best lead to date."

"I am sorry. I cannot help."

"Why not?"

"I did not see anyone."

Payne nodded in understanding. He pulled out an American twenty-dollar bill and placed it on the counter. He wasn't sure what the going rate for a shakedown was in Mexico, but he figured this would be a good place to start. "Does this help your memory?"

Eduardo tucked the money into his pocket. "Nothing wrong with my memory. I remember just fine. I was working in the back office all night. That is why I see no one."

Payne growled but didn't ask for the money back. "Who was working out front?"

"My son."

"Is he around?"

"No. But even if he was, he would remember nothing."

"Why's that?"

"He drinks on the job."

"You let him drink at work?"

Eduardo shrugged. "He works for free, so I let him drink."

"Wonderful."

"It is good system. It has been working for years."

Payne took a deep breath. This was going nowhere fast. "Maria! Time to go. He can't help us out. We'll have to look around the site."

"Hold up," she shouted from the back. "I'm getting supplies."

Eduardo smiled. "She is getting supplies."

"Yeah, I heard. Thanks."

He kept smiling. "While you wait, you look at tape?"

"Tape? What tape?"

He pointed at the security camera. It was barely visible above the counter. "Tape of customers. We keep tape for twenty-four hours."

"You have a security tape? From last night?"

He nodded. "Like I say, Mexico is *dangerous* place. Tourists cannot be trusted. They are worse than conquistadores. They come in here and steal my Twinkies right off the shelves. Do you know what we call Twinkies in Mexico? *Submarinos*."

Payne ignored the Spanish lesson. "Where's the monitor?"

Eduardo signaled for him to follow. "Come. It is in my office. I show you."

Five minutes later, Eduardo was rewinding the tape for Payne and Maria. Unlike the digital setup at the Fiesta Americana, this system was basic—one angle, no panning or zooming—but it was much better than a drunk witness. If the credit card statement was accurate, Payne knew the purchase had been made at 9:32 P.M. on Saturday night. They decided to start at 10:00 P.M. and work their way back from there, just in case the time stamp was off.

"What should we look for?" she asked.

Payne shrugged. "You'd know better than I would."

"Why's that?"

"Weren't you an unpaid intern in college?"

She nodded. "Yeah. I guess I was."

"And what did your fellow classmates look like?"

"I don't know. I guess they looked like me."

"Great. Then we'll look for hot Italian women."

She laughed at the description. "You think I'm hot?"

"Maria, this is *Mexico*. It's, like, two hundred degrees outside. *Everyone* is hot."

She taunted him softly. "You think I'm hot."

"Shut up," he whispered back. "I didn't say that."

Eduardo looked at them. "Are you two married?"

"What?" they blurted in unison. "No!"

"That is too bad. You have much potential. You argue like married couple."

"Don't I know it," Payne said.

"My son is married. He does not like it. *That* is why he drinks at work."

"What about you?" she asked.

Eduardo sighed. "I *used* to be married. I did not like it, either. That is why I let him."

Payne nodded. "Now it makes perfect sense."

Just then, a female customer flashed across the screen. Since the tape was still rewinding, everything she did was fast and in reverse. Eduardo tapped the PLAY button, but by the time he hit it, she had backed out the door. "Should I go forward?"

Payne shook his head. "Just play it from here. We want to see her face."

The camera, mounted high above the cash register, offered a clear view of the front counter but didn't show much of the store. If Eduardo was trying to catch the Twinkie thief, he was going about it wrong. As the customer roamed the aisles, all they could see was her waist and a pair of jeans. Everything else was obscured because of the angle of the lens.

"I can't see anything," Maria complained.

Payne reached into his pocket and pulled out his phone. "That's okay. The person we're looking for used a credit card. We'll see her when she comes to the counter."

The customer kept moving, up and down the rows.

"What are you doing with that?"

"I want to take her picture. That way we can show it around."

She nodded. "Good thinking."

After nearly a minute, the customer walked toward the camera. She had a bottle of water in one hand and a box of cereal in the other. She placed both items on the counter, then pointed outside, as if to say she also wanted to pay for a tank of gas. Unfortunately, her face was hidden by a floppy hat. The kind someone would wear if she were going to be in the sun all day.

"Look up!" Payne screamed at the tape. "Look at the camera!"

Maria shouted, too. "Look up!"

A moment later, they got their wish. The customer took off her hat, wiped the sweat off her forehead with the back of her arm, then glanced directly into the lens. She looked at the camera for several seconds, giving them a chance to memorize the freckles on her face and her distinctive red hair. Then she punctuated her stare with a sly smile.

Payne snapped a photo of her. "Gotcha."

In reality, it was the other way around.

54

NAMED ONE OF THE NEW SEVEN WONDERS OF THE World (taking its place alongside such monuments as the Taj Mahal and the Great Wall of China), Chichén Itzá is a pre-Columbian archaeological site in the northern center of the Yucatán Peninsula. Built and rebuilt by the Maya civilization over a span of nearly a thousand years, the ancient city is one of the most popular destinations in Mexico.

After parking near the entrance, the foursome hiked toward the site, where they hoped to find the mysterious redhead who had used Hamilton's credit card the night before. To aid their effort, Payne forwarded her photo to each of their cell phones, which allowed them to search more efficiently. They flashed Tiffany's picture to everyone they passed on the dirt path that led to the ruins, but to no avail. Despite the thick vegetation that blocked their view, they sensed something significant was looming just around the corner. And they were right. After a slight bend to the northeast, the trail opened into a large courtyard of dirt and grass.

In the center was a pyramid known as El Castillo.

All of them stopped and stared in awe.

Originally known as the Temple of Kukulkan, the stone pyramid stands almost a hundred feet in height, with a square base that is nearly twice as long. Built by the Maya sometime between A.D. 1000 and A.D. 1200, the pyramid honored Kukulkan—a feathered serpent deity that resembled the Aztec god Quetzalcoatl—and served as a solar calendar. Each of the structure's four stairways contains 91 steps. When counting the top platform as another step, the pyramid has 365 steps, one for each day of the year. But more amazingly, the pyramid is positioned at such a precise angle that a solar phenomenon occurs here in the spring and fall.

Cackling with delight, Ulster urged them to follow as he danced toward the north side of the pyramid. They weren't sure why he was so excited, but they couldn't wait to see. He called to them over his shoulder. "Tell me, are any of you familiar with the plumed serpent that attacks this pyramid twice a year?"

Jones joked, "That still happens? I thought Godzilla killed that thing years ago."

Ulster laughed. "I'll take that as a no."

"Yep. That's definitely a no."

"Wonderful! That means I get to tell you everything!"

Payne groaned softly. They weren't there for a history lesson. They were there for the redhead. "We don't have time for *everything*. You have to keep this short."

"Of course, my boy, of course! No problem at all. I'll give you the twenty-minute version instead of the two-hour lecture."

"Petr, I'm serious!"

Ulster laughed. "Don't worry. I'm just teasing. I promise I'll keep this short."

He led them to the bottom of a staircase that bisected the northern face of the pyramid. Stone balustrades, each ending in the carved head of a serpent, bordered the stairs on the left and the right. With his knees firmly against a restraining rope that surrounded the pyramid, Ulster reached out and tried to touch one of the serpents' heads, which jutted out from the pyramid. He wanted to feel the stone on his fingertips. Sadly, his round body and short arms prevented it.

He sighed dejectedly. "So close and yet so far."

Jones was amused by the effort. "No one's looking. Step over the damn rope."

Ulster shook his head. "If I do, you will, too. And Jonathon. And Maria. Before you know it, the pyramid will crumble, and I'll be the one to blame. I can't have that on my conscience."

"You're kidding, right?"

"Not at all."

Jones considered their options. "What if I pick you up and *throw* you onto the pyramid? Then it would be my fault, not yours."

Ulster patted his belly. "The pyramid would crumble even sooner, I'm afraid."

Payne tried to hurry this along. "What were you saying about a serpent?"

"Ah, yes! The plumed serpent of El Castillo! Thank you for reminding me." He turned his back to the pyramid and faced the group. "As you probably know, the Maya were phenomenal astronomers. Without telescopes or lenses, they predicted eclipses, the rise and set of the Pleiades, and the movement of planets and stars."

"How did they do that?" Maria asked.

"With carefully positioned window slats in their observatories."

"I don't follow."

To illustrate his point, he put his two hands together, as if he was about to pray to the heavens above. Then he separated his hands by half an inch. By staring through the space in between, he was able to focus on a narrow part of the sky. "The Maya constructed their buildings with such precision that they could chart celestial movement from a single room. One day the sun would move across the sky in one window slat. A month later it would move across the sky in the next window slat. And so on. By charting the sun's progress throughout the hours, days, and months, they knew where the sun would be with the accuracy of a marksman."

"And the snake?" Payne asked.

Ulster pointed at the serpent head to the west, the one he had been trying to touch. "As amazing as this sounds, the Maya angled this pyramid in such a way that sunlight, in the form of a serpent, crawls down this balustrade at sunset during the spring and autumn equinox until it is reunited with its head below. At any one moment, the snake is nothing more than sunlight and a series of triangle shadows—cast by the western corners of the pyramid—but viewed with time-lapse photography, the serpent of light appears to slither along this railing."

Jones blurted, "Are you serious?"

Ulster nodded as he walked toward the western corner. Then he turned back and pointed at the side of the balustrade. "Notice the cut of the stones. They were shaped to look like the scales of a snake. When the light shines upon them, it truly looks like a serpent."

"That's *really* cool."

"Twice a year, tens of thousands of people gather here at sunset to watch the return of Kukulkan. The biannual celebration is so popular, the Mexican government had to do something to lessen the massive crowds. So they started to hold nighttime shows throughout the year, using spotlights to simulate the serpent effect. In some ways, it's even more pronounced because they can do it after sunset when there's far more contrast between light and shadow."

Payne stared up at the pyramid. It truly was an architectural marvel. One of the most impressive buildings he had ever seen. "When was this built?"

"Approximately one thousand years ago—give or take a hundred years. The temple inside is even older, though."

Maria glanced at him. "The temple inside?"

He nodded. "In Mesoamerica, it was quite common to build one monument on top of another. The Aztecs did it. The Maya did it. Even the Spanish did it. Why rip something down and start from scratch when it's far more economical to build on top of what was already there?"

"They did that here?"

He nodded again. "Back in the 1930s, archaeologists didn't know what was inside El Castillo. Keep in mind this was less than a decade after Howard Carter's discovery of King Tut's tomb in Egypt, so the whole world was a little treasure-crazy at the time. The Mexican government, hoping for a possible windfall, dug several exploratory tunnels into the pyramid until they found a staircase *underneath* the one we're looking at now. The hidden stairs led to a temple chamber, where they found a Chac Mool and a jaguar-shaped throne."

"What's a Chac Mool?" she asked.

"A Chac Mool is a sculpture of a reclining figure holding a bowl on his lap or stomach. You'll see them throughout Mesoamerica. No one knows their origin or significance, but many believe that sacrifices—whether human or not—were placed in the bowl to appease the gods."

Jones looked at Ulster. "Just a sculpture and a throne? No gold?"

He shook his head. "Despite their expertise in other fields, the Maya were latecomers in the field of metallurgy. In some parts of the New World, the craft was practiced for two thousand years *before* the arrival of Christopher Columbus, yet as far as we can tell, the Maya never mastered the art. Though some gold disks and ornaments were found in the sacred well of Chichén Itzá, many archaeologists think that they were made by craftsmen from the lower isthmus, not from artisans who grew up locally."

Jones grumbled. "How disappointing! You know how much I like gold."

Ulster smiled. "I know you do. Unfortunately, it was the Aztecs, not the Maya, who had all the gold. At the time of the Spanish conquest, Montezuma the Second was receiving more than two tons of gold in tribute every year. Of course, the conquistadores never found most of it. To this day, the mystery of the Aztec gold has never been solved."

Payne rolled his eyes. This was how it always was with Ulster. He started on one topic—the shadow serpent of El Castillo—and ended up talking about something completely unrelated. If not for meals, the man would never shut up. "The Aztecs? *Really?* We're standing in front of a Mayan pyramid, and you're talking about the Aztecs? I thought you promised the short version."

Ulster nodded, admonished. "Jonathon, my boy, you are quite right! I'll save my Aztec lecture for another day. While we're here, let's focus on what's *truly* important."

Payne tested him. "Which is?"

Ulster shrugged. "I'm afraid I can't recall."

Payne held up his phone. "The redhead in this photo."

"Ah, yes! Now I remember. Let's go find that trollop before she disappears."

55

CHICHÉN ITZÁ WAS A MAJOR ECONOMIC POWER DUR-
ing its heyday. As such, it was the focal point of a major
trade route that brought unavailable resources—such as gold from
Central America and obsidian from the west—into the region. But
outsiders brought more than commerce inside the city's walls.
They also brought ideas for the city's design. Unlike many "pure"
Mayan cities in Mesoamerica, Chichén Itzá is a mixture of several
architectural styles, including the Puuc style found in the northern
lowlands and the Toltec style of central Mexico.

The buildings themselves are grouped in a series of architectural sets, which were separated at one time by a succession of low
walls. Most of the stone walls are no longer there, but the sets still
remain, spread throughout the city like tiny suburbs. The most
famous area is called the Great North Platform. It includes El
Castillo, the Temple of the Warriors, the Platform of Venus, and a
grass field that caught Payne's eye: the Great Ball Court.

Temporarily distracted from his search, Payne walked over to

Ulster, who was showing Tiffany's photo to a group of tourists. "Do you have a minute?"

Ulster nodded. "Of course, my boy. Of course!"

"I know I just chastised you for your lecture about the Aztecs, but . . ."

"Yes?"

Payne pointed at the field. "Is that what I think it is?"

Ulster grinned with delight. "I am *so* happy you asked. Knowing your background in sports, I was dying to tell you about it, but I heeded your warning and focused on the task at hand."

Payne shrugged. "After all of our adventures together—talking about art, religion, and whatever—this is *finally* something that I care about. Therefore, I'm officially calling a time-out with regard to the search. Please tell me about the field."

"With pleasure," he said as they walked toward the playing court. "Known as the Mesoamerican ball game, the sport can be traced to fifteen hundred years before Christ. The first fields were discovered—"

Payne cut him off. "Hold up! I'm stopping you right there. Do *not* ruin this moment for me. For the first time in our history, we finally get to talk about sports. I don't care about its origins, or its symbolism, or anything else that would fill a university lecture. Just give me the basics. The ball. The rules. The players. Nothing else matters. That's the beauty of sports."

Ulster scratched his beard in thought. "Just the basics?"

"Yes. Just the basics."

"I don't know if I can talk like that."

Payne smiled. "Try."

Ulster gathered his thoughts as he stared at the field. Measuring 545 feet wide by 223 feet long, it was the largest ball court in ancient Mesoamerica. Two stone walls, nearly 39 feet in height, ran the entire length of the end zones. High in the middle of each wall was a stone ring, carved with intertwining serpents. "Let's start with the field."

"Great."

"Unlike some modern sports, the dimensions of the field varied from place to place. This one is by far the largest ever discovered, more than five times as large as some other courts. However, some things remained constant. There were high walls on both ends, with rings in the middle. And the object of the game was to get the ball through the hole."

"Like basketball."

"Yes and no. Instead of scoring through the top of a hoop, the ring was turned on its side, allowing players to shoot through the left or the right. Points were accumulated by a team for accomplishing certain feats, such as hitting the opponent's wall or hitting the ring itself. Ultimately, though, the goal was to get the ball through the hole. If that occurred, the shooting team automatically won the game."

Payne walked toward the left wall and stared at the ring. With an approximate diameter of a basketball hoop, it was more than twenty feet in the air. "One goal and the game was over? That sounds pretty easy to me. Give me ten shots, and I bet I can make one."

"Trust me, my boy, it's harder than it looks. The sport is still played in parts of Mesoamerica, and a typical game lasts for hours. Oftentimes no goals are scored."

"Hours? How could it last for hours?"

"Unlike basketball, you can't use your hands. Players were forced to use their elbows, hips, and legs."

Payne laughed. "Yeah, that would do it."

"Plus the balls were rather unwieldy."

"How so?"

"They were eight inches in diameter and made of solid rubber.

No bladders. No air pumps. No inflation. Solid rubber balls that weighed eight to nine pounds each."

"That's like a bowling ball."

"A bowling ball that bounced rather high. Of all the inventions the Spanish found in the New World, they were most amazed by the rubber balls. They had never seen such a thing before."

"I guess that says something about the common man. Who cares about the giant pyramid? Tell me more about the bouncy thing. That cracks me up."

Ulster smiled. "Because of the ball's weight, they wore equipment like American football players. Helmets, arm pads, knee pads, and so on. The sport was so brutal that some players died during the game. According to the Spanish, head shots and stomach shots were particularly fatal."

"I bet they were."

"Of course, fatalities *were* expected in ceremonial games—particularly at the end of the match. According to some historians, the captain of the winning team was sacrificed to the gods."

"Wait! They killed the *winner*? What kind of incentive was *that*?"

"It guaranteed the captain's place in heaven."

"Thank God we didn't have that tradition at Annapolis. I was the captain of my football and basketball teams. I would have been killed for sure."

Ulster explained further: "This game has been played for more than three thousand years throughout Mesoamerica. Different cultures had different traditions. The Aztecs, for instance, sacrificed captives before their games to honor their gods. Then they killed members of the *losing* team as food for the gods after the games. Sometimes, due to a scarcity of rubber in Tenochtitlan, the Aztecs would use human heads or skulls instead of balls."

"That's disgusting."

"The Aztecs actually had skull racks positioned near their fields. The racks were rows of pointed sticks where the heads of the losing team would be placed after the game. Obviously, the sticks are long since gone, but I've seen some particularly gruesome artwork that depicted the practice." Ulster glanced at the wall, searching for something. "I believe the Maya had some grisly carvings somewhere near this court. If you'd like, I can try to find them."

"No, thanks. I've seen plenty of dead guys in my lifetime."

Ulster nodded. "I guess you have."

Payne pointed at the base of the wall. It was slanted toward his feet at a forty-five-degree angle. "Is this some kind of anchor to hold the wall up?"

"Architecturally, it might have had that purpose. Athletically, it had served as a bench for players who were waiting to enter the game."

"I'll be damned. The Maya had benchwarmers."

"No," he said, "I don't believe the benches were heated. However, thanks to the direction of the midday sun—"

Payne cut him off. "'Benchwarmers' is a sports term. It means backups. Substitutes. Second-teamers. They aren't on the field, so their job is to warm the bench with their butts."

Ulster laughed. "What a strange-yet-accurate word! I'll be sure to remember it. Here I thought I would be the only one imparting knowledge during this conversation, yet you've managed to teach me a colorful new term. Somehow I feel a tad bit smarter."

"As do I. Thanks for explaining the game to me."

He threw his arm around Payne's shoulders. "This is why we make such a wonderful team. I supply the academics, and you supply—"

"Everything else."

✠   ✠   ✠

WHILE PAYNE AND ULSTER searched for the redhead near the ball court, Jones and Maria focused on the buildings of the Central Group.

To reach that area of the site, they walked along a raised path known as a *sacbe*. The term, meaning "white road" in Yucatec Mayan, was used to describe the paved roads that were built by the Maya. White from the limestone stucco that coated the roadways, more than a hundred *sacbeob* were discovered in Chichén Itzá alone. Not only did they connect different zones inside the site, but they also fanned out to other cities in the region.

After a five-minute walk through a thick forest, they emerged in a large clearing that was shaped like a closing parenthesis. Grass and dirt filled the area between the stone buildings, which started in the north and arched along the clearing toward the south. Of all the structures in the Central Group, the one that caught their eye was the Mayan observatory.

Nicknamed "the snail" because of the spiral staircase inside the domed tower, El Caracol was built high above the surrounding vegetation in the early tenth century. Windows were angled with such precision that sight lines for more than twenty astronomical events—including solstices, equinoxes, solar and lunar eclipses, and the cycles of Venus—were discovered in the structure.

Marveling at the architecture, Jones and Maria strolled toward one of the stone staircases, where a young tour guide was finishing up a brief history of its construction.

"Thanks to the archaeologists at INAH, we are learning more and more about Chichén Itzá every single day," the tour guide explained. "One of the things we know with some certainty is the completion date of this building. According to a carving on the upper platform, this observatory was built in A.D. 906. That is the end of the Late Classic period of Mesoamerican cultures."

He paused for a moment, waiting for a question, then pointed at a ruin to the south. "Next we are heading to a stone temple called La Iglesia. That is Spanish for 'the church.'"

The tour group, which looked bored out of their minds, turned like zombies and started trudging in that direction. Jones hustled to show them a photo of the redhead. Meanwhile, Maria used the opportunity to grab the tour guide's arm.

"Excuse me," she said, politely. "May I ask you a question?"

He nodded excitedly. "Thank goodness! My first one of the day. I'm glad someone is awake. I was beginning to feel like a high school teacher."

"Actually, I'm not *technically* in your group."

He laughed. "That's fine with me. I'm not *technically* a tour guide. I'm just filling in for a friend who's sick."

"Well, it sounds like you know your stuff."

"I'm getting there. I still have a lot to learn, though."

"You're a student?"

He nodded. "Archaeology. I'm working with INAH for the semester."

"INAH? I heard you mention that. What does that stand for?"

"Instituto Nacional de Antropología e Historia."

"Which is . . . ?"

"A government bureau that protects and preserves the historical sites in Mexico. We're currently overseeing the archaeologists who are excavating Old Chichén."

She furrowed her brow. "Old Chichén? What's that?"

He laughed. "I thought you had *one* question."

"Sorry. If you have to go, I completely understand. It's just, well, I'm an archaeologist myself, so I'm kind of excited to learn more about this place."

"I bet you are. Chichén Itzá is a wonderful site, filled with all kinds of historical mysteries. Are you here alone? I'd be happy to show you around."

She shook her head and pointed at Jones. "I'm actually here with him. We were supposed to meet a friend of a friend, but we can't find her anywhere. Maybe you've seen her."

"Maybe I have. What does she look like?"

She pulled out her phone. "Actually, I have a picture of her."

"Wow. You're prepared."

"Let that be a lesson to you. Archaeologists are always prepared."

He smiled and glanced at the screen. "Hey, I *have* seen her. That's Red. She got here last night."

"You know her?"

"Not personally, but I saw her last night. Everyone called her Red."

"You saw her *here*?"

"Not *here*. At the campground by Old Chichén. That's where some of the archaeologists are staying. It's much cheaper than a hotel room." He laughed at himself. "Look who I'm telling? I bet you're staying in a tent yourself. Am I right?"

"Something like that," she lied. "So, how do I get to Old Chichén?"

He pointed at a narrow path that led through the forest to the south. "It's a long hike through the jungle. I hope you have water and bug spray."

She patted her backpack. "Like I said, archaeologists are always prepared."

56

Payne and Ulster caught up with Jones and Maria near a modern gate that led to a jungle path. Signs posted by the Mexican government warned visitors not to trespass. But the foursome ignored the warning and headed down the trail.

Known as *Chichén Viejo* in Spanish, Old Chichén is a relatively new discovery that isn't open to the general public. At least not yet. Archaeologists have been working on the site for nearly a decade, trying to clear the roots and vines that have overwhelmed the ruins, but progress has been slow. Pyramids that once stood above the trees are now buried underneath them. Buildings with exotic titles—such as the Temple of the Owls, the Platform of the Great Turtle, and the Temple of the Monkeys—were even more connected with nature than their names implied, because they were covered in plants, and leaves, and insects. Although many of the ruins have been excavated and restored to their former glory, many more are still waiting to be rescued from the tyranny of neglect and time.

As the group passed discarded columns and fallen shrines along the way, they felt like explorers in a forgotten land. Birds cawed overhead. Animals scampered through the brush. Everywhere they looked, they saw abandoned blocks, carved with serpents and Mayan faces.

Jones loved every second of it. "This. Is. Awesome."

Ulster laughed. "I was thinking the same thing myself. As much as I enjoyed the polished brilliance of El Castillo, there is something special about this. To see a lost city in an ungroomed habitat, it is more—dare I say it?—*authentic*."

Maria agreed. "Good word, Petr. This does feel authentic."

Payne swatted a bug on the back of his neck. "Yeah. Authentic."

After snaking through the jungle for half a mile, the trail opened into a large clearing. Guarded by two carved sentinels that were taller and wider than Payne, the main excavation site was a beehive of activity. Workers walked to and fro, hauling large stones in wheelbarrows and carrying handfuls of equipment. Refurbished temples, which looked like they had been transplanted from the Great North Platform, glistened in the afternoon sun. Orders were being shouted in Spanish, and English, and a few languages that Payne couldn't place. Despite their geographic differences, everyone seemed to be working as a cohesive unit—one unified team trying to put Humpty Dumpty back together again. In many ways, it was inspirational.

Maria glanced around the busy site. "Now what?"

"We demand to see their leader," cracked Jones.

Payne smiled. "*Or* we ask for Red. That was her nickname, right?"

Maria nodded. "That's what the tour guide said."

Jones shrugged. "I guess that would work, too."

Payne led the way, followed by Maria and Ulster, then Jones. Even though they felt safe among the workers, the two ex-MANIACs remembered why they were there. This wasn't a family reunion. This trip was to find a man who had vanished from a crowded hotel. A man who had a trunk full of weapons and artifacts. A man whose disappearance had triggered interest from the CIA. Payne and Jones didn't expect trouble, but they were ready for it just in case.

It took less than ten minutes to find someone who recognized the redhead. He directed the group to the southwest corner of the site, where a number of tents were nestled under a canopy of trees. During the daytime, the area was mostly deserted. But at night, it was filled with archaeologists from around the world, who shared exaggerated stories of their exploits while eating plates of beans and drinking bottles of cheap wine.

None of that was going on now.

As they approached the camp, Payne spotted Tiffany outside a small, camouflaged tent. Sitting on a carved rock that resembled a Mayan head, she was lost in thought as she sharpened a hunter's knife with a practiced hand. One stroke on the whetstone after another, shaping the blade to razor-sharp perfection. With a single glance, Payne knew she wasn't an intern. He didn't know *what* she was, but it sure as hell wasn't an archaeologist.

"Carousel," he whispered to Jones. It was a code from their military days. It told Jones to circle around behind the target. Immediately, Jones understood the situation and darted to his left into the trees. Something didn't sit right with his friend. He went on high alert.

Up ahead, Tiffany cocked her head to the side, like a predator processing information. She remained like this for a few seconds, listening to four sets of footsteps in the underbrush, trying to decide what to do next. Finally, she cast her eyes forward and stared at Payne.

A smile crossed her lips as she rose to her feet.

"Took you long enough," she said to him.

Payne slid his hand behind his back and reached for his gun, which had been tucked into his waistband and covered by his shirttail. "Excuse me?"

She continued to sharpen her blade. "I figured noon at the latest."

Maria and Ulster tensed when they saw the knife in her hand. They nearly panicked when they saw the gun in Payne's. Something bad was happening. Something they didn't understand.

"Do I know you?" Payne asked, unsure.

"No, but I know *you*. In fact, I know all of you. Been waiting for you all day."

Payne continued forward, one tentative step at a time. "Is that so?"

She lifted the knife in front of her to inspect the blade. "Yep."

To Payne, the movement was a sign of aggression. With the knife up high, he knew she could fling it at them with a simple snap of her wrist. It was a chance he wasn't willing to take. Payne whipped his gun out as Jones moved into position from behind. In less than a second, they had her covered from two divergent points.

"Would you mind putting that down?" Payne growled. It was a command, not a question. "It's been an interesting weekend."

She smiled at his request. "For you and me both."

"Drop the weapon," he said bluntly.

The grin never left her face as she flung the knife to the ground. It stuck in the dirt a few feet from the entrance to the tent. "Happy now?"

Payne shook his head. "Happier, but not happy. Who the hell are you?"

"I dropped mine, now you drop yours."

"Not until you tell me who you are."

Her smile waned. "I'm Tiffany Duffy. Now drop the gun."

From the corner of his eye, Payne saw Jones nod. He knew he

could lower his weapon because Jones had her covered. He tucked his gun into the front of his belt. "Better?"

"Better." She pointed at a log near the tent. "Go on. Take a seat. We need to talk."

"We'd prefer to stand."

She shrugged as she lowered herself to the carved stone. "Suit yourself. But I'm sitting down. I'm still recovering from yesterday's excitement. I'm not as young as I used to be."

"Tiffany," Payne said, "I can tell from the tone of your voice that you find all of this amusing, but every second that passes without an explanation brings us a little bit closer to a messy scene. Ain't that right, DJ?"

Jones finally revealed his presence in the nearby trees. "My hand is starting to cramp. Must. Squeeze. Trigger."

She glanced over her shoulder and laughed. "Wow! You guys are just like I imagined. I've heard stories, you know. Many, many stories."

"Is that so? From whom?" Payne demanded.

"I'm not at liberty to say."

"Really?"

"Yes, really."

He read between the lines. "Are you Agency?"

She smiled at him. "I'm not at liberty to say."

"What *are* you at liberty to say?"

She continued to grin. "We've been expecting you."

Just then, the flap on the tent flipped open. Acting on instinct, Payne pulled his gun before he had a chance to see who it was. Not that it really mattered. At this point in the game, he didn't know what was going on or who to believe. Other than Jones and Ulster, he didn't have faith in anyone at the site. That included Maria, who had emerged on his radar after years of dormancy. Although he didn't suspect her of anything, she certainly hadn't earned his trust. That would take a lot longer than a weekend, if at all.

"Are you all right?" said a man inside the tent. "I thought I heard voices."

He stepped out and saw the barrel of Payne's gun.

Then he saw Payne. And then he saw Maria.

If he was surprised or scared, he sure didn't show it. Instead, the emotion on his face was one of pure relief—as if the guilt he had been feeling for a thousand years had finally been released.

The guns didn't matter. Neither did Payne and Jones.

The only thing he cared about was Maria's safety.

Now that she was there, Terrence Hamilton could finally relax.

57

HAMILTON RUSHED FORWARD TO WELCOME MARIA. He hustled past Payne and greeted her with a warm embrace. "Thank goodness you're all right. I've been worried sick since the hotel."

She hugged him back, but the look on her face spoke volumes. She was thoroughly confused by his presence. "You were worried about *me*? We've been worried about *you*!"

He laughed it off. "Me? Why would you worry about me?"

"Why? Because you were kidnapped from the hotel."

"Kidnapped? How absurd! I wasn't kidnapped. I was *rescued*!"

"Rescued?" she blurted. "What are you talking about?"

He studied her face. "You mean your handler didn't tell you?"

"Handler?" she said, even more confused.

Payne interrupted. "Handler? I'm not her handler."

Hamilton glanced back at Payne, who was standing there with his gun raised. But instead of pointing it at Tiffany—who was still being watched by Jones—Payne was now aiming the weapon at him. In a flash, the guilt that had disappeared from Hamilton's face had returned, along with fear, doubt, and a hundred other emotions. "Wait! This *isn't* your handler? Good heavens! Who are you then?" He stepped in front of Maria to protect her. "Just let her be. She doesn't know anything about any of this. I promise!"

"That makes two of us," Payne admitted. Not only didn't he know what was going on, he had the unmistakable suspicion that they had been played. He didn't know why, and he didn't know by whom, but he knew they had been lured there under false pretenses.

Now it was up to him to figure out the specifics.

"Jon," Maria urged, "put down your gun. He won't hurt anyone."

Hamilton lifted his hands above his head. "She's right. I won't."

Ulster stepped forward. "Jonathon, my boy, I'll vouch for him. He has a sterling reputation in the field. Never a hint of controversy. Not even a whiff."

Hamilton looked over to see who was speaking on his behalf. He quickly did a double take when he saw Ulster. "Good heavens! They grabbed you, too. What's going on?"

Ulster said, "I'm not quite sure myself."

Payne glanced at Tiffany. "Care to fill us in?"

She shook her head. "I can't. I'm not at liberty to say."

"In that case, who *is* at liberty to say?" he demanded.

"Sorry. I'm not at lib—"

Payne charged toward her in anger. "I swear to God, if you finish that fucking phrase, I will knock you off that seat. And if you think I won't do it, look into my eyes."

She looked up at him and smiled. "No need for threats. I know what you're capable of. Like I said earlier, I've heard stories."

He raised his pistol as if ready to strike her. "From whom?"

She had to give him something. "My team leader."

"Aha!" Jones cracked from behind. "I told you we should have asked to see their leader. You thought I was joking, but noooooo! No one ever listens to the black guy."

Payne ignored him. "Give me a name."

She shrugged. "Don't have one to give."

"I don't believe that for a second."

She knew Payne wouldn't hit her—she was quite familiar with his background and his ethics—so she called his bluff. "Beat me all you want. I've been *trained* not to talk. You won't get a name until he arrives. He can tell you himself."

"He's coming here?"

"He's supposed to."

"When?"

She shrugged. "Soon."

Payne grimaced as he glanced around the site. They were isolated in the middle of the jungle. No maps. No surveillance. Limited ammo. If a battle erupted, he was confident that he and Jones would survive. Soldiers like them thrived in terrain like this. Unfortunately, they weren't alone in this mess. If shots were fired, they would lose track of Ulster, Maria, and Hamilton in a matter of minutes. After that, things would get ugly fast. "DJ?"

Jones read his mind. "Can't stay here."

"Thoughts?"

"Let's head to the main site. More people, less jungle."

"Less jungle means less cover."

"True. But more witnesses means less funny business."

Payne conceded the point. "Agreed. Which part of the site?"

"We can decide on the way."

"Fine with me. I'll lead. You follow."

"I'm ready when you are."

"I'm ready now." Payne glanced at Tiffany, who was staring at him with her mouth agape. "Come on, Red. We're waiting on you. Get your ass in gear."

She stood reluctantly. "What kind of conversation was that?"

"Efficient."

"I was thinking 'clairvoyant.' You barely used words."

"Words are overrated."

Payne slid behind her and frisked her for weapons. He found a pistol in her waistband and two cargo pockets full of ammo. He took the gun but let her carry the bullets like a pack mule. At this point, he didn't know whose side she was on or what they were up against. If she happened to be a CIA agent, they might actually be on the same team, facing a foreign threat of some kind. If so, he knew the extra ammo would come in handy.

As he finished patting her down, she playfully thrust her ass against his groin. She glanced back at him and said, "I think you missed a spot."

He shoved her forward, not in the mood for games.

⊞   ⊞   ⊞

CONVERSATION WAS LIMITED UNTIL the group passed the main excavation of Old Chichén. With so many workers running around, Payne told them to keep quiet until they were clear of everyone. Once they were back on the jungle trail, Maria turned to Hamilton for an explanation.

"What happened at the hotel?" she demanded.

"You honestly don't know?"

"Know *what*?"

He clenched his teeth in anger. "That makes me so mad! They *promised* me they were going to tell you everything. That was part of our agreement."

"What agreement? Who promised to talk to me?"

"The CIA."

She sneered at the name. "The CIA? You're involved with the CIA?"

He stared at her. For some reason, there was bitterness in her voice—as if working for the CIA was the ultimate betrayal. "I don't *work* for them, if that's what you're asking."

"But you're involved with them? Since when?"

"Since they saved my life at the hotel," he explained. "I went to my truck to get the document that I had told you about. As soon as I left the lobby, I was greeted by Miss Duffy and a few of her colleagues. They told me my life was in danger and I needed to come with them immediately if I wanted to live. I asked about your safety, but they assured me you would be fine. They said people were after *me*, not you. They said the less interaction I had with you, the better. They also told me a handler would be assigned to you for your protection. So I took them at their word and left the hotel without delay."

"Just like that?"

"Yes. Just like that."

She studied his face. He appeared to be telling the truth. "Why didn't you call me? The *least* you should have done was call me. I was worried sick."

"I wanted to—I truly did—but they told me the more contact we had, the more dangerous it would be for you. Besides, they *assured* me that your handler would explain everything." Hamilton called out to Tiffany, who was walking a few steps in front of Payne. "You promised someone would tell her!"

Tiffany looked over her shoulder. "Oops."

Maria shook her head in irritation. She'd had some previous dealings with the CIA, none of them good. From her limited experience, the organization was filled with liars. "Then what?"

"What do you mean?" Hamilton asked.

"That was Friday evening. What have you been doing since?"

"Hiding in a tent. Waiting for the threat to be eliminated."

"*Eliminated? As in killed?*"

He shrugged. "I asked, but they wouldn't say."

"What in the world are you mixed up in?"

"Me? I was about to ask you the exact same thing."

"What does that mean?"

He lowered his voice to a whisper. "In case you've forgotten, we're currently being led through a jungle by two armed men who appear to be friends of yours. I don't mind answering a question or two about my weekend, but I would appreciate if you could return the favor."

Her cheeks flushed with embarrassment. For the last few minutes, she had been focused on her situation. Meanwhile, Hamilton had no idea why a gun was pointed at his back. "I am *so* sorry! I should have explained that a while ago. You must be terrified."

"I don't know about terrified, but certainly uncomfortable."

She explained. "After you disappeared, someone trashed my room. I was worried for my safety, so I called two friends of mine from America. They were kind enough to come at once."

He glanced at her. "Your room was trashed? When did that happen?"

"While we were at the bistro. Why?"

He paused in thought. "It just, well, it doesn't make sense. Why would they do that?"

She shrugged. "We have no idea. That's what we've been trying to figure out for the past two days."

"And what did you find?"

"A whole lot of nothing."

Hamilton turned toward Ulster, who had been quietly listening to their entire conversation. "What about you? What on earth are you doing here?"

"I'm tremendously close to David and Jonathon—they're the two armed men who are holding you hostage. Please don't hold that against them. They're actually wonderful chaps."

Jones called from behind. "Thanks, Petr. Love you, too."

Ulster grinned. "I'm also an old acquaintance of Maria's. I've known her since her graduate school days, back when she was still an archaeologist-in-training. Actually, I met the three of them on the exact same morning. Funny story: They stole a helicopter in Milan and flew to the Archives unannounced. Just popped in for a friendly introduction and—"

Payne loudly cleared his throat.

Ulster got the hint. "Anyway, Jonathon phoned me for some background information on the Maya civilization. When I questioned him about specifics, he mentioned your disappearance. Obviously, I wanted to do whatever I could to help, so I hopped on my plane and came at once."

"Well, thank you," Hamilton said. "Thanks to all of you. I'm still not a hundred percent sure how you're going to help, but thank you nonetheless."

58

ANGEL RAMIREZ DID TWO THINGS AFTER HE SUR-
vived the smoke-filled battleground of the Zócalo. He
sought medical attention for himself and the kids, and he seized
control of Hector's operation before anyone in the city could take
advantage. But not necessarily in that order.

His first order of business was putting out a sizable reward for
Hector's killers. He managed to do so *without* revealing Hector's
death. He simply said they were thieves who needed to be punished and left it at that. People would find out about Hector's death
soon enough.

Although he'd seen glimpses of Bro and Chase while he was
underneath the SUV, Angel had seen Tiffany the clearest. He had
a perfect view of her face and her bright red hair. It was unmistakable in the haze. Despite his anger—or maybe because of it—the
image was seared into his brain. He described her in great detail to
a street artist, who sketched her over and over until the picture
matched Angel's memory. Afterward, he took a picture of the sketch

and sent it to everyone who worked for, or was connected to, his organization.

In his message, he called her *El Diablo Rojo*.

The Red Devil.

Unlike the olden days, when information took forever to filter across a country, her photo appeared on cell-phone screens throughout Mexico within minutes. As expected, a feeding frenzy erupted, from the Pacific Ocean to the Caribbean Sea. Hungry for money and the promise of advancement, low-level players rushed to the airports, train stations, and border towns, hoping to spot Diablo Rojo before she slipped away. But it didn't stop there. Because of Tiffany's interest in the medallion, Angel sent out word to the talent scouts who worked the archaeological sites—the men who searched for potential targets among the busloads of tourists who visited the jungle every day—and told them to be on the lookout for collectors. Angel figured if she cared that much about an artifact, she might surface in one of the areas around the sites, possibly to sell the Aztec medallion to the highest bidder.

Though he hoped for the best, Angel realized the odds of catching her in the immediate future were pretty damn slim. Not because his men weren't motivated but because her crew was bound to have an escape plan that was just as good as their plan of attack. And it had been precise, one that anticipated every move that he and Hector had made. Over the years, Angel had been involved in hundreds of kidnappings and had worked with dozens of men, many of whom were ex-military, but the expertise of her crew was on a completely different level.

There was no doubt: they had worked in black ops.

Nevertheless, within twelve hours of sending out his personal all-points bulletin, his organization was flooded with potential leads. Phone calls, e-mails, and texts came from nearly every state in Mexico and several border countries as well. Of course, most of the leads were fruitless. To earn the reward, Angel required photographic evidence of Diablo Rojo. This resulted in more false sightings than Bigfoot and the Loch Ness Monster combined. Pictures poured in at such an incredible rate, Angel was afraid his Internet connection was going to overheat. He sat there in his office—with one arm in a sling—clicking on picture after picture after picture.

A few of the women *did* resemble his target. One photo was close enough that he personally called its sender and asked for a few close-ups in better lighting. Unfortunately, when the next batch arrived, it was quite obvious that the woman was far too old to be the redhead that he was looking for. Despite the temporary excitement of that lead, most of the pictures were so far off the mark that Angel started to doubt the collective intelligence of his operatives. No fewer than five pictures were of men, not women. A sixth candidate was so gender-neutral that he couldn't tell what sex "it" was. Not that it really mattered, since it was abundantly clear that "it" wasn't his target. After a while, it became apparent that most people were taking photos of redheads with the same mind-set as a worker buying a lottery ticket. They figured, *You can't win if you don't play.* So they took pictures of everyone and sent them in.

Angel continued his hunt late into the night. He eventually passed out in his office chair from a combination of painkillers and exhaustion. Remarkably, he was back at it with the rising sun, awakened by the memory of his fallen friend and his desire for retribution.

Less than an hour into his morning search, he came across a photograph from a small village in the Yucatán. Not a fuzzy cellphone picture—like so many he had seen in the previous hours—but a series of clear shots of a redhead, taken with a telephoto lens. The instant he saw it, he recognized her face like a mother identifying her young. There was no doubt or indecision. He knew it was the woman who had killed his friend. Somehow, some way, she had been spotted half a country away, tracked to a tiny camp-ground near the ruins of Chichén Itzá.

Within seconds, he was on the phone.

Within minutes, he was rounding up troops.

Within hours, he was flying across Mexico to get revenge.

He didn't care who or what got in his way. The bitch needed to die.

      ✠   ✠   ✠

LED BY PAYNE, who kept a close eye on Tiffany, the group left the jungle path and marched through two zones (the Central Group and the Ossario Group) in the site as if they were on a field trip with guns. Payne and Jones did their best to conceal their weapons, but there was only so much they could do with so many witnesses around. Fortunately, most people were paying attention to the Mayan ruins, not the six foreigners who were about to be attacked.

They had just reentered the Great North Platform when Tif-fany spotted a man near the entrance who resembled Angel Ramirez. At first, she assumed her mind was playing tricks on her. She was in Chichén Itzá, nearly a thousand miles away from Mex-ico City. There was no way in hell that he could have found her that quickly. *Besides, didn't Angel die at the Zócalo?* She was pretty damn sure that Church had killed him at the beginning of the shootout. *Or did he?* Before she had a chance to ask Church, he had been shot himself. In the aftermath, she had assumed that Angel had been killed—either from a bullet to the head or the bomb in the SUV. Now she wasn't so sure. From a distance, the guy looked like Angel. Same face. Same build. Same mannerisms. And his arm was in an elaborate sling. Not the kind someone would wear for a simple sprain but the kind someone would wear if he had been shot and lived.

"Oh, shit," she mumbled to herself. "It can't be."

Payne heard her comment. "What's wrong?"

"Can we stop and talk?"

"Of course we can. Would you like some tea?"

"*I'm serious*," she pleaded.

"I'm not. Keep moving."

She stopped anyway. "Listen, I know you're not going to believe a word I say—"

He pushed her forward. "Exactly. So why even try?"

"Because we're walking into a trap."

"Speaking of traps," he said, "shut *your* trap and keep walking."

"*Listen*," she said urgently as she hid behind him. "If I wanted to make a scene, I could do it with ease. All I have to do is start running. Trust me, I'll scream so loud they'll hear me in Florida. I know it, and you know it. The only reason I'm playing along is because you're doing everything that we anticipated. Do you really think I would have used Hamilton's credit card at the gas station if we didn't want you here? I stared into the camera on purpose, you know."

Payne had figured as much. "Go on."

"See that man in the sling?"

He looked toward the entrance. "Yep."

"We tried to kill him yesterday. Apparently, it didn't work. My guess is he won't be happy about the attempt."

"Who is he?"

"His name is Angel Ramirez. He's a dangerous man with a lot of dangerous friends."

"How dangerous?"

"Let's just say there's a reason we left you a boxful of weapons in the Hummer. We didn't want you to be unprepared in case he slipped past us."

"Like he did."

She shrugged. "We're not perfect."

"What do you expect me to do about it?"

"That depends. Did you bring the AKs?"

"Nope."

"The C-four?"

"No."

"Shit."

Jones moved in from the rear. "What's wrong?"

Payne answered. "According to Tiffany, we're about to be attacked."

"By whom?"

"The guy in the sling."

Jones looked ahead. "No problem. I'll just shoot him in the other arm."

"He might have friends."

"How many?"

Tiffany answered. "More than us."

Jones grimaced. "I don't know. I'm on Facebook. I have a lot of friends."

She shook her head. "Unless they have guns, I don't think they can help."

"They might. Do I have time to update my status?"

Payne ignored him. "Does Angel know who we are?"

"Yes," she lied.

"All of us?"

"Yes."

"So hiding won't help?"

Worried about her safety, she continued to lie. "For the short term, maybe. But *not* for the long term. These are the type of guys who will follow you home. America, Italy, Switzerland—it really doesn't matter. They won't stop until we're dead."

Payne stared at her, trying to gauge the truth. Unfortunately, she was a trained CIA agent, someone who lied for a living. There was no way he could detect a lie with any certainty. "What do you recommend?"

"That depends. Are you as good as they say?"

"Yes."

"Then we can take them."

Jones interrupted. "What's this 'we' shit? We're not giving you a gun."

"Of course you will, if you want to live. You're severely outnumbered."

Jones shook his head. "Right now I count one guy in a sling. He may or may not be a bad guy, who may or may not be looking for us. How are we outnumbered?"

"I'm telling you," she assured them, "guys like this don't come alone."

Payne continued to stare at her, searching her eyes for any signs of truth. He simply couldn't tell if she was lying or not. "Petr, come here."

Ulster hustled over. "You rang?"

"How well do you know this place?"

"Quite well. Why do you ask?"

He continued to stare at Tiffany. "Where's a good place to hide?"

"From what?"

"Possible gunmen."

Ulster gasped. "The jungle, I would think."

He shook his head. "I don't want you leaving this site."

"Well, in that case, I would say—"

Payne cut him off. "Whisper your answer to DJ. I don't want the others to hear."

"But—"

"Just do it."

Ulster did as he was told. He whispered the answer to Jones.

"DJ, you got it?"

Jones nodded. "I got it."

"Good." Payne pulled out Tiffany's gun. He handed it to Ulster, who was tempted to object, but the look in Payne's eye kept him in line. "I want you to take Maria to that hiding place. Stay there until one of us comes and gets you. Do you understand?"

"Yes."

"If anyone else comes, shoot them in the face."

"Yes, but—"

"But what?"

"What about Terrence?"

Payne shook his head. "Sorry. Don't trust him. He's involved in this, but I don't know how. Until I do, he's on his own."

Maria objected. "That's not fair! Why do you get to decide everything?"

"Because you called me. The moment you did, you put me in charge of your safety. So that's what I'm doing. Trying to keep you safe."

She started to argue. "But he's—"

Hamilton cut her off. "He's right, Maria. He's right. I haven't earned anyone's trust. Go with Petr. He'll keep you safe. I'll be fine with Tiffany."

Maria glanced at Jones for support, but he was on Payne's side.

"Go," Jones said. "I'll come get you when this is over."

She took a deep breath and nodded. "You better."

59

PAYNE FOUND HIMSELF IN A PREDICAMENT. HE DIDN'T trust Tiffany, but he believed her story about the man in the sling. Angel Ramirez was there to kill her. She had just enough fear in her eyes to be convincing. Unfortunately, Payne didn't know what to do about it.

Had he trusted her story fully—that Angel was a dangerous man with dangerous friends who would systematically hunt them down until they were dead—he would have lured Angel to a private section of the site and put a bullet in his brain. No questions. No guilt. No problem. The crisis would have been over before it had gotten out of hand. But the reality was he *didn't* trust her. Not in the way he trusted Jones or Raskin. If one of them had warned him about Angel's intentions, Payne would have sprung into action because he trusted them implicitly.

But he couldn't kill a man on Tiffany's word.

He simply couldn't. He was more cautious than that.

What if Angel was there for her—but he had *legitimate* reasons to be after her? Perhaps he worked for the Mexican government, and he had been assigned to track her down for crimes she had committed in Mexico. Or maybe Angel worked for the CIA, and he had been tasked with stopping an illegal operation that she had been running? In that case, Payne's involvement would not only be reckless, it would potentially make him a traitor in the eyes of America. There was no way he could risk his reputation over a woman he didn't trust.

With that in mind, he did the next best thing.

He sent Jones to collect some intelligence.

Before departing, Jones whispered the name of Ulster's hiding place to Payne—so both of them would know it—then he dashed into the jungle between the Ossario Group and the main entrance to the site. From there, he hoped to learn as much about Angel as possible. Was he a Federale, a criminal, or something else? Was he acting alone, or did he have a team of gunmen at his disposal? And if he had a team, what type of weapons did they possess? Answers to those questions and several more would help Payne decide what they should do next.

Meanwhile, Payne realized he couldn't afford to stay in the open. Not only because he was a large target but because he didn't want to be seen with Tiffany. If she was a wanted woman, he didn't want to be linked to her in any way. He quickly surveyed their options, then he ordered her and Hamilton into the closest grove of trees, where the three of them could analyze the site while they waited for word from Jones.

✠   ✠   ✠

JONES RAN AND JUMPED and ducked and scurried through the jungle until he was hiding in the underbrush less than twenty feet from Angel, who had positioned himself near the main entrance to the site. He was standing there with a scowl on his face, staring at people in the passing crowd. His left arm was in an elaborate sling. It had multiple straps around his back and waist, which took the weight off his shoulder while keeping his arm anchored against his stomach—as if any movement at all would cause his wounds to reopen. There was also a thick wad of surgical gauze protruding from the collar of his shirt, some of which appeared to be stained with blood.

Standing by Angel's side were two thugs who looked like they had just escaped from a Mexican prison. They were covered in tattoos from head to toe, including teardrop tattoos under their eyes. In some Hispanic cultures, it meant the bearer had killed someone while incarcerated. From appearances alone, Jones didn't doubt it for a second. Everything about them screamed *danger*. If they were Federales, they were the best damn undercover officers that he had ever seen, because their ink probably took two years to complete, if not longer. They also had a look in their eyes that said, *If you touch me, I will turn your dick inside out.*

All in all, they were not happy men.

Jones stayed in the weeds for several seconds, trying to learn as much about them as possible. Although he felt ants and spiders crawling across his legs and into his clothes, he didn't flinch. He simply blocked it out of his mind like he had been trained to do in sniper school. Back then, he had been required to remain motionless for hours at a time under the harshest conditions imaginable. A few minutes in the undergrowth wouldn't kill him.

The three men didn't talk, but Jones still managed to learn a lot about them in a short amount of time. Under the back of their shirts, they had solid bulges that went halfway up their backs. Probably large-caliber handguns—the kind with serious stopping power—or smaller pistols with silencers already screwed on. Earpieces were visible in their right ears, which suggested a network of gunmen that extended wider than the three of them. After all, he assumed the two thugs were bodyguards who wouldn't leave Angel's side.

Unfortunately, Jones had no way of knowing who else was working for Angel. The odds were pretty good that they *wouldn't* look like Mexican gangbangers. Otherwise, they would be too easy to spot among the crowd of tourists. If he had to guess, he would say that Angel's scouts probably looked and acted like normal folk—with one major exception.

They would be wearing earpieces.

☩   ☩   ☩

JONES BACKED AWAY FROM his hiding place and called Payne, who listened intently as Jones described the three men near the entrance. He also detailed his theory about the earpieces. He felt they could be used to identify sleepers around the site.

Payne thanked him for the info. "Anything else?"

"Simple question: yes or no on Angel?"

Payne groaned. He knew the query would be coming. Unfortunately, he still didn't feel they had enough to go on to kill a man in cold blood. Just because Angel looked like a bad guy didn't mean he deserved to die. And even if he did, Payne wasn't going to ask his best friend to pull the trigger on a whim. They were soldiers, not executioners. Sometimes there was a fine line between the two, but Payne knew that they were on the wrong side of the line at that moment.

"That's a negative. Repeat. That's a negative. Do not shoot Angel."

"Are you sure? There are no friendlies in the way."

"Still a negative. Repeat. Still a negative. Fall back and regroup."

"Understood. See you soon."

Payne ended the call, only to find Tiffany staring at him.

She said, "You are such a pussy."

"Excuse me?"

"You heard what I said. *You're a pussy.* Jones had the shot, and you ordered him down. Why would you do that?"

"Why? Because I don't trust you. Not one bit. I'm not going to take a man's life on your word alone. For all I know, you lured me here to do just that."

She shook her head. "You are *such* a disappointment! I had heard so many stories about your exploits that I had you built up in my head. But now I know you're just a coward."

He shrugged it off. "I've been called worse."

She continued. "Actually, now that I think about it, I'm glad you gave the order to pull back. I learned more about you in those three seconds than I could in a hundred war stories."

"Is that so? What did you learn?"

She stood from her hiding spot. "If you don't have the balls to shoot an armed killer, then I know you don't have the nuts to shoot an unarmed woman."

He stared at her. "Try me."

She smirked at him. It was the same smirk that she had flashed at the security camera in the gas station. It let him know that she had figured him out. "And based on your indecision, I know you were *this* close to giving the order. That means if I make a play for Angel, you aren't going to stop me. In fact, I'd be willing to bet that you'll give me support."

"I wouldn't count on it."

"Don't worry, I won't. But it would be nice."

She tossed Payne an extra clip, then darted through the trees on her way to find Angel. She had missed the chance to kill him the day before. She wasn't about to screw up again.

Meanwhile, Hamilton remained behind. He sat there in silence, studying Payne like a poker player looking for tells. After several seconds, Payne glanced at him and winked.

Hamilton laughed. "I'll be damned! You played her. You gave the order *not* to shoot in front of her, because you knew how she'd react. You knew she'd go after him."

Payne fought the urge to smile. He didn't want to gloat.

60

Jones hustled through the jungle until he was back by Payne's side. Sweaty, dirty, and slightly out of breath, Jones was grinning like a child at an amusement park.

Payne stared at him. "Why are you so happy?"

"This is *so* much better than shoveling snow."

"Good point."

Jones glanced around the thick grove of trees where they were hiding. He spotted Hamilton but didn't see Tiffany. "Where's Red?"

"We broke up."

"Damn, Jon. You can't keep a woman to save your life."

"Actually, I let her go so she could *end* a life."

Payne explained his rationale, and Jones wholeheartedly agreed with the decision. Although there was some risk in letting her go, they realized that she had lured them to Chichén Itzá for a reason, and the quickest way to find out what that reason was, was to let her do her thing. In the meantime, if she happened to eliminate a dangerous criminal who might be after them, so be it. They also realized if she started a major shitstorm, everyone at the site would be in danger. So they pulled out the maps they had acquired at the visitor center and planned for the worst.

Jones eyed the different archaeological sites, which were spread out over several square miles of mixed terrain, and realized their best bet was to keep the violence contained in one area. That would allow frightened tourists to flee the battlefield and hunker down in the outlying zones until the carnage eventually stopped. In addition, it would also draw sleepers into the field of play, which would be the easiest way to eliminate them. Fighting a team of armed gunmen was one thing. Fighting a team of anonymous gunmen was quite another. The sooner they saw what they were facing, the better—even if it meant fighting ten shooters at once.

Jones pointed at the main entrance to the site. It was on the western edge of the Great North Platform, which spread out to the north and the east. This included El Castillo, the Great Ball Court, and hundreds of feet of flat ground between the other ruins. "Angel's standing here. The odds are pretty good she's going to engage him somewhere in this zone."

"Agreed."

"Did you give her a weapon?"

"Nope."

"Then she'll have to acquire one."

"My guess is that won't be an issue."

Jones looked up from the map. "Hey, Doc, get your wrinkled ass over here. I need your help."

Hamilton, who had been trying to stay out of their way, trudged over through the weeds. "Is there a problem?"

Jones tapped his finger on the map. There was a 980-foot-long path that led from the Great North Platform through the northern wall of the city to a small body of water in the jungle. It was labeled CENOTE SAGRADO. "What's this?"

He looked at the name and smiled. "Cenote Sagrado. That

means 'Sacred Well.' It is also called the Well of Sacrifice. A thousand years ago, when this city was thriving, the Maya used to sacrifice humans and treasures into the *cenote* in order to honor Chaac, who was the Mayan rain deity. According to Mayan mythology, Chaac produced rain and thunder when he struck clouds in the heavens with his ax of lightning. In the early twentieth century, an American archaeologist named Edward Herbert Thompson dredged the well. He found everything from skeletons and skulls to pottery and jade. If you're interested, he wrote a captivating book about the Maya called *People of the Serpent*. Really fascinating stuff."

Jones glanced at Payne, then Hamilton, then back at Payne. "We *have* to keep this guy away from Petr. Can you imagine how many years of our lives they could suck from us?" To illustrate his point, Jones spoke in a mocking tone. "Hey, look at that bird! Speaking of birds, did you know that birds are descendants of a specialized subgroup of dinosaurs? Based on biological evidence, birds are blah, blah, blah . . ."

Payne fought the urge to laugh. He knew Jones was making a serious point.

Jones stared at Hamilton. "Do you understand what's going on here? Bullets are about to start flying, and you're wasting my time with a history lesson. Meanwhile, I still have no idea what a fucking *cenote* is."

"Sorry. My apologies. I didn't mean to ramble."

"And yet I'm still waiting for an answer."

Hamilton nodded. "A *cenote* is a local term for a sinkhole that exposes the water table underneath the soil to the surface. This area is filled with them. Some are rather narrow, no more than a foot or two in diameter. Others are rather massive."

"And this one?"

"It's approximately one hundred and fifty feet in diameter and naturally circular. The limestone cliffs drop nearly seventy feet to the water below. It's one of the main reasons that Chichén Itzá was built here. An underground river gave the Maya a fresh supply of water."

"Is it fenced off?"

Hamilton shook his head. "Actually, quite the opposite. There are no barriers at all. Tourists are allowed to walk right to the edge and peer into the water below."

"Thanks, Doc. That's more like it. I can actually use that information."

He smiled. "Glad I could help."

⚜   ⚜   ⚜

TIFFANY WAS TEMPTED TO jog back to Old Chichén, where she had stashed some weapons around the periphery of the campsite. In her line of work, it was better to be safe than sorry. But the more she thought about it, the less she liked the idea of a long run, since she didn't know who had tipped off Angel. For all she knew, there was a spy waiting for her at the dig site.

Eventually, she decided to play it safe and hide in the trees that separated the archaeological zones. From there, she hoped to spot as many gunmen as possible. As a trained agent, she knew what to look for in large crowds of people. It went beyond the obvious (weapon bulges, earpieces, and inappropriate clothing). She also studied the way people moved—the rhythm of their steps, their interactions with others, and so on. Over the years, she had spotted more criminals from their body language than everything else combined.

It took less than five minutes to spot one of Angel's men. He was dressed in jeans and a T-shirt that was a little too tight to conceal his firearm. She also spotted his earpiece as he strolled past the woods in an area known as El Mercado (the Market). Located on the opposite side of the zone from the main entrance, it was one of the easternmost ruins at the site, far from most people. Several rows of stone columns—some as tall as thirteen feet—stood in the middle of a manicured grass field. The ancient columns once supported a thatched roof that had protected merchants and their goods from the elements. Unfortunately for the gunman, they offered him little protection from Tiffany. The moment he stopped to admire the pillars, she plucked a pointed rock from the turf and charged forward. Within seconds, she had bashed him on the head. Not once. Not twice. But several times. Over and over again until the white meat leaked out. Only then did she stop to take his gun and wipe the blood splatter from her face and brow.

Thrilled with the silence of her kill, she hooked her arms under his and dragged his lifeless body toward the nearby woods. She planned to dump him in the weeds before she hustled to the other end of the site, where she hoped to kill an unsuspecting Angel by the visitor's center. But it wasn't meant to be. Ten feet short of the woods, her plan went to shit when she was spotted by a group of teenage girls, who were doing everything in their power to avoid their parents. There was a brief moment of silence as the girls processed the murder scene in front of them, and then they did what Tiffany had threatened to do earlier.

They screamed so loud people could hear it in Florida.

✠   ✠   ✠

JONES WINCED WHEN HE heard the sound. "What the hell was that?"

"Howler monkeys," guessed Hamilton. "They're surly creatures that prowl the treetops of Central America. However, I must admit I don't remember their pitch being quite that high. Normally the sound is more guttural than bloodcurdling."

"Shut up!" Payne ordered as he tried to pinpoint the screams. He knew damn well they were human, but they were tough to locate from his position in the jungle. Trees and vines had a way of distorting sound. "I think they came from the east."

His guess was proven correct by a series of gunshots.

They occurred one after another in rapid succession.

"Definitely east," Payne said.

Jones cursed as he pulled out his map. Normally he would have considered this great news because there was only one group of ruins to the east. They sat nestled in a tiny corner of the site, isolated from the rest of the Great North Platform like a tiny peninsula in a sea of trees. If a skirmish broke out over there, there was a damn good chance the fighting could be limited to that small quadrant, which would keep civilian casualties to a minimum.

Unfortunately for Jones, this wasn't a normal circumstance, so he didn't view this as a positive development. In fact, he viewed it as the worst possible news, because the shootout was taking place next to a temple that he had never heard of until moments earlier. A temple he didn't care about until his friend Petr had whispered its name into his ear.

It was the temple where Ulster and Maria were hiding.

61

A NGEL HEARD THE SCREAMS, THEN A SERIES OF GUN-shots. He immediately used his radio to find out what was happening. They spoke in Spanish. "Who is shooting?"

"The Devil," answered Edgar, one of his gunmen.

"Where?"

"East of the pyramid. She just killed Pedro with a rock."

"A rock?"

"She bashed in his head."

Angel made the sign of the cross. "Can you see her right now?"

"Not this moment."

"Why not?"

"She has me trapped behind a pillar."

"Trapped? Are you *sure* she's still there?"

"Pretty sure."

"Make damn sure!" he ordered. "I won't send anyone to help unless I'm *sure* she's there. We can't let her slip past us."

Fearful of Angel's violent reputation, Edgar reluctantly agreed. He took a deep breath, then peeked around the stone column, only to find Tiffany standing twenty feet away with her gun raised. His heart sank at the sight.

"Shit," he mumbled.

Angel heard Edgar's final word over the radio. It was followed by a gunshot to the east, then radio silence. After a few seconds, he nodded in understanding.

"Okay," he said. "*Now* we know for sure."

PAYNE AND JONES SPRINTED through the jungle until they reached El Mercado. They found Pedro's body, ten feet from the edge of the trees. He was missing his weapon, his radio, and a chunk of his head. They assumed Tiffany was responsible for the scene.

Jones was impressed. "She has some skills."

Payne spotted a second body. It was crumpled next to a pillar on the other side of the market. He hustled over and plucked the earpiece from Edgar's ear. "A lot of skills."

Jones surveyed the area. She was nowhere in sight. "Now what?"

"Check on Petr and Maria. Make sure they're okay."

"And you?"

"I'll watch your back while you do."

Jones nodded, then hustled across the plaza toward a large ruin.

Known as the Temple of the Warriors, the building features a stone temple on top of three stacked tiers that resemble the bottom half of a pyramid. A Chac Mool is positioned between the temple and the main stairway that leads to the ground below. The complex is fronted by hundreds of carved columns depicting warriors.

At one time the columns were painted in bright colors, but now the pigment is barely visible in the afternoon sun.

Jones ignored the "warriors" and the restraining rope that protected them from the general public. He dashed through a gap on the right side of the complex and made his way to the back of the bottom tier, which was shaded by trees and concealed from the rest of the site. According to Ulster, this was where he and Maria would be hiding.

"Don't shoot," whispered Jones as he inched his head around the corner. He knew them well enough to realize that neither of them was comfortable with guns. "I come in peace."

Ulster stepped out of the jungle and breathed a sigh of relief. "Thank goodness it's you. We heard shots close by and didn't know whether to go or stay."

Jones jogged toward him. "Where's Maria?"

She emerged a few seconds later. "I'm right here."

"Good. I thought maybe you'd left."

"I was thinking about it. I'm not the type to sit on my butt and do nothing."

"I know you aren't," Jones said. "But I also know you're not a fan of bullets."

She reluctantly nodded. "Is there anything we can do?"

"You can stay put."

"I mean besides that."

"You can stay alive. That's a pretty important job."

"Indeed!" Ulster said.

"Come on," she whined. "Playing hide-and-seek with gunmen is not my idea of fun. Can't I help as a translator or something?"

Jones smiled at the thought. "Actually, now that you mention it, that's not a bad idea. Pull out your cell phone."

"My cell phone?"

"There was a sign in the visitor center that bragged about cell phone service here. You might actually have reception."

"We're in the jungle."

"Just check."

She glanced at her screen. "I'll be damned. I can't get reception at my house, but I have reception here."

Jones smiled. "The Maya were *way* ahead of their time. Their pyramid is actually a giant antenna. They were the first ancient civilization to have Wi-Fi."

Ulster laughed. "I realize you're just joking about the antenna. However, the Maya were innovators in many ways. Did you know they—"

Jones cut him off. "Not now, Petr."

"Yes, of course, how silly of me. More important things to deal with."

She pointed at her phone. "What did you have in mind?"

"Your translation skills might come in handy. Just be ready for my call. I'll let you know if I need you."

"Trust me, David. You need me. It's pretty obvious."

He smiled at her. "We'll see."

⌖　　⌖　　⌖

PAYNE CONCEALED HIMSELF IN a small grove of trees to the south of the stone warriors. He had barely settled into position when he spotted a group of armed men gathering near the base of El Castillo, approximately five hundred feet to the west. He tucked the earpiece into his ear, hoping to eavesdrop on their plans, but Angel and his men were speaking in rapid Spanish—way too fast for him to keep up with their conversation.

Frustrated, he plucked it out of his ear and stuffed it into his pocket.

A few minutes later, Payne heard footsteps in the loose gravel behind him. He turned and saw Jones sprinting across the Plaza of a Thousand Columns. At one time, the rows of columns supported a large thatched roof. Now nothing remained but the columns themselves. Payne signaled for him to stay low and to the south, just in case the men had binoculars.

Payne remained silent until Jones was next to him. "How are they?"

"They're fine. In fact, they're better than fine. Maria gave me a great idea."

"About what?"

"Dealing with Angel's men."

"Really? Does she have lots of experience dealing with foreign men?"

Jones growled softly. "That's the kind of comment I'd expect from me, not you. You should be ashamed of yourself."

Payne smiled. "Sorry. I hope you can forgive me."

Jones pulled out his map. "Actually, I hope you can forgive *me*. I'm about to ask you to do something dangerous."

"How dangerous?"

"I need you to draw their attention to the western side of the pyramid."

"Why?"

"Because Tiffany was just over here. If they come looking for her, Maria and Petr are going to be in the line of fire."

"Good point. Out of curiosity, how do you expect me to draw their attention? If possible, I'd prefer not to get chased by a bunch of angry Mexicans."

"I don't blame you."

"Good. I'm glad."

Jones smiled. "Don't get me wrong: I'm *still* going to ask you to do it. I just won't blame you for being pissed at me."

Payne said nothing. He simply growled.

Jones rolled his eyes. "Don't worry, you big baby. I have something in mind that will help your cause. If you do what I say, your odds of survival go up to, like, seven or eight percent."

"Up from what?"

"Two or three."

"Great."

"Do you still have the earpiece from the dead guy?"

Payne pulled it from his pocket. "I tried to listen in, but I couldn't understand them. Their Spanish is way too fast for me."

"You don't have to understand them. I want them to understand *Maria*."

"Maria? What's she going to do?"

Jones pointed at the map. "She's going to invite them to a ballgame."

62

As far as Payne was concerned, he viewed Angel and his men as potential threats, *not* targets. After all, they hadn't fired on Payne or his friends, or endangered them in any way. In fact, the only person who had hurt anyone at Chichén Itzá—at least to his knowledge—was Tiffany.

Of course, that didn't mean he thought Angel was harmless. Based on the number of gunmen who were gathering near the pyramid, Payne sensed they were out for blood and didn't care how many people got hurt in their effort to find Tiffany. Still, despite the mounting evidence against them, Payne's moral compass wouldn't allow him to open fire on anyone unless he was provoked. The moment that occurred, he would go after them with guns blazing. But until that happened, all he was willing to do was prepare for the worst.

In many ways, it reminded him of his mind-set in the military. His unit usually knew where their biggest threats were located—Afghanistan, Iraq, North Korea, et cetera—but they weren't allowed to engage the enemy until a line was crossed. In the meantime, they used their time wisely. They moved supplies. They cleared terrain. They probed for weaknesses. They did everything they could possibly do until they got permission from the Pentagon to attack.

Then they kicked some serious ass.

To prepare for the looming battle, Payne hustled through a cluster of trees that defined the southern edge of the Great North Platform. He moved with speed and stealth, two things that didn't seem possible for a man his size, and did so with little effort. Though he had worked hard to increase his strength and stamina over the years, he was a natural-born athlete who had been blessed with physical tools that would make an Olympian jealous.

Payne eased to a quiet stop a few feet from the trail that led to the Ossario Group to the south. In order to get into position for Jones's plan, he had to cross the path at some point and had hoped to do so there, where the trail was narrow and shaded by trees. He glanced left, then right. Everything looked clear on the path itself. He was ready to dart across the trail and continue his journey forward when he spotted one of Angel's men hiding on the other side. Wearing a camouflage jacket and pants, Jorge blended in with the foliage ahead. The main thing that had given him away was the movement of his hand as he attempted to swat bugs away from his face. If not for that, Payne would have run right past him and would have been shot.

Now he had a chance to take him out.

The decision to become aggressive was an easy one for Payne when he saw the weapon that Jorge was holding. It wasn't a handgun. It was an FN SCAR-L, a heavy assault rifle that was used by a few special operations regiments in the U.S. Armed Forces. Similar to the AK-47, it is a gas-operated, rotating-bolt rifle that is capable of killing a lot of people in a short amount of time. One look was all it took. Payne knew he had to do something about the weapon. There was no way in good conscience that he could let someone walk the grounds with that much firepower. Not with kids and families scurrying for safety.

It was an accident waiting to happen.

Fortunately for Payne, Jorge didn't hear his approach or see him in the weeds. He was too busy swatting at the bugs that had descended on him to notice anything but the gnats. This gave Payne plenty of time to figure out the best way to acquire the weapon. Eventually, he settled for the simplest method possible. He was going to run Jorge over and steal it. After all, the rifle was just dangling at his side, hanging from a strap around Jorge's neck. His hands weren't even on the trigger. That meant the odds of getting shot were pretty damn slim.

They were odds he was willing to take.

Payne burst from his hiding place and made it across the path in three powerful strides. By the time Jorge saw the blur headed his way, it was too late to do anything except raise his arms to protect his face. Payne buried his shoulder in Jorge's sternum with so much force that he cracked two ribs in the initial blow. Jorge cracked two more when they crashed to the turf. Payne scrambled to his knees and was prepared to knock Jorge out with a swift elbow to the chin, but that had been taken care of when the back of his head had bounced off the hard ground.

Wasting no time, Payne took the assault rifle, a few clips of ammo, and Jorge's radio, then scurried into the woods ahead.

There was somewhere he needed to be.

⚜   ⚜   ⚜

ANGEL DIDN'T HAVE MUCH experience in the ways of war. He was a criminal, not a soldier. Most of his fighting had occurred on the streets of Mexico City, not in the jungles of a Mayan city. The difference between the two was significant. There were no cars. Or houses. Or any of the things he was used to. Instead there were ruins. And trees. And wide-open spaces. Yesterday's battle at the Zócalo was his first shoot-out in two years, and he had barely made it out alive.

Here, against *these* opponents, he didn't stand a chance.

Neither did his men.

Sure, most of them were skilled with guns, but not like this.

It was one thing to hit a bull's-eye at a shooting range. It was quite another to hit a moving target that was returning fire with the accuracy of Payne and Jones.

They knew the tactics. They knew the angles.

They knew all the things that Angel's men didn't.

And they were more than willing to take advantage.

Angel made three major mistakes in his initial strategy. To begin with, he minimized the value of his superior numbers by bringing his men together in one place. They would have been far more effective scattered around the site, slowly closing in on Tiffany's last-known position like a hangman tightening a noose. Second, he chose a staging area for his troops next to the most visible building at the site. El Castillo stood nearly a hundred feet tall and was almost twice as wide. It could be seen from every corner of the ancient city. No matter where Payne and Jones went, they always knew where Angel's men were. In the middle of an open plaza, they were more visible than a lighthouse on a clear night.

Finally, and worst of all, Angel ordered his men to find and kill Tiffany at all cost. Had that order been given at the O.K. Corral, Payne and Jones would have sat back and watched the violence unfold without intervention. After all, it wasn't their fight. But everything changed when Angel's men gunned down four innocent tourists who had been hiding behind one of the smaller ruins. The instant they tried to scurry past the pyramid on their way to the main exit, Angel's men opened fire. No rhyme or reason. No mistaken identities.

They simply fired on them in cold blood.

⌖　　⌖　　⌖

JONES SAW THE INCIDENT from across the plaza. He was sickened by the sight. In a heartbeat, he went from an interested spectator to an active participant.

His initial plan had been to protect Petr and Maria by luring Angel's troops away from the market. His new plan was to protect everyone at the site. In his opinion, the best way to do that was to eliminate every criminal with a gun as quickly as possible.

He pulled out his phone and called Payne, who was still scrambling to get into position. The phone vibrated several times before he finally answered.

"Are you okay?" Payne asked.

Jones explained what had happened. He also stressed it was time to get involved.

Payne nodded in agreement. "I just picked up a weapon that will help our cause. I got a SCAR-L from one of his men. I also got another radio."

"How much ammo?"

"Enough to make them extinct."

"Good. Because that's what we need to do."

"What did you have in mind?"

"Same plan as before. The only difference: shoot to kill."

⌖　　⌖　　⌖

MARIA FELT THE PHONE vibrate in her hand. She glanced at the screen. It was a call from Jones. Her chest tightened as her heart started to race. She was being summoned to war.

"Hello," she whispered.

"You're on."

"What do you need me to do?"

"I need you to leave Petr and come here."

"You need me to leave him? Are you sure that's a good idea?"

"Trust me, he's safer there than he will be here."

"But—"

"Maria," he said, "give him the damn phone."

She did as she was told.

Ulster got on the line, curious. "Hello?"

"Petr, I need to borrow Maria for a few minutes, but she's reluctant to leave your side. Please tell her that you'll be fine without her."

Ulster gulped, unsure. "Will I be fine without her?"

"Of course you'll be fine. Otherwise, I wouldn't be doing this."

"In that case, she's all yours. I'll send her on her way."

"Feel free to keep the gun. She won't be needing it."

"All right, David. I'll do just that. I'll send Maria, but keep the gun."

"Perfect. Let me talk to her again."

Ulster assured her it was okay to leave as he handed the phone back to Maria. She complained briefly but eventually agreed.

"Okay," she said to Jones, "where do you need me to go?"

"Exit south through the jungle and meet me near the trees on the western side of the market. Do you know where that is?"

She glanced at her map. "Yes."

"Good. I need you here in two minutes."

63

EARLIER IN THE DAY, PAYNE HAD IMAGINED WHAT IT must have been like to play the Mesoamerican game at the Great Ball Court. With his size and strength, he figured he would have been an unstoppable force even though he had never played the game before. It wasn't hubris. It was genetics. They simply didn't make men of his size a thousand years ago.

Now he would have the opportunity to play a different sport on the famous court. One he knew how to play. One he had been playing at a world-class level for years. The rules were quite different from those of the original game, but there were similarities. It was a brutal, violent competition, one where blood would be spilled. Only in this case, players wouldn't be sacrificed *after* the match. They would be killed in the field of play as part of the game. No points would be tallied. No scores would be kept. The last man standing would be the winner.

He planned on being that player.

To prepare for the contest, Payne sprinted the entire width of the field—all 545 feet—and entered the building on the northern edge. Known as the Temple of the Bearded Man, it was where nobles and invited guests used to watch the games. It offered a perfect view of the field and, more important, protection from a side or rear assault. Covered with centuries of dirt and grime, the stones were slicker than he had expected. Payne slipped as he scrambled into position, banging his leg on one of the steps. A two-inch gash opened just below his knee. Before long, blood was trickling down his shin and soaking his sock.

If all went well, it would be the only injury that he suffered.

But the first of many that he would inflict.

⊞   ⊞   ⊞

MARIA STARED AT JONES as though he were crazy. "You want me to do *what*?"

Jones explained. "I want you to be Tiffany."

"I don't look anything like Tiffany."

"You don't have to look like her. You're *pretending* to be her on the radio."

"What good will that do?"

"If I'm correct, it will get Angel's men headed to where we want."

"Which is?"

Jones smiled. "In front of Jon."

"Does he know that?"

"Of course he knows. Are you willing to help or not?"

She nodded. "But what does this have to do with translating?"

"What do you mean?"

"You said you needed my translation skills."

"I might," he assured her. "I don't know if these guys can speak English. If not, you might have to be Tiffany in Spanish."

"That's it?"

"Yep. That's it."

"If that's all you needed, why couldn't Petr come along?"

Jones pulled out his map. He pointed at the Great Ball Court, which was located a few thousand feet from where they were crouching. "Why? Because I'm Jon's backup, so there's going to be some running involved. Petr's a lot of things, but aerodynamic isn't one of them."

⚜   ⚜   ⚜

PAYNE PUT JORGE'S EARPIECE in his ear, then settled behind Jorge's assault rifle. Although he had limited experience with the weapon, it felt comfortable in his hands. From his prone position inside the Temple of the Bearded Man, he had an elevated field of fire. In this case, it was literally a field, which was bookended by 39-foot-high stone walls that were more than 500 feet in length. Once his opponents entered the alley in between, there would be no escape.

He would mow them down like weeds.

⚜   ⚜   ⚜

ANGEL'S MEN HAD GATHERED on the southeastern corner of El Castillo. If it had been up to them, they would have launched their search for Tiffany several minutes earlier—as soon as Edgar's death had confirmed her location in the market. Instead, they had been forced to wait for an injured Angel to hobble all the way from the site's entrance to the staging area on the opposite side of the Great North Platform. With his arm in the elaborate sling, it would have been quicker if his bodyguards had picked him up and carried him across the plaza. Of course, no one had the cojones to tell him that, but everyone was thinking it.

Upon his arrival, their attitudes quickly changed.

Angel sat on the bottom step of the pyramid, his face flushed from the long walk. Blood had soaked through the patch on his shoulder and had stained his shirt bright red. No longer annoyed, his men stared at him with a combination of fear and respect. Most of them had never met Angel. He and Hector had rarely made it to this part of Mexico. They had allowed their lieutenants from Yucatán and Quintana Roo to handle the kidnappings in this part of the country. Local troops had heard stories about Angel, but this was the first time they had ever seen his face. To see him like *this* was inspiring. He looked like he could pass out at any moment, yet here he was leading them onto the battlefield. Whatever the Devil had done, they would make her pay.

Nevertheless, Angel did his best to motivate them.

"Yesterday afternoon," he claimed, "the Red Devil tried to kill Hector Garcia's family by blowing up his truck at the Zócalo. I managed to pull his children from the fiery wreckage, risking my life to save theirs. In the process, I took a bullet in the shoulder. Doctors wanted to remove my limb, but I wouldn't let them because I need both arms to fight the Devil. And that's what I intend to do until one of us is dead."

✠   ✠   ✠

PAYNE AND JONES HAD no knowledge of the kidnapping plot, the medallion, or anything else that had happened in Mexico City. All they knew was what Tiffany had told them—that she had tried to kill Angel the day before and he was gunning for revenge. They combined that information with everything they had learned on their own and came up with the best plan possible.

Now all they had to do was execute it.

Once Jones was in position near the southern end of the ball field, he told Maria what to say and how to say it. He needed her to pretend to be Tiffany, who she had met earlier that day. Maria didn't have to mimic the tone of her voice; she just needed to capture the cockiness that Tiffany had displayed at the Old Chichén campsite. In addition to being Tiffany's defining characteristic, Jones knew it would generate an emotional response from Angel. Ultimately, that's what they were hoping for. They wanted Angel to become so angry that he did something careless. And the moment that happened, they would be ready to pounce.

Jones stared at her. "You can do this."

"I know I can," she assured him.

He smiled at her confidence. "Keep that swagger, and you'll be fine. The more you taunt, the more unhinged he'll become. Trust me, I've dealt with plenty of men like him before. Pride plays a major role in their lives. Getting beaten by a woman will drive him crazy."

Maria nodded in understanding. She was an expert on the topic. Her father's pride had destroyed many lives and had torn her family apart. After all this time, she was still coming to grips with everything he had done—including killing his wife (her mother) in order to protect a family secret. The anger she felt toward him was still a major part of her life. She didn't want it to be. She truly didn't. She wanted to let it go. But it was still there, lurking under the surface, ready to bubble up at the worst possible moment.

For once, she could use the anger to her advantage.

She would use it to taunt Angel.

✠   ✠   ✠

ANGEL'S MEN WERE READY to charge toward the market when they heard a female's voice in their earpieces. Angel ordered them to shut up so he could hear what she was saying.

Maria drew out his name in a mocking way. "Annnnnnnnngel! Can you hear me, Angel?"

"Who is this?" he demanded.

She ignored his question. "Listen to me, Angel, because I am *not* going to repeat myself. I'm going to give you one chance to go away—one chance to forget about me. If you choose to ignore this offer, you and your men will regret it."

Angel struggled to regain his feet. "I'll kill you, *puta*! Show your face, and I'll kill you! Letting me live was the biggest mistake you ever made!"

"You can't kill what you can't find."

Angel climbed three steps of the pyramid to see over his men. He stared into the trees, looking for any sign of the Devil. "Trust me, *puta*! I'll find you—and I'll kill you."

"Sounds like fun," she taunted. "Unfortunately, I'm a little pressed for time. To speed things up, why don't I tell you where I am?"

"Don't bother. I never trust a whore!"

"You never trusted your mother? How sad!"

Physically injured and emotionally exhausted, Angel's anger continued to build. He unleashed a string of profanity that she could barely comprehend. When he paused to catch his breath, she went in for the kill.

"I'll tell you what, *maricón*. Why don't I give you a hint that you can trust?"

Angel bubbled with rage. In Mexico, *maricón* was a powerful word. Literally, it means "homosexual," but in the criminal world, it means something different. It means something stronger. It means you are less than a man. "What kind of hint?"

She nodded at Jones, who fired a single bullet into the ground. The gunshot roared like thunder. Angel and his men turned their heads toward the west, trying to pinpoint the exact location of the sound. But it was tough to gauge on one shot alone.

"Did you hear that, *maricón*? Or do you need *another* hint?"

Jones fired a few more rounds, just to make sure.

Angel pointed toward the southern end of the ball court. There was no doubt in his mind the shots had come from there. By this time, his men were raring to go, like sharks that had smelled blood and were ready to attack. All Angel had to do was open their cage.

She cooed at him. "I'm waiting, *maricón*. Do you have the balls to get me?"

Angel stared at his men and growled. "Kill the bitch."

THE *REAL* TIFFANY LISTENED to the taunts through her earpiece, the one she had stolen from her first victim. She laughed the entire time. Within seconds, she had figured out what Payne and Jones were attempting to do. They were hoping to lure Angel's men to a certain part of the site where they would be lying in wait. She wasn't sure if Angel would be stupid enough to fall for the trick, but if he did, she would be ready to take advantage.

ANGEL'S MEN CHARGED FORWARD en masse, riding a wave of passion and inexperience to their impending demise. Had Angel taken a moment to think things through, he would have come up with a better plan than a frontal assault in an enclosed space. Instead, he let his emotions cloud his judgment. It would be a fatal mistake. On the battlefield, guts can do only so much. At some point, brains are more important—especially when the enemy is using theirs.

Less than a minute later, Angel's men arrived on the southern edge of the playing field. They were keyed up and hungry for vengeance. They were also susceptible to deception. To complete the charade, Jones had asked Maria to wait for them at the northern end of the field, where she would taunt them upon their arrival. As soon as they spotted her, she turned and ran up the temple steps. The color of her hair didn't matter. Not from five hundred feet away. The only thing that mattered was catching the bitch who had tried to kill Hector's family.

Without thinking, the men quickly gave chase.

Payne eyed their approach through the front sight of his assault rifle. Elevated above the Great Ball Court, he was protected by one of the stone pillars that held up the temple's facade. His weapon had a standard effective range—the range to consistently hit and severely wound a human torso—of more than sixteen hundred feet. That was approximately three times the width of the playing field. From the moment they stepped onto the grass, Angel's men were in play. And yet he patiently waited until they had closed the distance to two hundred feet. More than halfway there—so they wouldn't turn back—yet far enough from him to pose little threat.

In his mind, it was the perfect kill zone.

Stuck between two walls with nowhere to hide.

Payne opened fire on the approaching horde and cut them down with ease. Head shots. Heart shots. Leg shots. Whatever. They tried to fight back by firing wildly toward the temple. Bullets hit the pillars, the steps, and the front wall, but Payne was too well protected to even flinch. A few men in the rear tried to run back toward the southern end of the stadium, but Jones was waiting for them. He picked them off, one by one, until the only person upright on the field was a man who had died while trying to climb the western wall. Now his body leaned against the slanted base of the wall in the area that had been designated as a team bench.

It almost looked like he was trying to check into the game.

But it was too late. The game was nearly over.

✠   ✠   ✠

WHILE ANGEL AND HIS bodyguards were focused on the west, Tiffany scurried around the base of the pyramid and came up behind them. One shot, then a second. Both from close range. The bodyguards died without raising their guns. Angel whirled and tried to get off a shot at Tiffany, but she was too quick. She fired a bullet through his "good" shoulder. He dropped his weapon and screamed in pain, no longer able to use either arm.

"Quit your crying!" she taunted. "Now you have a matching set."

"Fuck you!" he yelled in Spanish.

She pushed him to the ground and stepped on his wound. "No, fuck you."

He shrieked in agony, unable to speak. In her mind, it was a well-deserved punishment for the slaying of her teammates in Mexico City. She refused to ease up on him until she saw Payne and Jones in the distance. They had spotted her and were coming her way. There were things she needed to learn before they intervened.

She knelt next to Angel. "How did you find me?"

"Fuck you!" he screamed.

She grabbed his freshly wounded arm and twisted it behind his back. With her bullet still lodged in his shoulder, the pain was beyond excruciating. "How'd you find me?"

He howled in pain. "Your picture."

"What picture?" she demanded.

"Someone sent me your picture. They told me where to find you."

"Bullshit!" She twisted his arm deeper.

He screamed again. Blood poured from the wound.

"Prove it," she growled.

He was getting desperate. "The picture . . . It's on my phone. See for yourself."

She dug through his pockets. Sure enough, Angel wasn't lying. There were several close-ups of her on his phone. They were taken at the campground of Old Chichén. Sent to him via e-mail. As she had suspected, someone at the site had tipped him off. She had a pretty good idea who it was. She would deal with him when the time was right.

For now, she had to deal with Angel.

She knew she wouldn't be safe until he was dead.

She pulled her trigger and ended the threat.

64

FOR THE PAST SEVERAL MINUTES, PAYNE AND JONES had been on the same side of this war as Tiffany. Now that Angel was dead, she went back to being their adversary. They approached her cautiously, fully aware of her skills. Payne closed in from the northwest, the assault rifle aimed at her chest. Meanwhile, Jones looped farther south before converging on her location. She was standing next to the pyramid, three corpses at her feet. One was Angel. The other two were his bodyguards. The tattooed men had looked tough, but Tiffany had killed them with ease.

Payne kept that in mind as he moved in. "Drop the weapon!"

She scoffed at his request. "You've got to be shitting me."

"Drop the weapon," Jones echoed.

"Seriously? You *still* don't trust me?"

Payne moved closer. "Can't afford to. We saw you in action."

She smiled at the compliment. "What can I say? This isn't my first rodeo."

Jones took aim. "It will be your *last* rodeo—unless you drop your weapon."

"Wow! You guys are so serious. I thought you'd be more fun." She tossed her weapon to the ground and calmly raised her hands. "I'd heard that you were fun."

"From who?"

"I told you, Jon. I'm not at liberty to say."

The comment pissed Payne off. He charged forward and frisked her. Then he pushed her roughly onto the pyramid steps. Still keyed up from battle, he was sick of her games.

"I'm about to get a lot less fun," he assured her.

"Damn! What's your problem?"

"My problem?" Payne yelled. "Several tourists are dead because of you. Several more are injured because of you. And now you're going to force me to kick the shit out of you to get some answers. Unless, of course, you want me to skip the beating and go right to torture."

She laughed it off. "You won't torture me."

"Really? I saw what you did to Angel. Did it work?"

Jones chimed in. "Do the stick trick. That *always* works."

She glanced at Jones. "The *what*?"

Payne smiled. It was a tactic from the Vietnam War that involved a bullet hole and a very sharp stick. "Can't. She doesn't have an open wound."

Jones grinned. "No problem. I'll give her one."

Before Payne could respond, Jones fired a single round into the pyramid. The bullet hit the steps a few feet above Tiffany's head. The shot was so close that she felt the sting of debris on the back of her neck. She jumped in alarm, stunned that he'd actually fired his gun.

"What the fuck? I'm not the enemy!" she screamed.

"How do we know? You won't tell us who you work for."

"You *know* who I work for. Hamilton told you who I work for."

"Tell us yourself. Or I'll fire again."

"Fine! I work for the CIA—just like Hamilton said." She checked the back of her neck for blood. "Are you happy now? Or do you need me to spell it for you?"

Jones growled. "Wait! What are you suggesting? That black people can't spell CIA? You racist, redheaded spook. I ought to kill you just for that."

Payne nodded in agreement. "She deserves it."

Jones fired again. This time even closer.

"Stop doing that!" she screamed.

Jones shook his head. "Not until you tell us."

"Tell you what?"

Payne answered. "Who is running your op?"

She took a deep breath and nodded. It wouldn't hurt to tell them a little more, especially this late in the game. "I don't know his name. I swear to God I don't. But his code name is Explorer. He says he knows you from back in the day."

"From where?" Payne demanded.

"How the fuck should I know? Your records are sealed, and he wouldn't tell me."

Payne shook his head. "Not good enough."

"Sorry, Jon. It will have to do, because that's all I know about him. If you want to know more, you can ask him yourself. He should be here any minute."

"You've been saying that since the campground."

"What can I say? The guy is late. If I had to guess, I'd say he's waiting for the fireworks to die down. He's not the type to get his hands dirty—so to speak."

She punctuated her comment with a smile, as if she had made a joke that they would eventually understand. It was a feeling they didn't enjoy. Normally they were the ones making jokes. Not the other way around.

"What's so funny?" Jones insisted.

"Nothing," she assured him. "But if I were you, I'd round up Ulster and Pelati. Once Explorer arrives, we'll need to clear out of here in a hurry."

Payne laughed. "Clear out? We're *not* going anywhere with you."

She shrugged. "Suit yourself. If you'd rather stick around and explain to the Federales what happened here, that's fine with me. I'm sure they'll let you go with a warning."

Jones cleared his throat. He hated to side with Tiffany, but it was a valid point. They needed to clear out ASAP. "Jon, she's right. We don't want to be here when the cops arrive. I'm not saying we have to go with her, but—"

"Quiet!" Payne ordered. He turned his ear toward the sky.

"Damn, dude. You don't have to yell at me."

Payne ignored him. "Can you hear that?"

"Hear what?" Jones demanded.

He frantically searched the clouds. "Listen!"

65

PAYNE STEPPED AWAY FROM THE PYRAMID TO IDEN-
tify the source of the sound. But the scope of the building
was messing with the acoustics. "Is that a chopper?"

Jones listened. He heard a distant rumble. "Sounds like it."

She leaned back on the steps, cocky. "Told you he was coming."

Payne scanned the horizon. "You never mentioned a chopper."

She laughed. "Did you think we were going to take a bus? Come
on, Jon. Get serious. We're going to fly out before the Federales
arrive." She glanced at her watch. "Speaking of which, that should
be any minute now. If I were you, I'd get my friends."

Jones looked to Payne for instructions. "Jon?"

Payne continued to listen. The sound was getting closer. It was
definitely a helicopter. "Get Petr, but stay hidden. There's no telling who is coming for us."

Jones sprinted toward the east side of the plaza, where Ulster
was hiding behind the Temple of the Warriors. Maria was much
closer. She was waiting near a small ruin called the Platform of the
Eagles and the Jaguars. It was between the Great Ball Court and

the west side of El Castillo. She would remain there until Payne or Jones signaled for her to come over. After the violence of the past few minutes, she was inclined to follow their orders.

Payne stared at Tiffany, trying to read her face. "If you're lying to me, I'll gun you down before your buddy in the chopper has a chance to take me out. You know that, right?"

"Trust me," she said to him, "he's *not* my buddy. In fact, I have a strange feeling that he told Angel where I was hiding."

The comment piqued Payne's interest. "Why do you say that?"

"Why? Because Angel found me in the middle of nowhere in less than a day. He couldn't have tracked me without help."

"We found you."

She laughed. "No, you didn't. You found *Hamilton*, and only because I sent you an invitation. You wouldn't have found him if I didn't want you to."

"Maybe Angel followed the same trail."

"What trail is that? There's no connection between Hamilton and me. Absolutely none. Angel would have had no reason to check Hamilton's credit card. Not like you."

"Then how'd he find you?"

"Someone sent him my picture."

"How do you know that?"

"Angel told me before his, um, accident. I checked his phone and confirmed it. He had several photos of me at the campsite, taken with a telephoto lens."

"And you think your buddy sent them?"

"I told you, he's *not* my buddy. And, yes, I think he sent them."

"Why would he do that?"

"Why? Because he doesn't like loose ends, and Angel was a dangerous loose end. Hell, I didn't even know the bastard was alive until I saw him here. I thought I'd killed him yesterday. My guess is Explorer put Angel on my scent, so we could take him out together."

Payne furrowed his brow. "Together?"

She nodded. "Why do you think he brought you to Mexico? He viewed you as the ultimate safety net. If anything slipped through the cracks, he knew you and Jones would handle it. And you did. You cut down Angel's army in less than twenty minutes."

"No one brought us to Mexico. We came here on our own."

She laughed. "You still don't get it, do you? Explorer has been playing you from the very beginning. He knows you, Jon. He knows how you think. You, Jones, Ulster, Pelati. He needed your help so he brought you here, one after another."

Payne glanced at the sky. The chopper was approaching.

"Bullshit! No one knows us like that."

"Really? Then how did I know when you'd show up? How'd I know how to lure you here? I didn't plan that shit on my own. Explorer told me what to do and when to do it."

Payne tried to connect the dots, but things weren't clicking.

"Think about it," she said. "He enticed Maria with a job offer. Six hours later, Hamilton was gone, her passport was missing, and she had no one to turn to except . . ."

"Me."

"Actually, no. He thought she would call *Jones*, not you. He screwed that one up. But you two are connected at the hip, so he knew both of you would come running."

Payne grimaced. That's exactly what they had done.

She continued: "Without her passport, Maria couldn't leave the country. Then again, even if she could, she wouldn't abandon Hamilton because of her daddy issues. Explorer knew if Maria was given a father figure, she would cling to him like a baby on a tit."

"Hamilton was in on this?"

"Not knowingly," she admitted. "When I picked him up in Cancún, he honestly thought his life was in danger. And just so you know, he was asking about Maria the entire time. He truly was concerned for her safety."

"Great. I'll be sure to tell her."

"Please do. That girl has enough problems already."

The helicopter was ready to land. He only had time for a few more questions, so he changed the topic. "What about Petr?"

"What about him? We knew you'd call Ulster about the artifacts in the trunk. He's your go-to guy when it comes to history. We also figured he'd hop on a plane to give you a hand. And guess what? We were right."

"But why? Why do you want us here?"

She shrugged. "Unfortunately, that question is above my pay grade. I have no idea what he has in store for you. But I'll admit I'm kind of curious. I'm assuming it's something big."

"Why do you say that?"

"Why? Because Explorer used every trick in the book to assemble four of the top people in their fields, and he did it without you even knowing. Why go through all of that trouble unless it's to conceal something huge?"

Payne stared at her, suspicious. For someone who had been unwilling to talk, she was suddenly a fountain of knowledge. "Why are you telling me this?"

"Because Explorer sold me out. I *know* he sold me out. He led Angel here and didn't have the decency to warn me. A guy like that can't be trusted."

"And I can?"

She nodded. "Pardon me for saying this, but there are a lot of soldiers in the world who are ex–Special Forces. Maybe they aren't as good as you, but they're pretty damn close. And I should know because I've worked with some of them."

"What's your point?"

"Explorer brought you here for a reason. My guess is *trust*."

"Trust?"

"Even though he deceived you—even though he fed you a bunch of lies to get you here—he *still* feels he can trust you. That tells me a lot. That tells me I can trust you, too."

"He trusts me to do what?"

She shrugged. "You'll have to ask him that yourself."

66

PAYNE'S HEAD WAS SPINNING FROM EVERYTHING Tiffany had told him. At first, he had doubted that anyone could know him well enough to predict his every move, but when she broke things down for him, step by step, it sounded within the realm of possibility. Maria had turned to him and Jones for protection. Then the three of them had turned to Ulster for help with the artifacts. In less than a weekend, Explorer had assembled a top-notch team by pulling their strings.

Payne didn't know whether to be pissed off or impressed.

Just to be safe, Payne decided to meet Explorer alone. If he turned out to be someone from Payne's past, then he wanted to deal with him on the chopper before Jones, Maria, and Ulster learned his identity. The CIA was known for its elaborate missions, sometimes leaving sleeper agents in the field for decades before they were called into action, but this was something different. At least sleeper agents were *agents*. They were trained to do the assignment that the Agency had given to them, even if it occurred years after their placement. But this? In addition to *not* being agents, Maria and Ulster weren't even Americans.

Why had Explorer lured them here? What was his endgame?

Payne was eager to find out.

He waited for the dark green utility helicopter to land on the eastern side of the pyramid before rushing to greet it. He used one hand to shield his eyes from the dirt and sand that was kicked up by the chopper. He used the other hand to hold the assault rifle. If he sensed trouble of any kind, he was more than willing to open fire— if for no other reason than to give his friends more time to slip away.

The rear cabin door slid open, revealing an older man in khaki pants and a short-sleeved shirt. Aviator sunglasses covered his eyes. The man, concerned with Payne's mood, raised his hands and waved. Not only to greet Payne but to let him know that he was unarmed. It was a gesture that Payne didn't return. There would be no kindness until he knew what was going on.

Instead of leaving the helicopter, the man backed inside and took a seat on one of the three benches. The rest of the cabin was empty. Other than the pilot, who remained in the cockpit, no one else was on board. Payne made sure before he climbed inside. Only then did he focus on the man. Although his face looked familiar, Payne couldn't quite place it until the man took off his sunglasses and flashed a cat-that-ate-the-canary smile. Then everything clicked.

It was Dr. Charles Boyd, Maria's onetime mentor.

A man who had lived a double life for decades.

A spy who had been outed by Payne and Jones.

Payne groaned in recognition. "Son of a bitch."

Boyd smiled wider. "Hello to you, too."

✠ ✠ ✠

BORN CHARLES IAN HOLLOWAY, Explorer had been known by many names over the years. He had attended the U.S. Naval

Academy in the early 1960s. Upon graduation, he was loaned to the Pentagon for an "alternative tour of duty," after which Charles Holloway ceased to exist. Reborn as Charles Boyd, he majored in archaeology and linguistics at Oxford. He was eventually hired by Dover University, where he rose through the teaching ranks and was named head of the archaeology department in 1991. By that time, his reputation as a scholar was well established. This allowed him to travel the world without drawing attention. His cover as an academic allowed him to pursue his true agenda as a CIA operative. The CIA financed his intellectual pursuits; in exchange, he was obliged to do their bidding. Nothing too extravagant—mostly smuggling and simple intelligence—but important nonetheless.

Since Boyd truly enjoyed the activities associated with his cover, he continued to work as a professor and an archaeologist even after the CIA gave him the opportunity to move on. His research at one particular site, the catacombs of Orvieto, had attracted an inquisitive student with a passion for history: a much younger Maria Pelati. Familiar with her surname—and her father's influence in Italy—Boyd took her under his wing, where she quickly blossomed into his best pupil. He was so impressed by her abilities that he hired her as his teaching assistant. During the school year, they worked side by side in the classroom. During the summer months, they worked side by side in the field. Their relationship went beyond professor and student. She viewed him as a mentor and a surrogate father, someone she could look up to and trust.

But Boyd had been lying to her the entire time.

His double life finally came to light after they had discovered the catacombs of Orvieto. Inside the legendary site, they found a scroll that threatened the sanctity of the Catholic Church. Fearing the damage it would cause, Benito Pelati tried to fix the problem by accusing Boyd of murder and theft. In the course of a week, Boyd went from a respected academic to one of the most sought-after fugitives in all of Europe—and Maria was labeled as his accomplice.

Known for their ability to track targets, Payne and Jones were coerced by two CIA agents to find Boyd before anyone else could capitalize on his discovery. It took a while, but they eventually found Boyd and Maria in Milan. Payne and Jones were ready to turn them over when they sensed that something wasn't quite right. As it turned out, the men were actually working with Benito Pelati, and they had been paid handsomely to ensure that no one— including Maria—would bring the damning information about Christianity to light. To convince Payne and Jones of his innocence and to save his life, Boyd was forced to reveal his role with the Agency and his nonofficial cover status. This was done at gunpoint in front of Maria.

In a matter of minutes, Maria had learned that her father had sent two men to kill her *and* that her surrogate father was a longtime spy who had been deceiving her for years.

After that, it was tough for her to trust anyone.

Especially men.

☩   ☩   ☩

PAYNE HELD HIS weapon steady. "I thought you had retired."

Boyd shook his head. "Apparently not."

"Still with the Agency?"

"I am indeed."

Payne considered Boyd's claim. It would be tough to verify in the field, since CIA agents weren't issued credentials of any kind. Normally he would just call Raskin and ask him, but he was temporarily off limits. "Out of curiosity, how does someone stay on active duty after a clusterfuck like Orvieto? Your picture was on the front page of every newspaper in Europe. I'm guessing that much publicity would make it impossible to do your job."

"I guess that depends on one's job."

"You're no longer an operative?"

"Not in the conventional sense, no. Then again, nothing about my career has been conventional. You know that better than most."

Payne nodded. "I guess I do."

Boyd crossed his legs in front of him. He appeared to be calm, totally under control. "So, I guess you're wondering why you're here."

"The question had crossed my mind."

"I was hoping to share that morsel with everybody, but since you are currently pointing an assault rifle at my chest, I am going to assume that is highly unlikely."

"What gave it away? My rifle or my rifle?"

Boyd smiled. "Glad to see that your wit is still working."

"So is my trigger finger, in case you're wondering."

He laughed, not the least bit afraid. "Tell me, my boy, what can we do to speed this along? I realize you must have several questions to ask, but upon our descent, we happened to notice a congregation of flashing lights that were headed this way. Based on conservative estimates, I say we have less than a minute to depart before we are fired upon by the Federales."

"What's your point?"

"My point? I realize that attacks of this nature happen to you frequently—so often, in fact, that you have built an unnatural tolerance to the threat of gunfire. However, I have a sneaking suspicion that Maria and Petr do not share your cavalier attitude about such things."

"Probably not."

"Then what do you say we invite them on board for a mini-reunion? I'd be happy to whisk them away to safety before they have to deal with any violence."

Payne raised his voice. "The only reason they're facing violence is because of you."

"Touché," Boyd said with a laugh. "And yet somehow I think they'll forgive me once I tell them why they're here."

"Why *are* they here?"

Boyd shook his head. "That, I'm afraid, I must keep to myself until we are in the air."

Payne glanced out the cabin door and spotted flashing lights near the main entrance of Chichén Itzá. Boyd wasn't lying. The cops would be there any second. Although he didn't trust the man, Payne sensed they weren't in any physical danger from Boyd. If he had wanted to hurt them, he could have done so already. With that in mind, Payne decided it would be safer to go with Boyd than to take their chances with the Federales. He figured if they didn't like what Boyd had to say, they could always leave him later.

"We'll come with you on one condition," Payne said.

"Which is?" Boyd asked.

"I need you to stay in the cockpit until I have a chance to explain what is going on."

"Why is that?"

Payne stared at him, serious. "If Maria sees you before I have a chance to brief her, there's a damn good chance she will throw your ass out of the chopper."

Boyd laughed. "Trust me, I know Maria better than any of you. She doesn't have a violent bone in her body."

"Is that so? When was the last time you talked to her?"

"It's been several years, I'm afraid."

"In that case, you don't know her at all."

67

AFTER ROUNDING UP ULSTER AND MARIA FROM different ends of the site, Jones waited in the nearby trees for Payne's signal. Once the all-clear was flashed, the three of them hustled to the helicopter, where they were joined by Hamilton and Tiffany. Payne pulled them aboard, one after another, and ordered them to sit down and buckle up. It would be a bumpy takeoff. Police in riot gear charged through the front gate as the chopper left the ground in a cloud of dust. The pilot banked hard to the north, barely clearing the trees as they flew over the Sacred Well. Having missed the chance to see it from the ground, Ulster stared wistfully out of the cabin window. It was the last thing he recognized before the jungle swallowed the horizon.

The multipurpose utility helicopter had three bench seats and a small cargo area in the rear. Payne and Jones sat on the closest bench to the cockpit. Hamilton and Tiffany were in the middle. Ulster and Maria were way in the back. Payne had purposely seated them in this order. He wanted a chance to talk to Jones in private before they were forced to tell Maria about Boyd's involvement. Payne had a feeling that Jones would want to handle that conversation. At least Payne hoped he would. Otherwise, the ride might get even bumpier.

The droning of the rotors made it difficult to talk in the belly of the chopper. It would be even tougher to eavesdrop. Payne and Jones could chat all day, and they weren't the least bit concerned about being overheard.

Jones leaned in. "Who's running the op?"

Payne answered. "Boyd."

"Boyd who?"

"*Charles* Boyd."

Jones did a double take. "I thought he was retired."

"So did I."

Over the next few minutes, Payne told Jones everything he had learned in his conversations with Tiffany and Boyd. Jones listened intently, not the least bit amused about being played. He prided himself on being ten steps ahead of his opponent, yet he had failed to connect any of the dots. All along he had been saying that something was off—Hamilton's disappearance, the trunk of artifacts, the cache of weapons—but he hadn't seen this one coming.

"What does he want with us?" Jones asked.

Payne shrugged. "The cops showed up before he could tell me."

"Fuckin' cops. Always screwing things up."

"Tell me about it."

Jones paused in thought. "What's his role at the Agency?"

"He claimed he isn't an operative anymore. I tend to believe him. His name was dragged through the mud with all of those false charges. It would have been tough to continue after that."

"You can't be a spy if your contacts don't trust you."

"What else could he be?"

"Maybe an analyst. Maybe an instructor. With his teaching background, I could see him at the training academy."

Payne shook his head. "Those gigs would be near Washington. No way he'd be running a mission in Mexico if he were an analyst or an instructor. He has to be something else."

"Maybe he went rogue."

"Rogue?"

"It would explain a lot—including his need for cheap talent. He lured four of us to Cancún with a suite and a plane ticket. The crafty bastard."

Payne glanced at Maria. For now, she was sitting quietly next to Ulster. But he knew it was only a matter of time before she left her seat and asked what was going on. "Speaking of which, who is going to tell Maria?"

"I vote for Petr. *Definitely* Petr. It's tough to stay mad at Petr."

Payne laughed. "Chicken."

"You're damn right I'm chicken. She *knows* I won't shoot her. Without that threat, there's no way I can protect myself."

"Just so you know, *I'm* willing to shoot her."

"Then *you* should tell her."

Payne smiled. "In all seriousness, I will if you want me to."

Jones weighed the offer. "Thanks, but no thanks. She needs to hear it from me. It will go down easier coming from me."

"You're probably right."

"But do me a favor. Keep your rifle loaded, just in case."

✠   ✠   ✠

AFTER SWITCHING SEATS with Ulster, Jones filled Maria in on the pertinent details of the last few hours. Her face flushed with embarrassment when she realized that she had been manipulated. Jones assured her that she wasn't alone—that everyone, including

Hamilton, had been deceived in one way or another—and they would confront the mastermind together. For the briefest of moments, she felt better about the situation. And then she asked the question.

"Who set us up?" she wondered.

Jones grimaced. "That's where things get messy."

"Messy? What do you mean?"

"You aren't going to like it."

"Who is it?" she demanded.

"Charles Boyd."

She heard the name and winced. It hit her like a punch to the gut, one she didn't expect. After years of denial, she knew she would be forced to deal with some issues that had never gone away. She had done her best to bury them, but they were still there, lurking deep inside her psyche like a childhood trauma she had just remembered. Her heart raced. Her hands perspired. Her face turned pale. Jones wasn't sure if she was going to pass out or explode with rage, but he was prepared for either possibility. Instead, she did something that surprised him. She took a few deep breaths, then nodded in acceptance.

"Is he in the cockpit?" she asked.

He studied her face. "Why?"

"I'd like to talk to him."

He arched his brow. "Is this some kind of trick?"

"Trick?"

"Are you *pretending* to be calm so I lower my defenses?"

"Not at all," she assured him as the color gradually returned to her face. "I'd honestly like to talk to him. There are some questions I'd love to ask. It's been a long time."

"How long?"

"Years." Her mind drifted back to the days after their discovery in Orvieto. Back then, she was still in graduate school, a few years from her doctorate, and Boyd was still her mentor. "He told me he had to return to the States to clear his name from all the rumors. He said he would be back in a couple of weeks, but . . ."

"What?"

"He never came back. No calls. No e-mails. Nothing. I haven't talked to him since."

Jones swallowed hard. "I didn't know that."

She laughed bitterly. "How could you know? I didn't tell anyone. After that, I went into hiding for a very long time. I cut off contact from my friends. I was too ashamed to tell anyone."

"Ashamed? Why would you be ashamed?"

"Why do you think? My father made up those rumors about him. It cost him his job. It cost him his reputation. It cost him *everything.* I wouldn't want to talk to me, either."

"Hold up! You're blaming yourself for your father's actions? Pardon me for saying so, but that's crazy. The man killed your mother. He tried to kill you. He tried to kill all of us. None of us blame you for what he did. You have to know that. None of it was your fault."

Tears welled up in her eyes. "Yeah, but—"

He cut her off. "No buts. That's it. End of story. I'll shout it to the heavens until the day I die. You are *not* to blame for your father's actions. You are *not* to blame for your brother's death. And you are *not* to blame for Boyd's departure. The guy was an operative in the CIA. He lied to you for years. There are a million possible reasons for his disappearance, none of which have *anything* to do with you. And if he *tries* to blame you, I'm going to shoot the bastard."

Maria said nothing. Instead, she reached out with both hands, grabbed Jones behind the head, and pulled him in for a kiss. A long, passionate kiss. It was so unexpected it left him gasping for air. When it was over, she leaned back in the seat and flashed him a smile.

"Sorry about that. Had to be done. I hope you're not mad."

Jones shook his head, unable to speak.

✠   ✠   ✠

ULSTER SAW THE KISS from across the chopper. A romantic at heart, he was thrilled by the development. He was rooting for the pair to get back together. He elbowed Payne in the ribs to make sure he saw it. "I think David might get lucky."

Payne grumbled. "I hope they wait until *after* we land."

Ulster continued to stare. "I don't."

68

MÉRIDA, MEXICO
(74 MILES WEST OF CHICHÉN ITZÁ)

THE HELICOPTER LANDED IN A FIELD ON THE OUT-
skirts of Mérida, the capital city of the Yucatán. With
access to several ports to the north, an international airport to the
south, and a population of more than a million people, Mérida
was a great place for a safe house.

Boyd climbed out of the cockpit and signaled for everyone to
join him inside a small cinder-block building. Concealed by trees
and camouflage netting that had been draped over the roof, the
structure was invisible from the air. Payne eyed it suspiciously,
wondering what the CIA was trying to hide. He would find out
soon enough.

One by one, they filed into the lone room and took seats in col-
lapsible wooden chairs that sat underneath cheap banquet tables.
A portable chalkboard, covered by a canvas tarp, sat against the
wall across from the only door. Ulster rubbed his hands together
in anticipation, anxious to see what was written underneath.
Meanwhile, Maria was anxious for a different reason. She was
eager to question Boyd, who had done everything to avoid eye con-

tact with her. He realized they needed to talk, but he wanted to wait until after his briefing.

He walked to the front of the makeshift classroom and faced the group. He did not smile or frown. His face was neutral. Ulster and Hamilton were sitting at the first table. Maria and Jones were at the second. Payne remained standing by the door, the rifle in his hands. The only one who wasn't there was Tiffany, who had duties to perform outside.

Boyd cleared his throat and was ready to begin.

Maria never gave him a chance. "Where have you been?"

"Excuse me?" he said.

"None of us have heard from you in years. Now, after all of that time, you resurface to screw with our lives. Where have you been?"

"I'll get to that in a moment, Maria, but first—"

She interrupted him. "Actually, that's *Dr. Pelati.* Or haven't you heard? I finished my doctorate a while back. No thanks to you."

"No thanks to me?" The words stung, more than she could have possibly known. "I realize you're harboring some animosity toward me over my disappearance. However, I don't believe this is the time or place to discuss such personal matters."

Payne spoke up. "I disagree. I think this is the perfect time."

She glanced over her shoulder. "Thank you, Jon."

Jones nodded. "I'd like to know, too. Where have you been?"

Ulster chimed in. "I think it's a reasonable question."

Boyd clenched his jaw. This wasn't how he had imagined it. He had a detailed lecture planned, similar to the ones he had written when he was still a professor. Now he would have to scrap it for an informal Q&A. "All right, *Dr.* Pelati. I shall honor your request and answer your query. After all this time, it's the least I can do."

"You can say that again," she said bitterly.

He took a deep breath. This would be more difficult than he

had thought. He hadn't been expecting so much anger. "Where would you like me to start?"

"How about the moment you abandoned me? You left me at the Archives and said you would return in two weeks. But it's been—oh, I don't know—*years*. Why didn't you come back for me like you had promised?"

He shrugged. "I wasn't allowed."

"Why not?"

"The Agency felt my time had run its course in Europe. After all the negative publicity I had received, they no longer felt I could be an effective operative."

"You were fired?"

He shook his head. "Reassigned."

"Why didn't you call?"

"I wasn't allowed to call. I wasn't allowed to write. They ordered me to distance myself from Orvieto. They felt a clean break was the only way to proceed. They made me promise not to call or contact you in any way, so I did what they asked—as hard as that was to do."

"You should have made them understand! One call would have made all the difference in the world. At least I would have known you cared."

He spoke from the heart. "I *do* care about you, but I simply couldn't risk it at the time. They were watching me too closely. As hard as this is to accept, the CIA was my life. From the time I was a boy, the only thing I wanted to be was a spy. I never dreamed of being an astronaut or an athlete, a cowboy or a fireman. I just wanted to be a spy. Along the way, I picked up other passions— such as archaeology and history—but my main focus has always been the Agency."

"In other words, you cared more about your career than me."

"Maria, I hope you realize that working for the Agency isn't like working for IBM. There are codes you must follow, rules you must obey. If you don't, coworkers can die. Innocent civilians can die. If you stray outside the lines, the Agency won't fire you. They will lock you up and throw away the key. If you don't believe me, ask Jonathon or David."

She looked at Jones, who nodded reluctantly.

Boyd continued. "Think about what I gave up to follow the Agency's directives. You and I had just made a *major* archaeological discovery, one that threatened to rewrite the history of Christianity. Don't you think I wanted to be a part of that? After all the time we had spent in the field, do you know how difficult it was to walk away from Orvieto? It ripped my heart out, but I did it willingly and without remorse. Do you know why?"

"Because they asked you to."

"Partly. But also because of you."

"Me?" she said, confused.

He nodded. "The Agency is *very* territorial. If they knew I had discovered the catacombs on the company's dime, they would have demanded compensation. That would have affected you, and Petr, and all of the scholars who had a chance to study our findings at the Archives. Ultimately, I did the selfless thing and walked away."

"That's absurd! How could the CIA stake a claim in Orvieto? To get a piece of the pie, they would have to admit that you were an operative. There is no way they would've done that."

He shook his head. "They wouldn't have to admit anything. They would get their money through backdoor channels. They would funnel it through their shell companies."

To fund black operations (off-the-book missions), government organizations have to get their financing from nonpublic sources. Oftentimes fake companies are established to help foot the bills. The FBI has Red River Mining, the Navy has Pacific Salvage, and the Pentagon has several dozen, some of which enabled units like the MANIACs to carry out their missions.

Boyd continued: "While teaching at Dover, I received regular stipends from one of these shell companies. Had I stayed in Europe to study the catacombs, I am confident that the CIA would have made things difficult for all of us. So I did the honorable thing and fell on my sword."

"Meaning?"

"I told the director that *you* had made the discovery, and I was merely a faculty adviser along for the ride. If not for your surname, I doubt he would have believed me. In truth, I'm not sure he did believe me. However, due to the murder of your father and the scandal that followed, he ordered me to walk away to keep the Agency clean."

She stared at him, trying to decide if his explanation was plausible. Eventually, she decided that it was. "For the time being, let's *pretend* that's what happened—that you walked away from Orvieto for my sake, and Petr's sake, and all of the scholars of the world. You still haven't answered my original question. Where have you been?"

"I have been here."

She glanced around the room. "In this shed?"

He shook his head. "In Mexico."

"Doing what?"

"Working as an archaeologist."

"I thought you still worked for the Agency."

"I *do* work for the Agency. I work for them as an archaeologist. After the events of Orvieto, the director wanted me as far from Europe as possible. They considered the Far East for a while but decided against it, since I didn't have the language skills or the theological background to be effective. Africa was also considered, but once again it proved to be a poor fit for my skill set. Ultimately, they decided that Mexico was the best place for my rebirth."

"Why Mexico?" Jones wondered.

"I am an expert in Christianity, I speak fluent Spanish, and, above all else, I told them that I had some leads that I wanted to pursue."

"What kind of leads?"

"Archaeological leads."

Jones ordered him to stop. "Let me see if I got this straight. For the past several years, you've been working for the CIA as an archaeologist? Not an operative pretending to be an archaeologist but an *actual* archaeologist?"

Boyd nodded. "As I mentioned, my name and face were too recognizable to continue clandestine operations in the traditional sense, so the CIA redefined my position. With me at the helm, they launched a new company that specializes in archaeological endeavors. Technically speaking, it isn't a shell company that only exists on paper. Instead, it is a *front* company, one with legitimate operations that are used to conceal covert activities. The name of the company is Global Archaeological Enterprises."

Jones considered the acronym. "Your company's name is GAE?"

Ulster ignored the question. "I'm actually familiar with your enterprise. You've made some solid discoveries. I recall a decent haul in Chile. And another one in Malta."

"We've done pretty well—certainly well enough to keep the Agency happy. In addition to the income stream, we have placed operatives around the globe in a variety of positions. The company has been a win-win for everyone."

Payne spoke up. "Then why did you just blow its cover?"

Boyd glanced at him. "Excuse me?"

"As far as I know, DJ and I are the only people in this room with a security clearance. If your company is so successful, why did you just blow its cover?"

"Trust me, Jonathon, if there was any other way, I would have kept that information to myself. However, considering the business proposal that I'm about to offer, I could see no way around it. You needed to know the truth."

Maria rolled her eyes. "Proposal? After all this time, you're going to offer us a proposal? You have got to be joking! Why in the world would we get into business with you?"

"Because it's the right thing to do."

"The right thing? Coming from you, that means *nothing*."

"Actually, it will mean quite a bit once you hear my proposal. I'm fairly certain you will be happy with the terms."

She crossed her arms against her chest. "Happy? I doubt anything that you say will make me happy. I'm a *long* way from happy."

"Same here," Payne said, "but what have we got to lose? He's already lured us to Mexico. We might as well listen to what he has to say. That is, if it's okay with you."

Maria didn't speak. She just nodded.

"Go on, Charles. We're waiting. What's your proposal?"

Boyd glanced around the room, making eye contact with one person after another. Finally, his eyes settled on Maria. He stared at her for several seconds before he spoke. "We're *this* close to uncovering one of the most important treasures in the history of the Americas, and I need your help to claim the prize."

69

MARIA WAS CONFUSED BY HIS STATEMENT. "WHAT treasure?"

Boyd ignored the question. "Tell me, Maria, what do you know about shared perspectives?"

She groaned in frustration. Back when she was his student, Boyd had an annoying habit of evading her questions by asking questions of his own. Nothing was easy with him. He made her work for everything. One question from her would lead to five questions from him, each more difficult than the last. In the long run, it taught her to think for herself. But at the time, it was frustrating as hell. Even simple questions—such as *What time is it?*—would lead to ten-minute discussions. Eventually she learned the best way to shut him up was to front-load her answers. The more she appeared to know, the less he would question her.

"I know quite a bit," she said cockily, trying to rub his nose in all she had learned without him. "We were discussing the concept earlier today. Petr used a hypothetical bombing of the city of Jerusalem to illustrate the importance of different perspectives to understand the true history of an event. Up until now, everything we know about the conquest of Mexico has been told from the Spanish point of view. They wrote the history books, so they controlled what we know about that particular chapter. Without a detailed account of the Maya side of the conquest, we only know half the story."

He corrected her. "Actually, we only know a third of the story, because the Spanish conquered two major civilizations in this part of the world: the Maya *and* the Aztecs."

Jones came to her defense. "Not to argue semantics, but shouldn't the Spanish Conquest be viewed as two separate stories? The Spanish versus the Maya is one story. The Spanish versus the Aztecs is the other. As far as I know, there wasn't much interaction between the Maya and Aztecs. I don't see how they could offer details on each other's defeat."

Boyd smiled knowingly. "Unless, of course, they were defeated by the same object. In that case, their perspectives would be quite beneficial."

"The same object? What does that mean?" she asked.

He glanced at Ulster, who was sitting in the front row. "Tell me, Petr, in your long career as a historian, have you ever heard of an artifact known as the Death Relic?"

Ulster scratched his beard in thought. "The Death Relic? No, I'm afraid not. If I had, I'm quite confident I would have remembered it. The name is rather ominous."

Boyd nodded. "I thought so, too, when I came across the term a few years ago. I found it in the journal of a South American merchant who arrived in Mexico several decades after Hernándo Cortés had seized Tenochtitlan. During the course of the merchant's travels, the indigenous population of Mexico—the Tlaxcalans, the Totonacs, and so on—regaled him with stories of the demise of the Aztec Empire. Over and over, the natives spoke of a magical object that the Spanish had carried into battle, one that gave them power and strength. Eventually, this item became so feared by the mighty Aztecs that they associated it with death. Hence the name."

Ulster grinned at the possibilities. "A relic of death! How utterly fascinating! Obviously I am familiar with charms and amulets being described in pagan folklore, but rarely do you find one associated with Christian forces. Please, tell us more."

"Initially, there was nothing more to tell. Even though the object was mentioned several times in the merchant's journal, I was unable to find any secondary sources that backed his claim. As you know, the Spanish were very thorough in their destruction of native documents. That forced me to turn to the writings of the priests and conquistadores who dealt with the Aztecs in the early years of the Conquest—men like Bernal Díaz del Castillo, Diego Durán, and Bartolomé de las Casas. Unfortunately, there was no mention of the object. Not that I expected one. After all, their writings have been analyzed by scholars for centuries. If one of them had described a magical relic, I'm confident that I would have heard of it."

Ulster urged him on. "What happened next?"

"I was ready to write off the story as a myth, nothing more than the fanciful creation of a lonely merchant, when I decided to approach things from a different angle. Since Cortés and his men had landed on the Gulf Coast before their long march to the west, I wondered if the indigenous tribes of the east might have heard rumors about the magical object. My knowledge of the Maya was somewhat lacking, so I reached out to Terrence via e-mail. Much to my surprise, he informed me that he had recently come across an account of a similar object being used by the Spanish against the Maya. It had the same name and the same magical qualities. The Maya were so scared of the relic that they abandoned their cities when they saw it coming."

Maria grimaced. "They ran in fear?"

"Fear is an understatement. Like the Aztecs, they associated this object with death. They did everything in their power to avoid it and the men who carried it."

Hamilton entered the conversation. "Over the years, I have assembled a substantial database of Mayan glyphs—words and phrases that were carved in stone, painted on ceramics, or written in one of the remaining codices—that I use to translate documents and authenticate discoveries. Prior to Cortés, who arrived in Mexico in 1519, I could not find a single reference to an object known as the Death Relic. However, in the decades that followed the arrival of the Spanish, a new pictograph surfaced in the world of the Maya, a symbol that looks remarkably similar to their Death God. The differences are subtle, but once I knew what to look for, I found the symbol over and over again in artwork throughout Mexico."

To illustrate his point, Hamilton walked to the chalkboard and removed the tarp. On the surface underneath, there was a series of ancient words, glyphs, pictographs, and translations that had been scrawled in different colored chalks. To Payne, Jones, and Maria, it looked like gibberish. To Boyd and Ulster, it had significance. Hamilton tried his best to bridge the gap between the two groups.

He pointed at a drawing on the left side of the board. The creature had a skeleton face, grinning teeth, and an exposed spine. Bells and rattles decorated its wrists and legs. An ornament of some kind rested on its head. "This is a pictograph of the Mayan Death God. It goes by many names. It appears in art, architecture, and writing. It is one of the most common images in the history of the Mayan civilization, dating back more than a thousand years. We have found it at sites from northern Mexico to southern Guatemala."

Jones stared at the creature. "He's an ugly bastard."

Maria nodded in agreement. "He certainly is."

Hamilton moved a few feet to their right and pointed at a second image. Though it looked similar to the first, it had an important modification: two bones, in the shape of an X, hung from a cord around its neck. Hamilton picked up a piece of chalk and circled the necklace. "I realize the difference is small. Nevertheless, it is quite significant. In terms of the modern alphabet, think of it like this: The difference between an O and a Q is merely the tail at the bottom of a circle. In the language of the Maya, the difference between the Death God and the Death Relic is this necklace of bones. It completely changes its meaning."

"When did it first appear?" Ulster asked.

Hamilton answered, "It's impossible to tell, due to the inexact nature of carbon dating. The best that we can guess is that it first appeared here, in Mérida, in the mid-1500s, before the image spread throughout the Yucatán like a plague. Based on that assumption, we concentrated our efforts in Mérida, starting with a few contacts that I have at the Roman Catholic archdiocese in the city. Since the local monks were known for their detailed records of the Maya, we thought they might be able to point us in the right direction. We were hoping for something small, perhaps the scent of a distant bread crumb that we could follow to another source. Instead, they unwittingly handed us a whole loaf of bread: they gave us the diary of Marcos de Mercado."

70

Before discussing the diary, Hamilton filled them in on the basic history. Otherwise, Payne and Jones wouldn't understand the significance of the discovery.

"Diego de Landa arrived in the Yucatán in 1549 to encourage the Maya's conversion to Catholicism. The Spanish monarchy gave the Franciscans nearly unlimited discretion, and Landa took full advantage. In spite of his conservation efforts with regard to the Mayan languages, Landa is best remembered for his annihilation of the Maya and their artifacts."

"Hold up," Jones demanded. "He preserved the language but destroyed the artifacts?"

"Yes," Hamilton answered. "He was stationed as a monk in the mission at Izamal, a small city to the east of Mérida, where he took interest in the Maya's use of glyphs and decided to translate them into Spanish. With the help of Mayan elders, he established the base for their glyphs that is still used by scholars today. However, in July of 1562, Landa ordered an auto-da-fé in the city of Maní. It is said that he ceremonially burned more than twenty-five thousand artifacts that he deemed blasphemous. From that point on, the Maya and their culture were under constant threat, all because of Landa's desire to convert them to Catholicism."

Boyd added to the explanation. "Landa's action did not go unnoticed. The Council of the Indies took an interest in his behavior, going as far as forming a committee to determine whether Landa had committed any crimes. Even after Francisco de Toral had testified against him, Landa was cleared of any wrongdoing."

"Who was Toral?" Jones asked.

"Toral was the first bishop of the Yucatán and the first man to officially accuse Landa of unwarranted brutality. It was Toral who had first complained to the powers that be. Interestingly, when Toral died, it was Landa who was chosen to replace him. Somehow Landa had gone from a man accused of inhumane atrocities to the most powerful man in the Yucatán. Returning from his trial in Spain, Landa once again enacted a brutal crusade against the Maya. His cruelty was universally despised by the natives, the monks, and even by the Spanish soldiers."

Hamilton picked up from there. "Over the centuries, historians have speculated about Landa's return to Mesoamerica. No one could understand why the Church would grant him this freedom. That is, until we read the diary of Marcos de Mercado. Then it all made sense."

According to the journal, Landa bought his freedom with the promise of a vast treasure. He convinced the Church that he had assembled a massive stockpile of Mayan artifacts—items that he had deemed too valuable to burn. In exchange for his release, he was willing to hide these items from the King and smuggle them to the Church instead. To make sure that Landa followed through with his promise, Mercado was assigned by the Church to chronicle Landa's movement upon his return to the Yucatán. Prior to the priesthood, Mercado had trained as a soldier, so they felt he was the perfect choice to spy on Landa in hostile terrain.

"Initially, Landa didn't trust Mercado—and rightfully so. But everything changed in 1572 when a group of Mayan warriors tried to kill Landa in a small town near here. Mercado intervened and saved the bishop's life. After that, Landa trusted him implicitly."

Ulster raised his hand. He had read several pages of Mercado's journal, faxed to him by Payne, but couldn't recall that particular story. "Pardon the interruption, but is that anecdote in the journal? I don't remember any violence in the sections that I examined."

Boyd answered for Hamilton. "The journal is more than three hundred pages in length. It details everything from his voyage to the New World through his pilgrimage to the west and his return back to Mérida. It is a fascinating read, one that I'm sure you'll enjoy. We'll be happy to let you read it in its entirety. That is, if you choose to accept our proposal."

"Finally!" Payne blurted from the back of the room. "Tell me more about your proposal. What's our role in things?"

Boyd smiled. "I assure you, Jonathon, all of this history is necessary for you to understand your role in things. We'll be getting to my proposal in just a moment. Trust me."

Payne shook his head. "Actually, Charles, that's the problem. We don't trust you—not one bit. Why should we, after all of the crap that you've pulled this weekend?"

Boyd nodded in understanding. "Now that you mention it, I see your dilemma. I haven't earned the right to be trusted. Perhaps it is time to move things along?"

Payne patted his rifle. "Yes, perhaps it is."

Boyd continued the story, skipping years of history to describe the pot of gold at the end of the rainbow. "After gaining his trust, Mercado discovered that Landa had been truthful with the Church—that he had, in fact, saved several thousand Mayan artifacts during his earlier stint in the Yucatán. The cache included jewelry, statues, masks, icons, and hundreds of Mayan codices, all of which were stored in a cave near Mérida. Landa planned to ship some of the treasure back to Spain, thus staying in the good graces of the Church, while keeping the best items for himself. Because of his military training, Mercado was put in charge of selecting the most trustworthy soldiers in the Yucatán to accompany the treasure on its voyage across the sea. Instead, Mercado handpicked a squad of soldiers who were infuriated by Landa's atrocities and asked them to steal the treasure before it could be sent back to Spain."

Jones perked up. "Mercado stole the treasure? That's awesome!"

Payne asked, "Do you know where it is?"

Boyd answered, "His journal referenced an ancient pyramid that had been concealed by locals to protect it from the Spanish. We assumed he was referring to another location in Mérida."

"Why's that?" Maria asked.

"Because Mérida was built on top of an ancient city named Ichcaanzihó. In Mayan, the name means 'city of the five hills,' which refers to the five pyramids that once graced this region. We figured Mercado simply moved the treasure to another part of Mérida, but we were wrong. He actually put the treasure on a Spanish ship and sent it to the west."

Jones furrowed his brow. "The west? I'm not great at geography, but I'm pretty sure Spain is to the *east*—unless he was taking the scenic route."

Boyd shook his head. "Mercado had no intention of sending it to Spain, and he had no intention of selling it for profit. Instead, he was looking for the best place to hide it in Mexico, and that happened to be in the mountains to the west."

"Hold up! Mercado shipped the treasure *from* Mexico *to* Mexico?"

"That is correct."

"To who?"

Boyd replied: "To his older brother, Manuel. He was a conquistador who had assembled a team of compassionate soldiers that had discovered an Aztec treasure on the outskirts of Tenochtitlan. Manuel's goal was not to plunder but to preserve the history of the Aztecs before it was completely erased. In that regard, the Mercados were very similar to the Ulsters."

Ulster laughed at the comparison. "I do believe this is the first time I have ever been compared to a conquistador. Perhaps I should get a helmet?"

Payne smiled at the image. "Let me see if I've got this straight. The younger Mercado stole a Mayan treasure from Diego de Landa and sent it west. The older Mercado, who already had an Aztec treasure, unloaded the Mayan cargo from the ship and did what with it? He combined the two treasures into one massive hoard?"

Boyd nodded. "According to Marcos's diary, that's exactly what happened in March of 1574. Roughly a year later, he abandoned his post with Landa and traveled west to meet his brother. The two reunited in the summer of 1575, at which time they moved the Mercado treasure into its current resting place. The brothers lived together in Puebla for nearly two decades until Manuel died from a high fever. Marcos eventually returned to Mérida in 1596—seventeen years after the death of Landa—and served out his term with the archdiocese."

"But the treasure remained out west?" Maria asked.

"Yes. I'm quite confident it did."

"Why are you so sure?"

"Because we found it," Boyd claimed.

"You *found* the Mercado treasure?"

"Yes."

"When?" she demanded.

Boyd glanced at his watch. "About twenty hours ago."

Jones joined the conversation. "Then what in the hell are you doing here? Shouldn't you be rolling around in piles of gold?"

"I wish I could," Boyd admitted. "Unfortunately, it's not that simple for a man in my position. If I were to stake a claim on this treasure, the first thing I would be required to do is notify the CIA of my involvement. From that moment on, the Agency would take an active interest in the acquisition process—the thought of which is something I dread. Although I'm a company man, the last place I want a treasure of this magnitude to end up is in some bunker in Langley, Virginia. Instead, I want it to be studied by scholars from around the globe, academics who are searching for answers to the mysteries of the Aztec and the Maya. I want this treasure to be displayed at the Ulster Archives."

Ulster nearly fell off his chair. "Are you serious?"

Boyd nodded. "Quite."

"But wait, you want me to, I mean, you're giving me . . . *really*?"

"Yes, really. That is, if you're willing to accept the terms of my proposal."

Ulster leaned forward. "I'm listening."

"First of all, I want Terrence to be listed as the coleader of the team that discovered this treasure. Without his insight into the Maya and his connections in the Yucatán, I would still be searching."

Ulster nodded. "Done."

"Secondly, I want Maria to be listed as the other coleader. Instead of me, she will be given credit for my half of the discovery."

Maria balked at the idea. "No way! Not a chance! I didn't *do* anything to find this treasure. There's no way in hell I want my name associated with it."

Boyd stared at her. "Don't worry, my dear, your job is yet to come."

"My job? What job is that?"

"A moment ago, I mentioned that Terrence and I had located

the Mercado treasure. In reality, we have discovered the *location* of the treasure, not the treasure itself. The hoard itself still needs to be claimed. To do so, one final piece of the puzzle still needs to be solved—a piece that happens to fall into your area of expertise: Christianity."

"How so?"

"It seems that Mercado knew of the so-called Death Relic. He even mentions it by name in his diary and describes the impact it had on the Maya and the Aztec. To keep their treasury from being invaded, he writes that the location was protected by the Death Relic itself."

Maria returned his stare. "So you need me to figure out what the Death Relic is? If I remember correctly, Christianity happens to be your area of expertise as well. Of course, it's been so long since we've talked, I might be mistaken."

He smiled, trying to ease her anger. "No, my dear, you are correct: it *is* my area of expertise. However, as I outlined in my proposal, I cannot afford to be a part of this claim. Therefore, I will not be joining you on the next leg of this mission. When you make the discovery—and I know you will—I will be at a meeting in Washington, D.C., with plenty of witnesses."

"Why me? Why not someone else?" she demanded.

"Because I trust you," he said sincerely. "In my world, that's the highest compliment I can give. Not love, not admiration, but trust. And the truth is that I trust you implicitly. I trust you to solve the puzzle, I trust you to honor our agreement, and I trust you to hand the treasure over to the Archives. Of all the people I've ever met, I trust you the most."

"Me?" she said, surprised.

He nodded. "In addition, I also trust your friends."

"My friends?"

He pointed at Payne and Jones. "I'm confident that David and

Jonathon will get you to where you need to go. That is, if you gentlemen are willing to accompany her."

Jones glanced at Maria. "Of course."

Payne shrugged. "Got nothing better to do."

Boyd smiled. "Wonderful. Then it's time for me to bid you adieu."

"You're leaving?" she asked.

He shook his head. "No, my dear, it is *you* that is leaving. There's a plane outside. It's fueled and ready to take you to where you need to go."

"Which is where?" Payne wondered.

Boyd grinned as he answered. "Cholula."

71

BOYD HAD PROVEN TO BE A MASTER STRATEGIST DURing the past few days, but one thing he had failed to take into account was Payne's physical stature. Used to the spacious legroom of a military cargo plane or the first-class accommodations in his company jet, Payne felt like a sardine in the fixed-wing aircraft that flew them from Mérida to Cholula. Forced to sit next to Maria, who was half his size and the only one able to squeeze into his cramped row, conversation was limited for the first hour. She passed the time by reading a file that Boyd had assembled on the history of the Great Pyramid of Cholula while Payne stared out the window at the Gulf of Mexico below.

To get from the northern end of the Yucatán to their destination in central Mexico, they flew over water for most of the trip. In many ways, it helped Payne understand why Marcos de Mercado had used a ship to move the Mayan treasure westward in 1574. Not only did he shave several weeks of travel time by charting a sea route but he also avoided hundreds of thousands of natives who might have intercepted the fortune in the desert or the mountains.

Maria closed the file and tried to stretch. It was tough to do in the limited space.

Payne smiled at her attempt. "Sorry."

"For what?"

"For taking up half the plane."

She laughed. "Now that you mention it, things *are* kind of tight. Remind me to complain to the flight attendant the next time she comes by."

"When you do, tell her I'm still waiting for my drink."

She licked her lips at the thought. "Actually, I could go for a drink right about now. A pitcher of margaritas would definitely take the edge off."

"A whole pitcher?" Payne said, surprised. "In my experience, if a woman drinks a whole pitcher of margaritas, she usually takes off a lot more than her edge."

She laughed at the joke. "In your experience, huh? Out of curiosity, how many times has that happened to you?"

Payne flashed a devilish grin as he pretended to count the answer on his fingers. When he reached double digits, she grabbed his hands to make him stop.

"Forget it. I don't want to know."

"Good. Because I don't want to say."

✠   ✠   ✠

BOYD KNEW THE BUILDING in Mérida had to be "cleaned" before he left Mexico. To accomplish the task, he hauled a five-gallon can of gasoline from his SUV to the makeshift classroom, then splashed the accelerant on the walls, the furniture, and the floor. By the time the fire department arrived to put out the blaze, every shred of forensic evidence would be reduced to ash, and he would be on his way to America.

But Tiffany had other ideas.

She had wanted to confront Boyd about the photos ever since Chichén Itzá but had decided to wait until Payne and Jones were out of the equation. Now that they were gone, it was time to make her move. She raised her weapon and entered the classroom while Boyd worked with his back to the door. She called his name to get his attention.

Boyd turned and saw the gun. "What are you doing?"

"Getting some answers."

"Answers? To what?"

"Stop talking. I'm asking the questions here."

He placed the empty can on the floor. "As you wish."

"Why did you do it? Why did you sell me out?"

"Sell you out? I'm afraid you're mistaken. I would *never*—"

"Cut the bullshit! I know damn well you sent my picture and location to Angel. And don't even try to deny it. I saw the e-mail on his phone."

The corners of his lips curled into a smile. "Ahhh, that explains your hostility. You found out about the e-mail. I was wondering what you were referring to. Now your reaction makes perfect sense. I, too, would be upset if the same thing had happened to me."

✠   ✠   ✠

AFTER A WHILE, Maria's conversation with Payne shifted to the mission at hand. Payne knew very little about the city of Cholula and needed to be briefed for the journey ahead. Instead of reading Boyd's report, which was several pages long and looked less exciting than a history textbook, he decided to question Maria directly. According to Boyd, her knowledge would be the key to everything once they arrived at the site. Payne didn't know whether or not that was true. He sensed maybe Boyd had presented the challenge in that manner to make her more receptive to the credit that she would be given, but he wouldn't know for sure until they solved the mystery.

Perhaps her knowledge *was* the key to finding the treasure.

They would find out soon enough.

He pointed at the file in her lap. "What can you tell me about the site?"

She opened the folder and handed him a picture of a large orange-yellow church that had been built on top of a lush green hill. "This is Iglesia de Nuestra Señora de los Remedios. In English, that means Church of Our Lady of Remedies."

Payne stared at the picture. "That's a beautiful church."

She nodded in agreement. "Does anything about it stand out?"

"Tough to tell," he admitted as he tried to make out the details of the dome and spires. They could barely be seen in the photograph. "Do you have something closer?"

"I do, but the feature I'm referring to is quite visible in this photo."

Payne shrugged. "Sorry. Nothing stands out."

"Look at the hill."

"The hill?" He glanced at the ground underneath the church. Trees and grass covered the terrain, as if it were any other hill in the rolling landscape of central Mexico. "What about it?"

"It *isn't* a hill. It's actually a pyramid."

☩   ☩   ☩

"WHY DID YOU DO IT?" Tiffany repeated.

"Not for money," Boyd assured her. "Technically speaking, I did not sell you out. I am not the type of man who would sell information to scum like Angel Ramirez."

"No, you're just the type of man who would stab someone in the back!"

He shook his head. "There's a big difference between stabbing someone in the back and punishing someone for her mistakes. And you made *several* mistakes during this operation—the type of mistakes that have consequences."

"Mistakes? What mistakes? I acquired the medallion and millions of dollars for your front company. What else is there?"

He laughed at the absurdity of her statement. "What else is there? How about anonymity? I told you from the beginning that anonymity was crucial to this operation, yet you allowed Angel to see your face at the Zócalo. Within twelve hours of the ransom drop, a sketch of your face was sent to every criminal and border guard in Mexico. The entire country is looking for you."

"Bullshit! I wore a gas mask at the plaza."

"What plaza is that? Because the Zócalo that I remember is no longer there. All that remains is a giant hole and scorched stone. The damage is so bad that the Federales are treating it as a terrorist attack. As far as they're concerned, you're public enemy number one."

Tiffany had seen pictures of the aftermath. The damage was more severe than she had anticipated. "That's not my fault. My expert misjudged the explosives."

"But you hired the expert. Therefore, the fault lies with you."

"And you hired me, so ultimately you're to blame."

He smiled. "This isn't about blame. This is about containment. As long as you're alive, you're a threat to everyone who participated in this operation. We can't risk you talking to the Mexican authorities. That would make things, um, complicated."

"So you sent Angel to do something you couldn't. You coward."

"No, my dear, you have it all wrong. I put Angel on your scent so you could punish the man who revealed your identity. If you had killed him in Mexico City like you were supposed to, we wouldn't be in our current predicament."

"There you go blaming me again."

He shook his head. "I told you, this *isn't* about blame. This is about containment."

✠   ✠   ✠

Maria's last comment confused Payne. "You mean the hill is *shaped* like a pyramid."

"No," she countered, "it *is* a pyramid—an ancient stone pyramid. In fact, it's the largest pyramid, by volume, in the world. Its size is estimated at nearly four and a half million cubic meters. That's nearly twice the size of the pyramid at Giza."

He looked at the photograph again and tried to picture what she was saying. If not for her description, he never would have guessed that there was anything under the grass but dirt. It looked completely natural to him. "How tall is the hill?"

She corrected him. "The *pyramid* is two hundred and seventeen feet tall. Its base is nearly fifteen hundred feet on each side."

"Holy crap! That's almost the length of five football fields."

She knew little about football. "If you say so."

He pointed at the grass. "Is this common?"

"Is what common?"

"The grass. I know some pyramids were swallowed by the jungle and forgotten for centuries, but this is the first time I've ever seen one swallowed by a lawn."

She smiled at the comment. "Actually, the pyramid wasn't swallowed. It was hidden by the locals. According to legend, they were so convinced that the Spaniards would destroy it—like they had done to the great monuments in Tenochtitlan—that they covered it with soil and seed. By the time the conquistadores arrived in Cholula, the pyramid looked like a hill."

"That's one of the coolest things I've ever heard."

"The locals did such a remarkable job of concealment that the pyramid was eventually forgotten. It remained undisturbed for over three hundred years until a construction crew rediscovered it in the late nineteenth century. Since 1931, archaeologists have dug over five miles of tunnels through the heart of the pyramid. They have found altars, floors, walls, and human remains dating back to the ninth century, but no significant treasure."

He glanced at her. "Is that good or bad?"

"Neither," she said, "because we'll be focusing on the church, not the pyramid."

"Why's that?"

She flipped through the papers in Boyd's file until she found the document she was looking for. It was a photocopy of one of the pages of Mercado's journal. She had highlighted several of the dates. "Construction of the church began in the spring of 1574, approximately the same time that the treasure arrived in Cholula. According to this, Marcos's brother, Manuel, handpicked the work crew and oversaw the building process of the church. Upon its completion in the summer of 1575, Marcos himself became one of the clergy. He remained there until 1596."

Payne nodded in understanding. "From what I know about conquistadores, they were explorers and fighters. They weren't architects, and they weren't builders. If Manuel took the time to build this church, there has to be a reason."

She agreed. "Back then it was quite common to build churches on top of native monuments. It was Spain's way of claiming the land as its own. If Manuel had somehow learned about the pyramid, he would have realized the best way to protect it would be to build a church on top of it. The hill underneath would have been considered holy ground, which would have kept explorers away. By building one church, he hid the treasure and protected the pyramid."

"You gotta love the irony."

"What irony?"

Payne explained. "Bishop Landa was supposed to be a holy man, but he used his authority to kill the natives and to destroy their relics. Meanwhile, the Mercados—who were trained soldiers—didn't fight back with violence. Instead, they fought back by building a church. I wasn't an English major, but I'm pretty sure that qualifies as irony."

She nodded. "I think it does."

"What's that expression? *God works in mysterious ways?* That's a perfect example."

She gasped. "I can't believe you said that. That's my favorite saying of all time. My mother used it constantly when I was a girl."

"Really? I didn't know that. Maybe that's a sign."

She smiled at the thought. "If it is a sign, I bet it's a good one."

✠   ✠   ✠

TIFFANY AIMED THE GUN at Boyd's chest. "From my perspective, it's too late for containment. Everyone knows what I look like. For now, all I care about is punishment. You stabbed me in the back. Now you have to pay."

His smile widened. "Actually, my dear, it is *you* who must pay."

Before Tiffany could react, she sensed a presence behind her. It was one of the henchmen who had trashed Maria's suite in Cancún. He had been summoned to Mérida to silence Tiffany once and for all. And he enjoyed his work. He calmly put the barrel of his gun against the base of her skull and pulled the trigger. The bullet tore through her spine, killing her instantly. Her blood and brain prevented the muzzle flash from igniting the gas fumes in the room.

A minute later, Boyd would incinerate her body along with everything else.

Then he would head to America. Just like he had planned.

72

CHOLULA, MEXICO
(76 MILES SOUTHEAST OF MEXICO CITY)

THEY ARRIVED IN CHOLULA AFTER DARK, WHICH was fine with them, since they realized that several laws might have to be broken in order to complete their adventure. Even Ulster, a straitlaced academic who felt more guilt over parking tickets than some people did over felonies, was willing to concede that a thorough search couldn't be done during daylight hours. Not only was Our Lady of Remedies a major tourist attraction—drawing thousands of visitors per week—but his involvement was bound to draw attention from INAH and the Catholic Church, both of which would impede their investigation for several weeks. In the world of archaeology, Ulster learned long ago that it was easier to ask for forgiveness than it was to get permission.

Patrolled by a police equestrian unit, the single road that led to the church was well guarded. It forced the group to abandon Boyd's vehicle more than a quarter mile from the complex. After breaching the security fence that encircled the Cholula archaeo-logical site, Payne led the way up the side of the mound while the others followed. They marveled at the topography and the natural feel of the grass. In the daylight, the illusion would have been shattered by all of the layers of the pyramid that had been exposed for exhibits, but at night the reality was concealed by darkness. To them, it seemed as though they were climbing a normal hill.

No words were spoken until they reached the courtyard outside the church. Payne whispered instructions to Jones, who hustled into the shadows with lock picks in hand. Less than five minutes later, Jones opened the door from inside the church. Years ago, this would have produced applause and congratulations. Now it was merely routine. No longer amazed by his abilities, Payne and Maria walked past him as if he were holding a door open for them at a restaurant, and Ulster did the same. Hamilton was somewhat impressed, but he was too worried about being caught to say anything out loud. Instead, he simply nodded to express his thanks.

Jones shook his head in frustration. "Tough crowd."

Familiar with the sixteenth-century structure because of her research on the plane, Maria led the way toward the main part of the church. Having seen several pictures of the nave and altar in Boyd's file, she couldn't wait to see them in person. Her pace was so energized that the rest of the group struggled to keep up until she stopped in the center of the main aisle to soak it all in. As expected, the interior of the church was breathtaking. The entire nave, made of local stone and decorated with twenty-four-carat gold leaf, seemed to sparkle in the dim glow of the recessed lights above the altar. Everywhere she looked, she saw gold—lustrous and brilliant, even in the faintest of light. For a brief moment, her heart sank when she considered a possibility that hadn't crossed her mind until that very instant. What if the Mercados had melted the Aztec gold to decorate the interior of the church? What if the treasure had been in plain sight all along?

Ulster sensed her concern. He walked over and whispered reassurance in her ear. "Don't worry, my dear, the walls are merely gilded. The treasure is somewhere else."

She was taken aback. "How did you know what I was thinking?"

He smiled. "Because I was thinking it myself."

With that, Ulster continued forward toward the altar.

She was ready to join him when she felt a tug on her sleeve. She turned and saw Hamilton. He was standing there with his backpack in his hands and a strange look on his face, as if he had something that he needed to say. "Are you all right?"

He nodded. "Yes, Maria, I'm fine. It's just, there's something I need to give you. I wanted to give it to you *much* earlier—I swear I did—but Charles made me promise to wait until we were inside the church. You know Charles and his crazy schemes. He claims he has a reason for everything, although half the time I don't know what that reason is."

"Trust me, I know the feeling."

"Yes, I hoped you would."

Wasting no time, Hamilton sat in a nearby pew and unzipped the backpack that he had been carrying with him since Mérida. He reached inside and pulled out a hard plastic case that had been custom-fitted to protect a gold medallion that had once belonged to Marcos de Mercado. Just four days earlier, the medallion had been locked away in a secret vault belonging to Hector Garcia. Familiar with its history, he had been searching for the Mercado treasure for years but had been unable to put the pieces of the puzzle together. Unwilling to sell the item for any amount, Garcia was forced to trade the medallion for the safe return of his children, a price most parents would be willing to pay. In the end, Garcia also paid with his life.

Hamilton was aware of none of that. He knew nothing about the kidnappings, the bombs at the Zócalo, or the millions of dollars of dirty money that would end up in the bank accounts of the CIA. All Hamilton had been told was that Boyd had acquired the medallion from a private collector, and due to confidentiality agreements, the item should never be discussed in public. After witnessing the violence at Chichén Itzá, Hamilton assumed that they had acquired the item through illicit means, but at that point he figured it was too late to do anything about it.

Maria stared at the medallion. In the dim light of the church, it was tough to see all the details that had been carved into the gold. The one thing she did notice was a small, rectangular slot through the center of the artifact. "What is it?"

Hamilton explained. "This medallion was handcrafted by a Spanish artisan in the late 1500s. He made it from a detailed design that we found in the journal of Marcos de Mercado, who claimed the medallion was the key to unlocking the mysteries of the New World. On the front, there is an etching of the Death Relic symbol that I showed to you in Mérida. It is surrounded by several smaller glyphs of mixed origins. A few are Mayan, a few are Aztec, and a few are from the other indigenous tribes in Mesoamerica."

She turned on her flashlight and studied the front surface of the medallion. She had never seen an object quite like it. "What do the glyphs say?"

"Unfortunately, we just acquired the medallion yesterday. Charles immediately sent me a series of photographs, which I have been trying to decipher ever since. As far as I can tell, the glyphs say the same thing over and over again: *Death protects the treasure*."

"Death protects the treasure? What does that mean?"

"That, I'm afraid, is the riddle you must solve."

"Me? Why me? Why do I have to solve it?"

He smiled to ease her anxiety. "Look around you, Maria. We are inside Our Lady of Remedies, a historic Catholic Church. Your area of expertise is the history of Christianity. Who better to solve the riddle than you?"

She took a deep breath. "When you put it like that . . ."

He laughed. "Don't worry, Maria. I am confident in your abilities. If I didn't think you could do it, do you really think I would have allowed you to join the team? As I told you in Cancún, the task that we hired you for is right up your alley. Now all you have to do is *think*."

Maria thanked him for the information, then asked to be left alone for a few minutes so she could gather her thoughts on the subject. Hamilton quietly slipped out of the pew to give her the privacy that she needed. Before long, he was gathering the others to explain everything he had told her about the medallion. Although most of the burden had been placed on Maria's shoulders, Hamilton realized it would be foolish to keep the rest of the team in the dark about such an important clue. Unlike Boyd, who wanted Maria to be the one to solve the puzzle, Hamilton didn't care who found the prize as long as it was one of them.

73

U NSURE WHERE TO BEGIN, MARIA GLANCED AROUND the church in hopes of finding a clue. She stared at the arches, the vaulted ceiling, and the main dome but saw nothing of value except exquisite craftsmanship. Eventually, her eyes drifted toward the main altar. Decorated with fresh flowers and gilded with twenty-four-carat gold, it was truly a beautiful sight. Everywhere she looked, there were splashes of color—red, yellow, green, and pink—but the color that grabbed her attention was in the middle of the back wall. Remarkably, it was the same shade of turquoise as the water in the Caribbean Sea—the same color she had seen in Cancún, and Tulum, and the Mayan coastline in between. Prior to her trip to Mexico, she had never seen that particular shade before, but here it surfaced again a thousand miles from the distant shore. With nothing better to go on, she decided to glance through Boyd's file to see if the color had any significance.

She flipped through several pages of the church's history until she came across a photograph of the altar. She stared at the picture and realized the turquoise color was part of a carved figure that depicted the patron saint of the church. Anxious to learn more, she turned the picture over and read the description on the back. The tiny statue of the Virgin Mary—which resembled an elaborate doll in a long, turquoise gown—arrived in the New World in 1519. It was brought to the Americas by a Spanish soldier named Juan Rodríguez de Villafuerte, who viewed the idol as his protector for the dangerous trip. A year later, when Hernán Cortés was initially defeated by the Aztecs, Villafuerte hid the statue of Mary in a native temple, where it remained undisturbed for more than twenty years. Eventually, the indigenous people of the region, who were in the midst of being converted to Christianity, discovered the statue and worshipped it until it was "rescued" by a Spanish monk. Ever since, the statue has been considered the protector of the church.

Wait. What was the statue protecting?

The whole church? Or something else?

She turned the picture back over and studied the details of the image. Strangely, the only part of the carved statue that was actually visible was Mary's painted face. An elaborate gold crown, topped with a gold cross, rested on her head. The other features of the statue—Mary's arms, legs, and torso—were concealed by a turquoise gown that flared out from the collar. The end result looked like a turquoise pyramid with Mary's head glued to the apex. Stranger still, there was a single item draped around Mary's neck: a tiny gold medallion.

"Santa Maria!" she whispered, sensing she was on the right track.

Instead of rushing forward and making a scene, she held Mercado's medallion next to the image of the statue. Unfortunately, the medallion in the picture was far too blurry to make an accurate comparison. She cursed under her breath as she grabbed Boyd's file. Trembling with excitement, she flipped through the dozens of pictures in the folder, hoping to find a close-up of Mary's medallion. Amazingly, she stumbled across something even better.

The first photograph was a drawing of Diego de Landa, presiding over the auto-da-fé of Maní. He was holding a gold cross above his head as a group of natives cowered at his feet. In the background, Spanish soldiers were burning artifacts and chopping off the heads of Mayan rulers. The second photograph was an oil painting of a Spanish conquistador. He, too, was holding a cross in the air as dozens of Aztecs were slain around him. One native in particular caught her eye. He was kneeling on the ground, pleading for mercy, as a Spanish soldier prepared to pierce him with a lance. One end of the lance was sharpened to a deadly point; the other end was topped with a jewel-encrusted cross.

Picture after picture, drawing after drawing, all of them depicting the same theme in slightly different forms: the Spanish killing natives in the name of the cross. She had studied them all during the flight to Cholula, but she had not picked up on this common thread until that very moment.

"Oh, my God!" she blurted, louder than she had intended.

From various sections of the church, heads whipped in her direction—everyone concerned that they had been spotted by a guard. Payne happened to be the nearest person to Maria. He rushed to her side to find out what was wrong. He was expecting trouble, but she greeted him with the best news possible. She had solved the riddle.

"What is it?" he demanded.

"I figured it out! I know what the Death Relic was."

"Already?"

She nodded, fully confident. "It was the cross."

"The Death Relic was the cross? I don't follow."

By this time, the others had rushed to her side as well. She quickly took them through her theory, using the photographs to illustrate her point. "It's all about perspective. From the Spanish point of view, the cross was a relic to be worshipped. They took it into battle, where it gave them power and strength. They fought for the cross. On the other hand, the natives viewed the cross in a completely different way. From their perspective, it was something to be feared. Look at all the natives who were slain in the name of the cross. To them, the relic represented death."

Ulster stroked his beard in thought. "My dear, you might be on to something. In the minds of the natives, who had never seen this symbol before the Spanish Conquest, they had to define it in their own terms. In their eyes, the cross was evil. The cross *was* death."

Hamilton nodded enthusiastically. "That would explain the glyphs! The lone difference between the Death God and the Death Relic symbols was the necklace of bones around the Death God's neck. The bones were shaped like an X. It must have been their way of depicting the cross."

Payne glanced at his watch. He hated to dampen the group's enthusiasm, but he knew time wasn't on their side. "I know this is an important discovery, but given our current location and my desire to avoid a Mexican prison, I was wondering if this information will actually help us find the treasure."

She nodded. "As a matter of fact, it might."

He tapped his watch. "Then let's get moving."

She signaled for them to follow her toward the altar. As she walked, she explained what she had in mind. "Take a look at the statue. What does it look like from a distance?"

Jones guessed. "A really ugly puppet."

She glared at him. "David, that's a statue of the Virgin Mary."

He was ready to amend his joke but thought better of it.

Ulster bailed him out. "At first blush, it appears to be a pyramid."

She agreed. "I thought the same thing when I saw it. Not only that, but she's wearing a medallion around her neck. That can't be a coincidence."

Payne was confused. "You think the treasure is inside the statue?"

She shook her head. "Not at all. I think this statue has another purpose. It was discovered in the 1500s and has been on this altar for several hundred years. According to legend, this statue is said to be the protector of the church. But I don't think it's protecting the church. I think it's protecting what was *hidden* in the church. I think it's protecting the treasure."

Maria genuflected in front of the altar and quickly made the sign of the cross. Then she scooted around to the back wall, where the statue was kept in a gilded arch. Unfortunately, the arch started at eye level and soared more than fifteen feet up the wall. Resting on an elaborate stand that took the form of a dark serpent encircling a blue globe, the Virgin Mary statue was positioned halfway up the arch. Maria's mind quickly flashed back to the main pyramid of Chichén Itzá, the one that was attacked by a serpent during the spring and autumn equinox. She wondered if there was a link between that particular deity and the creature on the stand. If so, it would be another indication that the Christian and Mayan worlds were connected at that spot.

She stared up at the statue. "Can someone give me a hand?"

Payne was the strongest, so he picked her up and placed her on the stone ledge at the base of the arch. From there, she was able to lean forward and peek behind the statue.

After a few seconds of searching, she started to chuckle. "I'll be damned."

Jones heard the comment. "You *will* be damned if you keep swearing on the altar. That's the Virgin Mary you're talking to."

She ignored him. She was too focused on her discovery. "You're not going to believe what's back here. There's a carved circle in the wall. It looks to be about the same size as the medallion."

Payne furrowed his brow. "A carved circle? What's so exciting about that?"

She glanced down at the group. "Terrence, correct me if I'm wrong, but didn't Mercado's journal say that the medallion was the key to unlocking the mysteries of the New World?"

Hamilton nodded. "As a matter of fact, it did."

"At the time, I thought it was merely a figure of speech, but what if he meant it? What if the medallion is literally a key—a key that gives us access to the treasure?"

Ulster grinned. "Trust me, my dear, I've heard crazier things in my day. Did I ever tell you about the temple that one of my colleagues unearthed in the rain forest of Cameroon? In order to get inside, they had to shove a stick into the rectum of a hippopotamus."

Jones did a double take. "Excuse me?"

Ulster laughed. "Don't worry, David. It wasn't a real hippopotamus. It was the statue of a hippopotamus. Nevertheless, it was a crazy place to put a keyhole."

"Anyway," Maria said, "I think this will work, but I'm not quite tall enough to reach the slot. Unless we can find a ladder, one of you is going to have to do it for me."

Jones pointed at Payne. "Dammit, Jon. You heard the lady. Help her!"

"Don't swear," she said.

"But you just swore, like, two seconds ago."

She reached out her arms. "Be quiet and help me down."

He pretended to pout. "Yes, ma'am."

After moving the statue to the floor, Jones cupped his hands together and boosted Payne onto the stone ledge at the base of the arch. He studied the arch and saw the carved circle she had referred to. As she claimed, it appeared to be the same size as the medallion.

She handed it to Payne. "Good luck."

Payne took the medallion in his right hand and reached up high. The rectangular slot in the center of the medallion lined up perfectly with a tiny notch in the middle of the hole. Unsure of the physics, he tried to spin the medallion like a dial, but his hands slipped across the smooth surface of the gold. He tried again, this time pushing hard against the medallion as he twisted it to the right. This time, the dial moved. With every crank of the medallion, it went deeper and deeper into the wall until the arch behind the statue cracked open like a door.

Wasting no time, he swung the arch completely open and peered into the shadows ahead. There was a short hallway, then a stone staircase that curled into the darkness.

"What's back there?" Maria demanded.

"I can't tell. Someone give me a flashlight."

Jones held out his hand. "I'll let you use mine, but we're a package deal."

Payne looked down at Jones, Maria, Ulster, and Hamilton, and he knew what needed to be done. Having come this far, it would be unfair for any one of them to make the discovery alone. He nodded to Jones, who began to boost Maria to the ledge. Payne pulled the group up, one at a time, and helped them through the hidden door.

The space behind the altar was unremarkable in every way. It led to a storage vault that had been carved into the tip of the pyramid below. Made of simple stone, it wasn't painted or gilded, and it didn't have any of the architectural flourishes of the rest of the church. Of course, there was no reason to decorate a space that wasn't meant for visitors.

Instead, the space was designed to be warm and dry.

The ideal place to protect the piles of Aztec gold and the hundreds of Mayan codices that lined the alcoves in the vaults below the church.

EPILOGUE

BUILT TO RESEMBLE AN AZTEC PYRAMID, THE MAIN building of the Fairmont Acapulco Princess resort towers fifteen stories above the tropical landscape on the southern coast of Mexico. Surrounded by lush jungles, sandy beaches, and the Pacific Ocean, the Fairmont is annually recognized as one of the top resorts in Latin America. On most evenings, the Beach Club restaurant was the type of place that Payne and Jones would enjoy without hesitation, but as they glanced around the crowded bistro, they realized the significance of the date. It was Valentine's Day.

Or as it's known in Mexico: *El Día del Amor.*

The Day of Love.

Jones cursed under his breath when the hostess led them to a cozy table for two, which offered a romantic view of Revolcadero Beach. Lit by candlelight and sprinkled with rose petals, everything about the table setting was designed for romance—including the bottle of champagne that chilled nearby. He brushed the petals off his chair before reluctantly sitting down. If not for the growling in his stomach, he would have been tempted to leave.

"Just so you know," Jones declared, "it doesn't matter how much you wine and dine me: you're *not* getting laid."

Payne moved the ice bucket out of his way. "Don't worry. You're not my type."

Jones considered the comment. "You're *such* a racist."

"Yeah. That's it. You figured me out."

Unwilling to leave Mexico until Ulster had dealt with the politics of their discovery, Payne and Jones decided to fly to Acapulco for a few days of golf and swimming before returning to the snow and ice of Pennsylvania. After the confusion of Cancún, the violence of Chichén Itzá, and the excitement of Cholula, they felt they had earned an actual vacation.

One without gunfire. Or explosions. Or carnage of any kind.

The only thing they wanted to shoot was under par.

As for the treasure itself, the inventory process had yet to begin because of a major disagreement that was brewing between the Catholic Church and Mexico's Instituto Nacional de Antropología e Historia. Since the treasure was reached through Our Lady of Remedies, the Church felt the gold and artifacts belonged to them. Meanwhile, the INAH claimed the Mexican government should control the hoard, since the vaults were dug into the top of the pyramid. Ultimately, the two groups would come to some agreement, one in which both sides would prosper, but it would take a few more days.

In the meantime, Ulster, Maria, and Hamilton patiently waited for an opportunity to examine the treasure. On the night of the discovery, they were rushed for time, which prevented them from grasping the scope of the collection. They realized it was a major historical find—one that promised to address many of the unanswered questions about the Aztec and Mayan civilizations—

but they wouldn't be able to gauge its true significance until they were allowed to study the codices in a proper setting. Before Sunday, there were only three known Mayan codices in the world. Now there were more than three hundred.

Scholars would be busy for years to come.

For the time being, Payne was more concerned with his best friend than he was about the treasure. He eyed the couples at the other tables. It really was a romantic setting. "I hate to point out the obvious, but shouldn't you be here with Maria?"

Jones shrugged. "I don't know. Maybe."

"Maybe?"

"I thought I had everything figured out until she kissed me. Now I'm confused again. Honestly, I have no idea what she's thinking—or what I'm thinking."

"I saw the kiss. It wasn't a peck on the cheek."

He shook his head. "No, it wasn't."

"I'm guessing it meant something."

"Possibly," he admitted. "But even if it did, nothing has really changed since the breakup. The attraction has always been there. It's just, you know, the other stuff that got in the way."

"Actually, I don't know. What other stuff are you talking about?"

Jones groaned at the question. Although Payne had been asking him for years, Jones had never revealed the reason that he had broken up with Maria. He figured she was out of his life, so he saw no reason to upset his best friend over the details. However, now that Maria was back in their lives—regardless of how temporary or permanent her presence might be—he felt he owed Payne the truth.

Jones cleared his throat. "I know you aren't going to like this, but here's the truth: I ultimately broke up with Maria because of you."

Payne laughed at the comment. He thought it was a joke. "Because of me? Well, I guess that explains the romantic dinner. How long have you felt this way?"

Jones shook his head. "Jon, I'm trying to be serious. Maria and I were clicking as a long-distance couple until I asked her to visit me in Pittsburgh. She hemmed and hawed for a couple of weeks until I got sick of the runaround. Eventually, I confronted her about it on the phone. She told me that she didn't want to visit because she didn't want to deal with you."

"She didn't want to deal with me? What the hell did I do?"

"Come on, Jon."

"Seriously, what?"

Jones grimaced. "You killed her brother."

Payne raised his voice. "A brother who was trying to *kill* her. I saved her life."

"I know you did, and I tried to tell her that. Unfortunately, she was still coping with her father's murder, Dr. Boyd's desertion, and a bunch of other issues. I think you got lumped into that mess. Plus, if you remember correctly, you introduced yourself by shoving your gun in her mouth and threatening to blow her head off. That probably didn't help."

Payne took a deep breath. "Probably not."

"Anyway," Jones continued, "I told her that you were my best friend and a major part of my life. I let her know that I wanted to continue my relationship with her but *only* if she was willing to work things out with you."

"Let me guess: that didn't go over too well."

"Not well at all."

"And now?"

Jones shrugged. "Like I said, I have no idea what the woman is thinking. You know as well as anyone that negative emotions are hard to shake. If that initial encounter scared her or she still harbors animosity toward you over her brother's death, it would certainly explain her belligerence."

"She is feisty," Payne interjected.

"I can't help but think that her willingness to face you means she's still interested in me. It's taken years, but at least she's willing to deal with you. Hell, it's more than that. She trusted you, enough to call you when she was in trouble." Jones ran his fingers across his scalp. "I don't know, maybe enough time has passed to heal old wounds."

"Listen," Payne said, "if you care about Maria, you owe it to yourself to give it another chance. Don't let me stand in the way. I want you two to break up over *your* issues—like your immaturity or your bad breath—not because of me. I don't need that on my conscience."

Jones laughed. "Thanks for your confidence."

Payne encouraged him. "Seriously. This is the perfect day to express your feelings. What have you got to lose?" With that, Payne nodded toward the entrance of the restaurant. Jones turned and saw Maria talking to the hostess, who pointed to Payne and Jones's table. Maria stared at Jones from across the room and smiled warmly.

"Jon, what the hell did you—"

When Jones turned back toward Payne's seat, it was empty. His friend had conveniently vanished, as if by magic. Folded neatly on the table was a note that read:

THERE'S STILL HOPE FOR THE TWO OF YOU.

DINNER'S ON ME.

ACKNOWLEDGMENTS

As always, I'd like to start with my family. Without their love and support, I wouldn't be the person or the writer that I am today. Thanks for putting up with me.

Next, I want to thank my friend and agent, Scott Miller. Before we teamed up, I was a self-published author. Now my books are available around the world. It's quite comforting to have Scott, Claire Roberts, and the whole gang at Trident Media in my corner.

Over the past several years, I've had a chance to work with Natalee Rosenstein on seven Payne and Jones thrillers. I'd like to thank her for all that she's done for my career. I'd also like to acknowledge Ivan Held, Neil Nyren, Victoria Comella, Robin Barletta, and everyone else at Putnam and Berkley.

Next up is my good friend Ian Harper. I want to thank him for reading, rereading, and then re-rereading everything I write and for all the suggestions that he makes. His advice and expertise are invaluable. If anyone is looking for a freelance editor, please let me know. I'd be happy to put you in touch with him.

Finally, I'd like to thank all the readers, librarians, booksellers, and critics who have read my thrillers and have recommended them to others. At this stage of my career, I still need all the help I can get, so I would appreciate your continued support.

For more information about my writing, please visit: chriskuzneski.com.